HELL DIVERS X

FALLOUT

NICHOLAS SANSBURY SMITH

**BLACK
STONE**
PUBLISHING

Printed in the United States of America
Originally published in hardcover by Blackstone Publishing in 2021

ISBN 979-8-200-92418-9
Fiction / Science Fiction / Apocalyptic & Post-Apocalyptic

Version 1

Blackstone Publishing
31 Mistletoe Rd.
Ashland, OR 97520

www.BlackstonePublishing.com

For Josh Stanton,
the captain of the Blackstone ship, you are more than
my publisher; you are a friend and mentor. Your unwavering
support and passion for Hell Divers has elevated the series
to a level I never dreamed possible. I am forever grateful
for everything you do.

"Courage is not having the strength to go on; it is going on when you don't have the strength."

—Teddy Roosevelt

RECAP SINCE
HELL DIVERS IX: RADIOACTIVE

In a devastating betrayal, Captain Rolo has all but wiped out the Vanguard army with a nuclear warhead targeting the supercarrier *Immortal*. But he had no way to know that King Xavier and the surviving Hell Diver and Cazador teams from Brisbane were on the assault ship *Frog*. But in the race to escape the explosion, the ship was damaged, stranding X and his remaining forces on Australia's Sunshine Coast.

Outpost Gateway has suffered a different sort of disaster: an attack from carnivorous vines. Director Rodger Mintel sent out a desperate plea for help as the radioactive tendrils tore into the bunker, which X received just before Captain Rolo's betrayal. No one knows if Rodger survived the attack, and X and Magnolia fear the worst.

At the Vanguard Islands, Michael Everhart has been framed for the murder of Oliver and his son, Nez. Michael's wife, Layla, has been under twenty-four-hour guard as she cares for their son, Bray, and Rhino Jr., unable to help. Michael, unaware of X's predicament, has pinned all his hopes on his mentor returning to free him.

Back in Australia, Hell Diver Kade Long has been captured by the Knights of the Coral Castle. They dragged him to their leader, known as the Forerunner, who seems to be half-man and half-robot. As Kade's comrades all fight for their lives and freedom elsewhere, Kade sits in a cell in the underwater Coral Castle wondering what the knights' plan for him is—and hoping it's not execution.

Meanwhile, the truth of what happened at Brisbane is spreading, and so is the radiation from the nuclear blast. The fallout threatens to destroy everything in its path, including the king's remaining forces and the Coral Castle itself...

PROLOGUE
TWENTY-ONE YEARS AGO . . .

The *Hive* carved through altocumulus clouds twenty thousand feet above the surface. The nuclear-powered helium airship flew south, toward a zone never explored since the bombs of World War III turned the planet into a wasteland and created ongoing electrical storms that blotted out the sun.

Two hundred forty years had passed since civilization ended. For most of the 1,042 survivors living aboard the airship, the past wasn't a daily thought. Most passengers didn't think about the Old World at all—only how to survive another day on the airship.

But not everyone aboard remained in the dark about conditions on the surface. The Hell Diver teams knew exactly what was down there on that blasted surface.

In the launch bay of the airship, Hell Diver Xavier "X" Rodriguez sneaked a nip of shine from his flask and slipped it back into his locker while his best friend and fellow diver Aaron Everhart pulled on his chest armor rig.

"I saw that," Aaron called out.

"What?" X asked.

Aaron secured the side clips and turned his blue eyes on X. There was no judgment there today, just disappointment.

"Sorry, man, just taking the edge off," X said.

"You always say that."

Aaron snapped the last closure on his chest rig and went to the crate, guarded by two militia soldiers, in the center of the launch bay. The soldiers took out a key and opened it, then retreated to the double doors, where they waited with crossbows cradled.

X and Aaron pulled out weapons and ammunition from the cache normally stored in the airship's armory.

Each diver took a blaster—a sawed-off double-barreled shotgun with a third barrel for a flare. X picked out his favorite assault rifle. It had a scratched barrel, and duct tape on the grip. He stuffed extra magazines into the carrier vest over his armor.

Aaron pulled out a bolt-action rifle and slotted rounds into a bandolier draped like a sash over one shoulder.

Both divers stuffed extra shotgun shells into every pouch and pocket. Where they were diving, they just might need every round.

Normally X didn't feel predive jitters. He had eighty-one jumps under his belt, most of them in green zones—areas where radiation was minimal and the biggest concerns were failed chutes in the air, and sinkholes on the surface.

But today was different. Today they were diving into a yellow zone that no one had seen for over two centuries.

If Aaron was nervous, he wasn't showing it. The tall, lean diver ran through the checklist—if anything wasn't working right, now was the last chance to fix it.

"You good?" X asked.

"Just another jump into paradise, right?"

"Not exactly," called out a voice.

Both men straightened as Captain Maria Ash strode across the room, moving fast and with purpose, as usual.

"We're moving into position now," said the captain. "Our surface sensors are sending back some disturbing data."

"This isn't a yellow zone, is it?" X asked.

The captain shook her head. "The electrical storms are minimal, but the surface has high radiation," she said. "That's why I'm here: to give you the choice."

X almost laughed. He knew there was no choice. Hell Divers never had a choice. If they refused to dive, humanity died. If they died on the surface, humanity died.

The only way to survive was to dive.

Aaron looked at X, commander of their four-man team.

"I'll go; you stay," X said to Aaron.

"Nah, you know I can't let you go alone."

"You got Tin to worry about. I got myself."

"He's my kid, but he's your godson."

"Yeah, but a boy needs his father."

X looked back to the captain.

"So, you want to let us in on what this mission is?" he asked. She pulled out a tablet, clicked on the screen, and handed it over.

Aaron leaned down to look at the location of an Old World hospital.

"Medicine?" X asked.

"Not just any," Maria said. She brought up a new image. "This is a vaccine called Redotal, which I believe will eradicate the cough."

X and Aaron exchanged a look.

The airship was in the middle of a pandemic as a virus they called simply "the cough" ripped through both the upper and lower passenger decks.

"You find this, and you'll give us a second chance to continue sailing until the storms clear or we find a new home," Maria said.

"I'm in," Aaron said.

"I'm the commander—" X started to say.

"Tin's not immune to the cough, Xavier. I'm coming with you, for his future and for everyone else's."

Captain Ash held each man's gaze in turn, then lowered her head slightly in a rare display of emotion. In the glow of the lights, X saw the strain in her features. A cancer survivor, she looked older than her five decades, and he could tell she had more than her physical health weighing on her mind.

"I always thought it would be a storm, or perhaps engine failure, that sent us crashing to the surface like so many of the other airships since the war," she said. "But now this virus threatens our population just as much, if not more."

"Just one question," X said. "If this medicine is a couple of centuries old, it's gotta be past its prime."

"Stored in liquid nitrogen at minus 196 degrees Celsius—three-quarters of the way down to absolute zero. It'll be as fresh as the day it was made."

"I'll find…" X's eyes darted to Aaron. "We will find the medicine. Don't worry, Captain."

"I know you will," she said, with another rare form of emotional expression: a smile. "Be careful down there. You are two of our last heroes."

They moved over to the launch tubes, normally operated by technicians who were absent today due to the mission's secrecy. The two militia guards escorted the weapons cache and Captain Ash out of the bay.

X held up a gloved fist like an Old World boxer. "Let's save the world again, man."

"Don't let that juice get you cocky."

"Never, boss."

Aaron cinched his helmet and climbed down into his launch tube. X did the same, smelling the worn plastic and the lingering scent of the cleaning solution he'd used on his visor.

The heads-up display (HUD) flickered online, a small green subscreen showing both his and Aaron's life-support systems.

The dive clock blinked on: 2:00. *Two minutes.*

The warning siren blared as X looked down at the glass exit hatch beneath his feet. Wispy clouds drifted under his boots.

Red light bathed his pod, and he hit a button on his wrist computer to turn on his helmet lights.

Sixty, fifty-nine, fifty-eight…

X checked his HUD as the digital map of their dive came up. Once he confirmed all systems were online, he double-checked his rifle strap and gear—all snug.

Featherlight and strong as a sword. Featherlight and strong as a sword.

He squeezed his fists, but the alarm drowned out the cracking knuckles.

Twenty-nine, twenty-eight, twenty-seven…

The red faded away, replaced by a cool blue that did little to relieve X's anxiety. He wasn't worried about dying; he was worried about *failing.*

He had already lost his wife to cancer, and with a third of the ship sick, this was the most important dive of his career.

His headset clicked on, and the soothing voice of Captain Ash surged into his ear.

"Good luck, X and Aaron. You are the best of us," she said. "Good luck and dive safe."

"We dive so humanity survives," X and Aaron said simultaneously over the comms.

Ten, nine, eight…

X looked down just as the glass hatch whispered open. He tucked his arms by his sides and slid out into the dark clouds. For a moment, he had the sense of being truly as light as a feather, as if his body no longer belonged to him. Then his guts caught up and his blood warmed, prickling across his skin.

One hundred eighty pounds of flesh and bone, in addition to the hundred pounds of armor and gear, plummeted toward the dead surface.

He spread his arms and legs out through the puffy altocumulus. A single blue light glowed to the east, where Aaron fell at the same rate.

A little farther east, a fork of lightning arrowed through the black sky.

"Raptor Two, you see that?" X said over the comm.

Static crackled into his earpiece, hardly audible over the whistle of wind across his armor. In the green hue of his night vision, he searched for Aaron, but the other diver had vanished now.

X checked his HUD and saw the green dot representing the man he trusted most in life—a man who had stood by his side through the dark times. Aaron was there when X struggled with drinking. He was there when his wife died, and after, when the drinking got worse and resulted in more risk-taking on missions.

Some of the other thirty Hell Divers on the airship liked to joke that X had a death wish. He didn't correct them; maybe he did.

"Too close for comfort," Aaron finally replied. "You thinking what I'm thinking?"

"Race ya," X said.

Bringing his arms against his sides, X rotated head down, rocketing earthward in what they called a suicide dive. It was the fastest survivable way to the surface, but crazy dangerous when the electronics went out.

So far, so good, X thought.

His HUD displayed the data he relied on during a dive: *15,005 feet; 134 mph velocity; 8 degrees Fahrenheit; 105 beats per minute.*

X remained calm as he dived, his eyes flitting from his HUD to the shelf of clouds. He bit down on his mouth guard as he got batted around in a pocket of turbulence.

"God damn it," he grumbled. *Strong as a sword…*

Experience took over and X regained control, spreading his arms and legs out again before pulling back into a delta shape.

At eight thousand feet, the electronics suddenly went haywire, the data scrambling across his HUD and then winking off altogether.

"Son of a bitch!"

His shout was lost in the howling wind. Aaron wouldn't be able to hear him anyway. They both were now deaf and blind.

With his night-vision goggles offline, X could see only the blue glow of his battery pack and the lights from his helmet. They surrounded his body like a halo around a comet as he streaked toward the surface.

This wasn't the first time his equipment had fritzed out in an electrical storm, and that was why X had taught himself to calculate his altitude and velocity without the help of his sensors.

Aaron would be doing the same thing, looking for any sign of the surface before they smacked into it.

Flashes of lightning gilded the horizon, capturing the outline of a cloud in the beetle shape of the *Hive*.

X looked away as he broke through another wind shear, the turbulence tugging him in all directions. He stiffened his back, flexed his muscles, and used his arms to hold his position.

Thunder boomed so close his bones rattled.

He watched his HUD for a glimpse of his altitude. He tried to calculate the distance since he'd last seen it, but doing math while the wind beat him like a drum was nearly impossible.

Lightning flared to the east, where he'd last seen Aaron.

Every hair on his body rose up, and every muscle fiber seemed to tense.

"Aaron!" X shouted. "Aaron, do you copy?"

Static crackled over the comm.

X put his altitude at around two thousand feet or a bit higher. He began to come out of the nosedive in anticipation of pulling his chute.

Just as he fought back into a stable falling position, the HUD winked back on.

His heart skipped at the altitude reading of 1,500 feet.

"Oh shit!" he shouted. He bumped his NVGs back on with his chin and saw the wasteland burst into view.

To the east, X saw a glowing object falling far slower than he was. Aaron had already deployed his parachute.

"X!" the voice surged over the comm. "Pull your chute!"

X pulled the pilot chute, released it.

He expected to feel the suspension lines become taut and the sensation of being pulled skyward, but instead, he kept falling.

"You got to be fucking kidding me," X muttered. He pulled his reserve. "Please work."

The low-porosity reserve chute fired out, and the lines snapped taut.

He let out the breath he had been holding and took a moment to study their drop zone.

The Old World city was much smaller than the megacities they were used to diving into. It was much warmer here, too, almost eighty degrees.

Instead of the typical snowy ground, he saw mounds of sand.

They were in a desert, below the border of the former United States, deep in the land once known as Mexico.

But the terrain wasn't all desert. X spotted some sort of flora carpeting the outskirts of the city, some of it encroaching on the decayed structures. As he drifted earthward under his canopy, he raised his rifle scope to his visor and zoomed in on what looked like large snakes.

Not snakes, he realized. Vines.

"You seeing this?" X asked Aaron over the comm.

"Yeah. Never seen anything like it before."

There were trees also, towering structures with skeletal limbs that curled at the tips like melting candles.

"My God," Aaron said.

X didn't believe in God, because he didn't believe any supreme being would allow the world and all its animals, plants, and marine life to shrivel and die. And like most places, this Old World city was dead. Nothing except for mutant beasts could survive this radiation.

After securing his rifle, X grabbed both toggles to steer his canopy toward the hospital at the western edge of the town. A warning sensor beeped, and a new reading came on his HUD. He took his left hand off the toggle to grab the duct-taped grip of his rifle. His heart was ticking faster now than during the dive.

Aaron sailed overhead toward the drop zone—the roof of the hospital. X was low enough now that he could see that it wasn't going to work.

There was no rooftop.

"Follow me to a new DZ," X said over the comm.

He toggled over to a field outside the hospital, where the foundations of buildings poked out of the dust and sand. X guided his chute down, pulled on the toggles to slow his descent, and bent his knees slightly.

As the ground rose up to meet his boots, he performed a two-stage flare. He hit the ground hard, raising a puff of dust. He ran out the momentum, and with no wind on the ground, he easily kept his balance.

Halting, he went down on one knee, raised his rifle, and held security while Aaron floated down to the surface. Another cloud of dust billowed up where he touched down.

X scanned the structures all around them—mostly just foundations, which made spotting the three-story hospital easy. It seemed to be the only building still upright.

The area hadn't been hit by one of the nuclear warheads, but it had burned. Everything was charred, which made X worry the medicine would be destroyed if it hadn't already been looted.

X didn't see anything moving, but other divers had told him of camouflaged desert beasts—creatures that looked like stone, and man-size reptiles that could blend in with their surroundings.

Aaron packed his chute and brought up his rifle to cover X. Five minutes later, they had their gear slung over their backs and were moving out.

"Radiation is in the red," X said. "You all buttoned up?"

"Suit integrity is one hundred percent. You?"

"Same."

Side by side, the two men advanced through the ruins, along a street buried under a layer of dust and sand. X knew it was a road only by the rusted, windowless vehicles parked there.

They passed a rotting brown HOSPITAL sign.

X turned to watch their six, backpedaling while Aaron took point.

After crossing through the first block, they came to a road covered in vines. The creepers tendriled around the burned husks of vehicles and over ruined foundations.

Aaron kept going, but X walked over to one of the bloated red vines with spiky, twisted stems.

"Don't touch it," Aaron said.

X hurried to catch up with his partner.

It was as deathly silent as interstellar space.

Around the hospital, the vegetation thickened as if the structure itself were providing it nourishment. X and Aaron both halted at the edge of the property.

Vines curled out of the rooftop.

X bumped off his night vision, using the sporadic lightning flashes to see the mutant cladding of ropy red vines that enveloped the rooftop.

"This is remarkable," Aaron said.

"Not exactly the way I'd describe it," X said. "Come on, we need to find a way in."

X checked his radiation gauge and found it unchanged. As long as he didn't puncture his suit, he would be fine for an hour or two.

They brought up their weapons and slogged through the sand toward the building. Normally, X didn't like wind on the surface, but about now a nice gust to cover their tracks would be most welcome.

A cracking noise stopped X midstride. The hair prickled on his neck.

He moved his finger to the trigger.

Aaron turned. "What?"

X brought a finger to the mouth of his helmet to indicate silence.

The two men slowly played their rifle barrels over the blasted landscape where thick ropes of vine lay coiled like anaconda snakes, their hard skin covered in strangely curved barbs.

X scanned twice for any camouflaged beasts hiding amid the vegetation. Seeing nothing, he signaled to advance.

They crossed through a lot where vehicles stood parked on bare wheels, their tires long since rotted out and the bodies rusted to thin, fragmented shells.

The building was in much better condition. One door

remained at the emergency entrance. X went straight for it, entering a lobby with overturned chairs.

Most of the hospital seemed to have been spared from the flames that wiped this small town out. He made his way down a corridor framed with hospital beds. It wasn't until they got to the emergency wing that they saw the first bodies.

Two corpses lay in the hall, covered in dust, their clothing tattered over bodies mummified in the dry desert air.

X moved around the bodies and headed for the pharmacy, hoping the meds were still in their cryo–storage containers. Time after time, when they found supplies or nuclear fuel cells for their ship, they had gone bad over the 240 years since the bombs dropped. He prayed this was not one of those times.

Still, X pushed on, shining his helmet lights down the corridors. Vines grew over the ceiling and walls, the spiked barbs coming within mere feet of his armor.

Thirty minutes later, they found the pharmacy, its door propped open. At first, he thought raiders had hit this place already, but looking closer, he saw it wasn't people who had opened it.

Vines had burst out from the inside, forcing the double doors open.

X stepped over broken glass, some shards crunching under his boots. Aaron followed him inside, carefully stepping over the vines on the floor.

They entered a lobby with a counter. Beyond it were shelves, most of them stocked with generic medicines. X walked around the desk and started down an aisle. Pill jars and boxes littered the dusty floor.

He made his way to another open door, which led into what should have been an airtight room.

At the entrance, he froze.

"What?" Aaron asked.

X shined his light on two armored bodies.

Aaron walked over. "Holy shit, are those..."

"Hell Divers," X said.

The two men walked into the room, stopping about five feet from the armored corpses. They were both covered in some sort of gray-green moss.

X crouched down and shined his light on the helmets. Broken visors gave a view of bare skulls.

"Makes no sense," X said. "How could they be more decayed than the bodies in the hall?"

"I was wondering the same thing," Aaron said. He stepped around them and went to the cases on the shelves while X examined the skeletal remains.

He reached out with a gloved hand and touched an arm. The simple touch moved the armor, and the bone snapped, some of it turning to powder.

X practically fell on his butt in surprise. "What the hell?"

Aaron stood in front of a crate. "Leave them alone and come help me," he said.

X got up and noted the same mosslike substance clinging to the walls and ceiling.

"I'm not seeing any Redotal," Aaron said.

X pulled out his knife and cracked open a lock on a drawer. He pulled it out to find vacuum-sealed bottles, but not what they were searching for.

As they scoured the room, X heard the cracking sound again. Aaron froze too.

As X waited, he saw a door like that of a walk-in freezer. It was marked with an *R*.

"Found it," he whispered. "It's been in thermal isolation for two and a half centuries."

"Let's hope it worked," Aaron said.

"We're gonna find out."

X opened the door and searched until he found the medicine. Under his helmet light, he held up one of the bottles, confirming it was what they had come for. He carefully secured the bottles in a pouch.

On the way out, X picked up the pace as they walked past the dead divers. He wasn't sure who they were, only that they weren't from the *Hive*.

X hurried down the corridor, almost tripping on a vine. He hopped over it and then stopped.

Aaron kept going.

"Hold on," X said.

"What now?"

"That wasn't here earlier."

"So?"

"So if it wasn't here earlier, how'd it get here? I didn't put it there. Did you?"

"It moved."

"Vines move?"

"I don't know, man, come on, let's get gone…"

X backed away when the same cracking came again, this time behind him.

"X…" Aaron began to say. He turned and accidentally stepped on a vine, crushing it under his boot. Red liquid trickled out.

"Watch out," X said, pulling Aaron back just as the barbs on the vine began to burst. Pink mist puffed into the air. The cloud expanded right toward them, moving fast.

"Run!" X said.

They both took off down the hall. They could hear more barbs popping behind them, trailing them. X ran hard, but the sound grew nearer. He looked over his shoulder as barbs on the vines clinging to ceiling and walls burst, releasing yet more of the pink mist.

"Faster!" he shouted.

He leaped over vines that were now actively snaking their way across the corridor. One sagged down from the ceiling and tried to catch him in a loop. Another peeled off a wall and shot toward his leg.

They made it back to the hallway where the two corpses lay. The pink mist grew denser, darkening into a bloody red swirl as it enwrapped the bodies.

X shined his lights on the remains and was astonished to see the mummified flesh consumed in seconds, leaving nothing but clean, white bone.

Aaron stopped to look, but X yanked on his arm, pulling him into a hospital room. "Follow me!" he shouted.

X shouldered through a broken window, knocking out the remaining shards of glass. He fell three feet onto the sand, landing hard on his side.

His shoulder hurt, but it was the warning sensor in his helmet that made him almost piss himself. Data rolled across the HUD. *Suit compromised...* He had minutes to get out of here.

Aaron helped X up, and they dashed across the sand, away from the hospital building, hopping over the writhing, grasping vines.

More of the little pink explosions puffed into the air. X risked a backward glance to see an entire cloud of red, venting up from the top of the hospital.

"We have to get into the sky!" Aaron shouted.

X looked up at the lightning storm above them, then noticed that the radiation warning on his HUD had elevated. The readings were going up as the pink cloud rose above the hospital.

X didn't hesitate another second. Reaching over his shoulder, he activated his booster. Aaron did the same, and two balloons fired into the sky, quickly filling with helium. X grabbed his toggles as his boots swung up off the ground.

The storm of red reached out toward them, tendrils of spores swirling upward. The radiation gauge chirped louder.

X watched in horror as he shot upward toward the threat of lightning. He was stuck between a radioactive cloud and the electrical storms.

Heart pounding, he slowed his breathing and searched for Aaron. He was floating twenty feet away, his balloon pulling him higher.

"We're good, man, we're good," Aaron said over the comms.

Lightning flashed around them on the long ascent back to the airship. X watched for it in the darkness. Ice crystals formed on his helmet as he rose higher.

The radiation warnings finally ceased at two thousand feet. He looked down at the tear in his suit, praying he hadn't gotten a lethal dose.

Only time would tell.

For now, he was returning in one piece, with medicine to help save the sickest people on the ship.

X looked up as salvation hovered over them. The bay doors of the beetle-shaped airship opened, swallowing Aaron and his balloon. X floated up next to join him in the silo-shaped chamber.

A door sealed under their boots. The platform rose up as another door opened above them. Overhead, a plastic dome lowered from the launch bay to seal them inside. Chemical spray hissed out of jets on the platform, covering them both in white foam.

They turned with their arms out, leaving no square inch untreated.

Fifteen minutes later, the decon process was complete, and water rinsed off the chemicals.

The dome pulled away to a single person standing in the launch bay in a CBRN suit.

"We found it," X said.

"There was something down there," Aaron said. "Vines that move, and a radioactive mist that…"

Captain Ash listened but gave no visible reaction. It was almost as if she already knew about it.

"Well done," she said. "You saved a lot of lives today."

X and Aaron threw up a salute.

"Tell no one about what you saw down there," she said on her way out. "That's an order, divers."

ONE

The dream had come to King Xavier Rodriguez the past two times he rested his eyes. He let out a groan as he sat up in a briefing room on the CIC of the assault ship *Frog*, where he had fallen asleep from pure exhaustion.

As he stirred awake in his chair, he recalled the dive to the hospital all those years ago. He'd thought the carnivorous vines were a fluke of nature, but now he wondered if this was what had killed everyone else who ventured to the Panama Canal over the past two centuries.

X replayed Rodger's SOS message on a tablet.

"Help! Vines… coming through the walls… They're turning people…"

There was little doubt in his mind what had happened at the outpost. And X held out scant hope that Rodger or anyone else had made it out of there alive. The bunker wouldn't have saved them; it would have doomed them.

X got up and opened the hatch to the CIC. The place bustled with activity. He strode through, ignoring salutes, to stand at the remaining window. The broken ones had been sealed off to keep out rain and radiation.

Outside, he could see a shoreline littered with wrecked boats. The *Frog* was anchored off the northwestern shore of Fraser Island, adjacent to Kangaroo Island and 184 miles from Brisbane.

Seeing all those wrecks, X had decided to anchor the amphibious assault ship here for repairs, hoping some of those vessels contained what they needed to get her seaworthy again.

They had fled north to escape the radioactive fallout after Captain Rolo nuked the supercarrier *Immortal*. Almost two days had passed since then, and X was still in a homicidal rage.

For now, they were far enough from the fallout, they were safe to make repairs. First they had to find the parts. Behind him, the remaining crew worked swiftly to identify what was needed. The damaged ship had a slew of issues.

Waiting for a full briefing, X was getting more frustrated by the minute.

Over the years, he had experienced many betrayals and lies from superior officers. That list included Leon Jordan, former captain of the *Hive*, who had left X stranded on the surface for nearly a decade. Up until two days ago, that betrayal had topped the list. But Captain Rolo had officially surpassed Jordan.

The spineless old bastard was the *king* of betrayers.

Nuking the supercarrier hadn't just destroyed their most valuable ship. It had also killed hundreds of innocent soldiers and sailors. With one single bomb, Captain Rolo had all but wiped out the Vanguard military.

Eevi, Timothy, and other sky people loyal to X would have tried to stop him from this, and while X wanted to hope they were still alive, he didn't see how that was possible. Rolo would never have left anyone alive to tell the story.

No matter how much X thought about what had happened, he still couldn't quite wrap his head around it. These were sky people they had rescued from the machines. What could lead someone to such an evil act against the very people who had saved his life?

The answer was simple, though. Atrocities throughout history had the same cause: greed and fear.

The sky people from Tanzania had survived unfathomable horrors at the machine camp. They were rescued and brought to a paradise they would do anything to keep. And that meant Michael and everyone else back at the islands were in danger too.

But this wasn't over. Rolo hadn't won.

Not with breath still in the king's lungs, and blood pumping through his body. X would return to the islands and make Rolo, Charmer, and anyone else who had supported them pay with their lives.

He blinked the sleep from his eyes and went to General Forge, talking in Spanish with Captain Two Skulls across the room.

"Give me some good news," X said.

Captain Two Skulls and General Forge exchanged a look.

"What?" X asked. "You can't fix the ship?"

Forge looked uncertain. "Sir, we have a list of parts, and we think we can fix the ship, but…"

"But what?"

X looked to Two Skulls.

"What the fuck aren't you telling me?" asked the king.

"Sir, we don't have the *fuel* to get back to the Vanguard Islands," Forge said.

"You're just telling me this *now*?"

"There was a leak. We lost more on the way here."

"So we find more, or we find a new ship," X said. "Shit, I'll swim if I have to."

Forge and Two Skulls both looked at him but said nothing.

He knew how crazy he sounded.

These two men had just lost most of their troops, but neither of them was acting like a damned child. Hell, X wouldn't be surprised if they were both silently questioning his leadership. After all, it was his actions that had given Rolo the opportunity to nearly destroy them.

"I'm sorry," X said. "Let's get an advance team together to start looking for the parts. We'll find the fuel."

"I volunteer to lead the salvage mission."

X turned toward the voice of Magnolia.

She was dressed in her Hell Diver suit and armor, with her helmet tucked under one arm. Her electric eyes seemed to flash as she looked at X.

He could say no, but perhaps getting her off the ship was a good thing.

Or perhaps the wastes will take her, too...

"Captain Two Skulls, keep me updated on the status of the ship," X said. "General Forge, send out your best scouts to see what's out there and what kind of parts we can find. Mags, you come with me."

He left the CIC and headed belowdecks, straight to the sickbay.

It wasn't a complete shock to see Lieutenant Slayer up from his bed and talking with Sergeant Blackburn. The two remaining Barracudas were still on the mend from their near-death battle a week ago with the beast living on the submarine, but the color had finally returned to their faces.

Blackburn had his blond hair slicked back, and Slayer had a freshly shaved head.

"Attention," someone said.

The medical staff and both Barracudas saluted X.

"As you were," X said. "You should be resting, gentlemen."

Slayer heaved a sigh. "After what happened, hard to rest, sir."

"I understand. That's why I'm here. I need you and Sergeant

Blackburn to make sure you're doing everything you can to get better."

X glanced at Magnolia, then back to the soldiers.

"We're going to need every able body for what comes next," he said.

"We'll be ready to fight," Slayer said.

Blackburn gave a stern nod.

"Good, but for now keep resting," X said. "That's an order."

He pressed on with Magnolia into the medical bay until they located Corporal Valeria. She had a clipboard like the one the Cazador scribe Imulah used, and was reading a chart.

"Corporal," X said.

She turned and smiled. "Ah, King Xavier, you come for Miles, yes?" she said in her heavily accented voice.

She put the clipboard back on a slot on the bulkhead and walked over to a secure hatch. It opened to a small room with a prison cell on one side, occupied by Jo-Jo. The monkey lay curled up on the deck, her injured arm wrapped in a bandage.

Miles slept in a cage facing the barred-off cell, or so X thought. The dog lifted his nose and sniffed the air. He tried to get up, struggled.

X went over and bent down in front of the cage. "It's okay, boy."

"His ACL need time for recovery. Otherwise, he berry good," said Valeria.

"And Jo-Jo?" X asked.

"She makes a remarkable recovery so far, King Xavier." Valeria walked over to the cell. "She ready when you need her."

"How about now?"

Valeria turned to X. "Now?"

"We need her for a mission."

Jo-Jo stirred in the cell, and the oval black eyes looked up. She let out a grunt, then got up with her front knuckles.

Miles wagged his tail and licked at the metal gate of his cage.

"Can I let him out?" X asked.

"Sí, sí," Valeria said.

X unlocked the gate, and Miles nudged up against him. After a quick hug, the husky went over to Jo-Jo, who reached out her paw.

Magnolia cleared her throat. "Sir, can I ask you why I'm here..."

"Meet me in the cargo hold and gather the other Hell Divers," X said.

He kept his eyes on the animals as Magnolia left.

Jo-Jo was three times the size she had been when Ada found her in the wastes. The thought hurt his heart with a reminder of yet another person dear to him that he had lost over the years.

And that was why X could never give up. None of those deaths should be in vain.

"Get Jo-Jo ready to head outside, just in case," X said to Valeria.

"And Miles?"

"He stays put."

X bent down to scratch his dog behind the ears. He hated doing it, but Miles needed to heal, and right now X needed to lead without worrying about his best friend getting hurt while following him around the ship.

The king stood and made his way through the medical bay. He gave Slayer and Blackburn a wide berth so they didn't need to salute. It didn't matter—the men got up and came to attention.

"Rest," X growled.

He didn't stop until he got to the cargo hold where the Hell Divers had stored their gear from Brisbane. The APC was right where they had left it, decontaminated from radiation and the toxic jungle they had driven through.

A single technician worked on the vehicle. Hell Divers Edgar Cervantes, Jorge "Gran Jefe" Mata, and Sofia Walters were helping. Tia was here too, talking to Magnolia. This was all that remained of the Hell Divers now that they had lost Arlo and Kade.

X stood in the entry hatch for a minute, again feeling the overwhelming sense of loss. It struck him how many times he had stood in the launch bay of the airship *Vanguard* when it was the *Hive*, staring at the lockers once occupied by men and women he had known and loved.

"Gather round," X called out.

The unsuspecting divers rushed over to stand stiffly in front of X. His gaze swept over them. Edgar seemed collected, and Sofia too, but Tia was a mess after losing Kade. Magnolia also seemed to be holding on by a thread after getting news about Rodger's likely death.

But now was not the time to mourn or mope. He needed them functioning at 100 percent.

"I won't lie to you," X said. "Things are critical on this ship. Without parts, we are stranded."

"Stranded?" Tia asked.

"For now, but I'm confident we will find the parts we need to be seaworthy." He paced a few steps, then stopped. "We have suffered heavy losses and now face a new enemy back at home. An enemy who tried to kill us and who wants to take what is ours, purely out of personal greed."

Gran Jefe hawked and spat on the deck. "I flay that bug-eyed captain myself, Your Majesty. Skin him, make him into a drum, then beat him every day."

X couldn't keep back a smile. "*Gracias*, Gran Jefe, but I'll be doing the flaying when the time comes."

The big Cazador bowed slightly.

X looked through the portholes across the hold, out over Kangaroo Island. Lots of monsters out there, from the cyclopes and dingoes to the bat-like human monsters, and Tasmanian devils the size of grizzly bears. Plenty of things eager to kill more people, but someone had to get those parts.

X looked to Magnolia.

"Commander Katib, once the Cazador scouts return, I am sending out three fire teams on a scavenging mission, and I want you to go with them, using this APC."

"Yes, sir."

"Jorge, you will go with her," X said.

Gran Jefe walked over, tilting his head back and raising his pierced nostrils in pride.

"Things look very bad for us, King Xavier, but we will still win," he said. "You know why?"

X tilted his head, curious.

"*Porque el gordo* Rolo think everybody dead now." Gran Jefe grinned. "We are *fantasmas*, Your Majesty—ghosts—and they don't see us until too late."

* * * * *

Michael was led up the stairs of the capitol rig, where he had lived in relative harmony for the past two years.

Now he was a prisoner.

Two mask-wearing sky people from Tanzania stood with machine guns in the passage ahead. At one point, Michael had been their savior from the machines at the prison camp.

But these people were not returning the courtesy. They were not his saviors but his captors.

They said nothing as they marched Michael into a stairwell and up toward the top of the rig. The sheer ingratitude made him so mad he wanted to break out of the cuffs secured over his robotic hand and his flesh-and-blood hand. He could maybe do that and maybe kill both these men. But what then?

Charmer had his wife and son and the support of the Wave Runners. Their leader, Sergeant Jamal, had already killed Ton and possibly Lieutenant Wynn and the other militia soldiers. Michael still wasn't sure. What he did know was that Charmer had been planning all this for quite some time, including framing Michael for the deaths of Oliver and his son, Nez.

The evidence was shoddy, with eyewitnesses claiming they saw someone with a robotic arm. They had established a motive for Michael to kill Oliver due to their multiple confrontations over time.

But this was the Vanguard Islands, where justice was once dispensed inside the Sky Arena. Michael knew he was lucky even to be getting a trial.

For now, the only thing he could do was wait for King Xavier to return, and hope that the violence would be swift and limited to Charmer and Rolo.

The two guards took Michael to the top of the stairs. One of them then opened a doorway to the sun-swept rooftop.

Michael squinted and brought up his bound hands to shield his eyes.

"Go," one of the guards said.

Stepping out onto the rooftop, Michael heard shouting.

Not shouting...

Chants.

"¡Combate! ¡Combate! ¡Combate!"

As his eyes adjusted to the bright sun, Michael saw that the guards were leading him to the source of those chants: the Sky Arena, now packed with people.

Was he getting a trial by combat after all?

One of the guards shoved Michael, knocking him to the dirt. He quickly recovered, pushing himself up to face the soldier.

"Big man with a gun," Michael said. "Pretty courageous of you to hit me."

"Don't talk to me about courage. You killed a man and a boy in their *sleep,* you piece of Siren scat."

The man lifted his face shield to look in Michael's eyes.

"I would never do that," Michael said. "I would never kill—"

The man punched him in the gut, dropping him to his knees.

"John," said the other guard.

Gasping for air, Michael glared up at John, who cocked his fist for another punch.

The other guard grabbed his wrist.

"You're a liar," John said.

Michael's long hair blew in a gust of wind as John finally stepped back. The other guard, who had yet to lift his mask, bent down to help Michael up.

"Don't touch me!" Michael snarled.

The guard backed away as Michael pushed himself up to his feet. Still catching his breath, he followed the two men into the Sky Arena. They entered a gate at the top level, with a view of the sunken amphitheater.

Hundreds of people filled the stands—Cazadores, sky people, refugees from bunkers like the one in Rio de Janeiro.

Michael scanned the crowds for people he recognized. He saw several men and women he had grown up with. But their eyes weren't full of pity or sadness when they saw him with the guards.

They glared at him.

It struck Michael that if his own people thought he was guilty, he was as good as dead.

The soldiers guided Michael to a partially enclosed sky box, where Charmer stood with a white eye patch. A bright-white tunic covered his wiry frame.

"I should have known you'd be here, Carl," Michael said.

"Ah, Michael," Charmer said. "Glad you could join us. Make yourself comfortable ... oh, and please refer to me as sir, or Charmer. Carl is my *old* name. I'm a different man now."

He gestured toward a plush seat that Sofia and the other brides of el Pulpo had sat on during the gladiator battles below.

Michael looked at Charmer's outstretched arm and fantasized about ripping it off and beating him to death with his own limb.

"Your wife and son are nearby," Charmer said with a cheery smile. "If you cooperate, I'll let you see them."

Anger boiled up, but he suppressed it the best he could.

The guards stood on both sides of the sky box. Another guard pulled back purple velvet drapes while Charmer took a drink of wine from a glass.

Charmer grabbed a megaphone and stepped out in front of the metal rail fashioned with welded links of interconnected octopuses.

"Attention, friends of the Vanguard Islands!" Charmer boomed.

All the faces throughout the arena looked up at the booth.

"Today, we gather for two reasons, but I won't keep you waiting," Charmer said.

He motioned for Michael to join him in front of the rail.

"As you may have heard, Michael Everhart stands accused of a heinous crime," Charmer said. "Many of you know Michael as a Hell Diver, chief engineer, and council member."

Cries and shouts erupted around the arena.

"He's innocent!" someone yelled.

"He saved you all!" screamed another.

Charmer held up a hand.

"You are right; he did save us," he said, turning slightly to Michael before looking out over the crowd. "But Michael also lied to us. To all of us."

The crowd went quiet.

"Michael lied about something very important: a secret food source."

More shouts came from the crowd, and again Charmer silenced them.

"Yes, that's right. Michael and a group of his comrades hid a source of food discovered by King Xavier on the supercarrier *Immortal*," he continued. "We believe they meant to use it for their own—"

"He lies!" Michael shouted.

Charmer lowered the megaphone, his smile gone.

"You will have your time to speak," he growled. "Now, step back."

Michael remained where he was, his chest heaving. John tried to grab him, but Michael stepped out of his reach as a scribe entered the booth with a clipboard.

Not just any scribe. It was Imulah.

He looked at Michael but said nothing, then handed the clipboard to Charmer.

"Thank you, Imulah," Charmer said. He raised the megaphone again. "Unlike Michael, I am going to be fully transparent with you all," he said. "We have documented his arguments and fights with Oliver before his death, and have eyewitness accounts that include several people who saw a man with this…"

Charmer gestured toward Michael's robotic arm.

"We know that Michael had a motive to kill Oliver, but we believe the death of his son was an accident," he said. "We believe Nez woke up and was trying to protect his father and that is why he was killed."

Michael felt his heart thump. "I would never do that!" he shouted.

Both guards grabbed him, pulling him back as he screamed. The entire stadium went silent during his outburst.

"I would never kill a kid!" he shouted. "I've been framed, set up!"

He stared out over the faces of Cazadores and sky people, realization setting in. This was just another one of Charmer's tricks. Part of his plan. He wanted Michael to do this, to look crazy.

Another guard rushed inside and moved over to whisper something to Charmer. Charmer bent down, listened, then nodded. He raised the megaphone again.

"I apologize for this dramatic scene," Charmer said. "But now I'm proud and excited to announce that the main event of today has arrived. Take a look!"

He pointed south. All eyes followed his finger into the sky.

Michael squirmed in the grip of the guards, trying to make out whatever Charmer was gesturing toward. Squinting, he made out a beetle-shaped hulk as, for a moment, it eclipsed the sun.

The airship *Vanguard* floated across a clear blue sky.

Michael felt his heart thump again, but this time not from fear. If the airship was here, then the *Immortal* wasn't far. And neither was King Xavier.

Michael relaxed in the guards' grip, but they held on tight.

Everyone in the arena watched the airship carve across the sky. Charmer seemed unfazed by either the view or the prospect of what King Xavier would do.

He held up the megaphone.

"I ask you all to give a massive welcome home to Captain Rolo and his brave crew, who have returned with a gift for us all," Charmer said. "They have returned with hybrid seeds that will weather future storms and grow fast enough we won't have to fear famine ever again or ever have to venture out into the wastes."

Michael narrowed his eyes on the ship, his gut twisting. Something was wrong…

"That is a good thing. For unfortunately, King Xavier and the

Vanguard military were wiped out on their mission to find the Coral Castle. It seems that sea monsters took out their ships," Charmer said. "We are also told that Outpost Gateway was destroyed in an unrelated radioactive attack that we still don't fully understand."

Charmer looked to Michael—just a glance before turning back to the crowd. Michael felt his entire body going weak, as if he were about to pass out.

X was dead? And Magnolia... Rodger...

"No," Michael whispered. "No, it can't be."

"While we may never know exactly what happened, these tragic events prove what Captain Rolo has believed all along: that our future is here, not in the wastes," Charmer said into the megaphone. "Soon we will elect a new king, someone who will protect this sacred place without any more fool's errands into the darkness."

He lowered the megaphone and turned away from the crowd, the drapes closing behind him. As he left, he stopped to whisper to Michael.

"Sorry to break it to you, mate, but no one is coming to save you," Charmer said. "The king is dead."

TWO

Kade Long twisted and turned on the hard prison bunk with nothing on but a tattered blanket and some ratty shorts. He had spent the past day and a half inside, waiting for the "knights"—the strangely armored and well-armed men who had captured him— to take him to find King Xavier, as the Forerunner had decreed.

So far, only two people had come to visit him while he waited. The first was a doctor who had applied a gel on his injured leg and wrapped it with what he heard her call "hybrid seaweed." She had been accompanied by two guards, who remained outside the cell during her short visit.

The second person who came to see him was the knight who had taken his weapons. He had brought Kade a small meal of dried fish with rice and steamed seaweed. That was probably ten hours ago—he wasn't sure.

Kade had been awake the entire time of his imprisonment, and while he knew he should have been sleeping, it simply wouldn't come. Not since he met the Forerunner and learned the truth.

It was still hard to fathom that Captain Rolo had used a nuclear warhead on the supercarrier *Immortal*. If he was crazy enough to do that, there was no telling what he would do when he got back to the Vanguard Islands.

But if King Xavier was indeed alive, there was still hope that Rolo could be stopped.

The king and the Hell Divers were on the *Frog* during the destruction of the supercarrier. Knowing that X was still alive along with the divers—especially Tia—helped keep Kade from going mental.

They're all still alive, and you will see them again.

Kade had just begun to relax and drift off to sleep when he heard footsteps. Two sets, possibly a third. They stopped right outside his door.

He stood and positioned himself in front of it. A metal hatch pulled back over a viewport, and a guard wearing an iron mask with grilles for a faceplate stepped up to look inside.

"Back up," said a gruff voice that Kade didn't recognize.

He complied.

"More," said the guard.

Kade backed up until he hit the bunk.

"Put this on."

Clothing came through the viewport. First a sweatshirt, then a pair of blue sweatpants. They were baggy, and he had to tie the string to keep them on. The masked guard watched him the entire time through the grille of metal covering his eyes.

"Want to draw a picture, or what?" Kade asked.

The man grunted but kept watching.

The sweatshirt felt thin, as if it had been worn for years by ten men before him.

The guard watched him another minute, then backed away.

A key twisted, and the hatch opened to the sight of not just the guard but also a knight. Kade had yet to see his face, masked behind the visor of a gleaming suit of armor.

The doctor was also here, wearing a brown jumpsuit. She sat Kade down on his bunk and unslung a satchel from her shoulder as the guard and the armored knight watched from the open doorway.

She rolled up his pant leg over the seaweed poultice and cut it off with scissors. Pulling out a flashlight, she examined the wound. The redness was gone, and a scab was already forming.

"Does it hurt to put weight on it?" she asked in a concerned voice.

"No."

She held his gaze, perhaps sensing the lie.

"Is he ready?" asked the knight.

"He should rest another day," the woman replied. "Probably more than that."

"I'm fine," Kade protested.

The doctor looked back to the knight, who simply nodded.

She leaned down and pulled out a folded oilcloth from her satchel. Inside was another wet strip of seaweed. It felt cold when she wrapped it around his flesh.

Kade thanked her, and after she left, the knight motioned him to follow.

"Are we going to find King Xavier now?" Kade asked.

He didn't expect the warrior to respond, but he didn't give up and tried an easier question.

"You going to tell me your name, mate?"

"Piss off," said the knight.

"I'm asking for a name, not the geographical coordinates of this place."

"You talk a lot," said the guard.

"You do too," said the knight. "Why don't you both shut the bloody hell up."

It was clear who was in charge here. The men in medieval armor were at the top of the pecking order, and this one was a real mongrel. But there was still much that Kade didn't know. Like why they wore that heavy armor in the first place.

Obviously, it protected them in the wastes, but some of it seemed over the top. Perhaps it was ceremonial. The Cazadores certainly had their own traditions and customs when it came to fighting. So did Hell Divers.

On the trek through the facility, Kade kept his mouth shut and looked around him. The place was big—much larger than the airship where he had spent most of his life. The guard and the knight took him back up the stairs to the main chamber, where he had seen civilians on the way in.

"Unlock the door, and I'll take him from here," said the knight.

"On your own? I was told to accompany you."

"You think I need help with this hoon?"

The knight lifted his metal visor, and Kade finally saw his eyes: brown and middle aged, with crow's-feet at the outer corners. He had a sharp nose over a thick beard that was patchy on the right side, where a scar cleaved a half moon across his cheek.

"No," said the guard. "You know I have the utmost respect for—"

"And yet you question me?"

He bowed his head. "It won't happen again, sire."

"Unlock the door."

The guard fished out a key and inserted it, then spun the wheel to open the hatch. The knight stepped up and said, "Let's go, Kade."

Kade followed him through into the open passage with a view of the balconied levels above. It was early in the morning, and most of the lights were out in the living spaces.

A single person stood at a railing. It was an old woman, her wizened face illuminated by a candle. Her eyes were clouded by cataracts, yet she seemed to see them as they walked in the darkness below.

The knight led him back past the tanks full of sea creatures. Large overhead lights had been lowered over the glass containers of beautiful underwater ecosystems. Bright coral colonies of gold and fuchsia blossomed in one large tank; thick green-and-black seaweed grew in another.

Kade halted at the top of the ladder leading to the platforms.

"Come on," said the knight. He was already on the catwalk crossing over the tanks.

Kade slowly followed, taking in the sweeping view. To his left was a tank full of crabs, lobsters, and shrimp, swarming the carcass of a dead fish.

On his right, a shoal of live fish moved as one. Not the mutant or deformed specimens he had seen on bad catches at the Vanguard Islands—these were plump, vital fish with bright scales.

This seemed to be an underwater farm. He counted the tanks across the vast space, each illuminated by specialized lights. By the time Kade crossed the platform, he had counted forty-one and there were still a dozen more.

After leaving the room, he was led back to the bottom of a ladder in the vertical shaft he had climbed down days ago. He hoped they were going to find King Xavier, but what if the Forerunner had already decided to get rid of Kade?

"Go," said the knight. He motioned for Kade to start climbing.

Moving to the bottom rungs, Kade looked up the shaft, which was open at the top. Lightning cleaved through the clouds and outlined a helmet looking down at him.

"I said go, damn it," said the knight, behind him.

Kade knew he had no choice but to obey and hope he wasn't being led to his death. Although why would they have treated his wounds if they were going to kill him?

Maybe for more info first, and to get me to think I'm safe, he thought.

Kade didn't trust them for a second.

He started up the ladder. Halfway up, his leg hurt again despite the seaweed poultice. The pain grew worse with each rung.

At the top, the knight standing guard held a rifle on Kade as he climbed out into the gusting wind and rain.

"Easy, pal," Kade said.

He put his hands up as the knight pointed his gun muzzle at a boat bobbing up and down in the water. Bow and stern lines moored it to the concrete platform he had just emerged from.

Kade walked over to it, shielding his face from the rain while glancing about him. It was hard to see much in the storm, and there was nothing to indicate where this place was located. It seemed to be in the middle of a coral reef, of which there were millions of acres along this coast.

The other knight emerged from the ladder behind Kade and jumped into the boat, then waved Kade aboard. "Put this on," he said.

Kade climbed aboard and opened a crate containing his Hell Diver gear. Rain pelted him as he swapped out the sweatshirt and sweatpants for his jumpsuit and armor rig. Finally, he cinched the helmet and tapped his wrist computer.

He was not surprised to find his battery empty. That meant his life-support systems were offline, but the rad suit still offered some protection.

A minute later, the boat was pulling away, and as soon as they were out on the open water, a bag went over his head. He could still see through it when lightning flashed, but any storms were distant.

Engines rumbling, the craft thumped across the waves. Kade used the time to consider everything that had happened. It was hard to wrap his mind around it, but he had seen the footage.

All he could do was pray King Xavier was still alive.

If the king had died since the nuclear blast...

No, he's the Immortal.

Kade pushed aside his worries and tried to relax as the boat thumped across the choppy water. After what felt like about three hours on the ocean, he couldn't hold back the nausea from the turbulent trip, and his worries.

"Hey," he said. "Hey, I think I'm gonna puke."

At first, no one answered.

"Hey, I said I'm going to get sick! The bag…"

The bag suddenly lifted off his head, and he stared down the muzzle of a shotgun held by the same armored asshole. "Don't try anything, or you won't have a mouth to puke out of."

"I promise," Kade said.

The knight lifted the barrel away, then reached down and lifted Kade's helmet off. Kade heaved onto the man's boots.

"I—I'm sorry," he said.

The knight grunted as Kade retched up foam and bile noisily on the deck. When he finally stopped, the boat was coming up on a landmass.

"You done?" asked the knight.

Kade waited a beat before nodding. His helmet went back over his head. Then came the bag, but not before he saw a lighthouse on the island.

A few minutes later, the boat slowed. They bobbed up and down, and an anchor splashed into the water.

Kade felt a hand on him.

A rhythmic beating noise met his ears as he shuffled across the deck. He was led over to a ladder and told to climb down.

Kade descended the rungs into a rubber raft. The two knights followed. The one with his weapons went to the bow, and the other took the oars.

Lightning flashed over the island, the blue glow falling over thick jungles.

Over the roll of thunder came the beating sound again. He had never heard anything like this before. It was hard to determine the source of the sound, but it didn't appear to come from the ocean.

Kade looked to the sky, waiting for the lightning to improve his view. The rubber raft hit the surf and fell off the front of a wave, knocking him on his back.

The knight on the oars squared the boat toward shore while the man on the bow hopped out into the surf. They hit the beach with a crunch, sliding up onto the sand. The knight that had hopped out pulled them as far as he could. Then he waved at Kade.

"Out!" he shouted.

Kade got up and fell over the side, hitting the beach headfirst, but thankfully his helmet took the brunt of the impact. The percussive beating in his ears grew louder, until it seemed to be just over him.

When the bag came off his head, he saw the source: a dull-black helicopter—the first he had ever seen.

"Crikey," Kade said.

"What, ya never seen a whirlybird before?" asked the knight.

"Not a working one."

The machine set down on the beach, the rotors slowing but still whipping up grit. The cargo hold doors opened, and another knight stepped out in the same bulky armor. Two of his comrades stood in the open cargo hold as he made his way over to Kade.

Unlike the others, the knight had medals and battle ribbons hanging from his chest plate. Centered among them was a gold trident.

"Ah, so you're the lad that almost became dingo shit," the man said in a gruff old voice. "Name's General Jack Campbell."

"Nice to meet you. I appreciate you saving my biscuit," Kade said.

The general laughed. "You're lucky, I suppose. We've been watching your group for a while. Not sure how you made it as far as you did."

Kade still had no idea how the knights had seen his people without his people seeing them. Especially in their bulky armor that sounded like walking barrels. Then again, this was their land, and they had managed not only to survive but to thrive here.

The general gestured toward the helicopter.

"We call her the *Sea Queen*, although that model's actually an ancient Sea King," he said. "Twin-engine medium-size amphibious rotorcraft fueled by petrol and batteries. She flies great in this shit weather."

"You better not chunder in it," said the knight behind Kade, pushing him forward.

"Let's go find your king," said General Jack. "I'm excited to meet this bastard."

* * * * *

Layla looked through the glass peephole at the two guards posted outside her apartment in the capitol tower.

These were sky people from Mount Kilimanjaro, guarding her just as the machines had once guarded them until her husband dived in and freed them.

She wanted to open the door and wring their ungrateful necks.

With a sigh, she returned to the small kitchen table where she and her husband had shared so many meals over the past two years. It was almost midnight, and her stomach gurgled with hunger after she'd skipped dinner.

A plate of sliced bananas sat there, the edges browned. She had given some of the slices to Bray and mushed some up for

Rhino Jr., but she had no appetite. Her entire world had come crashing down. And it was all because of Charmer.

The cunning, lying bastard had framed her husband for murder. At first, she couldn't come up with a good reason why. Sure, Michael and Charmer had their beefs, but Michael had helped save them and then delivered them to what was basically paradise.

So what drove a man to do this singularly evil thing to the person he owed for saving his life? Only one reasonable explanation came to mind.

Now that King Xavier was dead and the Vanguard military was destroyed, removing Michael was the last step to controlling the Vanguard Islands.

All that mattered to Charmer was power and taking over. To do that, her husband had to go. And the only way to remove him without sparking a war was to frame him for something so terrible that no one would support him.

Layla clenched her jaw in anger.

She loved X and always would love him, but he had made a fatal error venturing out on a futile mission that had not saved them but doomed them. He had thrown away his life and the lives of so many others, including Sofia.

Rhino Jr. was now an orphan.

She went and checked on the baby and her son. They both were awake when she entered the room they shared.

"Da-da," Bray babbled.

Layla nearly broke as she hoisted him from his bed. The child had been saying the same thing ever since Michael's arrest. Constantly asking for his father.

"Da-da's going to be okay," she said. "He's going to come home to us, I promise."

Rhino Jr. whimpered from the adjacent crib, looking up at

Layla. He wasn't talking yet, but Layla was sure that if he could say a word, it would be "Ma-ma." She still couldn't make herself believe that Sofia was dead. "I'm so sorry," Layla said quietly. "I'm so sorry."

She tried not to cry, tried to be strong. Holding Bray helped, but then Rhino Jr. started to whimper. He broke into tears, wanting to be picked up.

"Layla."

The voice came from the hallway. Victor, who along with Ton had been King X's faithful bodyguard, looked in on her with exhausted eyes. His gaze and clear voice told her he hadn't been sleeping.

"Can I help?" he asked.

"Yes, please."

Victor walked into the room and picked up Rhino Jr., rocking the chubby baby in his muscular arms. He had spent the past few days staying with her and the kids to help out. He had been a godsend since Michael was imprisoned, not only protecting the kids but also helping look after them.

He seemed to like being here too, especially after what had happened to Ton. They didn't know details, only that Ton had died in the standoff with Charmer and the Wave Runners.

"It okay," Victor said. "You safe. You okay."

Layla and Victor walked with the children, rocking them and whispering softly until they both fell back asleep. Quietly they put the boys down and left the room.

Layla went into the kitchen to look out the window at the moon. She could see the other rigs in the distance—people who had grown to support King X and Michael over the past year and a half.

Surely, some of them would fight for Michael if they knew the truth.

But how?

How could Layla prove that her husband wasn't responsible?

"Want some orange tea?" she asked Victor.

"Yes, thank you," he replied.

She prepared the tea while he stared out the window.

"We must do something," he said. "They kill Ton, take Michael, Steve, and the boy, Alton."

Layla handed him a cup.

"We need allies," she said. "People like us that know Michael isn't capable of killing a child."

"Yes, but we must be cautious." Victor closed the shutters at the window. "I worry Charmer can hear everything we say."

Layla feared the same thing, which was part of the reason they had yet to discuss things in detail. For the past few days, they had held her under armed guard. She wasn't sure if she could even leave her quarters. But she knew that if she did, she would be followed.

Victor sat at the table and whispered, "Who can we trust? No one has even come here since…" His face twisted with anger and sadness, no doubt thinking about Ton.

He made a good point, too. Not even her friends, like Katherine Mitchells, the widow of Les Mitchells, had come to see her with their daughter, Phyl. Layla didn't blame Katherine, after all her family had been through with losing Les and their son, Trey.

"I know a few people," Layla said. Lieutenant Wynn for sure, but no one had seen him since the standoff that killed Ton. Pedro and his comrade Cecilia would more than likely support efforts to save Michael. But how could she even get to them without Charmer and his henchmen finding out?

"Pedro and his people might come to our aid, and we might be able to get some of the Cazadores to help us too," Layla said. "Someone like Martino, who is very fond of Michael. He told me that Martino said he owed Michael a favor."

Victor let out an uncharacteristic sigh. "I worry for you, Layla. The babies need you, especially if…"

"Michael is going to be okay," she said. "We're going to save him."

"Charmer has spies everywhere. He will suspect us both. Hard to get help. That is why I must—"

"Wait. What did you say?" Layla interrupted.

"Getting help will be very hard."

"Before that."

"Charmer has spies everywhere."

She sipped her tea as an idea formed in her mind. There was one person she hadn't thought of until now. Someone she wasn't sure she could trust, but a man who did seem to like her husband.

"There's someone with more spies than Charmer," she said.

"Who?"

"Imulah."

Victor raised a brow. "Will he help?"

"Maybe, but it's a huge risk." Layla shook her head, unsure. "Maybe we should try to feel out Pedro first. His people seem uncorrupted by Charmer and his pals. Maybe they will help."

"Maybe, but they went through a lot in Rio. They risk everything by helping."

A knock sounded on the door.

Victor popped out of his seat and drew the cutlass he had sheathed over his back. He pulled it out and started toward the door.

"Open up, Mrs. Everhart," said a silken voice outside.

Charmer.

She held up a hand for Victor to get back.

Then she walked over to the front door and looked through the peephole. Sure enough, Charmer stood there, peering back up at her with his unwavering eye. From what she could tell, he was alone.

She swallowed hard, unlocked the door. Opened it.

Charmer flashed that maddening grin, and once again she somehow resisted slapping it off his face.

"Ah, Mrs. Everhart, good evening," he said.

"What do you want, Carl?" she asked.

"Ugh, I really wish you and your husband would stop calling me that. I prefer Charmer, or…"

"What do you *want*?"

Charmer frowned. "No need to be rude. I was just hoping to have a word with you, but first we're going to need to search your apartment."

Raising a finger, he beckoned two men from the shadows. These weren't sky people. These were Cazadores, and one of them wore a helmet bearing the crown of a Siren's skull.

They both held drawn swords, but Charmer waved his hand.

"Put those ugly things away," he said. "You're not afraid of a woman and two babies."

The man with the Siren skull on his helmet said something in Spanish about Victor.

"Is Victor with you?" Charmer asked her.

She knew better than to lie right now.

"Yes," she said.

"And does he have a weapon?"

"Yes."

"Ah, kindly bring it to me, to make this less difficult."

Layla walked back inside to find Victor holding the cutlass. She reached out. "I need that," she said.

"What if they come to take you? I will defend you and the children," Victor said.

"And you will die," she whispered. "This is not the time to fight."

Victor seemed to hesitate a moment, then relaxed and handed her the hilt of the cutlass. She took it and went back to Charmer.

"The babies are sleeping," she said.

"We will be quiet, don't worry," he replied.

She considered reasoning with Charmer to set her husband free but quickly pushed the thought aside. It would do no good because her husband was more useful to him dead than alive. He had plotted this for a very long time.

"The sword," Charmer insisted.

She handed it over finally, and he strode into the apartment as if he owned the place.

She watched him, wanting nothing more than to kill him right where he stood. But she had to stay calm, stay collected. The lives of her husband and son depended on it.

Victor stood next to Layla as the Cazador soldiers lumbered inside. The one with the helmet took it off and held it under his arm. He walked over to Victor.

"*Tu … amigo de Ton,*" he said.

Charmer turned around. "Not now, Jamal," he said.

Jamal stepped up to Victor, looking him in the eye.

Layla felt a chill up her back. This was the man who had ambushed her husband and killed Ton.

Victor must have known it, too, judging by his clenched jaw and tense muscles.

"Sergeant," Charmer said.

Jamal glared at Victor another moment before backing away. The two Cazadores followed Charmer around the apartment, going not so gently through her things. Jamal opened a trunk and dumped the contents, including her old Hell Diver suit.

"Hey," she said.

Jamal glared at her for a long, uncomfortable moment. Then he slammed the trunk shut with a thud.

Crying came from the bedroom.

Charmer returned from the kitchen, shaking his head. "I told you to be quiet."

His tone and his face told Layla he didn't give a shit. He walked over to the door. Layla hurried over and blocked the way.

"Don't touch them," she said.

"We have to search this room," Charmer said.

"You hurt them, and I will kill you. Depend on it, you little worm."

"Don't worry, I'm not your husband. I don't hurt—"

Layla slapped Charmer in his face so hard he had to take a step back. Jamal and the other guard drew their swords as Victor surged forward—and found a cutlass blade at his throat.

"Halt," Charmer said. He reached up and wiped blood from his lip. "Not very nice of you, Mrs. Everhart. You do that again, and your son will be visiting his parents in jail," he snarled. "Now, get out of my way."

She looked at Victor, who still had a blade at his neck. There was rage in his gaze. He was ready to fight. *Not yet. Soon…*

She took her time stepping aside, letting Charmer walk around her. Sobbing came from the nursery room.

Layla went over to the cribs and picked up both children, holding one in each arm. The guard outside still held a blade to Victor.

Jamal and Charmer began their search of the room. Bray sniffled, but he had stopped crying and watched the two men curiously as they tore through the closet.

Charmer pulled out a bag that Michael had stored in case they ever needed to leave fast. He handed it to Jamal, who dumped the contents. The Cazador rifled through old diving equipment: ropes, carabiners, metal stakes, and a flare gun, which he handed to Charmer.

"I'm afraid I'll need to take this," Charmer said. He shoved it in his waistband, then continued the search.

When they finally finished, Jamal walked over to look at Rhino Jr.

Charmer joined the soldier, smiling at the two babies in turn. She backed away until her spine bumped against a crib.

"Beautiful son," he said. "It is a shame another child might be without a father, which is exactly why I have to do this."

Layla held in a breath, her heart hammering as icy fear gripped her. She held Bray back, but Charmer turned his gaze to Rhino Jr.

Jamal reached out and yanked the boy from her arms.

"No!" she shouted.

He left the room with the child, and Charmer blocked her from following. Victor also tried to move, but the guard kept the blade at his Adam's apple.

Bray cried out, reaching for his small friend.

"Jamal wants the child to be with his own," Charmer said. "With his mother and father dead, it's only right."

"No, he needs me," Layla said.

"He needs his people, Mrs. Everhart. Just as your son needs you."

Charmer smiled, then backed away.

Stunned, Layla watched in horror as they left the apartment. Victor rushed over to her when the Cazador finally pulled the blade away. Layla held Bray tightly against her chest. Her mind raced, but there seemed to be only one option right now. She needed council, and the only person who could give it was Imulah. She must find a way to sneak out and see him undetected.

Bray pulled away from Layla to look at her. "Da-da, Da-da," he murmured.

"It's going to be okay," she said. "We will see Da-da again."

But was she lying to her son?

THREE

"The scouts are returning."

The message crackled in Magnolia's headset. She stood at the aft hatches of the cargo hold at the stern of the ship. With her night-vision optics, she searched for the River Heads public boat ramp, which the three scouts had used to access the peninsula.

Clouds of fog rolled across the ocean, obstructing the view.

She turned from the viewports to a flurry of activity that had taken over the open cargo bay. Twelve soldiers in dense Cazador armored suits had broken into fire teams Eel, Knife, and Octopus.

Some of them held spears; others loaded magazines into their battered rifles. And each team had one trooper assigned with a flamethrower connected to a rusted tank that looked as if it could blow up at any minute.

Magnolia looked over the sheet of paper listing the parts they needed for the *Frog*. Belts, valves, piston rings, camshaft, and the biggest and by far unwieldiest thing: an entire engine air-cooling system. Thanks to the briefing she had just gotten from the two sailors responsible for repairing the *Frog,* she even knew what everything was.

Soon, if the scouts had been successful, they would have a map of the area, with some idea where to find those parts on wrecked ships and boats.

She tucked the paper into the magazine carrier over her armor and joined Gran Jefe to finish refitting the APC recovered from Brisbane. Technicians were making last-minute fixes and alterations.

The new windshield was already secured. Both front tires were replaced, along with the axles. The grille guard was bent back into shape after slamming into the hulking Tasmanian devil that had killed Kade. The memory was a blur, but Magnolia could still see the monstrous beast fling him into the jungle.

Thinking of his death wouldn't bring him back. Arlo either. She had to worry about people she could still help. And she had to get back to Panama, where she hoped Rodger would be waiting for her.

"We're almost finished," Edgar said, walking over with a wrench in his hand. "Scouts back yet?"

"Will be soon," Magnolia replied.

"You know, I should be going out there with you," Edgar said.

"Too big a risk."

"Without me, yeah, I agree." Edgar tapped the wrench head against his gloved palm and looked out through the viewports at the mist. "Let's hope the scouts found something."

Tia and Sofia walked over. "*Hope?*" Tia asked. "If they don't, we're stranded here, right?"

"No, we're going to make it home," Sofia said. "I promise you that."

"Not all of us."

Tia lowered her head. She was grieving for Kade, who had taken care of her for many years at the machine camp and before. Magnolia felt her pain, but they were all hurting. Sofia was desperate to get home to Rhino Jr. And Magnolia was going to make sure her best friend did just that. She would search every wreck out there by herself if it meant getting back to Panama and the Vanguard Islands.

"We'll find the parts to get out of here; trust me on that," Magnolia said reassuringly.

A message surged over her headset.

"Prepare to intercept the scout team," said an officer.

Magnolia went to the viewports overlooking the aft weather deck. The two guards on sentry duty aimed the two mounted machine guns at the water. The elevator on the deck lowered to the water to retrieve the three scouts.

When it came back up, only a single man stood on it. Blood was smeared across his chest.

"Only one made it back?" Edgar asked.

Magnolia didn't answer, but Gran Jefe did. "*Malvado*," he said, pointing outside.

"Evil?" Sofia asked.

"*Sí, sí, muy malo*," Gran Jefe replied. He was the only diver wearing armor today and would be accompanying Magnolia on their mission, assuming the scout had returned with useful intel.

A pair of soldiers went out to the weather deck and returned with the man a few minutes later. By the time they were inside, King Xavier and General Forge had gathered with the fire teams.

X walked over to the scout, scratching his beard as he examined the man. "What the hell happened out there?" he asked.

"*Mon... struos*," was all the soldier said.

With shaky hand, he reached into a vest stretched over his bloodstained armor. He pulled out a piece of paper that must be a map of the area. Magnolia was close enough to see the boats identified there.

"What kind of monsters?" X asked.

The scout spoke in Spanish about *"perros grandes"* to General Forge, who translated what X already suspected.

"They encountered some dogs," Forge said. "Big dogs."

X paused a moment, then ordered the map duplicated for the three teams. "We lost two good men for that intel," he said to them all. "Let's put it to good use."

Magnolia knew that the odds of finding all the needed parts were slim, but the scouts had identified the most promising boats that might have them.

"It's going to be hell out there," Edgar said. "I really should be going. You know it, Commander."

"Not this time, Edgar," Magnolia replied.

He frowned and then looked to Gran Jefe. "Be careful and watch each other's backs."

Magnolia felt it was really Edgar telling Gran Jefe to watch *her* back. Everyone knew she was worried about Rodger.

Her heart thumped at the thought of him being gone. She tried not to think that way, but now she wondered if Captain Rolo had somehow attacked the outpost, too, as he had the super-carrier *Immortal*.

Was he really that deranged?

Of course he was. The bastard wanted to destroy the Vanguard military.

She still had no idea what had happened to Timothy, or Eevi, or anyone else on the airship. But she agreed with X: Rolo had probably murdered them all.

Magnolia looked at the techs who had stopped working on the APC. "Get back to work!" she barked.

They all looked in her direction, then promptly returned to the task.

Some time later, an officer ran over with three separate maps of the area. He handed one to Magnolia.

"A'ight, listen up everyone," X called out.

The three Cazador fire teams came to attention, standing like statues in front of the king and General Forge.

"Two of our men died to bring us the intel you all have seen. Those parts will determine whether we make it home or not," X said. "Make no mistake—to find the parts, you'll have to deal with beasts out there."

Forge tapped his breast plate and thrust his sword into the air.

"*¡Matamos los monstruos!*" he shouted. "We kill the monsters!"

The soldiers thumped their chest plates and raised their spears in the air. But those deep voices lacked the brash fearlessness Magnolia was used to hearing. These were the voices of a cowed army.

As those voices faded and the warriors stepped out onto the weather deck, guttural barking and howls rang out from the mist. The beasts were answering with their own war cries.

Gran Jefe stayed inside the cargo hold, his helmet still clutched against his chest. He raised his nose to the air, sniffing like an animal.

Then he turned.

"*No sólo perros,*" he said. "*Diablos*—devils out there."

"We're all devils," Magnolia said.

"Ready to roll!" Edgar shouted.

He got in the front of the APC and fired the engine. The sound reverberated through the cargo hold. Then he got out and gestured for Magnolia and Gran Jefe.

"All yours," he said. "Good luck."

Sofia and Tia stepped up with him.

"It will be okay," Magnolia said.

"Be careful, Mags," Sofia said.

The divers walked away as X made his way over to the APC. He scratched the beard clinging to his haggard, scarred face. His eyes met Magnolia's, and in them she saw the same pain she herself felt.

"Keep your head on a swivel out there," he said. "I can't bear to lose you."

Reaching out, he embraced her and whispered, "We'll get through this."

She hugged him back and felt the strength that was still there.

"I'll be back as soon as I can," she said.

Gran Jefe bowed slightly to the king, then got into the vehicle with Magnolia. She closed the door, which had been reinforced with an additional armor plate. Bars now crisscrossed the side windows.

She drove through the wide-open hatches, out onto the weather deck, and parked with the soldiers. A loud clank rang out as the elevator began lowering them down to an assault craft on the water.

X nodded and she nodded back, holding his gaze until he was out of view. When the elevator clicked to a stop, a ramp lowered from the deck to the assault craft. As carefully as she could, Magnolia drove the APC aboard. Bite marks from crocs marred the hull, reminding her of the rescue mission in Brisbane. The craft pulled away a few moments later, into the fog.

Opening the door of the truck, Magnolia got out and looked as the elevator returned to the weather deck. X still stood there, watching until the mist swallowed the assault boat.

Vicious barking and yowling erupted suddenly in the distance.

Magnolia got back into the truck and closed the door.

"¡Los dioses pulpos!" Gran Jefe said. He pounded his chest. "We have Octopus Lords to watch over us!" The sharpened teeth grinned, and he winked at Magnolia before putting on his helmet.

The assault craft approached the old River Heads public boat ramp. When they got close, the soldiers on the deck unlatched the cargo gate. A small wave lifted the boat as the driver eased off the gas. He got them right up to the concrete landing, where the men swung the gate down.

Magnolia fired up the APC and followed the warriors out onto the fractured concrete of the boat launch. The overhead lights stabbed the darkness, illuminating the backs of the Cazador troops fanning out to begin the search.

Gran Jefe climbed up into the turret with the recently added .50-caliber machine gun. He turned on a spotlight attached to the barrel. The beam lit the shattered road twisting away from the boat ramp.

The Cazador soldiers moved in combat intervals, with the flamethrowers up front. Warriors equipped with shields and spears also took the lead.

Magnolia drove slowly behind them. The idea was to stay close to the teams in case they needed backup. All scavenged parts would be stored in the back of the APC.

The first location on the map wasn't far. Ten minutes into the trek, Fire Team Eel peeled off the road. They hiked down the rocky shore toward a row of beached small craft.

Magnolia looked over the side of the road that had a good vantage of the shoreline. Gran Jefe's beam swept over cracked-open ships, yachts, barges, and fishing boats. All that remained of some of them were a rusted hull, a few spars, and maybe a propeller.

The spotlight raked over several blackened skeletons— human from what Magnolia could tell. She watched the light move to a ship lying on its port side like a beached whale.

The aft section was submerged in the water, but the bow was fully above the surface. A smaller naval ship about the same size as the *Frog*, it was one of the most promising wrecks the scouts had found.

Fire Team Knife started down toward the ship, leaving only Team Octopus ahead.

The barking came again, and Magnolia spotted movement just ahead of Octopus. A gangly quadruped shape darted past. She tracked it with the headlights as it stopped about two hundred feet in front of Fire Team Octopus.

Three of the soldiers stopped, but the one with the flamethrower aimed into the fog and launched a wide arc of flame.

The beast stayed out of the range, eyes glowing red in the darkness. Then it turned and vanished into the fog.

"All clear," Magnolia said. "For now…"

The four members of Team Octopus fast-walked down to a boxy ship lying on its starboard side against a rocky shore. Open hangars on the hull showed a cargo of wheeled vehicles.

Magnolia drove to the side of the road as the team of Cazadores climbed over a sagging concrete wall. Their boots hit the sand, and they slogged toward the vessel. She killed the engine to conserve gas. The only sounds were of wavelets lapping the shore.

The radio crackled with a message in Spanish from Team Eel. Gran Jefe translated from the turret.

"They say all boats are shit," he called down. "No parts. *Nada*."

Waiting for Fire Team Knife to report in, she heard more of the crazed yapping. Multiple dingoes this time—a pack.

She closed the door and grabbed the rifle she had propped against the passenger seat. Macabre memories flashed in her mind as she sat there. The first was an image of Arlo being torn to pieces in midair by baby bats. Then came an image of Ada falling to her death.

Next, she pictured Rodger sitting cross-legged while whittling a stick at Outpost Gateway. This wasn't a memory but what her mind had come up with for his final moments, when the vines had writhed in through the walls. Creeping silently down the hallways and through windows, enwrapping him in their snakelike coils and consuming him whole.

Barking jolted her from the horrific images that plagued her. The APC's spotlight speared through the darkness, chasing the beasts away.

The radio crackled again. Fire Team Knife had found some valves and piston rings that might work. They were gathering up parts before meeting up with Team Eel. Still no air cooler yet, though.

"I'm going to drive ahead and scope out the road," Magnolia said. "Keep your eyes peeled."

"Eyes ¿qué?" Gran Jefe asked.

"Watch out."

"Ah, sí, cierto."

She drove up over a hill, where some kind of shell lay in the middle of the road, just beyond the reach of her headlights. Gran Jefe put his spotlight on an armored torso. They had found one of the two missing scouts.

Blood was streaked across the cracked pavement, leading to limbs bare of armor and chewed to the bone. From a clump of mutant palmettos just off the road, glowing red eyes watched the vehicle. In the green hue of her night-vision goggles, Magnolia could make out the long snout of a dingo. Saliva dripped from jaws that held a human wrist and hand as, behind the beast, four of its brethren ripped pieces from the legs and feet.

"Fire or no?" Gran Jefe asked Magnolia.

"No, save your ammo. These pose no threat to us."

Ignoring the feeding monsters, she backed away in the APC. She reversed all the way to where Team Octopus had boarded the cargo ship.

"Octopus, do you copy?" Magnolia asked.

Static crackled.

"Octopus, come in. Do you copy?"

Again nothing.

Magnolia waited another second, starting to grow nervous, before a response finally crackled back over the comms.

"We have located an intact air cooler."

"Well, halle-fucking-lujah!" Magnolia crowed. "Copy that. Great job."

Magnolia parked on the shoulder of the road overlooking the shore. Gran Jefe aimed the spotlight at the rusted hull that Team Octopus had boarded.

She could see no way down with the APC.

Though she wanted to get in and out as fast as possible, she wasn't leaving the vehicle unless she had a damned good reason. Team Octopus was trained for salvaging. Her job was to get them and the air cooler back to the landing craft and onto the *Frog*.

She killed the engine and waited. A few minutes passed. Then fifteen. Thirty.

She scanned the darkness the entire time.

Just when she thought the monster dogs had departed, another bark came from the road behind them. Multiple pairs of red eyes glowed like coals in the mist.

All at once, the dingoes seemed to go wild in a cacophony of ferocious barking. She grabbed her rifle.

Something yelped in the darkness, and the vicious growls and snarls grew louder. Then came howls of agony from not one but two of the creatures. The loud yelping and yowling hurt Magnolia's ears.

It ended as abruptly as it began—silence once again, with only the distant sigh of the waves. She was almost afraid to whisper into the comm.

"You see anythi—"

Before she could finish her sentence, something came sailing through the fog and smacked into the windshield. It rolled off onto the hood, where it stopped.

Magnolia didn't need Gran Jefe's spotlight. They had found the other scout.

The helmet was broken open, the head inside it mangled and mashed. Only the lower jaw was still fully intact. It hung low in a mocking half grin.

A deep roar emanated from the mist.

Magnolia squinted at a meaty figure lumbering down the road.

"Jefe!" she called up. "Fire!"

Gran Jefe's spotlight hit a pitch-black Tasmanian devil galloping up the road. Its face was covered in warts and tumors. Tracer rounds split the darkness. Gran Jefe's initial shots missed, giving the beast time to leap over the concrete wall that bordered the road.

When she realized where it was heading, Magnolia opened the APC door. She shouldered her rifle and moved through the fog to look down at the ship. The monster crossed the fractured tarmac and entered an open hangar.

"Team Octopus," she said into the comms, "you got incoming."

Magnolia listened for a response but heard only the distant roar of the beast. Perhaps her signal was being blocked by the half-buried hull, or the storm could be interfering. Or maybe the team had already encountered hostiles.

She looked out over the ocean waves. The other teams had collected vitally needed parts to get them home. But they weren't going anywhere until they got that air-cooler unit out of this ship.

She couldn't sit here and wait.

"On me," she called up to Gran Jefe.

He shouted to her as she hopped over the wall. "Commander, orders to stay here!"

"Stay there, then," she called back. "I'm going to help!"

FOUR

"Team Octopus has located the air-cooler unit but is no longer responding," Magnolia had said.

The rest of her message was muddled but clear.

There was a Tasmanian devil out there—a big one.

The report came in ten minutes ago, and since then, the line to Magnolia and Team Octopus had gone dead.

X stood in the CIC of the *Frog*, looking out at the misty coast of the River Heads, waiting impatiently for the comm officer to get him a line to Mags. After losing the two scouts, he knew that the Cazador teams would encounter hostiles. But in the wastes, they were in their element—hunters, raiders, and experienced salvagers all. Forge continued to assure him of that.

"They know what they are doing," said the general. "Patience, King Xavier. It's probably the storms that are interfering."

Patience, X thought. He looked down to Miles, who sat on his haunches, just content to be out of his cage.

"Commander Katib . . ." X said into his headset. "Mags, do you copy?"

Static crackled, then a hiss of indistinct chatter.

X growled, "Can someone get me a solid line to anyone out there?"

"Working on it, sir."

The voice belonged to a twentysomething corporal with black hair pulled back into a ponytail. The man, who went simply by the name Tiger, reminded X of Michael. Not just his youthful features and long hair but especially his energy level and eagerness to help.

X thought of Michael and hoped he was holding things together back at the islands. He was irreplaceable in keeping the rigs running, which made him invaluable to everyone. His skills and knowledge were such that no one in their right mind would try to sabotage him.

Tiger swung around from the radio equipment. "King Xavier, Teams Eel and Knife have both reported back but have had no recent contact with Team Octopus or the Hell Divers."

"Something must have happened," X said.

"We could redeploy Teams Eel and Knife to search for them after they return with the parts, or send out the reserve teams now," Forge said.

X thought about sending the teams on standby but decided against it. They couldn't risk more people until they knew what was going on.

"Tell Team Knife and Team Eel to hurry up with the parts and then get back out there," X said.

"Yes, sir," said the general.

Waiting for news, X paced, his mind a mess of worries. But as much as he wanted to go out there and send more troops, he had to stay calm and trust in the training of his people. There was too much at stake to make half-cocked decisions.

Having Miles by his side helped. He patted the dog on the head.

Just when X was starting to calm down, he saw Captain Two

Skulls and Tiger speaking rapid Spanish in worried tones. General Forge joined them.

"What's wrong now?" X asked.

"There is another *problema*," Forge said. Tiger and Captain Two Skulls both looked at him with clenched features.

"Radiation, sir," Forge announced. "The winds have changed, bringing much of that radioactive fallout in our direction."

"How bad?"

"The rads are already going up; we shouldn't stay here much longer. Maybe a few hours before it gets really bad."

X felt the heat of anger rising in his chest. He wanted to kick the radio equipment but suppressed the urge. *Calm. Just keep the fuck calm.*

His pounding head didn't help. He counted to ten, then counted backward. Then, despite his best efforts, X let out a blue streak of curses.

"Son of a brokedick, dumbshit asshole!"

Miles let out a whine, and everyone in the room looked at X. He was losing it again. And for the first time in months, he felt the urge to drown himself in shine.

No, you're stronger than that. Your people need you! Magnolia needs you.

X went back to the window, searching the ocean for any sign of the other teams. In the fog, he saw movement in the bow of the weather deck. Figures, some in Hell Diver armor, some in Cazador armor.

He squinted, and they vanished.

What the hell?

The headache was getting worse, settling in behind his eyes. He stared out at the mist and saw movement again.

This time, he could make out the gigantic figure.

"Rhino," he whispered. "But I saw you die."

The great Cazador warrior, two years dead now, stood on the deck below, gripping his double-bladed spear. He looked up at X, raised his spear, and stepped to the side.

In the mist in front of Rhino, an entire team of Hell Divers emerged. Aaron, Rodney, Will... All members of Team Raptor. All dead from what was supposed to be a green dive.

Cruise and Murph appeared next. Both divers were part of the team that X had led to the surface not long after losing the entirety of Team Raptor. Both men died on that mission.

Katrina joined them; then came Les and his son, Trey. Arlo was there, too. So were Erin Jenkins and her father, Militia Sergeant Leonard Jenkins.

Commander Rick Weaver, from the airship *Aries*, appeared. X had hardly known the man but knew he was one of the best divers in history.

More Hell Divers and soldiers from the past decade crowded the weather deck.

Ghosts from the past...

A bright-white figure in a suit with gold feathers embroidered on the shoulder pads walked out in front of everyone. A sword hung from her duty belt.

Captain Maria Ash's serious but kind features looked up at X. He could hear her bold, clear voice in his mind.

"You have passed every test of your life, Xavier," she said. *"You dived so that humanity survived. You brought your people to habitable land. You defeated the machines and the Cazador cannibals. But now you face your most difficult test—one that requires you to fight with your head, not your heart."*

She took a step forward as, one by one, the divers and warriors behind her vanished.

"You must use the utmost care to get home and save your people," she said. *"There is no room for mistakes. No room*

for heroes. Use your head and not your heart. For humanity to survive, you must live."

Another voice sounded, this one not in his mind. X turned toward General Forge.

"Sir, Team Eel and Team Knife are almost back with piston rings, valves, a replacement camshaft, and four drums of synthetic engine oil they found," he said.

"Any word from Octopus or Commander Katib?"

"Nothing yet."

When X went back to the window, the ghosts had wandered off, replaced by an actual support crew readying the deck for the first batch of scavenged parts.

He stood there watching, thinking about what Captain Ash had said to him.

He knew what she was telling him: Stay back and keep out of the fighting. Lead from behind, not from the front. But it wasn't his style. Never had been.

Still, Magnolia was out there and might need his help.

"I'm heading down there to wait for the teams," X said. "Let me know if you hear anything from Commander Katib or Team Octopus."

Forge took off, and X bent down to Miles. "Stay put, boy. I'll be back soon."

Miles licked at his face and whined.

"I know, buddy, but staying here beats that cage, right?" X asked.

The dog's tail whipped eagerly.

X left the CIC. The two guards assigned to protect him followed with cutlasses sheathed. X knew their names and little more: Sebastian, a young Cazador skilled in sword fighting, who could move like lightning. And Nicolas, a thin Cazador so adept with a spear he was said to have knocked a male Siren out of the sky from twenty yards.

Both men rushed to keep up with X as he raced down the interior stairwells. At the bottom, he opened a hatch to the cargo hold.

Valeria was across the cargo hold with Jo-Jo. The beast knuckle-walked over to X, grunting. He stroked her neck and looked to Valeria.

"Everything good?" he asked.

"Sí, King Xavier. Do you need anything for Miles?"

"No, he's fine for now, but thanks, Corporal."

X went to the ten soldiers, who were already suited up and armed with rifles and spears. None of them had helmets on yet, and he could see their faces clearly in the well-lit hold.

Like so many times before, he saw men and women—boys and girls really, too young to have seen the horrors of war and the evil in the wastes. But older men were also here. Men who had fought wars before the kids among them were even born. Geezers like X, with bad backs, arthritis, and shit for hearing.

And like X, these warriors had not seen the end of war.

If he could find a way to get them home, another war awaited them at the Vanguard Islands—one that X wasn't sure he could win.

"Teams Eel and Knife are almost back," X said. "Everyone, get ready to pitch in."

Technicians and engineers wearing coveralls and tool belts stood by to take the found parts inside and start repairs.

X walked over to Edgar, Sofia, and Tia.

"Sir," Edgar said, "any news on Mags and Gran Jefe?"

"Not yet," X said.

"I volunteer to go search for them," Sofia said.

"Me too," Edgar added.

"I'm in," Tia said.

"Denied," said X. "Everyone stays here for now." He averted his eyes, not wanting to see the betrayed looks on the divers' faces. He felt it himself.

"I'm sure they are okay," Sofia said. "Probably hunkered down."

"We'll be on standby if you change your mind," Edgar said.

The divers stepped back from the viewports. X stayed to watch activity out on the weather deck. Even from inside the hold, his Geiger counter showed a significant uptick in rads from last time. Without proper protection, it wouldn't take much exposure to make a lethal dose.

They had to get out of here before the wind brought more fallout. The only way to survive was to run.

X watched the support team at the edge of the elevator deck waiting to intercept Teams Eel and Knife. There were only five people: three sailors with ropes, and two soldiers with mounted heavy machine guns angled down at the fog.

The elevator deck had already been lowered to the water.

"King Xavier, Team Eel and Team Knife have docked," Forge said over the comms.

"Copy that," X said. "I'll send soldiers down here to help with the supplies."

He put his helmet on and waved the soldiers onward.

"Okay, let's get those supplies unloaded pronto!" X shouted.

The hatches opened, and the troops filed out onto the slick deck. X followed them out with the divers.

A sudden howl startled him. But this wasn't coming from outside the ship.

X turned back to the cargo hold, where Jo-Jo was clearly agitated.

Something was wrong.

His heart jumped at another bestial sound. The trumpeting call of what the Cazadores were now calling "*cíclopes*" for their single eye.

"King Xavier, you must get back inside," said the guard named Sebastian.

A guttural scream pierced the evening. X moved with the troops toward the sound, which seemed to be coming from the water. The warriors formed a phalanx of spears and gun muzzles around him, and the two soldiers on the mounted .50-caliber machine guns kept their weapons pointed out at the water.

"Hurry!" one of the gunners shouted. "Get them out of the water!"

Panicked voices drifted across the weather deck.

"Move, move!" shouted another soldier.

Clanking came from the stern, where the elevator was rising back up.

"Sir, we must go," Sebastian said.

X hesitated, laser rifle cradled, straining to see what was on the elevator.

"Command, anyone got eyes up there?" he asked.

"Negative—fog is too dense," came the reply.

The trumpeting call came again, but there were no human answers to the horrifying sound. That told X they were either trying to keep quiet or already dead. Once he was inside with Edgar and Sofia, the guards shut the hatches. They stood there looking out the viewports in nervous anticipation.

The elevator finally clanked to a stop. Soldiers inched forward through the mist, spears and machine guns at the ready. X clenched his teeth and readied his blaster. He narrowed his eyes at movement in the dense fog. Out of the curtain came four men from the salvage team carrying crates. They hurried across the weather deck. And that was it. Nothing else emerged from the elevator.

X lowered his head. Another four men lost to the wastes.

Soldiers escorted the survivors. They all had injuries, and all were spattered with the blood of their dead comrades. Technicians in hazard suits moved the salvaged parts and gear inside the cargo hold. As they stowed it all away, X realized that the most important equipment was still out there. So was his best Hell Diver, a woman he loved like a daughter.

He turned to the open hatches and peered out through the mist.

"Come on, Mags, where are you?" he whispered.

In his mind, he pictured where she was, out in the suburban wilderness where dingoes, cyclopes, and the bear-size Tasmanian devils lurked.

"King Xavier."

General Forge came trotting across the bustling cargo hold.

"What is it?" X asked, fearing the worst.

"We picked something up on radar, sir," Forge said.

X looked back out the viewports, toward the water.

"You mean sonar?"

"No, up there," Forge said. He pointed up.

"What, in the sky?"

"Sí."

"What is it, an airship?"

"I don't know, sir, but it's moving fast."

X stepped up to the hatches as they closed. Bending down, he searched the storm clouds. Had the *Vanguard* returned to finish them off?

* * * * *

Inside a cell in the capitol tower, Michael bowed his head in despair. This was the same place they had kept Ada after she dropped a container full of Cazadores into the ocean, just after the last war.

"Last war," he whispered. They had hoped it would be the last, but it seemed humanity simply couldn't find a way to coexist. Now their one hope was gone.

He still couldn't believe that X had perished in the wastes.

And Magnolia. And Rodger... So many of his friends, people he loved and considered family, were dead.

Michael curled up on the slab of concrete, trying to keep from drifting into the darkness of despair. Up until yesterday, he had believed that King Xavier would return to save him and crush Charmer like a coconut shell. But if Charmer was telling the truth, then King Xavier wasn't returning and the Cazador army was all but wiped out. Only the Wave Runners, who were in league with Charmer, remained.

It seemed the chances of anyone coming to Michael's rescue were slim.

Lieutenant Wynn had been relieved of duty and was God only knew where. The remnants of militia from the *Hive* had seen the writing on the wall and had sworn allegiance to Charmer.

Which left Layla and Victor—assuming Charmer hadn't taken Victor into custody, or worse. Michael could only hope his wife was safe with Rhino Jr. and Bray. He didn't want her trying to mount a rescue, not on her own.

But who would come to her aid if she sought it? Michael kept trying to figure that out.

Maybe she could get the sky people from the *Hive*, Pedro and his people from Rio de Janeiro, and Cazador allies. But the chances were slim. Why would they risk their lives and all-out war to save someone who might be guilty of murder?

Now the Cazadores knew all about Ada sinking the shipping container. That meant that a sky person had murdered their own and, moreover, that King X had known about it, choosing to banish Ada to the wastes and then accepting her back.

Charmer had spread that story across the rigs. And now every citizen of the Vanguard Islands knew about Michael's alleged crime. The ceremony at the Sky Arena was the perfect way to paint Michael as the villain and Captain Rolo as the hero.

He shook his head in agony, his long hair whipping across his face. He'd never seen any of this coming. Who could have? While the Cazadores and his people were off setting up in Panama and trying to find the Coral Castle, the sky people from Tanzania were sitting here, getting healthier and stronger. Charmer had plotted and waited for his chance to strike.

Michael looked at the cell across the hallway. Moonlight streamed through from the windows down the hallway, falling on the sleeping form of Steve Schwarzer. The deputy chief engineer had stood by Michael, declaring his innocence and getting himself thrown in the clink.

Charmer was smart. He was cunning. He knew that letting Steve go could spark a rebellion. The old Cazador bladesmith had a lot of friends across the rigs. The only way to keep him quiet was by keeping him here.

Or killing him. Perhaps they still would.

Michael closed his eyes and tried to sleep. Finally, sometime after midnight, he must have drifted off, only to jerk awake a few hours later.

The sun was not yet up when the hatch opened. Heavy footfalls came from the passage outside.

Two guards wearing black pull-down face masks walked inside. Charmer was behind them, unmasked.

"Get up," he said.

Michael stood in front of the cell door. Steve was also awake now. He pushed himself up and staggered over to grab the bars.

"Coming to kill us in the middle of the night?" he asked.

"Coming to move you for your own safety," Charmer replied. "Put your hands out."

"Where's my wife?" Michael asked.

"She's safe with the kids. Unlike you, I wouldn't hurt a child. Now, hold out your hands."

"You won't get away with what you've done," Michael said.

"Away with what?" Charmer asked. "You're the one who will stand trial, not I, amigo."

A guard fastened cuffs around Michael's wrist and prosthetic arm. He wasn't sure he could break out of them, but this might be his only shot. If he could take down these two guards and Charmer, maybe he could free Steve and get to Layla and the kids.

That thought ended when Charmer pulled an Uzi submachine gun from under his tunic and aimed it at Michael's forehead.

"Don't get any thoughts in that evil little head of yours," he said. "I don't want to end up like Oliver and his son."

"You really are a prick," Michael said.

"To survive in this world, you have to be willing to break a few eggs. Or heads."

"That's not true," Steve called out. "You can still be a decent human being."

"Shut up, old man."

The guards unlocked the cells and took the two prisoners out, but instead of going down, they headed up to the rooftop.

"Where are you taking us?" Steve asked. "You going to have us fight in the arena now?"

Charmer didn't answer. He didn't need to. Michael already knew where they were going.

The airship *Vanguard* was mounted across the roof, past the Sky Arena, and that was where they were heading. What Michael didn't understand was *why*.

For your safety… The words rang in his mind.

It took only a few more minutes before they got to the open ramp. Sky people stood guard. But these weren't the faces he had known his entire life. These were men and women from Tanzania.

Some of them wore militia gear; others were in plain clothes. Each held a weapon: pistols, bolt-action rifles, submachine guns.

They watched Michael as he approached. It was clear these weren't the eyes of hope and awe that had greeted him when he dived through a lightning storm to save them at Kilimanjaro.

These were looks of fear and disgust. They all thought he had killed Oliver and his son. Charmer had convinced them of Michael's guilt before the trial even started.

As Michael staggered up the ramp to his former home, he felt dizzy. Anger coursed through his veins, filling his heart with rage.

He should have tried to take Charmer and the guards down when he had the chance. Now there were too many. Not to mention that he was going to be in the sky.

In the sky… Maybe this wasn't a bad thing, after all.

Memories filled his mind as he walked through the old, familiar passages. He passed a hatch leading to the gas bladders. In one of them, he had helped save the ship when he was just a boy. He knew this ship better than any living sky person.

The anger remained, though happily, the light-headed feeling faded as he was taken to the brig with Steve. Charmer stopped in front of an open cell.

"This is where you will remain until your trial," he said. "Don't worry, it won't be long. We have just a few other things to deal with first."

He shut the barred gate behind Michael. "Stick your hands through. Sorry it came to this, mate," Charmer said, unlocking the cuffs.

"Wait," Michael said.

Charmer stood there, watching him.

"Promise me you won't hurt my wife and kid," Michael said. "That you won't take vengeance against my people. You've won, Charmer. No one else needs to get hurt."

"That all depends on whether people cooperate." Charmer gave his mirthless grin. "I assure you, I won't hurt anyone who doesn't have it coming. And for now, as I said, Layla and the kids she watches are safe. I've even allowed Victor to stay with them."

Michael resisted the urge to let out a sigh of relief—he dared not show any emotion.

Charmer turned, then hesitated. The brow rose over his good eye. "You know, if you confess, it might avoid what you fear... for most everyone."

"You're slipperier than eel shit, you know that?" Steve said. "A confession would be a lie!"

The guard holding Steve punched him in the gut, dropping him to his knees.

"Stop!" Michael shouted. "Don't..."

His words trailed off when Charmer pointed the Uzi at him again. "Did you have something else to say?" he asked.

Michael glared back but said nothing more.

"Get him in that cell," Charmer said.

The other guard shoved Steve backward into the holding cell, then locked the door.

"I guess the adventure is over," Steve said when the guards left. He lay on the floor of their cell, drooling blood.

"Are you okay?" Michael asked.

Bending down to examine Steve, he noticed someone in the cell at the end of the brig. Someone had come over to the bars, their cut and bruised face almost unrecognizable in the darkness.

"Michael..."

The voice was female, but it wasn't until he stood and pressed his face against the bars of his cage that he recognized the battered features of the ship's former XO.

"Eevi," he whispered. "What did they do to you?"

"I tried to stop them..." She lowered her head and sobbed. "Timothy did too. We tried."

"Stop them from what?"

She glanced up at Michael with one eye swollen shut. In the other, he saw sadness but also raw fear.

"They said if I talk, they'll kill everyone I love," she said. "But they already did that."

"What do you mean?" Michael asked. He felt the dread rising inside him. It reminded him of the day his father died on a dive.

Eevi sniffled and wiped the hanging strand of snot from her broken nose.

There was anger in her gaze.

"They deactivated Timothy," she said. "Then they launched a missile at the *Immortal*."

"What?" Michael reared back. "That's impossible. Why would Rolo do that?"

"To take the throne," Steve said.

Michael stared at his older confidant in horror.

"That's why Charmer has done this to you, amigo." Steve ran a hand over the stubble on his head. "Holy shit, they smelled blood in the water and attacked."

"What about the Hell Divers?" Michael asked. "What about everyone else on the airship?"

"The greenhorns probably don't even know, and the other divers were in Brisbane. If they were alive, they're stranded there," she replied. "I'm the only one who knows the truth about what happened, and I'm the only one who refused to swear loyalty."

"And that's why you're here?"

Michael fought past the anger and confusion. "Surely Charmer knows you will tell us, even with the threats against those you love, which means—"

"He wants you to know," Steve said.

"Because he knows we can't do anything and no one will believe us," Eevi replied.

FIVE

"For shit's sake, keep us steady, Garrett," said General Jack. "I want a better look at this ship."

"Working on it, General," replied the pilot. He sat in the cockpit, flipping switches and manipulating the cyclic stick and collective lever.

Thunder rattled the helicopter as it dipped lower over the ocean. Kade sat strapped in with his back to the hull, hands now cuffed. He turned for a better look out the viewports but couldn't see bloody anything in the darkness.

Secured in the other seats throughout the troop hold were six knights, plus General Jack. Kade didn't know the full names of the other men but had heard one of them called Mal, another called Nobu, and a third called Zen. He still didn't have a name for the knight who had accompanied him for most of his imprisonment.

That soldier was on his right, wearing the holstered pistol he had taken from Kade, as well as his laser rifle.

The chopper yawed to the left after hitting another patch of turbulence.

"Garrett!" the general called out.

"Doing my bloody best, sir," Garrett shot back.

"Do better!"

The pilot reached out to the dashboard of ancient-looking equipment, flipping chipped plastic switches and tapping controls with iffy interfaces. It felt as if they were keeping this bird in the air with duct tape and baling wire. Hell, the thing had to be 270 or even 280 years old. He was amazed it still worked.

They flew lower again, rattling like the old jack-in-the-box toy he'd had as a kid. Black waves stretched as far as Kade could see out of the cockpit. It seemed something was down there.

"Be advised, I got eyes on a small ship," Garrett announced. "Looks similar to what our scouts saw."

It had to be the *Frog*, Kade thought.

General Jack peered through the cracked Plexiglas. "Watch out for any antiaircraft," he said.

"Copy that, General. Got my eyes peeled, and weapons are hot."

Lightning flashed outside the cockpit, illuminating the interior of the troop hold. The knights all sat with their crossbows and rifles cradled over their plate armor. They looked ready for a fight.

"General, I thought you were going to take me to King Xavier," Kade said.

General Jack craned his neck but said nothing, then quickly turned back to the windshield.

Kade looked past him as the pilot took them down toward the ocean.

"Keep your distance," the general said.

"Roger that, sir."

The chopper roared out of the clouds. Kade searched the whitecaps for the *Frog*.

"The target isn't moving," Garrett reported.

"You're sure?" General Jack asked.

"Positive. It's anchored off the River Heads public boat ramp."

The pilot flipped a switch that turned on the radio. "Got an incoming transmission from our scouts."

"Go ahead with it."

The radio crackled with a voice Kade had not heard.

"Queen One, Queen One, this is Knight Two. Do you copy? Over."

General Jack picked up the receiver. "Copy, Knight Two. This is Queen Actual; go ahead."

"Sir, we have a unit with eyes on multiple hostiles along the shoreline of River Heads."

Kade fidgeted in his seat, trying to hear over the rotors.

"They must be salvaging," Garrett said.

"Good luck findin' 'em down there. Bloody hell, those broken-down boats are home to a sampling of local wildlife," the general said with a laugh. Several other knights joined in.

"We should help them," Kade suggested.

That quieted the entire troop hold.

"*Help* them?" the general asked. "They're lucky I don't ram a missile up their biscuits right now."

"Give me the order, and I will," Garrett said.

"You don't understand—none of you!" Kade yelled. "The king didn't drop that warhead. He was trying to—"

"To find the Coral Castle so he can add us to his empire in the wastes?" General Jack shook his head. "Not on my watch, mate."

"We were searching for help, General."

"Shut your mouth," said the knight next to Kade.

Kade glanced over, eyeing his pistol on the man's duty belt.

"This king of yours," General Jack said. "You think he's out there scavenging with his troops, or is he the type of guy to stay on the ship?"

To Kade, the answer was obvious. The king would probably be out there with the soldiers. But it might be better to play ignorant, especially now that he wasn't sure whether they were taking him to X or going to blast the *Frog* to kingdom come.

"Now you speak," said the knight beside him.

"I don't know," Kade lied.

Jack went back to the pilot and said something Kade couldn't make out.

A moment later, the bird pulled up, back into the clouds.

Kade relaxed as they flew away from the *Frog*.

Looking over his shoulder again, he noticed they weren't heading back out to sea, where the Coral Castle was. They were going toward the mainland.

Kade tensed up again. Maybe they were headed to find the scavenging party. He sat in silence for another ten minutes until General Jack finally returned to the troop hold.

"Get ready for landing at the Starfish," he said.

That was the first Kade had heard the name of the place they were headed. He noted it as he watched the knights cross-checking their weapons. He felt naked without one, but he knew better than to ask. These people were nothing if not cautious.

"Landing zone looks clear, General," Garrett reported. "I've circled twice."

"Circle again."

Cautious indeed, Kade thought. He tried to peek out the cockpit windows but saw only the storm on the horizon.

The chopper made another circle before finally descending. It set down with a jolt.

"Okay, let's move!" General Jack boomed over the roar of the twin turboshaft engines.

Two soldiers went to the door and slid it open before hopping out into the darkness. Keeping low, they moved away with their crossbows up.

The knight with Kade's weapons started to put the bag over

Kade's head again, but the general stopped him. "Too danger-ous," he said.

"General, all due respect, but the Forerunner said—"

"The Forerunner doesn't have to fight monsters, Lucky."

The knight stuffed the bag away in his vest and gestured for Kade. "Let's go."

"Your name's Lucky?" Kade asked.

"I said let's go." The anger in his voice was impossible to miss.

Kade jumped out onto the cracked runway and moved away from the chopper. With his night-vision optics offline, he relied on the lightning to see. The sporadic flashes lit up a passenger plane, its fuselage split in half on the broken asphalt.

"Stay close," Lucky said. "There are things that live in the dark here."

"You don't say," Kade muttered under his breath, not that the knight could have heard him over the beat of the rotors. The draft gusted against them as they hurried away.

Lucky shouldered the laser rifle he had taken from Kade. They kept near the front of the formation. General Jack stayed in the middle, cradling a drum-fed submachine gun with a suppressor on the barrel.

The Sea King lifted back off. With no running lights, the hulk-ing machine blended into the dark storm above them.

The team double-timed it toward destroyed hangars across the airfield. Lightning forked over the rubble, capturing several of the collapsed structures, which looked like turtle shells.

The knights picked up speed. Kade tried to keep up, but his ankle hurt, and the handcuffs made running awkward. He scanned the hangars ahead and noticed something new: a fence that somehow was still standing. Not your usual chain-link affair, either. This was made of steel and stood at least ten feet high, topped with metal spikes and coils of barbed wire. This wasn't just an airport. Kade had a feeling this was a base of some sort. They had kept it up, securing the perimeter with the fence.

The knights opened a gate in the fence that surrounded the destroyed hangars, and waved everyone forward. Ahead, Kade saw something with a tiny red light, rotating on a pole.

A camera, he realized. It followed them as they went to the rubble that was once used to house airplanes. Sticking out of one of the mounds was an airplane wing. The knights ducked under it and then into what looked like an excavated tunnel.

"Watch your step," Lucky said.

Kade reached out with his cuffed hands to hold on to Lucky's shoulder as he entered a pitch-black staircase that went underground. A beam came on, lighting up the stairs that seemed to have no end. They went down six or seven flights.

At the bottom, the knight on point stood sentry outside an open blast door. Lights were already on inside. Kade followed the others into a large chamber where three more Sea King helicopters sat in various stages of repair.

"Bulldozer, you here?" shouted Lucky.

"Who's the new bastard?"

The voice came from above, and all the knights looked up at a man lowering toward them in a harness. He wore a welding hood and armored knee and elbow pads.

"The hell you doing up there?" asked General Jack.

"Fixing the door so Garrett can land. It's gonna be another hour before I get it open."

"An *hour*?"

"You didn't give me much warning you all were coming," Bulldozer said.

His heavy black boots hit the ground with a thud. The man was short and stocky and didn't appear to be a soldier like his comrades. He glanced up at the ceiling. "Damned track is off. Can't get her to open all the way."

"Hurry that shit up," the general said. "We're wasting fuel."

"Tell Garrett to put down at the Crab Nest. I checked; it's secure."

"And risk being seen? You been down here in the dark too long, mate."

"There are more hostiles out there, Bulldozer," Lucky said. "Allies of his."

He jerked a thumb toward Kade, but Kade was hardly paying attention. He continued to stare around him in awed silence.

If he hadn't gotten up close, he would never have seen the fence around the hangars. From any distance, this place looked destroyed and abandoned.

"Come with me," said Lucky.

Kade followed him across the subterranean hangar to a door on the other side of the three helicopters. The knights settled in, placing their weapons against the wall and drinking from their water bottles.

Lucky led Kade to the door that opened to a small barracks furnished with bunks, crates, and shelves stocked with jars of food and jugs of water. He checked the jars and found pickled fish. Other jars were marked *Seaweed*.

An adjoining room served as a command center. Lucky flicked on the lights over a dozen monitors displaying feeds from this compound.

"Have a seat," Lucky said.

Kade found a metal chair.

Lucky stayed at the door so he could keep an eye on Kade and still watch the chamber.

"How long we staying here?" Kade asked.

No response.

At the click of approaching footsteps, Lucky moved from the door to let the general into the room. Kade rose to his feet, but General Jack motioned for him to remain sitting. He removed his helmet and set it on the adjacent table. Then he grabbed a chair and pulled it over so they were face to face.

"I'm going to ask you a few questions, and you're going to answer," he said.

General Jack leaned in and stared at Kade. "You got a family?" he asked. "Or anyone out there waiting for you?"

Kade looked down.

"He asked you a question," Lucky said. He moved over and glowered at Kade, who looked right back at him.

"A man with a family can be a dangerous thing when he's trying to get home," General Jack said. "Then again, men can be dangerous no matter what."

"Mine's gone," Kade said. "Been gone awhile."

Lucky seemed to soften some, judging by his less-stiff stance.

"Sorry for your loss," said the general. After waiting a beat, he asked, "How long has your king been king?"

Kade wasn't sure he wanted to answer that either.

"I'm not your enemy. Neither is King Xavier. You have to believe me, I—"

"You're a prisoner," Lucky said. "The general is talking. You listen, and you answer his questions."

General Jack frowned. "Leave us."

"Sir?" Lucky asked.

"I said leave us."

Lucky strode off and shut the door a bit hard, perhaps.

"The Coral Castle exists because of men like him, so while he's a bit rough around the edges, he's an important sentry along the ramparts," the general said. "Same with the Forerunner. He's been around a *very* long time, and while I don't agree with everything he orders, I follow those orders because those orders keep us alive."

"I understand orders all too well," Kade said. "I also understand men like Lucky. We have several like him."

"Hell Divers?"

"Yes."

"So riddle me this." General Jack leaned forward again. "The Hell Divers and King X were not originally part of the Cazador Kingdom at the Metal Islands; is that correct?"

"Yes," Kade said. He feared that telling them what had really happened would make him even more of a target. It might make these knights believe the sky people had invaded the Metal Islands; killed the king, el Pulpo; and taken over. But it was far more complicated than that.

"I need to understand the history," Jack said.

Kade didn't see a good way to do that, because history made them look like conquistadores. How could he justify King Xavier's alliance with the Cazadores? Brutal warriors known for hunting and kidnapping survivors by baiting them in the wastes and then eating them.

Sure, King Xavier had killed their leader, but there were still soldiers in the ranks responsible for heinous crimes.

Maybe there was a way, though...

Kade cleared his throat. "My people lived on an airship that took off from Australia during the collapse," he said. "We traveled the globe for hundreds of years until I led a team of Hell Divers to the surface and discovered a promising message. That message led us to Mount Kilimanjaro in Tanzania."

He spent the next few minutes describing what had happened to his family, and his time imprisoned there. Finally, he got to the part where his people were rescued by Michael Everhart and a team of Hell Divers who defeated the machines.

"It was Hell Divers who ended the threat of the defectors," Kade said. "King X was one of the most legendary divers before he became king, and he risked a lot to bring more survivors from around the world back to our home."

"This home—you have yet to tell us where it is."

"And I won't," Kade said. "I'll protect it just as you have protected the location of your home."

"I see…" The general leaned back, taking it all in. He promptly stood and walked over to the supply crates. "You hungry?" he asked.

"Yeah, I could eat."

The door opened, and Lucky stepped back inside the underground hangar.

"Bulldozer thinks he fixed the door, and Garrett is about to land," he said.

"Okay, I'll be right there."

Grinding sounded in the distance. General Jack tossed Kade a sealed pack of something freeze-dried. He caught it in his bound hands.

"Hope you like bananas. You guys got those back home, right?" Jack asked.

"Yeah," Kade said. "Thanks."

As Kade crunched down on the first delicious bite, the grinding noise morphed into a whine, followed by clattering, then shouting.

Getting up from his chair, Kade moved over toward the door and looked up at the retracting ceiling. Sparks shot out from one of the wheels rolling along the tracks overhead.

Lightning flashed far above, its blue glow capturing the frame of the Sea King helicopter. Garrett held the position, hovering and waiting to touch down.

But something seemed to be wrong.

Bulldozer used a harness connected to a pulley system to raise himself toward the grinding wheels. On the ground, the knights and the general waited, watching. The huge overhead door opened about a quarter of the way before jolting hard and stopping altogether.

Indistinct shouting came from all directions.

Kade recognized a few words from where Bulldozer hung in his harness. "Brokedick!" seemed to be the interjection of choice.

The beating of the chopper made it all but impossible to hear anything else as it lowered toward the partial opening.

Jack waved for his men to get back.

The Sea King continued to lower, but the huge aircraft didn't seem as if it was going to fit through the opening.

An alarm blared.

Kade dropped the bag of dried bananas. *Not an alarm…*

A distant shout confirmed his suspicions.

"We got hostiles coming from the east!"

"How many?" Jack yelled back.

"An entire pack—maybe a dozen!"

"Get Garrett out of there and close the door!" General Jack reached out as Lucky tossed him his rifle.

Kade held up his hands. "Can someone uncuff me?"

None of the knights seemed to hear him, or they ignored him as they moved out under the open hatch.

Garrett pulled up. The whining grew louder, until it seemed to be just above them.

Kade flinched when he saw a winged creature slam into the cockpit of the helicopter. The Sea King jerked violently.

"Get back!" the general shouted.

The knights ran away from the opening.

Kade watched as the chopper pulled up with the Siren still attached to the hull. The mounted M60 machine guns blazed, spewing green tracer rounds into the night. Bullet casings rained from overhead, clinking on the concrete floor.

Three creatures swooped through the opening in the ceiling. They dispersed down into the hangar as the six knights raised their rifles.

"Down!" Lucky yelled.

A Siren flapped over him as he ducked. The creature picked up another knight and flung him into a wall. His visor shattered with an audible crack.

Gunfire drowned out the electronic-like wails of the monsters.

"Watch your fire!" General Jack shouted.

Kade crawled under the gunfire with the three monsters flying overhead. He got behind a crate with Lucky, who used the cover to fire at the monsters. The general slid next to them, turning his suppressed submachine gun on a creature that had swooped down with its wings out.

The eyeless beast snarled, spittle dripping from its twisted maw. Bullets punched into the rubbery flesh. It jerked from the impacts as it tried to pull up, but a head shot dropped it before it could fly away, and the beast crashed lifeless to the floor, not far from Kade.

Hearing a new wail, he looked up to find two more Sirens dropping through the hole in the roof.

"Watch out!" Kade yelled.

General Jack and Lucky turned a torrent of lead on them. Sparks pinged off the ceiling and door. That was when Kade saw Bulldozer, still in his harness, trying to unbind the still-grinding wheels.

Kade ducked as a beast came out of his peripheral vision. So the creature went for Lucky instead. It slammed into him and General Jack, knocking the general to the concrete.

Then the beast scrambled over to Lucky. He rotated on his back with his rifle, only to see a clawed hand slap it away.

Kade ran over and jumped onto the Siren's spiked back. He wrapped the chain of the cuffs around the grizzly neck of the beast and pulled as hard as he could.

All around him, guns fired, muzzles flashed, and monsters screamed in their emergency-siren-like voices. Knights yelled right back as they cut the abominations down.

The eyeless monster snapped at Kade as he pulled back on the chain. It reached up, clawing at his armor. He watched in horror as its other clawed hand slashed at Lucky, cutting through his vest and duty belt.

Kade grunted, pulling harder so the creature couldn't slash Lucky again. The monster bucked backward and then launched into the air. Kade lost his grip, landing on his back as the creature flapped upward, right for Bulldozer.

Rolling onto his side, Kade fumbled at Lucky's torn duty belt. He pulled his Monster Hunter revolver from the holster. He pulled back the hammer, closed one eye, and aimed. The beast flapped up toward an unsuspecting Bulldozer, closing in with outstretched claws.

Kade squeezed the trigger.

The heavy bullet broke the creature's spiny back. It let out a roar of agony and fell over the tail rotor on one of the disabled Sea King choppers.

Kade got up to his knees, holding the gun in his cuffed hands and looking for another target. Three of the monsters lay dead.

The other two flapped away through the opening in the rooftop.

"Drop the weapon," Lucky said.

When Kade turned, he saw Lucky aiming a rifle at his helmet.

"You're welcome," Kade said. He flipped the pistol around and handed it to the knight.

The other soldiers shook off the adrenaline and spread out to hold security while General Jack and Lucky checked the injured knight.

They carefully removed the helmet from a youthful face. The young soldier, a man named Mal, was choking on his own blood.

General Jack bent down and put a hand on his chest plate. He whispered a few words, then got up and nodded at Lucky.

Before Kade even knew what was happening, Lucky aimed the pistol between Mal's eyes. They widened just before he pulled the trigger.

SIX

A violent radioactive storm battered the beached cargo ship. The wind howled like a monster, keeping Magnolia awake and alert.

Beeping resonated in her helmet, and a check of her wrist computer confirmed the Geiger counter as the source of the warning.

The radiation was spiking—the first fallout from the nuclear detonation.

Two hours had passed since she and Gran Jefe joined Team Octopus inside the ship. Magnolia had climbed to an unstable mezzanine that extended over the engine equipment. The big Cazador Hell Diver was up here, watching the two hatches into the large space.

On the deck below, the Cazadores of Team Octopus worked to dismantle the air-cooling system from its mountings in the rusted, stifling engine compartment. Three of the four soldiers quietly attended to the disassembly while the fourth organized the air-cooler components below.

"How much longer?" Magnolia called down.

One of the salvagers held up two fingers.

"*Veinte minutos,*" he said.

"Twenty minutes," Gran Jefe said.

"Yeah, I got it," Magnolia replied.

She bumped on the comms to Command again but got only static.

Due to the weather, they had lost contact after Teams Eel and Knife returned to the *Frog* with valves, piston rings, and step-down transformers. She had a feeling X and General Forge would send the two teams back out here to help.

All she had to do was keep Team Octopus and Gran Jefe alive.

Magnolia used her flashlight to check the room again for any sign of the Tasmanian devil that she had followed with Gran Jefe. The beast had vanished somewhere inside the ship.

These monsters were smart. It knew they were here and was waiting for its chance to pounce. She could feel it in her bones.

"You hear anything?" she whispered.

"My stomach." Gran Jefe patted his gut. "*Tengo que cagar.*"

"What—you gotta take a shit? You got to be kidding me."

Magnolia raked her light from the entry hatch on their left back to Gran Jefe.

"You watch," he grunted. "I can wait *no mucho.*"

Magnolia might have laughed a few days ago, but not now.

"You can't hold it?" she asked. "That thing is still out there."

"I can no fight when I have to shit," Gran Jefe said.

"Fine. Go, then."

Magnolia followed him over the mezzanine. Their clanking boots drew glances from the Cazadores below.

"Hurry it up," she said.

Magnolia turned as Gran Jefe went down the ladder they had taken to access the platform. She heard the clatter of his armor coming off at the bottom, followed by what must be the roar of the wind outside.

But this wasn't the wind—it was Gran Jefe emptying his bowels.

"Why don't you just tell every beast on the coast where we are?" she said when it finally ended.

"They smell, they no come," Gran Jefe said with a laugh.

He climbed back up a few minutes later, looking perky.

"I can fight now," he said.

"Glad to hear it."

The radio in her helmet crackled.

"Team Octopus, this is Eel Actual, does anyone copy? Over."

"Copy you, Eel Actual, this is Commander Katib," Magnolia replied. "What's your twenty?"

"We have dropped off the first round of supplies to the *Frog* and are headed your way, over."

"Thank the Octopus Lords," Magnolia replied. She looked over the railing and quietly said, "We got support headed our way. Look alive."

The soldiers below were loading up the crate with the pieces of the air-cooling unit.

If they could get out of here with it, without losing anyone aside from the scouts, then it was a good day. They needed this morale boost after losing everything and everyone on the *Immortal* supercarrier in the blink of an eye.

Apparently, she wasn't the only one thinking about their losses.

"I sorry about Arlo," Gran Jefe said. "I miss him. He make me laugh."

Magnolia faced the big Cazador, seeing his dark eyes behind his visor. "Me too," she replied. A wave of guilt ripped through her at the memory. "I should have been paying attention to the sky. It should never have happened."

"No your fault." His voice held a serious and rueful tone that

Magnolia wasn't used to hearing. It almost seemed as if the guy did have a heart.

"He die because *la muerte* is part of *la vida,*" Gran Jefe said. "He funny, but lucky to be alive so long. He make too many mistakes. No your fault, Commander."

Gran Jefe put a hand on her shoulder.

"It like Ada—not my fault," he said. "Her fault. She make decision, and decision get her dead."

Magnolia was going to reply when a distant rattle broke her train of thought. Gran Jefe pulled his hand away and clutched his rifle. The gusting wind pierced the inside of the ship, whistling down the abandoned corridors.

The rattle continued, but this wasn't from the storm or the soldiers working below them. Team Octopus fanned out. They had heard the same thing.

A guttural roar echoed through the ship.

Another roar answered.

The noises made Magnolia clench up for an attack. The monster was waiting for them to move so it could strike them when they were in the open.

"Guess your *mierda* explosion didn't scare them off," Magnolia said.

Gran Jefe snorted.

"Follow me," she said.

Magnolia took a ladder down to Team Octopus as two soldiers finished putting the salvaged parts in a crate.

"Ready?" Magnolia asked.

"*Sí, listo,*" said the salvage boss.

Shouldering her laser rifle, she started walking. Gran Jefe fell in behind the group, holding rear guard. They worked across an open deck still clogged with vehicles, many of them still fastened by their moorings from when they were being transported centuries ago. Others had somehow, amid cataclysms unknown, flipped onto their roofs or lay on their sides. There had to be over a hundred automobiles on this deck alone.

The beams from tactical lights flitted over the broken windows and rotted interiors.

As they got halfway across the sea of cars, a distant growling resonated through the damp chamber.

Magnolia bumped on the comms. "Calling Team Eel and Team Knife—what's your twenty?"

They reported back from the road—both groups near the APC that Magnolia and Gran Jefe had left behind.

"Do you have eyes on hostiles?" she asked.

"Negative."

Across the elongated cargo space, they heard a thud, followed by breaking glass.

The team of Cazadores set the crate down and raised their weapons.

Magnolia moved ahead, sweeping the area with her laser rifle. The infrared scanner on her scope didn't reveal any heat signatures. But something was in here with them.

She checked the ceiling just in case the hulking devils could also, somehow, climb.

Seeing nothing suspicious, she turned to look for a way out. It didn't take long to find a jagged opening, blown in the hull by some long-ago missile. It was all the way across the deck, on the port side.

Magnolia gave the signal to advance. Two of the Cazadores picked up the crate while the other two joined the security watch.

Lightning flashed outside the ragged breach in the hull. From what Magnolia could tell, they were at least two decks above the beach. That meant getting down was going to be an issue, but she wouldn't risk getting trapped in one of the corridors while trying to find a way out. If they had to lower the crate and themselves on a rope in the storm, it beat getting cornered by the monster hunting them.

Magnolia looked over her shoulder at Gran Jefe, who was still watching their six. He backpedaled toward her, keeping his rifle trained on the hatch they had entered through.

Thunder boomed as they approached the riven opening in the hull. Rain pooled on the deck. Her helmet chirped another warning as the Geiger counter detected yet another uptick in radiation. But the distant scratching of claws that followed made radiation a secondary threat.

She turned again and spotted movement at the far end of the cargo hold: a hunched back of spikes protruding through wet fur. The dark bulk vanished among the vehicles.

"Behind us," she whispered.

"I see," Gran Jefe replied.

"Keep going," she said to the Cazador team.

They maneuvered around a car, heading for the opening while Magnolia kept her light on the vehicles at the other side of the hold. The monster had somehow ducked out of view.

"Where the hell'd it go?" she whispered.

She heard a muffled shout behind her, followed by a fading voice and a sharp crack. When she turned to check, three of the four members of Team Octopus had stopped around an opening in the deck.

It hit Magnolia then.

The hole in the bulkhead wasn't the only breach on this level. And the monster seemed to be using them as doorways to move through the levels.

She retreated with Gran Jefe to the gaping hole in the deck. The Cazador soldier who had fallen through was ten feet below, gripping his ankle.

A rope with a bowline loop already tied was on its way down when the shriek of claws on metal came again.

"Better move it," she said.

The soldier with the broken ankle threw the rope over his shoulders and held on as his comrades hoisted him upward.

In the respite between thunderclaps came heavy panting, then a throaty growl.

Magnolia crouched and aimed her rifle and tac light into the shadows. Thunder cracked outside, masking whatever the creature did next.

"Faster!" she yelled.

The Cazadores pulled harder, joined by Gran Jefe. The injured man was almost up now.

You can't lose a soldier, Magnolia thought.

Moving her finger to the trigger, she fired as the terrible panting seemed directly below.

A clawed paw swiped up at the Cazador's dangling feet, only to be shorn off by a laser bolt. The soldiers heaved the man up onto the deck as Magnolia fired another burst into the darkness.

A furious screech arose from the deck below.

The soldiers got back up, two grabbing the crate while the other helped the injured man.

"Go, go, go!" Magnolia shouted.

Wind slammed into them as they approached the jagged opening in the hull.

Gran Jefe and Magnolia stood back to cover the soldiers. She checked that they weren't being flanked, but all she could see outside were storm clouds over the ocean.

Waves crashed against the shore, and thunder boomed steadily.

"On our way outside," she reported over the comms. "Prepare for evac."

"Copy, Commander," said the leader of Team Eel.

At the edge of the hole in the portside hull, the Cazador soldiers set the crate down. Working swiftly, they got out the ropes and tackle. To Magnolia's relief, they were fast and competent.

They sent the crate down first. When it was safely on the sand, the first soldier rappelled down, readied his rifle, and put his head on a swivel.

The distant howl of the maimed Tasmanian devil made Magnolia shudder. The monster was out to feed, and she didn't think the wound was going to keep it from bringing back fresh meat to its pups.

She kept her rifle aimed into the cargo hold while the rain and wind beat against her armor. The third and then the final member of Team Octopus rappelled down. They called up, but Magnolia turned to wave them onward.

"Get to the evac!" she yelled.

"Now you go," Gran Jefe said.

As Magnolia reached for the rappel line, she heard claws scrabbling. She turned just as a hunk of metal came flying across the space, too fast for her to duck.

A car door slammed into her shoulder, spinning her around and smashing her into the hull. Warning sensors beeped in her helmet again.

Her heart hammered with fear. Stunned on her knees, she wiped the rain from her visor and blinked. Something huge and furry was climbing out of the hole the Cazador had fallen down. One arm was missing its paw.

And the beast wasn't alone. Another creature jumped onto a car across the cargo hold, crushing the hood. Gran Jefe fired a burst, forcing it down. Then he trained his barrel on the beast with the still-gushing wrist. It came at Magnolia as she tried to find her feet.

The shots stitched up the monster's spiked back, hitting the armorlike flesh with audible thunks.

Magnolia had time for one move. Reaching down to her thigh, she drew her blaster. The creature clambered toward her in an awkward tripod gait with alarming speed.

She aimed the triple-barreled weapon at the creature's tumorous mouth.

The beast lurched aside, but not enough in the half a second it had to avoid the spray of pellets that blew out the back of its throat.

The monster hit the ground and skidded into her, rolling up over her legs.

Pinned, she watched Gran Jefe fire at the other Tasmanian devil, which was now on the run. It jumped into a hole across the cargo hold, hitting the deck below with an audible thud.

Gran Jefe kept his rifle up and backtracked to Magnolia.

"You okay?" he asked.

"I'm stuck," Magnolia replied.

He put his rifle down, and with much grunting and some colorful Spanish expletives, he managed to heave the dead corpse off Magnolia.

"*Gracias*," she said.

"*De nada*," Gran Jefe replied. "You okay?"

"I think so."

He helped her to her feet. She holstered the blaster, switching back to her laser rifle. As the adrenaline began to dissipate, she felt pain in her right arm, shoulder, and neck.

She staggered back to the opening and was gratified to see that the team had left with the crate.

"You go," Gran Jefe said.

Magnolia grabbed the rope, wincing as she rappelled down the hull. Looking up at Gran Jefe, she wondered, was this what

Ada saw before the crab beast reached out from a tunnel to snatch her, snipping her rope?

Gran Jefe turned to head back into the ship.

A second later, he gave a loud war whoop. Gunfire cracked over his voice, and then he stumbled, arms windmilling. He fell past her, landing on his back on the beach two floors below.

Magnolia glanced up at the furry, tumor-ridden face of a devil. It grasped the rope with its paw, but she let go, dropping the last six feet to land beside Gran Jefe.

Before she could bring up her rifle, the beast leaped down after them. It swung an arm into her chest, smacking her to the sand. She landed hard on her side, looking at Gran Jefe.

Somehow, he was back on his feet, holding a cutlass. The tumorous abomination towered over him, dripping blood from one arm.

It slashed at Gran Jefe with enough force to take his head off if he hadn't ducked. Magnolia fumbled in the sand for her laser rifle. She grabbed it and aimed as the monster lifted Gran Jefe off the ground.

"Shoot!" he grunted.

She sighted between the wide shoulders and fired into its furry, spiked back. The laser worked better than bullets, boring instantly through the flesh. The thing screeched in agony, spitting blood into the rain.

It dropped Gran Jefe and turned toward her, again lifting its arms. Magnolia took a step back and fell on her butt. Chest muscles flexed as the monster prepared to strike her with its remaining clawed paw.

Gran Jefe didn't give it a chance. He swung his cutlass into the gory wounded wrist. The beast jerked away, letting out a frightful roar.

The big Cazador did not relent. He thrust and swung again, severing the arm above the elbow with a sickening crunch.

It clamped its other paw around the gushing wound and opened its black hole of a mouth rimmed with jagged teeth. Gran Jefe struck again.

As it began to let out a final roar, he thrust the sharp blade into that hole, through the palate, and up into the brain. That roar turned into an odd, alien shriek of pain and rage that died away in a hiss of escaping air.

The monster twitched several times, blinking vacant eyes at Gran Jefe. He withdrew the sword with a quick yank, and it collapsed facedown in the sand, dead.

Gran Jefe brought up his rifle and put a round through the head just to make sure, then walked over to Magnolia. She was still on her back, her helmet chirping away, her right arm pulsating with pain.

Movement caught her eye where the road almost touched the shore. The other Cazador teams flooded onto the beach, shouting catcalls at the other devil as it fled into the wastes.

"*Gracias* again," Magnolia said as Gran Jefe helped her up.

He brushed sand off her armor.

"*Gracias*, you too," he said. "We make *buen equipo*—good team."

SEVEN

Layla kissed Bray on the head, prompting a smile that showed his two lower teeth and single wide upper. He reminded her of a hippo.

"Ma-ma will be back soon," she said. Bray reached up to her from the floor, and she lifted him, rocking him for a few moments. Once he had relaxed on her chest, she put him into his crib. She tried not to look at the empty crib where Rhino Jr. had slept.

It was hard to imagine him somewhere out there with another caretaker. She missed the baby terribly. Even though he wasn't hers, she had formed an emotional bond.

And now he was gone.

She watched as Bray finally went down, relaxing his chubby cheeks as he drifted off to sleep.

The boy needed her now more than ever, and if something should happen to her…

Nothing will happen to you.

She convinced herself that was true, but deep down she knew she was taking a massive risk going to see Imulah—especially the way she was doing it.

She watched Bray sleep for a few minutes before slowly shutting the door. She went to the bathroom and changed into her black fatigues and black raincoat. Then she went to the kitchen, where Victor waited at the window.

"You sure?" he asked.

"Yes. This may be my only chance to talk to Imulah."

He propped open the shutters in the kitchen window, and they both looked out through the sprinkling rain. Storm clouds drifted across the moon, dimming its glow.

Layla was a bit concerned about slick surfaces, but she had climbed and dived in far more dangerous conditions. She grabbed a gear bag that Michael had kept for her in case they ever needed to bug out.

She was surprised Charmer and Jamal had never confiscated the knife when they searched her apartment for weapons. She uncoiled the rope and tied a treble grappling hook to the end. Then she sheathed the knife on her belt. Now she had at least something to defend herself with.

She put up her hood and stepped to the window. Rain peppered her face and coat. She looked down again, still not seeing any boats.

Lightning forked over the horizon, illuminating a distant rig.

Glancing up, she checked balconies for posted guards, or people outside. But it seemed no one wanted to get wet, and that was exactly what she was hoping for.

"Watch over Bray," she said. "If something happens to me, you know what to do."

"Please be careful, Layla," Victor said.

She climbed out the window and put her feet on the ledge just below. Then she unsheathed the knife and thrust the blade through the metal skin of the rig. She twisted it in, making sure it was secure. Now she had a handle. Once she felt safe, she checked the ocean again, then the balconies on the larger apartments above.

Still nothing.

Layla studied the exterior of the building. The balconies started two floors above her apartment. They were the fancier dwellings, once used by el Pulpo's wives, wealthy merchants, and the few high-ranking soldiers who made it to old age. A handful of scribes, including Imulah, also had the nicer living spaces.

Another arc of lightning flashed on the horizon. In the glow, she located the scribe's balcony, four floors above her and another four over to the right. She wasn't even sure he would be there, but this could be her only chance to talk to him without Charmer and his henchmen finding out.

Of course, they could still find out if the scribe spoke of her visit, but she had a plan to keep him quiet.

Holding on to the knife with one hand, she swung the grappling hook on the end of the coiled rope. Thunder boomed as the storm grew stronger.

"Okay, let's go," she said.

Giving the rope a final hard swing, she flung the hook up to the balcony above. It caught the railing with a clank that made her wince. She flattened her body against the wall. If someone glanced outside, they wouldn't see her.

Hearing nothing, she waited for another beat, looked up, and pulled the line taut. After pulling the knife free, she sheathed it once again and started climbing.

You got this.

With the rope running around her left leg and between her feet, she inchwormed her way up. Driven rain stung her face, but the wind bothered her more, pushing and tugging on her small frame.

It took a few minutes to reach the first balcony. She climbed over the railing, relieved to see blinds drawn over the glass window. She quickly unhooked the rope, this time waiting for thunder before she tossed it.

As the clap sounded, she swung the grapnel to the balcony above. Hook and thunderclap hit simultaneously, masking the clang of metal on metal.

She wasted no time climbing up to the next rail. This window had no blinds, and she saw directly into the apartment. The dwelling was dark, but she saw the occupant in a lightning flash.

A heavyset man was sleeping on a couch, turned in the opposite direction. There was no mistaking him, though. It was Captain Rolo.

She stared for a few seconds, hating this man who had been at odds with King Xavier since the beginning. But then again, Rolo had been right. The king had led his army to death—everyone, including Sofia and the other Hell Divers who had died to retrieve the seeds from Brisbane.

She looked away and tossed the rope up to the balcony on the right, swung over, and started up again. Candles burned inside the apartment, and she held on to the railing instead of hopping over. The blinds were pulled slightly along the right edge of the glass door. Through it, she could see a half-naked tattooed woman massaging a pale but muscular man on the floor. His eyes were closed, but his head was turned toward the glass doors to the balcony. Layla recognized him as another of Charmer's henchmen.

The woman looked down as she massaged his back. If she glanced up from her work, Layla would be directly in her view.

Easing herself down, Layla hung under the balcony. She reached up and used the bottom of the bars to pull herself around, out of the woman's line of sight. After moving under the balcony to the right side, she pulled herself up again, in front of the blinds.

Layla bent down, trying to keep out of view but keeping a line of sight into the apartment. The man was yelling at the woman about something. He suddenly slapped her, knocking her to the floor.

Thunder boomed, and Layla tossed the rope again. The hook connected to Imulah's balcony. She pulled it snug, then started climbing.

Layla shinnied up the exterior to Imulah's balcony. Once she was over the railing, she coiled the rope and set it down. There was no turning back now.

She stepped up to the glass. Inside the living room, a single candle burned. She tried the sliding door. To her surprise, it opened.

Soaking wet, she stepped onto a red rug.

"I'm surprised it took you this long."

Her heart skipped at the deep tone, and she half expected to find Charmer sitting there in the corner.

But this wasn't Charmer. It was the old scribe she had come to ask for advice.

"Please, just hear me out," Layla said.

"Come in," Imulah said. The glow of the candle illuminated his shaved head, graying beard, and dark eyes.

Tonight, those eyes were full of concern, perhaps even fear.

"You put us both at risk by coming here," Imulah said.

"Forgive me, but I don't know who else to turn to," Layla said. "I'm here for your counsel."

"I know why you are here. Please, have a seat."

She went to one of two chairs, taking a long look around as she walked over. She admired the shelf packed with hardbound books and the clay figurines of an octopus and a dolphin. A painting of an ancient Mayan city hung on a wall. In the corner, next to the chair, was a desk with a single framed picture on it: a male teenager, standing with his arm around a girl and a boy a few years younger.

It took her a moment, but she realized this was Imulah long ago.

"Your husband has been charged with the murder of Oliver and his son," Imulah said. "The evidence against him right now is mostly just from eyewitnesses, but there is motive."

"I know all this," Layla said. She considered her words carefully, then just blurted out, "I've come to see if we can rally people to our aid and free him."

She leaned forward and locked eyes with Imulah.

"You know Charmer is a murdering tyrant," she said. "He framed Michael, and with Xavier dead he plans to take the crown. You also know how the islands operate. You know everyone. You and only you can help me stop them. The Cazadores must come to our aid."

Imulah let out an uncharacteristic sigh. He turned toward the picture on his desk. "My brother and sister," he said. "We were kidnapped on a Cazador raid not long after that picture was taken. They both died on the journey here—killed by radiation poisoning."

"I'm sorry. That's awful."

He gave another little sigh, clearly anxious. "I never speak of it. It took me many years to put that picture out. I felt guilty working for the regime that caused their deaths. My heart has always been broken. Children are the light of our world. When they are taken before their time, it makes our dark world that much darker."

"That is very true."

Imulah folded his hands on his lap. "I tell you this for a reason, Layla. I tell you because of Bray. The Cazadores will never rally to your side and help your family."

"How do you know?

"Because they know that Ada sank a shipping container filled with their people, and they know that X allowed her to live. They also know he exiled her instead of executing her and then allowed her to return. The leader of the Wave Runners had a cousin on that container she dropped in the ocean."

Layla hated hearing it, but Imulah was right. The Cazadores would never help her.

"Do you know where Lieutenant Wynn is?" she asked. "Maybe he can rally the last of the militia soldiers from the airship."

"You can't count on him," Imulah said.

Layla swallowed hard.

"They have compromised his family, and Wynn has already sworn allegiance to Charmer. You know better than most what you would do for family."

Layla let go of her anger and nodded. It wasn't Wynn's fault.

"Charmer now has much of your militia," Imulah said. "And even more importantly, he has Jamal, the highest-ranked soldier left in the Cazador army back at the islands. With the rest of the military destroyed and King Xavier dead, the only way to save your husband is to prove his innocence—something you will need help doing."

Layla snorted. "How can I do that? I can't even leave my home without being followed. I had to climb here in the storm, for—"

"There is a woman," Imulah interrupted. "My spies have seen Charmer with her on many occasions. He has kept their relation-ship a secret, but I am told he is infatuated with her, that he tells her everything. She could be the key."

"Who is she, a Cazador?"

"No, she is one of your people, a woman named Jacquelyn."

Layla knew her right away. She was in her twenties—dark hair, dark eyes, silent and beautiful. She had been a lower-decker on the *Hive*. Now she worked as a horticulturist.

"What makes you think she will help me?" Layla asked.

"Because she does not love Charmer. I see her much as I saw Sofia with el Pulpo: a good soul trapped in a relationship she did not ask for." He shrugged one shoulder as if to suggest he had known many such relationships over his years. "She might know the truth, and if you can get her to talk, perhaps Michael can call her as a witness at the trial."

He walked over to his desk.

"If you can't prove it, and you can't fight, there is only one option to save your family," Imulah said. "You must find a way to free Michael, then flee the islands into the wastes. But I fear that out there, no matter how well prepared you are, you will meet the same fate as my brother and sister."

He picked up the picture of his family.

"You will need help freeing Michael if that is the route you choose, but anyone who helps you will pay a heavy price if they are caught. I respect your people, and I see Charmer for what he is. That is why I'm going to share something my spies have told me."

With bated breath, Layla drew closer.

"Pedro and his people believe in your husband," he said. "They know he did not commit these murders, and believe that Charmer has framed him."

"You think he might help me free Michael?"

"Perhaps."

"I have to get to him, then."

Imulah walked over to the window, hands clasped behind his back. "It will be a half moon tomorrow night," he said. "I will arrange a meeting, on a boat that will be a mile east of the capitol tower. I trust you will find a way to get there?"

Layla looked out over the water. She could never swim that far. But maybe she wouldn't have to.

"Yes." She smiled for the first time in a week. "I've got just the way."

* * * * *

King Xavier walked into the engineering room to check on progress. Crews of technicians, engineers, and even soldiers were working on the damaged tech. Some of the salvaged parts looked like junk to him, but the Cazador sailors knew how to make the best of everything, just as the sky people did on the airship.

Damaged plates were welded back together, stripped threads retapped, conduits bent for new wire runs. Slowly, one jerry-rig at a time, they were putting the ship back together.

But before they could sail again, they needed the air-cooling system that would keep the power plant from overheating once they reached the open water. Magnolia and her team were on their way back with it now.

He switched on his headset. "Captain Two Skulls, what's the ETA on our teams?" he asked.

The reply came back a few beats later. "Ten minutes, sir."

"Copy that. And the radar—you picking up anything?"

"Negative, sir. It's gone now."

"On my way back to the CIC."

X still had no idea what they had picked up on radar, but he doubted it was the airship *Vanguard*. There was no way in hell Captain Rolo would have returned.

But if not the airship, then what was up there?

X had plenty of other things to worry about right now. He left the engine compartment with his guards, Sebastian and Nicolas.

Moving through the cold, dim-lit corridors, X heard shouting in Spanish. The voice drifted from a connecting passage—something about medics.

"What did they just say?" X asked Sebastian.

"Requesting medical teams in the cargo hold," Sebastian said.

X switched back to the command channel. "Captain, was there another attack?" he asked.

"Negative, King Xavier, but there is a request for a medical team to treat some injuries."

"What injuries?"

Static cracked over the channel, then the reply.

"Unconfirmed, sir," Two Skulls said.

X gave his guards new orders and headed aft. He didn't know exactly what had happened out there with Magnolia, Gran Jefe, and Team Octopus, just that they had run into two Tasmanian devils on the cargo ship, with only minor injuries sustained.

When he reached the stern, the sprawling cargo hold looked far different.

A quarantine area partitioned off almost half the space.

Some of the soldiers from Teams Eel and Knife were already back and going through decontamination in a makeshift plastic chamber. Inside, the Cazadores scrubbed their naked, tattooed bodies with chemical soap. To his surprise, X heard laughter as he approached the sheeted-off area.

Laughter was good.

They had lost two scouts and two more infantry soldiers on the mission, but now that the others had returned with the parts, there was hope. Hope that they were leaving this accursed wasteland that had taken so much from them.

All around the space, technicians and soldiers worked efficiently, cleaning and stowing gear. A medical team of three rushed through the cordoned-off area.

X went over to the door, where Edgar, Sofia, and Tia stood behind the plastic sheets of the quarantined sector, waiting for their Hell Diver friends to return. They watched the hatches for Magnolia and Gran Jefe.

"King Xavier," Edgar said. He stood at attention along with Sofia and Tia.

"At ease," X grunted.

He hated the formalities that came with his position—especially on a day like today, when he felt deserving of little respect. If anything, his people should be questioning his leadership more than ever.

On the other hand, most everyone seemed to be focusing their attention on staying alive. And all their anger was directed at Captain Rolo.

"Any word about Magnolia and Gran Jefe?" Sofia asked.

"They should be back soon," X said. "Mind if I wait with you?"

The Hell Divers stepped back. X could see everything, from the soldiers scrubbing down in the decontamination chambers, to the workers in hazard suits carrying away parts. At the end of the cargo hold, two soldiers opened the hatch to the weather deck.

"Here we go," Edgar said.

The heavily armored soldiers backed away from the hatches, letting in a new surge of soldiers and gusting rain. At the front of the group, four hulking Cazadores lugged a large crate containing the air-cooling unit, X assumed.

He allowed himself a tentative sigh of relief. The salvage mission had been a success. Now they just needed to get out of here before the fallout baked them all.

He looked to the group of soldiers. Not all of them were standing. The medics on standby hurried toward the group.

Gran Jefe limped into the chamber with Magnolia in his arms.

"Mags!" X yelled.

He started toward the quarantine door, but Sebastian and Nicolas moved in front of him.

"We must remain here," Nicolas called out.

"What happened to her?" X yelled. "What's wrong with Magnolia?"

He tried to get through, but both soldiers held him back, now with help from Edgar.

"She'll be okay, sir." The familiar relaxed feminine voice finally got X to back off. He turned to find Valeria approaching. Dressed in hazard gear, she went through the cordoned-off space to a secondary clean room before proceeding.

X watched her cross over to the medics, who were walking with Gran Jefe, who still carried Magnolia like a child in his massive arms. They were both covered in mud, blood, and grit.

"I thought she was okay," Sofia said.

"I did too," X said.

"She's tough; she'll be okay," Edgar said.

X watched Gran Jefe set Magnolia down in one of the decon chambers. The showerheads opened up, spraying them with white foam.

A message came over the headset. "King Xavier, this is General Forge. Respectfully requesting your presence in the CIC."

"Why?"

"I'd rather tell you in person, sir."

X could hear background chatter, including the deep rasp of Captain Two Skulls. Conflicted, he wanted to stay behind. But Magnolia was safely back and conscious; she would be okay.

"Update me as soon as you know something," X said to Edgar.

"Will do."

Once again X found himself rushing through the corridors, wondering what was so urgent in the CIC. He arrived to find General Forge and Captain Two Skulls near the weather station with Corporal Tiger.

They all came to attention.

Miles, who had been sleeping, jumped up and ran over to X.

"Skip the formal shit," X said. "What's going on?"

Two Skulls nodded to the corporal sitting in front of the weather station. Miles followed X over.

"What ya got?" X asked.

"The worst of the fallout will be on us in an hour, maybe two," Tiger said in English better than X's.

"How long until they get the air cooler up and running?"

"I need three hours, maybe four," replied the captain.

"Obviously, we don't have that much time."

"I know. We'll have to make do, and test the engines as we go. I'm prepared to do that."

"Do it," X said. "I also want crews working to seal up this ship and buy us more time."

"On it, sir."

Two Skulls barked orders across the room.

"I have a sitrep on the estimates you were asking for," said General Forge.

He handed a ledger out. X took it and started reading the numbers of remaining troops and rations: *Twenty-five crew members. Seventy-five soldiers. Six injured. Five Hell Divers. One injured. Two weeks of food and provisions—maybe two and a half if we're careful with rations. Enough fuel to cross the Pacific.*

X felt some hope after reading through the notes. They had the means to get to Panama. The real question was, what would they find there? If the outpost was destroyed, then they wouldn't be able to reprovision before going back to the Vanguard Islands.

But first, they had to get to there. They were running out of time to escape the fallout.

He handed the ledger back to General Forge. The crew stood at their stations, waiting for orders. X scrutinized them all. From what he could tell, they were still with him and believed in him, even when they had every reason to doubt him.

Forge turned his eye to X. The burns on his face seemed to tighten. X could almost feel the rage radiating off the general.

X hated Captain Rolo and had promised to tear the old scorpion limb from limb, but maybe he would let the general deal with

Rolo. After losing over half his forces in Rolo's cowardly attack on the *Immortal*, Forge had the stronger claim.

"We're almost on our way home," X said. "Keep the faith. We will get back to the Vanguard Islands, one way or another."

"Prepare to test engines," said Captain Two Skulls.

The crew returned to their work with newfound enthusiasm.

X stuck around for a few minutes to watch, all the while thinking about Magnolia. There was little he could do belowdecks, though. This was where he needed to be.

Miles followed X across the room.

A flurry of shouting announced the first tests of the engines. Judging by the crew's reaction, everything was going to plan. Or at least, X didn't detect any panic suggesting imminent disaster.

After fifteen minutes, he asked for an update on Magnolia.

"She's been moved to medical," Forge replied. "Don't worry, she's in good hands, but go visit her if you wish. I will keep you updated."

"I'll stay here," X said.

As he started to sit, a tremor passed through the ship. A metallic ding echoed into the CIC. At first, X thought it concerned the engine test.

Faces across the command center looked up. The vibration and ding came again, catching the attention of more officers. Even the guards posted at the hatches seemed unsettled by it.

Chirping followed from the area of the sonar and radar stations. Corporal Tiger was already there, checking the monitor. Two Skulls and General Forge hurried over with X.

"We're picking up contacts," said Tiger.

"In the air again?" X asked.

Tiger brushed a strand of hair from his face and studied the screens. "No. In the water." He motioned to another officer and said something in Spanish. The officer replied in a panicked voice, but X couldn't make any of it out.

"Uh," Tiger said. "We've switched to our bioscanners on the ship's hull, and these are definitely sea creatures."

"More of those cyclops monsters?" X asked.

"Maybe, but some are much bigger in size." Tiger spoke again to one of the officers sitting at the stations. The man nodded and tapped at his screen.

"The computer is working to form a digital image. Stand by," Tiger explained.

X went to the cracked windows, now taped up to keep the rain and storm from getting inside. Through the panels, he could see the ocean clearly now that most of the fog had retreated.

He searched the whitecaps for beasts but saw nothing in the choppy water.

"What is that?" said General Forge.

X went over to the screen to find a digital recreation of whatever was out there. This was no cyclops.

"The computer says this is a . . ." Tiger leaned down, struggling to pronounce the words. "*Lethocerus insulanus* from the family Belostomatidae."

"Come again?" X said.

Tiger looked up at X. "Big-ass water bug, or what was once called the giant fish killer. It says they live in fresh water and use a snorkel to breathe underwater, but I guess these have mutated like everything else. And I've got more bad news."

"They are attaching to the hull," X said.

"*Sí*, King Xavier."

The dings echoed through the vessel over the next few minutes.

"*No hay problema*," said Captain Two Skulls. "No chance they get through."

"Really? 'Cause Corporal Tiger just said they aren't supposed to be able to breathe underwater, and here we are."

"The hull is three inches of steel plate, King Xavier, and that is just the exterior. It should hold back these bugs."

X hoped the captain was right. He watched as a dozen of the man-size beasts seemed to concentrate around a single area.

"Where is that?" X asked. He tapped the screen where they seemed to be gathering.

It took Captain Two Skulls a moment to identify the location. He confirmed what X had suspected. "Outside the engine room," said the captain.

"Fuck, they must be attracted by the engine testing you're doing. Can you stop it?"

"If we stop the test and just fire up the engines, they could burn out."

"You're sure they can't get through the hull?"

"*Sí.*" There was a slight hesitation in the captain's voice.

"Put all security teams on high alert," X said. "Seal up the ship the best we can."

"Yes, sir."

X went back to the windows with Miles. He still couldn't see anything in the water, but he could feel and hear them clatter against the hull. Miles growled. He could feel them too. The dog was ready for a fight.

X felt his heart quicken with the realization that the chances of their getting out of here without a fight were shrinking by the second.

EIGHT

Kade cursed himself for not bolting into the wastes when he had the chance. He might not have made it far, but maybe it would be better than sitting on his ass in the storage room. The door was shut, but was it locked?

Outside, voices and grinding machinery kept him from even trying to sleep.

Five hours had passed since the Sirens' attack, and the knights were still busy repairing the helicopter door. He finally got up and tried the regular door. Unlocked. Ever so gently, he eased it open just a few inches, letting in the clank and clatter.

Bulldozer was back in his sling, fixing one of the tracks in the ceiling.

The door was closed, but apparently, they now couldn't get the damned thing open, stranding their helicopter pilot, Garrett, out in the wastes.

Kade had picked up a conversation between General Jack and Lucky about the pilot putting down at the Crab Nest.

He watched the knights for a few moments, then lay down on the floor and curled up on the pad. Sleep finally came but wouldn't stay. Nightmares from the past haunted his dreams for hours.

A voice woke him from restless slumbers.

"Get up and get ready to move."

Kade pushed himself up in front of Lucky.

"Are we finally going to find King Xavier?" he asked.

"That would be impossible at this point," Lucky said.

"What do you mean?"

"Garrett isn't responding on the radio. We're sending a party out to his last known location, and you're going."

"On foot?"

"Yeah. We leave in ten, so rattle your dags."

Kade packed up his meager gear and joined the knights out in the chamber. With the loss of Mal, only six knights remained, including General Jack.

Bulldozer lowered himself back to the floor. He unbuckled his harness and went to a table, where he plucked the battery unit for Kade's armor off what appeared to be a jerry-rigged charging system. Kade's helmet was there as well, with the rest of his armor.

"You'll need this, mate," he said. "Sorry to say, I had to get rid of a few systems on your heads-up display, though."

Bulldozer tossed the helmet. Kade fumbled for it, nearly dropping it.

"Thanks," he said.

"Try the battery. Gave it some juice," Bulldozer said.

Kade put on his helmet, then inserted the battery into his armor chest slot. The unit glowed blue, and his HUD flickered to life. Raising his wrist, he checked his computer as his systems rebooted.

"Ninety-nine percent charge," he said. "Not bad."

"You'll need it, I reckon, considering we got more radioactive fallout coming our way," Bulldozer said.

"More fallout?" Kade asked. *Of course*, he thought. *The nuclear blast from the* Immortal.

"That's right," Lucky said. "Your people have poisoned our land."

"Not my people."

Bulldozer climbed back in his sling while Kade crossed over to the broken-down helicopters, where General Jack and Nobu were standing and drinking from a flask. For the first time, Kade saw Nobu without his helmet. He was middle aged, with a dark complexion and short-cropped hair, and he was watching Kade like a bird of prey.

Zen wasn't far away. He looked a lot like Nobu, with buzzed hair and dark eyes, though a bit younger. He was the best shot of anyone at the Coral Castle, or so Kade had heard. His eyes went to the bolt-action sniper rifle that Zen carried.

"We're ready to go," Lucky said.

The general took another drink from his flask. "I don't like this," he growled, "but it's our only option right now."

"You sure you can handle him?" Nobu asked, jerking his chin to Kade.

Lucky snorted. "Yeah, but feel free to go out there in my place."

Nobu looked away.

"Be careful. His people brought the monsters—like sharks to blood in the water," said General Jack. "That attack was the most brazen I've seen in over a decade."

The general drew his sword, and Lucky got down on one knee and bowed his head.

"May the Trident protect you," the general said.

"I will protect the Trident," Lucky replied.

General Jack eyed Kade up and down.

"This is your chance to prove you aren't an enemy," he said.

"You help us, and it will help your case when you head back to the Forerunner for judgment."

Kade was anxious to prove himself if it meant getting back to his people.

"I'll do whatever I can," he said.

"Good luck," Zen said.

Nobu nodded.

Kade dipped his head in respect. Then he followed Lucky, who didn't wait around. He was halfway across the chamber already, forcing Kade to trot and catch up.

Kade put his helmet on, checking his HUD. Most systems were online and working properly. He checked the time—almost midnight. The maps were gone, though—wiped, obviously, so he wouldn't know where this place was.

"Don't even ask—you aren't getting a weapon," Lucky said. "You're lucky we took off your cuffs."

He opened the door, then turned slightly. "And while I appreciate you saving my arse, that doesn't mean I owe it to you."

"Didn't say you did, mate," Kade replied. "But I definitely owe you for rescuing me from that dingo nest. I was a shark biscuit."

Lucky snickered at the slang for kids at a beach with shark-infested waters. It was true, though; Kade would have been torn to pieces if it weren't for the knight.

The man started up the stairs, giving Kade a good look at the weapons he had taken from him during that rescue. His Monster Hunter revolver was holstered around Lucky's waist, along with a tac knife and another pistol. Over his back he had a slung crossbow, and he carried Kade's laser rifle in front of him.

They climbed the stairs all the way to the surface, where lightning greeted them, flashing over the runways.

"So we're going to the Crab Nest?" Kade asked. "How far is it?"

"If we're lucky, we'll be there by morning," Lucky replied.

"Well, you are Lucky."

"Comedian, are ya?"

"Not really. Just trying to be friendly."

Lucky stopped just outside the door, then stepped up to Kade.

"We aren't friends, or mates, or whatever you call it, so get that through your dense cranium, okay, Hell Diver?"

"Don't worry, I got no illusions."

"Keep close to me out here, but just know, if you try anything, I'll kill you and sleep just fine." And before Kade could reply, Lucky started off across the runway.

The knight easily skirted the various barricades and traps. Kade got close enough to a stake pit to see that the trap had worked. Skewered on one of the spear-length spikes were the remains of a Siren that had reached for the dangling bait before falling and impaling itself.

As they advanced, he got a better view of the surrounding area. In the green hue of the night-vision goggles, he could make out what looked like a long-ago residential area on the western edge of the airport. Most of the structures appeared to have collapsed over the years, but he could see enough peaked roofs to know that these were once houses.

He looked away from the structures to a river at the southern edge of the runway, where Lucky seemed to be headed.

Towering trees spread their mutant branches over the dark stream. Along the bank, mushrooms grew out of the dirt, their caps ranging in size from automobile tires to satellite dishes.

Lucky cleared the area with his rifle, then went to a chain wrapped around the base of a tree. He grabbed hold and pulled up, exposing the sunken links that stretched across the hundred-foot-wide stream.

The two men followed the chain down to a small covered

boat. Lucky motioned for Kade to help. They stripped the tarp off, exposing a rickety skiff with long strips of weathered tape covering cracks along the hull.

Lucky pushed it down to the water, then waded out up to his knees and climbed into the bow while Kade held the boat steady.

"What about those cyclops things?" Kade said quietly.

"You just worry about pulling us across the river. I'll take care of any critters." Lucky crouched in the bow, laser rifle at the ready. He held the chain while Kade climbed into the stern.

The current caught the unstable craft, drawing them downstream.

"Come on, ya dumb bastard, start pullin'!" Lucky said.

Kade grunted and started pulling them along the chain. He was developing a strong dislike for Lucky, but right now he was in no position to do anything about it. Even if he could escape, where would he go?

Kade still didn't know where his comrades were, only that the *Frog* was somewhere out there, damaged. Even if he managed to escape, searching for it would be no better than searching for the Coral Castle—especially alone and on foot, without provisions or weaponry.

For now, Kade just had to help Lucky and deal with his attitude.

The boat rocked as the current grew stronger midstream. Rapids churned around them.

Kade kept pulling, getting them closer to the other side with each tug.

Just past midstream, he thought he heard something over the clanking chain and the slurp of water around the boat. He pulled all the harder, keeping the opposite bank in his view, focusing on the goal line.

Then he heard the unmistakable call of the monsters. It reminded him of recordings he had heard of elephants trumpeting.

Lucky heard it, too, and rose up to a crouch, holding on to both gunwales as he searched the water. Then he jumped over the side, into waist-deep current. He helped pull the boat the rest of the way to the shore, where Kade also hopped out.

They dragged the boat out of the water before slogging up a hill. At the crest, Lucky motioned Kade down at the edge of a clearing. Weeds shaped like cutlass blades moved lazily in the breeze.

Kade got up just enough to look over the vegetation. He saw dense clusters of short mutant trees, and the occasional giant mushroom growing in the open field.

Radio chatter came from Lucky's location.

"General, any word from Garrett?"

There was a pause.

"Copy that," Lucky said. "We're across the Mary River and heading east."

Mary River. Kade didn't have a map of the area on his HUD anymore—*thanks, Bulldozer*—but he remembered that river from studying maps back during the search for the Coral Castle. And there were only so many airports in the area.

This had to be the Maryborough Airport.

He got up when Lucky motioned again.

Crossing the field without a weapon was worse than crossing the airfield. At least there, one might lead a pursuer into a trap. Out here, they were at the mercy of Mother Nature—a horrible, mutant, lethal version of her.

Kade felt old injuries flaring up during the long trek. An hour and several miles later, Lucky finally sheltered at the remains of the first structure they had encountered. There wasn't enough left of it even to figure out what it had ever been used for. All Kade saw was a pile of rusted scrap metal and a few broken brick walls.

They hunkered down behind one of these.

"We're over halfway there," Lucky said. "But this last stretch is the most dangerous."

"Why? What's out there?"

"A few known lairs of the Tasmanian devils, and some dingo dens. Plus, those cyclops creatures, as you call them, are known to hunt the dingoes."

"So basically everything? We got *all* the monsters?"

"There are others too—rarer beasts."

Kade was glad he didn't explain further. The knight got up and started around the wall with his rifle up.

"Son of a bitch," Kade whispered.

He eyed his pistol, holstered on Lucky's duty belt, and quashed the urge to draw it and take the knight hostage. Maybe that was the way out of this. Take Lucky hostage and have him take Kade back to his people.

The idea marinated in his mind during the walk, pulling his attention from his surroundings. He almost didn't see the trench carving through the dirt ahead. A stagnant stream filled the bottom.

Lucky got there first and slid down the bank. At the bottom, he waded out into muck that came up to his waist. He worked his way across, keeping the laser rifle above his head, then climbed up the other side to the top of the slope.

Kade followed him to the bottom of the trench and struggled to get across. The thick muck slurped and nearly pulled his boots off, but at last, he fought his way through the mire and clambered up the far slope. Lucky was on his belly, looking out over another open field. An intact fence surrounded three intact buildings and the operational Sea King.

This had to be the Crab Nest. Kade stared for a moment before Lucky yanked him down.

"Stay out of sight, numbnuts," Lucky hissed.

Kade got down on his belly and stared through the weeds

while Lucky pulled out a pair of binos. Holding them to his helmet, he glassed a swath of about 90 degrees—another perfect opportunity for Kade to take him out.

And yet, he hesitated.

His gut told him something was wrong, that they weren't alone out here, and that Garrett was either hiding or dead.

"Stay here," Lucky said. "I'm checkin' it out."

"*What?* Oh, hell no. I'm not staying here unarmed. Give me a knife at least."

Lucky seemed to consider it, then shook his head. Kade reached over and grabbed him by his leg. He kicked free, then whipped the laser rifle around.

Kade stared up at the laser weapon, unflinching.

"You and I both know something's wrong," he said to the knight. "You go out there and get into trouble, I can't fucking help you. Leaving me a knife, you risk nothing."

"Except maybe a knife in the back," Lucky replied.

"If I wanted to hurt you, I already had a dozen chances just in the last hour."

Lucky kept the laser rifle on him for another moment, then finally lifted it. He reached down to his sheath and tossed the knife on the dirt.

"If there's a monster out there, you're better off using that on yourself," Lucky said. "Beats getting eaten alive or, worse, dragged back to a nest like the one I pulled you out of."

Kade picked up the knife and nodded.

"Be right here when I come back," Lucky said.

And with that, he climbed out of the trench and headed toward the *Sea Queen*.

Kade went down on his belly and watched the knight advance toward the fence. He went for a gate, unlatched it, and moved inside, sweeping his rifle left to right, back again.

He went straight to the chopper and opened the cockpit door to an empty interior. The knight then went around the aircraft and headed toward one of the buildings.

Kade got up slightly but dropped back to his stomach at a distant sound. Straining to hear the source, he picked up a slithering, crunching noise. But it wasn't coming from the direction of the helicopter.

He looked to the left of the trench, where some sort of tailed beast was advancing in the waterway. That wasn't the source of the noise either.

He whirled to his right, to see another monstrous figure slogging through the mud a hundred feet away. It was moving so fast, it had already gotten this close undetected.

Kade jumped up from the trench and legged it for the fence. A trumpeting wail pierced the night as he squeezed through, tripping and falling to the ground.

As he pushed himself up, he saw Lucky emerge in front of a building. He raised his rifle in the direction of the trench.

Looking over his shoulder, Kade saw the single bulging eye of each beast homing in on them. Lucky saw it too and opened fire, drowning out their screeches with the sizzle of the laser rifle.

Kade clambered toward the knight as another of the one-eyed amphibious beasts started to flank them.

"Behind you!" Kade shouted.

Lucky didn't have time to turn and fire at the approaching beast. The monster rose up on its tail, its clawed forelimbs wound up to strike.

Kade cocked his arm back and threw the knife right past Lucky's head. The blade cartwheeled and smacked into the ribbed, soft belly of the monster. It roared and grasped at the blade, giving Lucky time to turn and blast the creature in the eye.

"Run!" Lucky shouted.

He took off toward the chopper and the open cargo doors. Kade beat him there, but instead of climbing into the cockpit to fire up the bird, he went straight to the M60 machine gun.

He trained the barrel on the two cyclopean beasts charging toward them from the trenches. Kade sighted up the closest one and squeezed the trigger.

Green tracer rounds tore into its back as it hunched down, blowing off spikes and punching through armor. A limb sheared off, and a burst of rounds punched into the scaly chest.

The other monstrosity seemed to hesitate slightly, giving Kade just enough time to sight up the single eye and fire a burst. The head exploded like a meat grenade.

He eased off the trigger, his ears ringing as he searched for more hostiles.

A hand grabbed him and pulled.

Kade could hear Lucky yelling but couldn't quite make it out.

The knight pulled harder.

"Let go of the weapon!" he shouted.

Kade released the taped grip of the gun and put his hands up. "Okay, okay, relax."

He hopped out of the chopper with Lucky. He could hear the knight sending a message on the radio.

"General, we found the chopper, but no sign of Garrett," Lucky said over the comms. "What are your orders?"

Kade stepped over and fetched the knife from the monster's belly, missing the crackly response. He turned and saw Lucky stopped in front of the other carcass. Then he saw what they both had missed earlier.

The dead monster was still gripping what remained of Garrett: his head and spinal column, hanging out of a flight suit.

Lucky kicked the dirt, cursing. Then he crouched down, putting his hands to his head.

Kade walked over with the knife. After wiping the blade on the dead monster's fur, he handed it back to Lucky.

"Here," Kade said. "Your knife."

Lucky didn't even look up. He kept focused on the gory remains of the pilot. "Keep it," Lucky said after a pause. "You're going to need it, and I figure if you were going to use it on me, I'd already be dead."

He was right about that.

Kade hovered behind Lucky. From this angle, it would be nothing to slit his throat. Perhaps this was a test, to see if he could trust Kade.

It didn't matter; he wasn't going to murder the guy. Kade put the knife in his duty belt. "What's the plan now?" he asked.

"Bulldozer is working on one of the choppers back at base. It's almost ready to fly—just needs a few things from this one, including the storage batteries."

"Wait, Bulldozer can fly?"

"Yeah, he has a few hours logged."

"Then why doesn't he just come out here and fly it back to base?"

Lucky pointed at the sky. "You see that storm?" he asked. "General Jack says we got even worse fallout heading our way, and he isn't going to risk our last pilot by sending him out here to get cooked with us—or ripped in half like Garrett."

The knight dropped his arm and headed to the chopper.

"Our only chance is to get back to base on foot," he said over his shoulder. "Ride out the storm, then fly back home."

"What about finding the king?"

Lucky scoffed. "Your king? Hate to break it to you, Hell Diver, but if he's stranded here, him and the rest of your people are gonna bake like tits on a beach in a heat wave."

NINE

The first rays of sunlight crept up the hallway in the brig of the airship. Remodeled after the *Hive* was damaged in the war with the Cazadores, the brig had only three small cells now.

Two of those three cells were occupied—one by Michael and Steve, and one with Eevi. Michael couldn't see her right now and didn't want to wake her if she was still sleeping.

He lay on the thin sleeping pad, watching the day come. It was shaping up to be another beautiful morning at the Vanguard Islands.

Michael closed his eyes, thinking back on all those days he had spent at the kitchen table with Layla, watching the sunrise.

She was probably sitting there now, worried sick.

The good memories were replaced by this nightmare he found himself in, caused by the very people he had helped save and who had now betrayed him and King Xavier.

The Vanguard military wasn't lost to the monsters in the wastes. They were *murdered* by a pudgy, glum, cowardly monster named Captain Rolo.

The sky people from the machine camp were hell bent on

taking the Vanguard Islands for themselves, which meant removing the only two people who could stop them: King Xavier and Michael.

He let out a deep sigh of anxiety.

"You get any sleep?" mumbled a gruff voice.

The old man looked somewhat better today. The swelling over his good eye had gone down, but the bruising was worse.

"I got a few hours," Michael said. "How about you?"

"Slept like a baby."

"You serious?"

"Hell, no. I got up to take five pisses in the corner bucket, and each one felt like I was shooting needles out of my dick," Steve said.

Michael felt a grin coming and gave in to it, welcoming the momentary reprieve from the dread that assailed him.

Steve smiled right back. "Everything's going to be okay, Chief," he said. "We're going to figure this out. I still got a few tricks up this old sleeve."

"¿Qué?" said a voice from out in the corridor.

Out of the shadows came a man in leather Cazador armor. Seeing the black helmet with a Siren's jaw attached, Michael knew who it was.

"Jamal," he whispered.

The sergeant in the Wave Runners was the cousin of Hell Diver and former Cazador soldier Jorge "Gran Jefe" Mata. It was Jamal who had ambushed Michael, Wynn, and their team at the food depot, killing Ton in the process.

Steve pushed himself up off his sleeping pad and spat at the bars. "You're a fucking disgrace," he said. "Nothing but a pirate with a stupid hat."

Jamal stepped up to the bars of their cage, reaching for his cutlass.

"A very rich pirate," said a silken voice. "And if you spit one more time, you will be a very dead blacksmith."

Charmer appeared next to Jamal and slapped him on the shoulder plate.

"Jamal is simply here to escort you, Michael," he said. "I figured you need better security since so many people want you dead."

Michael joined Steve at the bars.

Another soldier walked into the passage carrying two small pails. He put them down in front of the cell.

"Eat and drink up," Charmer said. "I wouldn't want anyone to think we're treating you poorly."

"What about Eevi?" Michael asked. "You going to feed her too?"

The guard who had brought the food left.

Steve bent down and fished out three bananas and some fish jerky from the pail. He offered Michael some, but Michael didn't eat, and not because he wasn't hungry. Something seemed off.

He remembered hearing something during the night—footsteps and a voice—but when he sat up, no one was there.

"Eevi, you awake?" he called out.

No answer.

Steve held up a half-gnawed stick of fish jerky.

"Eevi?" he asked. "You there?"

"Eevi, talk to us," Michael said.

Still nothing.

"She's not available to speak right now."

Charmer came melting out of the shadows at the end of the hallway, a sly grin on his face.

"Finish your food," he said. "We're leaving in a few minutes."

Michael grabbed the bars. "What did you do with her?"

"She was told to stop making up lies, and I would strongly urge you not to repeat anything she might have told you," Charmer said. "If you do, it will only make things worse for you."

Jamal moved into the sunlight with his cutlass out. He ran a gloved finger across the edge.

"Everything you say will have consequences," Charmer said. "For yourself and for those who care about you."

"You touch my family, and I'll gut you alive," Michael said.

Charmer gave his typical icy smile, though this one seemed to twist with anger.

"Making threats really isn't a good idea for a man in your position, mate," he said. "In fact, I would—"

"Oh, it's no threat. I will happily gut you. Carefully so you don't bleed out—give you a few hours to behold your intestines before I strangle you with them. Bet on it, asshole."

The smile shifted to a scowl. Charmer pulled his eye patch up, showing the recessed pink flesh.

"You think I'm a coward, boy?" he said. "You think what's happening is because I want it? If so, then you know nothing about me or the bravery of my people. You can't know what we suffered, or what we're willing to do to survive in this paradise."

"Framing me for murder, for starters, and taking out the…" Michael let his words trail off as he looked over at Jamal. Surely, the fool had no idea that Captain Rolo had used a nuclear weapon on the *Immortal*, destroying the bulk of the Cazador army and navy. If he knew, he couldn't possibly support Charmer.

"That's right—you'd best be careful with what you say," Charmer said. "Rumors are spread by fools, and they have a way of resulting in unnecessary death."

"Yeah? And what about rumors spread by liars?" Steve asked.

"I'm not talking to you, old man," Charmer said. He put his eye patch back on, then snorted. "You know what? Skip the food. You're coming with us now."

Michael and Steve moved away from the bars as Jamal sheathed his cutlass and took out a key ring.

He spoke in Spanish and gestured for them to back up.

When the gate opened, Jamal stepped in and put heavy steel cuffs around Michael's robotic arm and his flesh-and-bone wrist.

"Make sure it's tight," Charmer said.

"Fuck you," Michael said.

"Shall I have Jamal tighten them a bit more?"

When Michael didn't respond, Jamal grabbed him and pulled him from the cell, then kicked the gate shut in Steve's face.

"Stay strong, Chief," Steve said.

Jamal pushed Michael out of the brig and down passages that Michael had walked thousands of times as a citizen of the *Hive*. Memories surfaced as they passed places where he had spent much of his youth.

On their right was the Wingman bar, where X had spent too many nights drinking away his sorrows. Around the corner was the trading post, which had been cleared of all the old stalls to reduce weight.

Next up, they came to the farm. The hatches leading in were all open. Farmers worked inside, tending raised mounds of dirt under the bright grow lights.

"Some of those new seeds will be planted here, just in case," Charmer said. "We have the Hell Divers to thank for those."

Michael thought of a nice riposte but kept it to himself. The Hell Divers had no doubt been conveniently left behind. Maybe Magnolia, Kade, and their teams had even made it back to the *Immortal*, right before it was nuked.

He also knew better than to hold on to hope that somehow Mags and the others were still out there, fighting for survival.

Charmer entered an enclosed stairwell that led to the launch bay. He raised a small handheld radio. "Take us down and open hatch four," he commanded.

"Copy that," came the crackling response.

The airship groaned, the turbofans whirring beneath them as they began to lower in the sky. The double hatches marked with a yellow 4 clanked open, letting in the brilliant morning sun.

They brought Michael up to the edge as the ship hovered over the capitol tower. Wind gusted in, blowing his long hair. He reached up and brushed it back with his cuffed hands. Farmers were down there, working on plots of dirt, planting more of the hybrid seeds.

In the end, the divers had saved the islands after all, bringing a new food source that would help them recover from storm-brought famines. And with the loss of the military, who had eaten up so much of the reserves, food was no longer going to be the problem it was.

The airship put down on the eastern edge of the rooftop. On the dirt, a group of militia soldiers with rifles waited. They watched Michael as he crossed the rooftop, passing the forest, gardens, and Sky Arena.

Once inside, he was guided down to the grand hallway, lined with statues of former generals, Hell Divers, and Captain Les Mitchells.

Two guards waited outside the double doors of the king's chamber, where Michael had attended so many late-night council meetings.

The doors opened, allowing him into the sprawling room. The rows of seating were empty, along with the wood council table.

Behind that table, a single person stood in front of the raised throne where X once sat, bored usually, as he listened to the council report on problem after problem. The man who was no longer king.

Captain Rolo walked away from the chair, eyes trained on Michael.

"Michael Everhart," he said, "you are here to be tried for the crime of murdering Oliver and his son in cold blood. You will be granted a trial by a jury comprising members of each major population group."

Charmer moved ahead as a side door to the chamber opened, admitting five people. They took seats, along with Charmer.

"These five jurors will render your verdict after being presented with evidence," Rolo continued. "This trial will take place over two days, at a secure and confidential location."

Michael looked at those who would judge him. All familiar faces, some of them even friendly—or they had been at one point. There was the well-fed businessman Martino, a disabled Cazador soldier with a deformed skull named Salamander, and a scribe named Ensio.

Behind them, Michael saw a sky person from Mount Kilimanjaro named Donovan and a man named Bailey from the former *Hive*. They were not people Michael would consider friends, and he was sure they were put here for appearances.

There was no way this would be a fair trial. It was all for show.

Still, Michael couldn't just give up.

"How do you plead?" Rolo asked.

Michael considered shooting the question back at the captain and spilling everything he knew about the man's crimes. It would create chaos and perhaps rally some allies. Maybe it would even get people questioning what really had happened out in the wastes.

He felt a cold stab of dread at the other thing it would do: put his family at risk.

"Not guilty," Michael said.

* * * * *

"You're going to be okay, Mags."

She recognized that rough voice but couldn't quite place it.

She tried to make out the blurry figures hovering over her. Then she tried to speak, mustering barely a croak from her scratchy throat.

"Can't you give her some more pain meds?" someone asked. That was a familiar voice, too—female and kind.

Sofia?

"She's already had a lot," replied an unknown voice.

"You all need to get out of here and let us work," the same person continued.

"What about potassium iodide?" said the rough first voice. "Have you given her enough?"

Magnolia lost track of the conversation and let the voices jumble and bend as her head pounded like a Cazador drum. She felt a new wave of nausea and remembered why her throat was scratchy. She turned on her side and heaved. The taste of blood hit her tongue. She retched again, harder this time, breaking more small blood vessels in her throat.

"Ugh," Magnolia moaned. She knew she was sick, but with what and how bad, she couldn't quite put together.

"Mags, look at me," said the same rough voice from earlier.

She blinked over and over until her vision cleared enough to see the scarred, hard face of King Xavier. He looked down at her with concern in his gaze.

"Mags," he said.

"X... what's wrong with... me?"

"Radiation poisoning," he said.

Right—the potassium iodide.

"You're gonna be fine," X said.

Magnolia sure didn't feel as if she was going to be fine. She felt as though her insides were melting. She had experienced radiation poisoning in the past, but nothing remotely close to this. She closed her eyes after a fresh drumroll rocked her skull.

Again spoken words turned to indistinct chatter as the pain took over.

She tried to pick up on some of the words but couldn't make out much. One of the voices sounded angry. She made out some of the words.

"You can't let anything happen to her." X again.

"Sir, I'm doing everything I can," someone replied.

"Do more!"

Magnolia opened her eyelids again, trying to focus on the man who had in some ways been the father she'd never had. But that pounding headache and the burning throughout her body were too much to bear.

She groaned and turned on her side, curling up in a fetal position and drifting into a state somewhere between reality and fantasy. The last thing she heard was, "Don't let her die."

The pain vanished, and Magnolia drifted into a dream world.

Or was this death?

On the horizon, lava burst into the dark sky, sending up plumes of fire into the electrical storms. Magnolia speared through the clouds, diving head down like a rocket toward the geyser of lava.

This wasn't death.

This was the memory of a dive not two years ago outside Antigua, where Team Raptor had deployed to search for an SOS, on repeat in Spanish, that translated to *"We are trapped, with no way out of our shelter."*

Magnolia dived through darkness, where the blue glow of lightning was dull compared to the brilliant red-orange lava pouring from the volcano on the surface.

Rodger, Edgar, and Arlo dived with her, spreading out as they maneuvered into a nosedive. The altitude ticked down on her wrist altimeter, while her eyes stayed glued to the fiery mountain.

"It's beautiful," she whispered.

Rodger's voice crackled over the comms, fading in and out. Something about whether the volcano was going to blow big.

"We'll be far enough away it won't matter if it does," Magnolia replied.

She led the team away from the lava-spewing cone, toward the ruined city of Antigua, in the central highlands in the former republic of Guatemala.

Using her night-vision goggles, she could make out the ruins below. The bunker's location took a few hours to find under the rubble, and another hour to blow their way in.

By the time they got to the security door, Magnolia knew there was no one alive. They hacked into the system that opened a vault door, revealing bodies sprawled out in a vast living space. Shattered glasses lay throughout the room, the poison they'd once contained long since evaporated.

The Hell Divers searched and found more skeletal remains throughout the vast bunker. Finally, they located the source of the repeating SOS, in a radio hooked to a pack of ITC batteries designed with cores to last five hundred years.

That was the only major thing they scavenged, but they did grab a few old rifles and bagged a few thousand brass cartridge casings for reuse.

On their way out, the ground rumbled.

This part of the dream became vivid, as if it were happening to her in real time.

"What is that?" Arlo asked.

Everyone knew it was the volcano.

They hurried out the way they had come, moving past the smoky hallway they had blasted through to get in.

The team quickly hauled the scavenged loot out into the city street and up to a shattered tile rooftop, to load into the supply crate. As the helium booster lifted it back up to the airship,

Magnolia turned toward the volcano, watching in awe as lava spewed skyward.

Rodger stood by her, his hand brushing hers. "That isn't going to get all the way here, is it?" he asked. "I used to play this game with my dad where we wrestled on my bunk and whoever fell off would fall into lava."

Magnolia chuckled and held his hand.

"You guys gonna kiss too?" Arlo said with a snort. "Shit, you're like two horny Sirens."

"Come on, let's get out of here," Edgar said.

"I'm with you, boss man."

Both men tapped their boosters, launching into the sky, but Magnolia and Rodger stood there a moment. Hand in hand, they watched the distant eruption.

The memory shifted to the airship, when she was in her twenties. Those were some dark years, having lost all her family and living belowdecks like a rat. Stealing and bartering to stay alive. It felt like a lifetime ago.

She remembered the day her world changed, when she had been caught stealing and thrown into the brig. Sergeant Jenkins had told her this was it; she was out of options. There was only one left: become a Hell Diver.

Then she had met X.

Her mind raced with memories of the man that she had grown to love like a father. He was more than that, even. He was a mentor, a leader, and a warrior she had followed into countless battles and dives.

She remembered departing on the *Sea Wolf* with X and Miles. Spending those days cramped inside the boat, eating shark, fighting the mutant octopus.

Then came the memories of the Metal Islands. El Pulpo and his wife, Sofia, who later became one of Magnolia's dearest friends.

She remembered General Rhino, his death, and the birth of the son he never knew about. An image came to mind of Sofia holding the baby, just a few days old, and handing him to Magnolia.

How tiny he had seemed! How fragile. How innocent. And she recalled how much she had wanted to protect that life.

That was during a time when things could have changed for Magnolia. She could have chosen to have a life with Rodger, to settle down with him in the Vanguard Islands. To have their own child. But she had chosen to dive. To come to Australia.

She was transported somewhere dark and wet. Somewhere underground, in a tunnel of concrete with an emergency alarm echoing. Walking down the passage, she heard a voice call out over the noise.

It was Rodger, and he was calling for her.

"Mags! Help me! Please, Mags!"

She ran toward his voice, moving around a corner to find a pulsating red glow at the end of the next tunnel. The light guided her to another corner. There, she slid to a stop in front of a wall of moving vines. They hung from the ceiling, others tendriled across the ground, and more snaked out of cracks in the walls.

They flashed brighter red when she took a step forward, some of the ends twisting up toward her as if they could sense her.

"Mags!" Rodger yelled again.

She searched for him through the mass of tangled coils.

"Rodger!" she cried. "Rodger, I'm coming!"

She jumped over the vines snaking toward her on the ground. A limb whipped after her leg, nearly snagging it. But she was fast and fought her way through before the vines could ensnare her.

The snaking, squirming vegetation chased her down the passage. In the winking glow, she finally saw a figure suspended in midair, wrapped in the spiky coils. All she could see of him was a small section of face and a pair of eyeglasses.

"Rodger!" she yelled.

The vines pulsated as they pulled on him. His screams grew louder and more anguished. She reached out for him, but the limbs caught her legs and snatched her up off the ground.

"Rodge!"

Her voice choked as a vine wrapped around her neck. She squirmed and fought, but it was no use. The vegetation had her now, and there was no escape for either of them.

"Mags, I love you!" Rodger shouted, his words muffled by the vegetation that engulfed him.

His glasses fell off his nose, into the carpet of vines. He held her gaze as she tried to tell him she loved him back.

Then he was gone, yanked away into the darkness.

Magnolia screamed, her voice drowned out by the emergency siren in her dream.

"Hold her down!" someone yelled.

Still squirming, she found herself in a white room with a bright light overhead. Several faces hovered over her, but one suddenly hurried off.

"I have to get to the cargo hold. Sedate her if you have to."

That rough voice was X.

She heard a hatch whine open, then clank shut.

"Commander, you have to relax," said a voice she remembered from earlier.

Magnolia recalled she had radiation poisoning, but why were the alarms from her dream still . . .

"What's happening?" she asked.

"Monsters," someone said. "Monsters are trying to come aboard the ship."

TEN

"Giant bugs and cyclops lizards," X muttered. "What's next? Kanga-roos with ten-pound inflatable testicles they bounce on?"

General Forge let out a nervous laugh. He stood beside X in the observation tower on the highest deck of the *Frog*, scanning the choppy sea with a pair of infrared binos. The king didn't need the optics to see the lizard tails and spiked heads poking out of the water. The monsters were swarming around the vessel, having chased the salvage teams back here. Large single eyes homed in on the ship, watching. Waiting for a chance…

Beneath the waterline, the giant bugs that X had yet to lay his eyes on were clamped onto the hull.

"The defenses are all in place," said General Forge. "Now we get ready to fight."

X was ready. Dressed in his Hell Diver armor, he held his helmet under his arm. His hatchet hung behind the pistol on his belt, and his laser rifle was strapped over his back armor. A blaster was holstered on his left thigh. On his right thigh, he had a sheathed knife mostly hidden under a dangling cutlass.

He was ready to fight, though he wasn't sure his weapons were going to do much against the giant water bugs or even the cyclopean lizards. It wouldn't be long now before they assaulted the ship.

X radioed Captain Two Skulls. "How are the tests coming?" he asked.

"We ran into *muchos problemas,* but we turn the engines on *muy pronto,*" replied the captain.

"Good. Get us the hell out of here."

X took the binos from Forge and centered them on the bow weather deck below. Two Cazador warriors manned the mounted machine guns at the port and starboard rails. Turning to the stern, X checked the other two guards, posted on the weather deck with mounted machine guns.

Gran Jefe was also down there, carrying a large flamethrower that looked like a child's toy in his huge paws.

"Tell everyone to hold their fire unless we are attacked," said X. "We can't afford to waste any ammo. We're going to need every bullet for when we get back to the Vanguard Islands."

If *we get back . . .* Right now that seemed less likely by the minute.

The last of the Vanguard military were thousands of miles from home, surrounded by an army of mutated creatures and about to face the worst radioactive fallout since the world ended.

On top of all that, Magnolia was fighting for her life belowdecks with several other soldiers who had also gotten severe doses of radiation.

X tried to put the injured and dead out of his mind. He had removed all distractions, even Miles. The dog was safe with Valeria and a security patrol in the cargo holds belowdecks.

The comms flared with a message from Captain Two Skulls to all hands, first in Spanish, then in English: *"Engine tests have been completed. Prepare for departure. All hands to their stations,"* he said.

"Finally some good news," X said.

The wind howled, slamming the glass viewports. X remained behind the reinforced panels, watching the waves and the spiked backs of monsters with Forge.

"Why aren't they striking?" X asked. "What are they waiting for?"

"I'm not sure, but we've done all we can, King Xavier," he said. "Our fate is in the hands of our warriors now. We should get back down to a safer area of the ship."

"Yeah…" X said. He remained another moment at the window, studying the storm clouds. He still had an odd feeling about whatever they had picked up on the radar earlier.

Could someone really be out there with an airship or other aircraft?

He had pretty much ruled out this being the airship *Vanguard*. No way in hell would Rolo return after already getting away with the seeds—especially if he thought X was dead.

Still, X couldn't help but wonder as he studied the raging storm.

"Something's out there, though," he said.

An alarm blared.

X hurried down the ladder after General Forge, to the CIC. They were greeted with panicked chatter and one stern, calm voice amid the sea of shouting.

"Sensors have detected damage to the orlop deck," said Corporal Tiger. "We have a team heading down there now."

"From those bugs?" Forge asked. He looked to Captain Two Skulls.

There was a pause from the corporal, then, "If I had to guess, yes."

Two Skulls grunted.

Clearly the captain didn't buy it, but X wasn't in the mood to argue. If there was even a gnat's ass of a chance that the monsters could get through the hull, he had to stop them. A single beast inside put their fragile equipment at risk. Losing anything crucial would put them dead in the water, and not just in a figurative sense.

"Send in our fire teams. If the bugs get in, they can't get to the engine room; we must protect it at all costs."

"Yes, sir," said Forge.

Another alarm chirped, drawing X over to monitors where Tiger stood with his staff. Before X got there, he heard the trumpeting call of a cyclops in the distance. It seemed to be coming from the bow of the ship.

X hurried to the only porthole that wasn't sealed off by boards or paneling. He tried to look out through the sheeting rain. Through the blur, he saw a lizard tail whip above the bow rail.

Both machine guns fired, blasting the creature back into the churning waves.

Another tail slapped over a railing near the gunner on the port side, knocking him down. He fell to the deck but quickly got up and thrust his cutlass, impaling a meaty body that had climbed up over the railing.

That cyclops stood up on its hind legs, roaring in agony. It snatched the man's armored wrist, crushing it and forcing him to drop the sword as he too screamed in pain.

The other machine gunner fired a long burst, stitching half-inch holes in the thick hide. Bleeding from multiple wounds, the beast raised two arms above its head and let out a screech.

X knew it wasn't a roar of agony. This was a tactical call to its comrades.

Three cyclopes skittered over the rail, onto the weather deck.

The Cazador swung the machine gun around and fired into the head of the shrieking beast, blowing off a horn and chunks of skull. It slumped to the side as the three newcomers slithered toward the soldiers.

The Cazador with the crushed wrist fired a pistol while his comrade kept laying down fire with the mounted machine gun. Bullets pounded the fast-moving cyclopes, disabling legs and shearing off patches of thick, armorlike scales.

But the three beasts kept coming.

"Get the gunners out of there," X said to Forge.

Both soldiers abandoned their guns and fled toward the hatches.

To cover their escape, three more Cazadores ran across the weather deck with rifles blazing.

"Send a message for all troops to prepare for battle," X said to Forge.

He stepped away from the window, where two crew members waited with a sheet of metal. They placed it over the glass.

The whine of power tools sounded behind X as he crossed the room with General Forge calling after him. "Sir, wait!"

X slowed, drawing his cutlass as he turned toward the general. "No one sits out this battle today," X said.

"I will fight by your side, King Xavier," said Forge.

X gave him a single nod and turned to Captain Two Skulls. "Keep an open line of communication and let us know where the monsters penetrate our defenses."

The captain nodded his tattooed head.

After securing his helmet, X left the CIC with General Forge and both men's guards. More warriors in the hallway followed X and his team. Pulling them from this position wasn't a worry for X. Everyone in the CIC was armed and knew how to fight.

And if the monsters made it this far, everyone was royally screwed anyway.

Heavy footsteps echoed as a fast-moving Cazador strike team in light armor crossed through an intersection ahead. X and company followed them all the way down to the cargo hold, where the cyclopes were now trying to break through. Their scaly bodies slammed into the hatches, thudding with their trumpeting calls.

When X got inside the sprawling hold, the steel hatches of the sealed-off quarantine space were already dented. If the monsters got in, the plastic sheets wouldn't stop anything.

A group of twelve Cazadores waited with spears and shields. Gran Jefe was there, too, along with Sofia, Tia, and Edgar.

They all knew they had to hold these beasts back here. To make things worse, the warriors had to make their final stand with just swords and spears. Bullets and laser rifles were just too damned risky—too easy to do irreparable damage to the ship.

X holstered his blaster and unsheathed his cutlass. The group followed him through the plastic door, closing it behind them.

"Everyone, get ready!" X shouted. "We can't let them get past us! We hold them here!"

A beast trumpeted on the other side of the hatch as it pounded against the dual doors. The battering continued, echoing louder and louder.

Everyone around X kept focused on the door, but he noticed the fear in some of their body language—including Tia, who held a shaking crossbow.

The left side of the double hatch finally gave way, breaking inward and disgorging the first monster. It burst inside, halting in front of the small human army. The single eyeball flitted back and forth at the enemy.

It blinked as if it was confused, or perhaps terrified.

The front line of soldiers attacked, thrusting their long spears into the scaly hide. The creature roared as the sharp blades found weak points, including the eye, which popped in a burst of gore.

The creature collapsed to the deck, making way for the next one to join the fray. The second beast lurched inside, sliding across the deck right in front of the line of soldiers. Spears lanced into its side and belly, impaling it over and over. It took three warriors to bring it down, and only after repeated thrusts of spear and sword.

In a final roar, it swiped out with a clawed arm, breaking the leg of a soldier stabbing it. He fell to the ground screaming as his comrades pulled him back behind the shield wall.

"Hold the line!" X yelled.

He moved up in the throng of warriors as two more cyclopes squeezed through the broken hatch. The right side of the hatch fell, and a third and a fourth beast barged into the space.

Their tails whipped, one snagging the foot of a Cazador holding a shield. It pulled him from the line of warriors as spears jabbed forward. The monster yanked the soldier backward, out through the missing hatch and onto the deck, where two more of the abominations waited.

Within seconds, the man was ripped in two, his screams ending in a clap of thunder. When it passed, a message surged over the comms.

"Orlop deck has been penetrated. Repeat, orlop deck has been penetrated."

The trumpeting of the beasts drowned out the rest of the report, but X had heard enough. They had to get the hell out of here.

X bumped on the command channel. "Get us moving!" he roared.

"Engines are online. We are sailing," Captain Two Skulls said.

It didn't feel as if they were moving, but X couldn't tell.

Two more monsters shambled into the room and rammed into the shield line. The Cazadores kept them back, making calculated spear thrusts to maim the beasts, using their shields to deflect blows from clawed hands and whipping tails.

A raucous trumpeting call rose above all the screams, both

human and monster. X was near the shield wall when he saw a behemoth creature lurking in the rain on the weather deck outside. This giant was twice the size of other cyclopes and had a mohawk of spikes over its oval eye.

Unslinging his laser rifle, X tried to move into position to get a shot through the open hatch, but every time he got close, a Cazador helmet or shoulder plate would block his shot.

He reslung his weapon and pulled out his hatchet.

The creature lowered its shoulders and charged, knocking two of its own brethren aside. The smaller beasts clambered away, fearful of what had to be the alpha beast.

The gargantuan creature swiped through two spears, snapping them like the old frail herb sticks from the *Hive* right before it slammed into the center of the shield wall.

The impact knocked the front-line soldiers in all directions. Several on the outer edges managed to hold their ground, including X, who threw his hatchet at the eye.

The blade missed, hitting the spikes on its skull and caroming away.

He went for his cutlass, then decided that protecting the important gear from an errant shot didn't matter much if this beast killed everyone.

Reaching down, he unholstered his blaster as the monster punched and kicked at the fallen Cazadores. It slapped others with its tail, launching them into the air. One of those hit X, knocking him to the deck.

As he got up, he saw a blur of motion heading toward him. It hit him, knocking him back down hard.

He pushed himself up on his prosthetic arm, dazed.

All around him, soldiers had broken off into groups to fight the smaller monsters, of which there were at least six now. The larger beast continued its powerful attack, crushing all challengers.

A voice called out to X. He found Nicolas bending down to help X up. The young guard was suddenly slapped away by the tail of a smaller cyclops.

Sebastian hacked at the tail with his cutlass, barely penetrating the scaly hide. The beast grabbed him and made to pull him apart.

X fired the blaster into its head, blowing off the upper half. It dropped Sebastian to the deck, beside X. The Cazador pushed himself back up, dazed but apparently unharmed.

A warning beeped on X's HUD, and he saw another problem: radiation ticking higher. He stole a moment to take in the battle raging around him—Cazadores and Hell Divers fighting a free-for-all in the cargo hold against the ugliest abominations he had ever seen. Blood flew, and agonized voices filled the air as warriors fell to the terrible claws.

How had it come to this? Maybe Rolo was right. Maybe he didn't deserve to be king. Maybe his people would be better off without him.

"Protect the king!" a voice boomed.

Sebastian and Nicolas crowded around X to fend off a beast that had sneaked up behind. They screamed as they slashed with their swords at the monster, opening riven gashes in its legs and belly.

Familiar howling came over the enraged trumpeting call of the beast as they cut it down with X. He finished it off with a slash of his sword across the neck. When it crashed to the ground, he turned to see Valeria with a grunting Jo-Jo. They were moving over to help a group of three soldiers who had one of the monsters down on its side.

It suddenly broke free, and the tail lashed outward, sending all three soldiers sprawling. Valeria got there before it could kill them, and hacked into an arm with her cutlass. Then she ducked another arm and swung the blade in a wide arc, opening the belly.

The beast headbutted her even as its guts were falling out. She crumpled to the deck, not moving.

"Valeria!" X shouted.

Somehow, the mortally wounded creature managed to remain standing. With its insides squirming out, it picked Valeria up with both hands.

It pulled on her feet and head, stretching her unconscious body in what seemed like slow motion.

Time seemed to bend around X. He holstered his blaster and unslung the laser rifle again, only to be knocked back to the deck. He could only watch as the beast gripped Valeria in its attempt to pull her apart.

"No!" he yelled.

From out of nowhere, something black and furry slammed into the cyclops from the side, pulling it down to the deck. Valeria rolled away.

X got up to see Jo-Jo hammering the deformed monster's skull into mush with both fists.

With Valeria safe for now, X turned back to the battle near the broken hatches. Gran Jefe shouted for people to get back. He slung the flamethrower straps over his arms and raised the nozzle at the huge monster in the center of the room, past a trail of dead or injured Cazadores.

Gran Jefe unleashed a torrent of flames at the abomination as it strode toward him, right into the blast. It swiped at the flames with one hand and held the other hand over its single eye as it gave an enraged cry.

The group around X formed another shield wall, advancing on the four beasts remaining throughout the room. He picked up the dropped blaster and shot a cyclops's legs out from under it.

The Cazador phalanx advanced as one, stabbing the smaller monsters as Gran Jefe sprayed the alpha beast with flames. The leathery hide finally caught fire, forcing it back toward the exit hatch as it held up its arms and let out a high-frequency shriek.

X winced at the horrifying noise but kept his focus on the monster. It was only ten feet from the weather deck when the spiked tail whipped out at Gran Jefe. The spike hit him in the side, but he somehow kept on his feet.

A second slap knocked him to the deck. Flames sprayed up into the overhead before Gran Jefe released the trigger. He turned onto his back as the monster charged at him, its clawed hands ablaze.

X flipped open the breech of his blaster and fumbled for shells. He dropped one, picked it up, slotted it. He went for another but could tell he was going to be too late.

The beast was almost on Gran Jefe.

"Shit, shit," X said. He closed the breech and aimed the blaster just as a furry body rushed across his field of fire.

Once again Jo-Jo emerged to save the day. Or so X thought.

The animal barged right past the monster and barreled into Gran Jefe, knocking the Cazador out of the giant beast's path.

X blinked, trying to make sense of what he was seeing. But there was no mistaking it.

Jo-Jo straddled Gran Jefe, pounding him with her fists.

The phalanx of warriors around X charged the blazing cyclops, stabbing it with spears while Sofia, Tia, and Edgar fired their blasters. The buckshot blew off pieces of the thick spikes on the armored head.

Finally, the monster turned and fled, its scales smoking.

Two soldiers broke off from the shield wall to pull Jo-Jo off Gran Jefe. The big man rolled onto his side, gripping his dented helmet.

Chest heaving, X turned to find the quarantine wall still sealed off. He looked around him at the many unmoving Cazadores strewn about. Some had lost limbs; two were torn in half.

He counted four dead, but there were many injured—at least a dozen, from what he could see. It was bad, but it could have been far worse.

X helped the injured soldiers out to the open hatch. The deck was clear of monsters. Even better, the ship was cleaving the waves, heading out to sea.

"Clear the cargo hold and seal it back off," X ordered.

He went back inside to check on Valeria. She was dazed but sitting up.

"You okay?" he asked.

She managed a nod. "Miles is safe," she said. "I take him to storage room belowdecks."

X checked Valeria over again as a message came across the command channel.

"Orlop deck is secure, but *los cíclopes* are loose inside the ship," said Captain Two Skulls. "I deploy hunter-killer teams to get them."

X froze when he heard that the last sighting was near the medical ward. Not only was that area virtually unguarded, but the people in there, including Magnolia, were too sick to fight.

"Secure this space and then head to the lower decks," X shouted.

He started to run back inside but halted just shy of the second quarantine wall—a reminder that he was covered in radioactive fallout.

Heading inside would put everyone at risk until he was cleansed.

The fate of Magnolia, Miles, and everyone else in sickbay was out of his hands.

ELEVEN

The distant trumpeting calls resonated across the terrain, silenced only by the barrage of thunderclaps. Kade felt the tremors from the near-constant rumble of the storm. Lightning sizzled across the dark sky, and rain dumped from the angry clouds.

He had never seen a surface storm this bad.

Out of breath from running with a heavy bag of batteries and salvage from the abandoned Sea King, he hunkered behind the thick trunk of a mushroom. The cap provided shelter from the downpour.

According to his wrist monitor, the rads were getting worse, prompting a continuous chirp in his helmet. Without his rad suit, he would already have a lethal dose. He couldn't stay safe out here forever.

His battery was already down to 60 percent. Without it, his life-support systems would fail.

Lucky joined him under the mushroom cap.

"General Jack, do you copy?" the knight said.

Lightning flashed across the field they had come from, splitting a mutant tree and setting it afire.

Lucky tapped Kade on the shoulder. "Storm's screwin' with my transmissions," he said. "Come on, we gotta keep going."

Kade got up just as the trumpeting came again, followed by a sound like the tone from an electronic oscillator.

Lucky heard it too and pointed his rifle into the clouds.

"Sirens," Kade said.

"That what you call 'em? Clever…" Lucky said. "Storm's bringing everything."

"The beasts aren't afraid of it?"

Lucky looked at Kade. "*Afraid* of it? Mate, they'd jump over you and me to eat one of those things."

The knight started through the jungle of trees and mushrooms. Kade searched the sky again before moving out with the heavy bag.

They pushed ahead, their boots sinking in the radioactive muck. Every step, it hit Kade more and more. They were experiencing the same thing as their ancestors—warring over the same things they had fought over for thousands of years: land and resources.

It was too late to change what had happened. He needed to get back to the king before X returned to the Vanguard Islands for what could be the final war.

That was all he cared about: making it home and protecting Tia, Alton, and the just society that X and his allies had created.

Lucky waved at Kade to get down. They both ducked behind a tree. It took Kade only a moment to see what had spooked the knight. The humped, furry back of a Tasmanian devil moved through the shadows.

Kade pulled out his knife, but Lucky motioned to be still.

A glance around the tree was all it took for Kade to see why.

This beast wasn't hunting. It was fleeing with its family. Tucked into a front pouch were several pups, their heads poking out.

Bloody gashes marred the beast's shoulders and neck.

A cyclops trumpeted in the distance, in the direction they were supposed to be heading.

Kade got up with the bag and followed Lucky deeper into the forest, taking a detour back to the airport. The cries of the monsters came in the respite of thunder that reminded him of artillery fire.

Wind blasted through the canopy, shredding leaves and shearing off limbs overhead. Kade kept close to Lucky. The knight kept his rifle shouldered, sweeping constantly for hostiles.

Finally, they came to a clearing with a snaking view of the river beyond a cluster of ramshackle houses. Lucky didn't stop to look.

Kade ran to catch up with him, taking shelter inside an old stone dwelling. The second floor had collapsed over half the house, but stairs provided a way up to the still-intact section.

Lucky knelt at a broken window and scoped the river with binos while Kade stood behind him. Yet again he had an easy opportunity to slit the knight's throat.

But it dawned on Kade that he needed these people now more than ever. The radioactive fallout, storm, and monsters made Lucky Kade's only hope of getting back to his people.

Lucky handed him the binos, then pointed toward the river.

Bringing the infrared binos to his visor, Kade centered them on the swollen river choked with debris.

But it wasn't debris.

Kade shuddered at the sight of cyclopes swimming toward the coast. He counted five of the creatures, but that was just the section of river that he could see.

"Bugger," Lucky muttered. He crouched down, his back to a stone wall. "General Jack, do you copy?"

Kade moved for a different angle of the riverbank. When he peeked around a rusted window frame, he saw a cyclops on the opposite bank with its bulging eyeball on their location. He quickly slid behind a wall for cover, expecting a trumpet call to rally the forces against him, but nothing came.

Gesturing for Lucky to stay down, Kade then stole another glance through a hole in the wall. The creature slithered back into the river to swim after its brethren.

"We're clear," Kade whispered. He handed the binos back to Lucky. The knight stood and glassed the river again.

"Let's keep moving," he said. "Get them bloody batteries and shit back to Bulldozer."

"Wait, what?" Kade said. "You want to cross the river in the boat?"

"No, I want to bloody *swim* across it."

A long, hooting call interrupted Kade's thoughts. They both ducked, but this monster was way off in the distance.

As they got back up, it started to sink in with Kade just how terrible a plan this was on multiple fronts. Not only because the monsters were using the river as a highway to get out to the ocean, but because the river was surging from the rain.

Kade picked up the bag and followed Lucky. The knight had a pissy attitude that wouldn't let up—just like the storm. They crept through the ruined village on the riverbank, staying behind an ancient stone wall covered in vines and red moss.

Kade recognized the trees where they had crossed the river hours earlier. He felt his heartbeat ramping up as they approached the muddy bank.

Lucky crouched behind a tree and watched the churning rapids. Nothing moved.

"We're clear; let's go," Lucky said.

The ferry chain crossing the river was buried deep in the slough, compelling the knight to sling his rifle and get muddy.

"Oh shit," Kade said.

The boat was gone, taken by the river.

"Use the chain," Lucky said. "It's our only shot."

Kade almost laughed, then realized the knight was serious. They were going to cross *in* the swollen river, in full armor, with monsters on the prowl.

With a huff, Kade slung the heavy bag over his back. Once it was balanced, he grabbed the chain and started down the muddy slope. On the second step, his boots slid, but he managed to hold on to the chain, stopping himself before hitting the water.

Lucky was already wading out into the current.

Kade followed right behind. The river bottom sucked at his feet, trying to hold him down in the murky flood.

Lucky was already nearing the middle, brown rapids churning around him. Where it grew too deep to touch the bottom, he started kicking. A moment later, Kade was kicking too.

At midstream, the current grew stronger, threatening to rip them free of the chain. But they both held on, pulling themselves across hand over hand.

Every passing second was one more that the cyclops could snatch him in its jaws and rip his spine out. Lightning flashed, illuminating the far bank. He didn't see any monsters waiting.

Lucky was almost across now. No longer kicking, he had all four limbs wrapped around the chain as he hauled himself to shore.

Kade tried to get his legs around it but lost his footing. He kicked his way back over, water slapping his visor. This time, he saw something in the blurred view.

A spiked head was coming right for Lucky. Moving with the current, the cyclops plowed into the knight. Lucky was gone before Kade could even call out a warning.

Looking over his shoulder downstream, he glimpsed the

spiked beast and its prey. The monster pulled Lucky out of the water and onto the bank, where it held him down with two limbs as the other two began to pull on his helmet.

Kade knew he had seconds to react before it ripped the man's head and spine from his body. There were two options: continue across, or…

Letting go of the chain, he went for option two—basically, suicide.

The water took Kade so fast he had no time to do anything but pull for the riverbank. He ended up a few feet away from Lucky and the beast, which also had little time to respond.

Kade reached for the knife to find it gone, swept away in the river.

Scrambling, he went for his pistol, strapped to Lucky's leg. He pulled it from the holster and brought it up toward the spiked head just as the single eye turned on him.

Kade pointed the muzzle into the large iris, turned his head away, and fired. The pistol bucked, and gore spattered Kade as the beast slumped off Lucky and slid back into the river.

"Get up," Kade said.

He reached down and hauled the knight to his feet. Lucky seemed unsteady at first, then seemed to shake off the pain.

Kade helped him up the muddy bank, both of them sliding several times in the slick mud. They clawed their way up to the flat and saw the airfield in the distance.

At the top, Kade looked back to the water. The carcass was gone, and he didn't see any of the other creatures behind them.

"You… I…" Lucky tried to say.

"Don't talk. Breathe," Kade said.

He helped the knight all the way to the airfield. When they were past the minefield, fences, and staked trenches, Lucky stopped. He bent over, hands on his knees, panting.

"My name isn't Lucky," he said, sucking down air. "It's a nickname."

Kade wasn't sure why he was saying this now.

"Real name is Gaz."

"That a first or last name?"

"Both. I've always been Gaz."

Lucky stood and put a hand on Kade's shoulder.

"What you did for me back there went beyond anything any of my comrades have ever done, and that I won't forget. I'll do what I can for you, mate," Lucky said. He unstrapped the holster and handed it back to Kade. "Thank you, Hell Diver," he said.

Kade grinned as he took the holster and buckled it around his waist. "I guess you're lucky I've got a death wish."

Lucky snickered and started across the airfield, not stopping until they reached the hidden entry to the bunkers. On the way, he used the radio again.

"General, we're almost back," he said.

He paused, listening.

"Copy that. I understand, General," Lucky said.

When they reached the underground hangar, they went through a decon room, where their armor and suits were sprayed down with chemicals.

After several steps, the sensors chirped that they were clean. Lucky opened the blast door and entered the main chamber. The other knights were standing around Mal's corpse, heads bowed. They all looked up at Kade and Lucky.

"You got my parts?" Bulldozer called out. He was in the troop hold of a chopper, crouching with a skein of wires in his hands.

"Got 'em," Kade said, unslinging the bag and handing it to Bulldozer.

General Jack crossed over to the chopper to meet him and Lucky.

"I'm sorry about Garrett, sir," Lucky said.

The general glared at Kade, then turned to Lucky. "Glad you made it back," he said.

"You can thank Kade for that," Lucky replied.

"Oh?"

Lucky took off his helmet. "Kade risked his biscuit for me three times. And the last one was the ballsiest thing I've ever seen. I was dead meat without him."

He scratched at his patchy beard.

"Got to admit, I was wrong thinking he was a hoon," Lucky added. He explained what had happened out there.

General Jack looked to Kade.

"Appreciate that, Hell Diver, 'specially after losing Mal and Garrett," he said. "Come on, Lucky, we're doing our send-off now."

Kade remained at the blast door while the knights surrounded their dead. The general bent down and laid the sword on Mal's body, with the hilt just below his throat. Then he stood and bowed his head.

"The souls of our brothers have already left their bodies, and we pray they travel safely, wherever their paths may lead them," he said. "They defended the Coral Castle with honor and bravery and brought us all hope."

They all lifted their swords, the blade tips touching.

Then they all lowered their heads and repeated after the general: "May the gods watch over our brothers on their journeys into the black."

General Jack pulled his sword upright, held it in both hands, and solemnly touched his forehead to the blade, holding it there. "For honor, honesty, and hope. For the Trident."

"For the Trident," repeated the other knights as they too brought up their blades.

General Jack sheathed his sword and went to the command center. "Hell Diver, come here," he called out.

Lucky and Nobu accompanied Kade over to the open room. The monitors inside were all active, showing locations around the airfield.

"We know where all the monsters are going," said the general. He handed a datapad to Kade.

"Crikey," Kade said when he saw an aerial view of the *Frog*.

"The Forerunner deployed a drone after learning we lost Garrett, and this is what we discovered."

Kade stared in horror as the ship was overrun by monsters. There had to be dozens of the one-eyed alpha predators on the weather deck. There also appeared to be some sort of giant bugs attached to the hull at various points.

"We have to do something," he whispered.

"And risk the lives of more men? I think you know that isn't going to happen," the general said. "The Forerunner has given me explicit orders to head back to the Coral Castle as soon as it's safe."

"But the king—"

"Is about to be barbie from that storm, and tea for the monsters." The general shook his head. "No one could survive all that."

"You still don't know King Xavier, then."

* * * * *

A silvery half moon vanished and reappeared as pale clouds drifted across the jeweled sky. Layla, in a black jumpsuit, looked at her watch. It was time.

She opened the windows and once again started climbing. This time, she had no climbing equipment. She wore a parachute and a booster. It felt odd to put on Hell Diver gear again. She was glad she had kept it just in case.

"You don't want me to go?" Victor asked.

"I would if you knew how to dive," she said.

Standing in the open windowsill, she looked over her shoulder and smiled at him. "I'll be back before Bray wakes up."

She scanned the water again. Searchlights raked over the whitecaps, watching for unauthorized boats.

Layla waited until the lights swung past, then leaped out the window. For a moment, she felt the pure weightlessness. But this was no normal dive.

Within a second of jumping, she pulled her chute. The black canopy bloomed out, the lines pulling taut, tugging on her shoulders. She grabbed the toggles and sailed away from the capitol tower, twisting to look at the machine-gun turrets.

She tensed, prepared to hear voices calling out or the crack of gunfire. Luckily, her escape had gone undetected for now as the wind took her out of visible range of the guns. It had been over a year since she'd deployed a chute, but it was one of those things you never forgot.

Again she looked back at the tower.

Searchlights speared over the water to her left, but none were angled her way. The only thing up here besides her was the airship *Vanguard*.

Floating off to the east, it looked like a beetle in the moonlight.

She steered toward it, hoping the boat Imulah had arranged would be there. If not, she was going to have one long swim.

Her heart thumped at the thought of this being a trap. She was glad for the knife tucked away in her vest—not much, but it was something.

The canopy sailed over the water, slowly descending. Searching the whitecaps in the weak moonlight, she finally spotted a small boat in the water—probably a fishing vessel. She steered toward it using the toggles.

As she flew closer, she could see poles on the back with lines out. *Smart.*

Pedro had thought ahead.

She prepared to flare onto the aft weather deck and noticed someone down there, watching the fishing poles.

What a surprise it was going to be if this turned out to be just a random fishing boat!

"Heads up!" she called.

Six feet from the deck, Layla pulled on her toggles and flared. It was a short space, only about fifteen feet, and the person there darted out of the way.

She stepped out of the sky.

"Layla," said a familiar voice.

She paused from gathering her chute and looked up at the face of not Pedro but Cecilia. The woman helped get Layla free of the chute and lines. A second figure approached, wearing a dark hooded cloak.

The hooded figure said, "I was no expecting that." Pedro gave his usual wide grin, then reached out to hug Layla.

She embraced him tightly. Having an ally made the impossible seem less daunting.

"We don't have much time," he said. "Come, let us talk."

He motioned toward the open cabin door. Cecilia followed them down a ladder into the cabin of the small boat. It rocked in light chop as they took seats around a wood table with rusted trim. Cecilia lit a candle and stuck it on the tabletop.

Layla pulled back a shade to look outside at the water.

"You no followed?" Pedro asked.

"No chance."

"Good. We are all at great risk coming out here."

"I know, and I thank you," Layla said. "Both of you."

Cecilia, who didn't speak much English, seemed to understand and nodded.

"We owe you and your husband," Pedro said.

"He didn't do what they said." Layla took in a deep breath. "Michael would never hurt a kid."

"We know, but the question is, how can we prove that? How can we help him?" Pedro pulled the hood away from his head. "The king is dead, and he is the only one who could have spared Michael."

Layla lowered her gaze, feeling the absence of everyone they had lost. "And the Hell Divers…"

"Our people are strong, but the Wave Runners have sided with Charmer," Pedro said. "Word of what they did to Ton, Steve, and Michael has everyone nervous."

He translated to Cecilia, who nodded.

"If we try and take out Charmer, it will start a war we can't win," Pedro said. "And there is no guaranteeing we could free Michael and Steve."

"Victor will fight. I will fight," Layla said.

"You are two people," Pedro replied.

"Yes, but we only need to kill Charmer."

Pedro and Cecilia exchanged a glance as he translated again. The flicker of candlelight gave away her feelings. It was evident in her frightened features that she wasn't behind what Layla had suggested.

Neither of these people was.

Waves lapped at the sides of the boat while Layla considered what to say next. She had come here wanting to feel these two out, and now that she had, it was obvious they didn't share her fighting spirit.

Not that she blamed them.

"After everything your people have been through, I understand not wanting to start a war for Michael," she said. "I won't ask you to fight. It's wrong; I'm sorry. There might be another way, one that Imulah told me about."

Layla told them about Jacquelyn, Charmer's lover, who might know something about what had really happened to Oliver and his son. It was a long shot, and Layla wasn't counting on it.

Pedro relayed this to Cecilia. When she finished replying, she reached across the table and put her hand on Layla's.

"She says you have been through much, too, and we want to help, but fighting a war is not the answer," Pedro explained. "I agree with her. We no ask that of my people, but I am ready to give my life for Chief Michael."

Layla stared at the man who, to protect his people in the launch bay after they were rescued from Rio, had single-handedly killed a Siren using *the leg of a cot*. There was strength in his eyes now, and the same fighting spirit she had hoped to see.

"If we can't free him through other means, then I will help break him out of prison," Pedro said.

Cecilia waited for the translation. When Pedro gave it, her eyes got wide. She spoke rapidly.

"What?" Layla asked.

"She says what then?" Pedro said. "If we free him, do we hide him?"

Layla had considered this very thing and realized that living with her husband and son was all that mattered. It didn't matter where, even if it meant they had to flee into the wastes. At least then they would be together.

"We will leave the islands," she said. "I'm willing to do that if it means he is spared."

"And go where?" Pedro asked.

"Anywhere—back to your bunker if we have to."

Pedro seemed to consider this, then nodded. "You will find a way, but first we have to figure out where they are keeping him, and come up with a plan."

"We won't have much time," Layla said. "His trial starts soon, and I doubt it will take long to convict him."

"Leave that to me," said Pedro. "I will find him. You work on this *amor* of Charmer to help prove Michael's innocence."

An engine suddenly rumbled. Pedro swiftly leaned forward and blew out the candle, plunging the cabin in darkness.

Layla tensed as she pulled back the shade to see lights flitting over the water.

"I thought you no followed," Pedro said.

"I didn't think I was," Layla said.

She looked around but didn't see anywhere to hide.

"My parachute," she blurted.

Pedro ran up the ladder and pulled it down into the cabin while Cecilia opened a trunk that was buried under life jackets and rope.

"*¡Para dentro!*" she said, waving. "You get in!"

Layla climbed inside the trunk as Pedro returned with the chute and lines. He stuffed them into her arms. Crouching down, Layla tried to flatten her body.

The engines rumbled closer. Lights flashed through the window.

Voices called out over the water.

"I will buy time," Pedro said.

Cecilia dragged the table over in front of the chest, then repositioned the chairs. She tried to close the lid, but it hit Layla's head. No matter how hard she tried to reposition, Layla couldn't get down any farther.

The sound of voices came on the deck above her. Pedro, then someone else.

Cecilia went to the ladder and climbed up.

Layla listened to the indistinct chatter and caught snippets of the conversation in Spanish. Something about fishing and how late it was.

Footsteps sounded overhead, clanking back and forth.

She eased the knife out of her vest pocket, peeking out the gap in the trunk lid. She could see the ladder, faintly distinguishable in the moonlight.

Boots hit the first rung, then brown fatigues, then a duty belt with a hatchet, knife, and pistol. The Cazador jumped down to the deck with a thud.

Layla readied her knife, listening to his grunting and sniffing.

As the boots clomped closer to her hiding spot, she saw a piece of the suspension line sticking out. No wonder the trunk wouldn't close.

There was no time to pull it back inside.

The Cazador shined his light over the floor, hitting the table and then the trunk. She closed her eyes, praying her pounding heart didn't give her away.

When she opened them, the man pulled back the table and tossed it aside. He leaned down and flipped open the trunk lid.

The man's eyes widened as the knife entered under his chin. With an audible crunch, it punched through palate and sinuses and up into the brain. His surprised eyes blinked once before he collapsed, pinning her on top of the trunk.

Footsteps sounded above, and the other soldier jumped down, brandishing a speargun. He looked down at his dead comrade, then aimed his bolt at her face. Unable to move, she waited for the fish spear to nail her to the cabin wall.

Another body leaped down, crashing onto the Cazador's back. He fired the spear into the deck in front of her chin.

The man hit the table and crashed into a wall. Pedro grabbed a handful of the squirming soldier's hair and then slammed his head into the deck once, then twice. Teeth flew on the third hit, brain tissue on the sixth.

Pedro stood over the limp corpse, chest heaving. Then he staggered over to Layla and helped pull the other Cazador off her.

Reaching down, Pedro helped her to her feet just as Cecilia climbed down the ladder. As she looked around in horror, Pedro said, "We have to get rid of bodies. And sink the Jet Skis."

Layla, still in shock, managed to nod.

Cecilia spoke in Portuguese with Pedro. He snapped back at her, clearly angry. For a moment, Cecilia stared at him, then shook her head in dismay. When she looked to Layla, resentment sparked in her eyes.

"I'm sorry; I had no choice," Layla said.

"No one can ever know about this, or we will have no choice but to fight a war," Pedro said. He spoke to Cecilia again.

Cecilia spoke rapidly, words laced with anger.

"What?" Layla asked.

"She says it's too late for that; we have blood on our hands," Pedro said.

Layla looked down at her black uniform, which was covered in blood.

Maybe Cecilia was right, but this was the blood of the enemy. The Cazadores had taken the side of Charmer, and she would kill every single one of those enemies if it meant saving Michael. Because saving Michael was also saving her people.

Reaching down, she dragged the dead body away from the trunk.

"Help me find my husband," Layla said. "I'll figure out the rest."

TWELVE

The distant trumpeting of a cyclops resonated through the ship. Magnolia froze, trying to determine whether the sound was real or if she was dreaming it. The distant clatter of claws on metal confirmed that this was no dream.

The monsters were inside the *Frog*.

A comm speaker crackled nearby, and she heard the familiar voice of Captain Two Skulls. "Hostiles on decks two, three, and four…" Something about soldiers needed, then a statement she couldn't make out.

She lingered on the threshold of consciousness, blinking at the blurred shapes of the other injured people inside the medical bay. There were two soldiers from the salvaging mission, but only one was in bed. The other man had joined Lieutenant Slayer and Sergeant Blackburn at the hatch, which they had managed to seal off. There were also two nurses and the ship's only doctor, Ray Keller.

Magnolia had heard that Keller came from the same bunker where Cazador forces had kidnapped Rhino many years ago. But unlike the late general, Keller was a small man and seemed terrified.

Slayer hit the comm button, transmitting to Captain Two Skulls in Spanish that Magnolia couldn't understand.

Shivering there on the bed, she curled back into a fetal position. Even with the two blankets, she couldn't get warm on the outside. On the inside, however, the radiation poisoning seemed to be slowly cooking her.

She drifted back into a dream—some real events from her life, some nightmares. All of them seemed to feature Rodger in some way.

The wail of a monster pulled her back into the medical bay. It sounded closer this time. Teeth chattering, Magnolia tightened her arms across her chest.

In between the eerie hooting calls, she heard intermittent shouts from sailors and soldiers in other rooms of the sickbay. Magnolia wanted to help, but she could hardly move. And with her head pounding so, she could hardly think either.

"Lieutenant," she mumbled.

Slayer limped over to her with a pistol in hand. "It's going to be okay," he said. "Those things won't get to us here. A team is on its way to clear this deck too. They shouldn't be far now."

She gripped her stomach and leaned off the bed to vomit into a bucket.

"Ugh, Octopus Lords, I'm sorry," Slayer said, leaning down to put a hand on her back. "Can I get you something? Water, pain meds—"

"A weapon," Magnolia croaked.

He pulled a knife from his duty belt and placed it on the bed.

"Thank … thank you," she said.

"Good news is, we're moving again. You feel that?"

Feeling the motion, Magnolia resisted the urge to vomit again.

"We're going home, Commander," Slayer said.

"Home…" Magnolia tried to focus on that word. She pictured

the Vanguard Islands, the trees and flowers growing on the rigs under the brilliant sun, the clear blue ocean, the pods of cavorting dolphins.

It seemed so far away.

The images vanished and she saw Rodger again, his body ripped apart by the vines in her nightmare.

Magnolia groaned again.

Another message in Spanish crackled over the comms.

"Oh no," Slayer said.

"What?" she asked. "What are they saying?"

"The team heading here was ambu—"

Distant screams cut him off, followed by a roar that resonated into the sickbay. Something big thudded against a bulkhead nearby.

Slayer limped back to the closed hatch with his pistol. Blackburn stepped back and raised his shotgun while the medical staff retreated over to Magnolia. She gripped the knife, wishing she had her curved blades.

A guttural scream sounded from the next room, but Magnolia couldn't tell whether the source was monster or human.

Clatter and breaking glass followed the noise. Then came what sounded like a body being torn apart.

Magnolia recognized that noise.

A cyclops had found prey and was removing the spine from the body.

"We have to do something," Slayer said.

"Don't open the hatch," said the nurse.

Blackburn raised his shotgun, ignoring the woman.

Shivering, Magnolia sat up, one hand on her stomach, the other holding Slayer's knife, as the sergeant opened the hatch. Slayer went inside the next room. Gunshots cracked out immediately, along with a boom from a shotgun.

A shriek rang out as an unseen monster took fire.

Magnolia tried to swing her feet over the bed and nearly fell out. She glimpsed Slayer firing with his pistol in one hand and raising his cutlass in the other.

The nurse and assistant backed up to Magnolia's bed. Not far away, the bedridden Cazador soldier also tried to sit up. He winced in pain from moving his broken leg and broken arm. This guy wasn't going to be any use in a fight if Blackburn and Slayer failed to kill the monster.

The fighting continued in the next room—more gunshots ringing out, the crunch of claws on armor, and armor hitting the deck.

Blackburn flew across the open hatch with a tail whipping past a moment later.

"AHHHHHH!"

The war cry that followed was from Slayer. Then the crack of a pistol.

The racket made Magnolia's pounding headache worse, and she felt her eyelids growing heavier. Would she be forced back into an unconscious state?

The comms crackled again with another indistinct message. She fought the red encroaching on her vision.

The nurse by her bed screamed. Magnolia raised her knife just as the cyclops squeezed through the hatch, snarling. That bulging eye blinked as it searched the room for more prey.

Blood flowed from multiple gunshot wounds. A blade stuck out of its back as it ducked under the hatch frame.

Magnolia raised her knife as the medical staff scrambled away. The injured soldier with the cutlass moved in front of them, hunched over, clearly in pain. He held his ground and slashed at the giant one-eyed freak of nature. It towered a good three feet above the man, raising muscular arms with gushing wounds.

Snarling, it strode forward, blocking the blade with a scaly wrist. Then it whipped its tail, knocking the man down and into the side of a bed. Again the eyeball flitted back and forth, settling on Magnolia.

A glistening black forked tongue shot out.

As the thing clambered forward, Slayer leaped onto its back. Grabbing the handle of the weapon lodged in its furry back, he pushed deeper and twisted. The beast wailed and tried to buck him off. He yanked the sword out, sending up a geyser of blood.

Slayer tried to bring the blade down on the back of the neck, but the monster swung an elbow and bashed him in the side.

He fell to the deck and rolled onto his back. The cyclops charged, slapping its tail against the hull and anything in its path. Stands of medical equipment toppled, and monitors shattered.

Slayer tried to crawl under the bed next to Magnolia as the creature swung at her with a clawed hand. She parried the blow with her knife but lost her grip. The weapon sailed away, clanking on the floor.

The beast grabbed her around the neck while simultaneously slapping the bed away from Slayer with its tail. Magnolia felt the cool tendrils of adrenaline as the abomination raised her into the air. She gripped its scaly wrist with both hands, choking as it tightened its death grip.

Looking down, she saw Slayer with the knife she had dropped.

The creature was leaning down to grab him with its other clawed hand when he lurched upward and jabbed the blade into its belly. The knife cut through the soft flesh. Then he twisted it and yanked to the side, and the guts flopped out on the deck.

The monster let go of Magnolia, dumping her back onto her bed. Reaching down, it held the gurgling wound. Blood squirted in all directions as it kicked and flipped like a fish out of water.

Slayer got up and walked over to the disabled creature,

picking up his cutlass on the way. Lifting up the blade, he drove it down through the face, killing the thing instantly.

He panted with both hands on his knees.

Magnolia collapsed back onto her blood-soaked mattress. The adrenaline was wearing off, and her head was throbbing fiercely. In her blurred vision, she saw Slayer reaching out to her, his lips moving, but she couldn't hear a single word.

"I'm okay," she said. Or at least, she thought she was saying it.

She blinked away stars as Slayer returned with Blackburn, helping the injured soldier walk. The nurse went to them while Keller attended the unconscious soldier the cyclops had slapped with its tail. He was injured but still alive.

"I'm out of ammo," Slayer said.

Blackburn bent down, groaning as he loaded his last two shells into the shotgun. Slayer shut the hatch as more trumpeting calls echoed closer.

He went to the comms again, but the device was hanging loosely from a wire, taken out by a monster's tail. The lights flickered, then blinked off altogether. A few moments later, they came back on.

Banging and crashing came again in the distance. It sounded like two more cyclopes, and Magnolia knew that the two injured men couldn't hold them both back. The stars and red shadow crept back across her field of vision. She was in bad shape.

As her world spun, she pictured Rodger again. This time, he was standing in the medical bay, smiling his goofy smile, his glasses hanging on the tip of his nose.

She knew that it was a hallucination, that he couldn't be real.

But he looked so real, and his voice sounded real.

"Be strong, Mags," he said. "You have to. You have to come find me…"

He vanished as loud pounding came from the hatch. Slayer and Blackburn moved into position. Magnolia fought to stay awake, watching the men, knowing they would die to protect her and the others.

Words from long ago echoed in her mind. *"I love you, Mags. You are my person..."*

"I love you too, Rodger," she whispered.

The hatch opened, disgorging pale, wrinkled flesh—not of cyclopes but of Sirens. Magnolia held in a breath as she tried to catch up to this new threat.

She couldn't hear anything—not the boom of the shotgun, or the ethereal cry of the beasts that had somehow made it onto the ship.

And suddenly, she realized why she couldn't hear those things.

These weren't Sirens.

Two figures in hazard suits strode into the room with swords dripping blood. Slayer and Blackburn both collapsed to the deck as more of the CBRN-suited soldiers arrived.

One of them held a device that looked like a Geiger counter; another had what looked like a fire extinguisher. From it, he sprayed a mist over the space.

She heard a voice she knew, and a person in a CBRN suit rushed over to her. Through a fogged-up visor, Magnolia saw it was X. He put a hand on her arm.

"You're safe now," X said.

The trumpeting call of a cyclops suggested otherwise.

"Stay here and protect them with your life," X said to one of his guards.

"Wait," Magnolia said, reaching out as X pulled away.

"I have to take back the ship," he said. "I'll be back as soon as I can."

* * * * *

"Get up!" an angry male voice shouted.

Still groggy, Michael hardly had time to react before a Cazador hauled him out of his cell. The guard barked something in Spanish to Steve, who had gotten up from his own bunk in the shared space.

Another Cazador shut the gate behind Michael and cuffed him. Charmer waited in the dark, watching with his one eye.

"Where are you taking him?" Steve asked through the bars as the gate clanged shut.

"We're going for a stroll, mate—relax," said Charmer. "Why don't you lie back down and get some rest, old man."

"Why don't you just step in here alone with this old man?" Steve said. He put his fists up. "We can settle things the old way."

Charmer laughed hard at that. "That would be quite the spectacle." He continued to chuckle as he turned away. Another guard stood in the dimly lit hallway, holding a crossbow.

Michael followed Charmer and his soldiers while Steve called out after them. "It's gonna be okay, Chief," he said.

Charmer led the way through the passages on the airship, down to the launch bay. As far as Michael could tell, only a day had passed since he pleaded not guilty to the crime of murder. He was told the trial wouldn't start for several days.

But perhaps something had changed.

The little procession went through the launch bay doors. The Hell Diver banners hung over lockers lining the wall beneath the portholes. Some of them fluttered in the wind streaming through open hatches. Across the sprawling room, the double doors were also open, with the ramp extended.

It was predawn, with no sign of sun yet on the horizon.

Michael felt a shiver of fear, which he had mostly managed up to this point. But being led here in the dark, he couldn't help feeling that Charmer was up to something evil.

Wind gusted into the bay, rustling the black jumpsuit Michael wore as he stopped.

"So the trial is off, and you're going to make me disappear; is that how it is?" Michael asked.

Charmer unfolded his arms. "You really think I would do that?"

"Oh, I know you would."

Two of the Cazador guards stepped up on Charmer's flanks, wearing masks to conceal their features. This was another tactic he used for his henchmen, who seemed emboldened because no one knew who they were.

"We're going on a short field trip, as one might have said three centuries ago," Charmer said. He took a radio off his belt. "Take us down, Captain."

The airship groaned.

"This way," Charmer said, pointing to the ramp.

Michael walked cautiously toward the yellow warning line and looked out over the ocean. He could faintly see the water in the moonlight, but not much else.

The airship lowered, the turbofans whirring under them.

"I still can't believe you people used to dive into the storms," Charmer said. "An honorable profession, indeed."

He stepped up to Michael's side.

"I always respected Kade for that, but he rather lost his mind after we crashed at Kilimanjaro," Charmer said. "Losing your family will do that, though."

Michael thought of Layla and Bray. He was inching ever closer to losing his family, too, and he still wasn't sure what he could do to fight back. In the past, X was always there for support and to fight, but his mentor was dead.

Not immortal, after all. The thought filled Michael with dread.

As the ship moved through the sky, his gut twisted with the thought of never seeing Bray and Layla again. Handcuffed, there was nothing he could do right now that wouldn't end in his death. But he could take Charmer with him if he wanted.

Be smart, Michael. Be smart.

The airship lowered over the ocean, and Michael finally spotted the concrete and rusted steel of an oil rig in the distance. It was miles away, but he could see pinpricks of light on the different levels.

"There's been a slight modification for your trial," Charmer finally explained. He pointed to a boat on the horizon.

As the airship continued to lower, the hull came into focus. Torches burned from mounts along the railings, illuminating the deck of a pot-fishing vessel. The midsize fishing boat pushed through the waves. From what Michael could tell, the crew wasn't fishing. The pots were stacked at the stern. The cranes protruding off the two-story cabin were idle.

"We decided having a trial at the capitol tower was too risky, due to a few of your friends," Charmer said. "But we found the perfect place."

The boat was a genius venue for the trial. They were out in the middle of the ocean, miles from the nearest oil rig. Out here, it would be difficult if not impossible to mount a rescue or attack. And no one would expect them to be here.

The turbofans whirred as they hovered two hundred feet above the boat. Their wind whipped against the nets on the deck below and even shook the carefully stacked pots in the stern.

One of the guards handed Michael a rope and a glove for his flesh hand. Michael put it on, then moved into position so he could fast-rope to the deck below.

He scanned the ship as he waited. The only people he spotted were Cazador soldiers of the Wave Runners.

Jamal stood directly below the airship, his black helmet angled upward. Two others of his posse were manning the sails.

Charmer said, "As you can see, there is nowhere to go. Aside from the ocean…"

Michael nodded toward Charmer, then backpedaled into the darkness, sliding down the rope to the deck of the pot-fishing vessel. He landed a few feet in front of Jamal. The sergeant reached forward and grabbed him, and the rope was retracted to the launch bay.

Spanish voices sounded across the ship as Jamal led Michael away from the center to the port side and pointed toward a stash of nets near the port rail. Another guard stood there, wearing a sash of throwing knives across his leather armor.

Michael heard a chirping noise and looked over the side of the boat. Waves splashed against the hull of the rocking vessel. Not far out, a single dolphin poked its head out of the water and eyed Michael.

The turbofans whirred louder as the ship descended. Charmer was next down. By the time his feet hit the deck, the dolphin was gone.

The first gleam of sun fired the horizon with purple and orange.

"Going to be a beautiful day," Charmer said, walking over. Gripping the rail, he drew a deep breath.

The airship rose back into the sky.

Michael scanned the water, searching for another boat. "Where's the jury?" he asked.

Charmer ignored the question and walked toward the two-story cabin. Behind a window stood a single Cazador. The man nodded as Charmer raised a hand.

Jamal went over and opened a hatch that was used as a wet well for lobsters, crabs, and other catches.

Michael's heartbeat quickened. Something was wrong. Had they brought him out here to execute him after all? Quietly and without witnesses?

He flexed his wrists inside the iron cuffs, prepared to defend himself.

"Get her up," Charmer said.

Michael narrowed his eyes as Jamal climbed down a ladder into the storage area. He returned with a woman soaked up to her waist.

What sort of game was Charmer playing?

The woman looked up, and Michael practically gasped when he saw the battered face of Eevi. Jamal pushed her to the deck as Michael rushed over.

"Stop!" someone shouted firmly.

A throwing knife suddenly whizzed past Michael's head and hit the mast behind him. The Cazador who threw it had another in hand.

"Stay where you are, or the next one is in your neck," Charmer said.

Eevi pushed herself up to her knees. Despite her swollen eyes, she held a look of defiance.

"As you may have guessed, we're not here for your trial today," Charmer said. "We're here for *her* trial."

He nodded to Jamal, and the Cazador hauled Eevi to her feet.

"Eevi Jones returned on the airship *Vanguard* with Captain Rolo, carrying news that would have made her a hero, as it has our beloved Captain," Charmer said. "She could have had a place here on the islands and enjoyed the fruits of the seeds recovered from Brisbane by the valiant efforts of Captain Rolo and his crew."

Charmer gave Eevi a cold stare.

"Instead, she chose to spread lies about Captain Rolo, making the slanderous claim that he massacred the Vanguard military and King Xavier," Charmer said. He shook his head. "These lies cannot be allowed to germinate in our soil."

"They aren't lies!" Eevi shouted. "Rolo is a murderer! *You* are a murderer!"

Jamal smacked Eevi in the back, knocking her to her knees. Charmer bent down in front of her. "Let's talk about murderers," he said. "Let's talk about Ada Winslow and what she did to a container ship of Cazadores after a peace treaty was signed. You were there that day. The day Ada dropped the shipping container into the water."

Eevi looked down, but he lifted her chin so she met his gaze.

"Were you there?" he asked.

She spat in his face. "What Ada did doesn't compare to what Captain Rolo did."

Charmer wiped the spittle from his face, then stood.

"You're right, because that's not what Captain Rolo did," he said.

It was insane to think the captain had done what Eevi was claiming, but Michael knew she had no reason to lie.

"You're all the same," Eevi said. "You and Rolo—greedy, sniveling cowards, the both of you."

She looked to Michael.

"I've known him since he was a boy. He would never kill a child."

"The time for his trial will come. Today is yours, and you've just admitted your guilt once again," Charmer said. "This bitch is all yours, Jamal."

The Cazador lifted his visor, a wicked grin on his face. He grabbed Eevi and hauled her toward the stern.

"No. Stop," Michael said. "You can't do this. You can't—"

"Punish her the same way her people decided to punish the Cazadores?" Charmer asked. "That's exactly what we're going to do."

Michael lunged forward, only to be tackled to the deck by two soldiers. Sprawled on the deck, he watched in horror as

Jamal grabbed a pot off the stack. He dropped it on the deck and opened the grate covering its opening. Then he grabbed Eevi by the hair and dragged her over to the pot.

"No, stop!" Michael yelled.

Eevi fought Jamal, hitting his arms. But it was no use. He stuffed her inside and shut the grate.

A third Cazador walked over and handed a speargun to Charmer. He pointed it at Michael as he squirmed and tried to break free.

"Fighting is a waste of energy," Charmer said. "This is justice."

"This isn't justice!" Michael yelled. "She didn't drop those Cazadores into the ocean!"

Charmer bent down so only Michael could hear. "Her lies are worse than killing one or even twenty people," he hissed.

Jamal kicked the pot as Eevi struggled inside. She grabbed the bars, peering out while he kept his boot over the grate.

"Don't do this," Michael said. "Please, Carl, I implore you. For what our people did to save yours, let Eevi live. She will take what she said back and never say it again. Right, Eevi?"

There was a hint of consideration in her eye that filled Michael with hope, but then she shook her head. "I spoke the truth," she said. "Someday, it will come to light, and you will be remembered as a murdering coward."

Michael heaved a sigh of defeat.

Jamal dragged the pot over to the port rail.

Eevi, crouched inside like a trapped animal, stared at Michael. He could tell by her defiance there was no turning back now.

"Please, Carl," Michael said. "Don't do this. There has to be another way."

Charmer looked over to Jamal and nodded.

"The decision has been made," he said.

Michael turned back toward Eevi as Jamal and another Wave Runner picked up the pot and balanced it on the rail.

"NO!" Michael shouted.

He pushed up from the deck, tossing the two men off his back with a strength he had forgotten he possessed. Fueled by rage, he ducked under a cable and rushed over to the side. As he grabbed the lobster trap with his bound hands, he felt a sharp prick in his back.

"Another inch, and this goes through your heart," Charmer said.

The two guards Michael had flung off grabbed him again.

"Let him watch," Charmer said.

Michael stared as Jamal tipped the pot over the rail, and Eevi vanished in a flurry of bubbles.

"No," he moaned.

"Justice is done," Charmer said. "Soon, it will be your turn."

Music from a wooden flute carried over the waves. Michael spotted a man on a Jet Ski bobbing in the waves. He started the engine and then drove circles around the spot where Eevi had gone under.

The Cazadores next to Michael backed away as a long arm, lined with suction cups, whipped out of the ocean and wrapped around the railing. In their eyes, this wasn't only justice; this was a sacrifice to the Octopus Lords.

"Bloody hell," Charmer said. "I didn't believe the legend was true."

The beast surfaced and glided over to the boat to examine them with saucer eyes before slowly vanishing into the depths to claim the sacrificial gift.

Michael felt the spear point come away from his back as he stared at the water, grieving.

A radio crackled behind him.

"We're done here. Send down the winch line for Mr. Everhart," Charmer said. "I'm heading to the capitol tower to prepare for the ceremony."

THIRTEEN

"I need another hour, maybe two," Bulldozer called out.

The mechanic and amateur pilot was working on a broken-down Sea King chopper in the middle of the underground hangar. The other knights were helping, except for Lucky, who stood with General Jack in front of Kade.

Above, the wind from the violent storm howled over the closed hangar doors. Thunder boomed.

Kade tried not to focus on the danger that King Xavier, Tia, and everyone else who'd survived the nuclear blast were still in out there. According to the general, they were dead meat.

Don't write them off yet, Kade thought.

He paced and watched the knights work, knowing he could do nothing to help his people right now. He had to hold out hope they would fend off the attack by the one-eyed lizard things and escape.

And right now hope was all he had.

Loud clicking drew Kade's attention to the chopper, where Bulldozer hopped out of the troop hold with a Geiger counter.

"The radiation readings are the highest I've ever seen," he

said. "We're not safe here, and I'm afraid we're going to lose this facility."

General Jack appeared to be turning red, as if he was about to blow. And then he blew.

"Bloody fucking cocksucking BASTARDS!" he shouted.

Everyone turned toward the fit of rage from the normally calm general. Kade had never seen this side of the man. His eyes, bright with anger, swept the room. They centered on Kade.

"*Your* people did this!" he shouted. "The Forerunner was right about them! They are bloody barbarians!"

Kade gulped. Any goodwill he had earned in the field seemed to fade away. General Jack had started to shift from calm and almost humorous to fearful and angry after the loss of Mal. When he found out about Garrett, his ire turned to rage, probably fueled by more fear. But it was the threat from this fallout that sent him over the edge.

The general raised his drum-fed submachine gun. He leaned in close with the suppressed barrel hitting Kade in the chest.

"The Forerunner made a fatal error by sending us to find your king," General Jack whispered in a low voice, like he didn't want the other knights to hear. "Your people stirred up every goddamned monster along the Sunshine Coast and then set off a nuke that will make this place uninhabitable."

He plucked the pistol from Kade's holster that Lucky had returned back on the riverbank. Kade didn't move, and he said nothing, not wanting to further enrage the general. After all, the general wasn't wrong about what Captain Rolo had done. Kade didn't blame these people for being furious. It was an act of war.

"Nothing to say?" General Jack said in a raised voice.

Kade shook his head. This seemed to make the knight even more furious. He poked Kade in the chest with the barrel, hard enough it hurt. Now Kade was mad. He stiffened and looked the general dead in the eyes.

"Sir, I've explained what happened and that it was a betrayal we could never have seen coming," he said. "I've apologized, and I mean it from my heart. If you want to kill me, then kill me. But do it knowing that if I had the chance, I'd kill Captain Rolo myself, and those who carried out his orders. Either way, I'm confident King Xavier will do exactly that. The prophecy was true about the Immortal."

"The Immortal." General Jack snorted. Then he looked down at Mal's body. "Forgive me if I don't believe your king is some divine leader, after all the death he brought to us."

The general looked back to Kade.

"A good leader sees betrayals and avoids them," he said.

"A good leader with a good heart sometimes is unable to predict the horrendous actions of leaders with evil ones," Kade said, treading carefully with his tone. "I believe that is why the Old World ended."

"And this is why our leader does not have a heart. He uses *this*." He tapped his temple.

Kade saw Lucky watching him, but he glanced away when Kade turned in his direction. They were hiding something from him—a secret, perhaps, about their own leader.

"Tell you what—if your king survives what our drone saw, then I'll buy he is immortal. Because he'll bloody well need to be considering he's brought the entire wrath of all that is evil to his ship," General Jack said.

Again Kade thought back to the images he had seen. He tried to remain stone faced as the general stared into his soul. Finally, the general pulled the suppressed barrel away.

"You're a good man, Hell Diver," said the general. "That doesn't mean I trust you, though."

The screaming storm above them seemed to grow louder, clawing at the door. Water dripped down from a crack, pooling on the floor behind the other broken-down Sea King.

Kade checked the Geiger counter on his wrist computer. The radiation was already inside the facility. All he could do was sit by and wait while the knights prepared. He used the time to think of Tia and the promise he had made her father long ago. Somehow, he had to get back to her. But right now she seemed so far away. All his people did.

A distant boom shook the floor. Everyone looked up from their work.

"What was that?" Kade asked.

"I think that was a land mine," Lucky called out.

"Defensive positions!" General Jack ordered.

The knights dropped whatever they were doing and ran to grab rifles.

Bulldozer hopped down from the cockpit and ran for the command center, with Lucky and the general. Kade hurried after them, stopping in the entry, within view of the multiple screens showing locations around the hangar.

"Oh no," Bulldozer said.

On every screen, pale, hairless, eyeless forms skittered and scrabbled toward the airfield. Bulldozer took a seat. The ancient chair creaked under him. He tapped the keyboard, switching between monitors that revealed more of the encroaching monsters.

"Bloody hell," the general said. "That's an entire colony. Bulldozer, get that fucking bird ready to go!"

The mechanic hopped up and ran out of the room, nearly knocking Kade over. He stumbled back as the man bolted for the Sea King.

"I thought we were going to ride out the storm down here," Kade said to Lucky.

Lucky scoffed. "We won't survive down here for even half the storm."

"Our only chance is to get in the air," the general said. "I want two knights on the entrance... Actually, no..."

He turned to look at Kade.

"You really trust this man?" General Jack asked Lucky.

"He saved my life three times out there," Lucky said. "He coulda killed me six times over."

The general scrutinized Kade for a long moment. "Don't make me regret this," he said.

Lucky handed the pistol to Kade.

"Get him a rifle too. And extra magazines. If those things get through—"

Another muffled boom cut him off.

Kade checked the explosion on the monitors. When the dust settled, hunks of Siren lay strewn around a smoldering hole.

Three more beasts galloped past the carnage, undeterred.

More explosions boomed as other land mines went off.

On another screen, a herd of maybe twenty raced across the airfield, already past the defenses.

Kade watched as the larger monsters swooped down from the sky. He stepped out of the command center and looked at the closed ceiling.

"May the Trident protect us," Nobu said.

"May the Trident protect us," the other knights chorused.

Lucky and Kade went to the rack of rifles across the room. Kade took one and checked the ammo—hollow-point rounds with red tips. Locally manufactured, probably at the Coral Castle.

He slapped in a magazine, chambered the first round, and held up the weapon. God*damn*, did it feel good to have a rifle again!

The roar of the storms sounded over the racket of machinery.

"Almost there!" Bulldozer shouted.

The unmistakable two-tone blare of an emergency siren seemed to answer. Thunder boomed, drowning it out. When it faded, Kade heard what sounded like footsteps. Dozens of claws clattering on the overhead door.

"They're up there!" Nobu yelled.

Zen played the sniper rifle's long barrel back and forth, waiting for a target, but Kade could see that the Sirens weren't getting in that way. He doubted they were going to be able to find a way through the blast door either.

For the next hour, the Sirens bashed and clawed at the ceiling, their alien screeches rising and falling over the clap of thunder and howling wind.

"Okay, I think we're ready!" Bulldozer shouted from the cockpit.

"Hell Diver!" General Jack yelled. "You head topside and clear the roof."

Kade was used to dangerous orders from his days diving, but this sounded like a suicide mission. He gaped at the general.

"You want deliverance? Do this, and I'll vouch for you to the Forerunner."

"Sir, if he goes up there, he's dead," Lucky said.

"Better him than us," the general said. "Enough of us have died for his barbaric people's greed."

All the other knights except Lucky pointed their rifles at Kade.

"You want out of here?" Jack said. "You clear the sky for us."

"You're wrong about King Xavier, and you're wrong about my people," Kade said.

"Really, mate?" General Jack snorted. "You know why Lucky here hated you so much?"

Kade looked to the knight.

"'Cause the Cazadores killed his dad when he was just a boy. Now, I don't know much about King Xavier or his people, but I know enough about the Cazadores and about these sky people that nuked your ship. Far as I'm concerned, they're pirates, the lot of them."

Kade understood the general's attitude, but it didn't make him right.

"Well, guess I'll just have to prove you wrong," Kade said, turning toward the hatch.

Lucky walked over and handed Kade a radio. "Tell us when it's clear," he said.

"I'm sorry about your dad," Kade said. "I didn't know."

Lucky nodded and tapped the keypad to open the blast door. "Same code to the one above—four-nine-one-nine-pound-four-nine," he said. "Good luck."

The big five-bladed main rotor on the Sea King turned, quickly whipping faster and faster. The draft created pressure on Kade's ears. Knights brought out the last of their gear from the storage rooms and piled it inside the troop hold.

Lucky tapped the code again, and the hatch began to close behind Kade. Kade backed away until it thumped shut. Then he turned and looked up the stairs, wondering how he could survive this.

* * * * *

X moved through the ship with Sebastian and Nicolas. Gran Jefe was also with them. Their armor glistened after going through decon back at the cargo hold. Their suits would protect them from radiation exposure for now, but the rest of the ship was getting dosed by the radioactive beasts prowling the decks.

"Give me a sitrep, General," X said over the comms.

"Teams are engaging hostiles on the lower decks," Forge said. "We still don't have control of the orlop deck, and I've moved most of our additional forces to protect the engine room, but with so many of our forces injured, we had to abandon sections of the ship."

"What sections?" X asked.

When the general explained, X realized that Miles was in one of the abandoned sections.

"I sent a guard. Haven't heard anything," Forge said.

X pictured Miles alone, in a cage, unable to fight back against beasts that would eat him as a snack.

"I'm heading there now," X said.

"Understood. Be careful, King Xavier."

The lights flickered as X made his way down the next passage with the small entourage of Cazadores. He heard a distant shout and what sounded like the thud of a cyclops tail against a bulkhead, then a decisive crunch.

X moved up next to Gran Jefe. The man had a fat lip, a black eye, and dents in his armor from Jo-Jo's fists but was basically intact. He led the way with a spear in his hands and a laser rifle slung over his hazard suit. He paused at the next intersection, where a cyclops lay sprawled on the deck.

Smoke curled away from a smoldering laser tunnel through the head. X had asked the teams to limit their interior shooting earlier, but now with the beasts inside, they would do whatever it took.

He steadied the laser rifle on his prosthetic right arm, which Steve had designed with a groove for a gun barrel. With the weapon up and ready, he moved into the passage with Gran Jefe. They found the Cazador who had fired the laser bolt. He was sitting on the deck, with his back to the hull and a hand on his gut. Blood leaked from his armor.

"Get him back to medical," X said.

"Sir, we have orders to stay with you," Sebastian said.

"And *I'm* ordering you to get this man to sickbay," X said.

"*Ándale,*" Gran Jefe said. "I protect the king."

Sebastian and Nicolas helped the injured Cazador up and took him away.

Gran Jefe continued down the next corridor, toward the hatch that would take them down a deck. Valeria had moved Miles down there just hours ago and locked him away in a storage space. At the time, X wasn't worried about the monsters getting into the ship, and even if they did, he'd thought the dog would be safe. But now he wondered if they had actually doomed Miles.

X moved past Gran Jefe with a newfound sense of urgency. They weren't far away now. He started running.

Reaching the corridor to the storage area, X stepped around another dead cyclops on the deck. A black forked tongue drooped from the open mouth.

"Check it," X whispered.

Gran Jefe thrust his sword into the eye; the beast didn't even flinch.

"*Muerto*," he said. "*Muy* dead."

He stepped over the carcass as X cleared the left side of the next corridor, then the right. There was no sign of the guard sent to check on Miles. X shined his light down the passageway.

Not waiting for Gran Jefe, he rushed down the corridor toward the hatch. He listened over the pounding in his ears for Miles—some indication of life. Whining, barking, *growling*…

When X got to the door, flecks of blood marked the hull just left of the hatch, over deep gouges from the claws of a cyclops. He could hear raspy breathing on the other side.

X grabbed the handle. It was unlatched.

"Miles…"

Sweeping his light over the long room, he found an almost impassable jumble of boxes and toppled storage racks. He moved inside and again heard labored breathing. His boots slid in a puddle of blood, and X went down on his back.

Gran Jefe rushed in after him, also skidding in the blood but keeping on his feet.

X saw the source of the blood. Another downed Cazador lay on the other side of the racks, next to another cyclops. The heavy breathing was coming not from the beast but from the wounded Cazador who had brought it down. Gran Jefe went over to help the man while X got up off the slippery deck.

Hearing a faint squeak, X glanced over at a cage that had fallen off a rack not far behind the two bodies. Two glowing eyes stared back at him. Then came the bark as familiar as X's own voice. Miles was up on his feet, tail wagging.

Beside the cage was another body. Dressed in a hazard suit, it was much smaller than the bulky Cazador Gran Jefe was checking on.

"It's okay, boy," X said to Miles. "Sit, sit."

He bent down and lifted the bowed head of the soldier. To his surprise, it was Valeria. But unlike the other Cazador, she didn't seem to be breathing.

"Corporal," he said.

Miles whined louder as X slowly turned Valeria on her back. Blood dripped down the inside of her cracked visor.

He put a gloved finger to her neck, finding a weak pulse.

"We have to get them out of here," X said. "You help that guy; I'll carry Valeria."

Gran Jefe hoisted the injured man onto his feet, wrapping one arm over his shoulder. X wasn't sure what to do about Miles. Letting him out of the cage would expose him to more radiation, but then, the hybrid animal was genetically modified to survive in these conditions. That didn't mean he was invincible, though, especially at his advanced age.

X bumped on the command channel.

"General, I've located Miles," he said. "Give me a sitrep."

"All hostiles have been tracked down and killed except on the orlop deck," Forge said. "We've almost regained control of the ship, and I've deployed a team to begin decon."

X heaved a sigh of relief. "Copy that. I'm headed back to medical, then to the CIC."

He motioned for Miles to stay, hoping he wouldn't burst out of the cage. The dog went down on his haunches, but when X opened the door, the dog jumped into his arms, orders be damned.

X resisted the urge to hug the dog too hard, not wanting to hurt or contaminate him further.

"Sit," X said.

The dog obeyed, and X bent and gently picked up Valeria. Holding her in his arms, he moved out of the room, into the corridor. From there, he backtracked to the medical bay.

Two guards stood sentry outside with spears crossed. They lowered them as the king approached.

The hatch opened to a scene of barely controlled chaos. X set Valeria gently down on a bed. Clearly, she wasn't getting help right away. There were too many injured—over fifteen already in the beds, and three medical staffers.

Another message came over the comms as X took in the scene. "King Xavier, do you copy?" said Captain Two Skulls.

Before X could respond, a new group of injured arrived, including a sailor wearing a hazard suit. X recognized him as one of the cooks. The man was mumbling, "La comida," over and over.

"Oh no," Gran Jefe said.

"What?"

"The food," Nicolas said. "The cook says the food has been contaminated."

A rumble seemed to come from all sides. The ship trembled.

People stopped to look up as an emergency alarm whined. X had a feeling it wasn't the food Captain Two Skulls was trying to contact him about.

Something was wrong with the ship.

FOURTEEN

Tritons blew from the top of the capitol tower, summoning every boat within earshot. This was one of only a handful of times the Cazador horns had sounded since Layla and her people had settled here. Sometimes, the deep, throaty note heralded a great celebration, and sometimes it was a call to war.

The tritons had last sounded when King Xavier departed with the Vanguard navy and army to Panama. Hearing the noise this morning had taken her back to a dark place. At first, Layla feared it had something to do with the two Cazadores she and Pedro had killed last night. But now she realized it must be something else.

It wasn't soldiers circling the capitol tower below. Those were civilian craft crowding the rig from all directions. Dories, johnboats, rafts—she even saw a canoe. It seemed every citizen of the Vanguard Islands had shown up.

Layla held Bray in her arms—or tried to. The growing boy squirmed, pointing and babbling, not wanting to miss anything. Even he knew something was up.

Victor stood beside her. She had told him of last night's meeting on the boat, and the two Wave Runners she and Pedro had killed. The news seemed to unsettle Victor, who didn't say much in response. He knew as well as she that her actions, if discovered, could spark a war.

They stood at the window, watching the boats arrive. Civilians got out wearing colorful clothing and hats.

Loud pounding on the door snapped her to attention.

Victor rushed out of the kitchen, returning a moment later. "Soldier," he said.

Layla felt her heart in her throat.

She handed Bray off to Victor and went out to look through the peephole. Standing in the hallway was a single Cazador soldier in light leather armor.

He pounded again and said, "Open."

"Hold on," Layla said.

She went back to Victor and took Bray back. The curious boy babbled and said, "Da-da."

"No, honey, I'm sorry, but it's not Daddy."

"Open!" the voice called again.

Bray recoiled slightly, curious but also wary.

Victor motioned her back. Then he went to the door, unlatched the locks, and opened it.

The Cazador soldier remained in the hallway but moved for a better view of the living room. He pointed a filthy fingernail at Layla. "You come," he said.

Victor stepped out.

"I say *her* come. You stay," the Cazador barked.

"I go where she goes," Victor replied.

He used his six-inch height advantage to good effect, looming over the soldier. The Cazador peered up with a grin, undeterred. His hand went to the hilt of the cutlass on his belt.

"Victor, it's okay," she said. "Watch Bray. I'll go."

"But—"

The Cazador cut him off. "*El niño*. Baby come too."

"What?" Layla asked. Her heart rate increased. What if, somehow, Charmer and the Wave Runners had discovered what she'd done last night? What if they had come to take her and Bray just as they'd taken Rhino Jr.?

"Baby come," the Cazador said with a jagged yellow grin. Bray smiled back and reached out, thinking this was a game.

Layla held her ground, and the soldier seemed to recognize she wasn't going willingly.

"I say bring baby. Come, no waste time," he said.

Layla tried to get a read on him for his true intentions. He was dangerous, that much was certain, but did they know what she had done?

Even if they did, they would never do anything to Bray . . . would they?

Another thought crossed her mind. What if they planned to keep Bray during the trial, then take revenge on him for Nez's death if Michael was found guilty?

The thought made her cold with dread.

Another chill came with the next thought. What if Imulah had gone to Charmer about her visit?

"No be afraid," the Cazador said. "I take you to rooftop for grand ceremony."

Layla saw truth in this man's eyes, but still she couldn't quite let go of the fear in her heart. She finally looked back to Victor and nodded.

"Give me a minute," Layla said.

"No minute," the Cazador said.

Layla held up her son. "He needs his diaper changed, so unless you want to smell shit the whole way . . ."

"No shit. *Vaya*." He waved her off.

She took Bray into the bedroom, once again trying not to

look at the empty crib where Rhino Jr. had slept for months. Even though he was not her own, she had grown attached to him and missed the baby terribly. There was also the guilt of letting Sofia down, after Layla had promised to care for her son.

Layla put Bray down and took off his shorts and then his cloth diaper.

"Da-da," he repeated.

She held back tears as she changed him. Her heart felt as if it would burst each time she thought about losing Michael. She had steeled herself so many times, preparing to lose him, but not like this. To think he would be executed for a crime he hadn't committed, by people he had risked his life to save, filled her with a simmering rage.

After she finished changing Bray, she grabbed the knife she had shoved into the Cazador's brain last night, and stashed it in her boot. She put on her chest carrier, and after strapping Bray in, she walked back to the living room and said goodbye to Victor. Bray reached out to Victor as they left.

The Cazador led her up a stairwell. As they neared the top of the tower, she could hear the buzz of many voices. At the top, Layla shielded Bray's eyes with her hand as they walked out into a light breeze and dazzling sunlight.

When her eyes adjusted, she saw maybe a hundred civilians filing across the rooftop. Militia soldiers in leather armor and tan fatigues patrolled with automatic rifles.

She noticed that the Vanguard logos had all been removed. New yellow sun symbols marked some of the armored plates. She didn't see the Vanguard flag blowing in the wind either. What she did see across the rooftop made her do a double take to make sure she was seeing properly.

The artillery cannons Michael and his teams had deployed were no longer pointed at the water. They were pointed at the surrounding oil rigs.

"Move!" yelled the guard.

Layla shifted Bray to her other arm as they trekked around cultivated plots, where farmers wearing round hats worked on their knees, planting the hybrid seeds from Brisbane. She searched for Jacquelyn, the woman Charmer had apparently fallen in love with. But a quick survey of the gardens revealed that the horticulturist wasn't working right now.

More soldiers patrolled around the fruit trees, lest some civilian try to steal an apple. The stream of Cazadores, sky people, and other rescued populations continued into the Sky Arena.

By the time Layla made it up to one of the entry points, the stands inside were packed. Over half the population of the islands had shown up, and still more boats were arriving.

The guard took her up a stairwell to one of the box seats. In some of the other elevated booths, she saw the usual wealthy Cazador businessmen, including Martino. There were also sky people in them now, people associated with Charmer. But she had yet to see that silken-voiced snake of a man.

The guard took her into one of the boxes overlooking the arena. She sat down with Bray, eyeing the glass of water and plate of fruit on the glass table.

"Drink; eat," said the Cazador.

She picked up a wedge of pineapple and gave it to Bray. He bit into it with his square upper tooth, taking out a small chunk. Gurgling with delight, he mashed the chunk until juice ran down his chin.

Layla scanned the audience for friendly faces. It didn't take long to find Katherine Mitchells and her daughter, Phyl. They were both looking up at the booth at the same time Layla was looking down. Phyl raised a hand to wave, but Katherine discreetly motioned for Phyl to lower it as Layla went to raise her own hand.

That was all Layla needed to see to know how alone she really was. Danger was everywhere, and everyone felt it.

"I'm sorry," Katherine mouthed before looking away.

Layla lowered her gaze, holding back a tear.

Ten minutes later, the horns blared one last time, silencing the entire arena.

"Time to begin," said the Cazador, favoring her with another sharpened, yellowed grin.

Across the arena, the crowd stood looking toward the largest booth, where el Pulpo used to watch the gladiator fights with his many wives. The drapes parted, and Charmer stepped up to the railing.

He wore a white tunic with a red tippet around his neck. Layla could vaguely make out the sun symbol on either end of the tippet.

"Stand," growled the Cazador.

Layla stood up with Bray in her arms.

Static crackled from unseen speakers, followed by the mellifluous voice of Carl Lex.

"Good morning, amigos, mates, friends," he said, holding out both arms. "Welcome to the first ceremony of the new order that will ensure the survival of our home."

Charmer lowered his arms and clasped his hands behind his back.

"Thanks to the courageous efforts of Captain Rolo and his crew, and those who paid the ultimate sacrifice, we now have the means to grow new crops that will sustain every mouth across the islands. You may have seen these special hybrid seeds being planted on your way here."

He looked around the arena and smiled. "These seeds will germinate within just months, but fear not. The rationing you all have endured will not get any worse. To tide us over to the next harvest, we will tap into the food supply that the former king and Chief Everhart hid from you all. Starting today, we will provide new rations to everyone."

Excited shouts filled the stadium.

Bray clapped his hands and laughed too.

Layla thought back to Michael's decision to keep the secret food from the supercarrier hidden at King Xavier's request. The idea was that the food would serve as an emergency cushion in times of want. They had taken it to an island and stored it in an old silo. Then, when Michael decided it was time to tap the food reserve and announce it to the citizens of the islands, the Wave Runners had been waiting to ambush them.

But for X and his original orders about the food, that would never have happened.

"With the death of King Xavier in Australia, we no longer have a king of the islands," Charmer said. "Today, we will vote for a leader, and I would like to be the first to nominate Captain Rolo, a man who has dedicated his life to his people and will dedicate the rest of it to serving you all."

A second figure emerged in the booth, this one wearing the white flight suit of an airship captain. Captain Rolo's wispy hair floated like gossamer in the breeze as he squinted into the sunlight.

This wasn't just a ceremony. It was a full-on regime change, and Layla had a front-row seat.

Captain Rolo held up a microphone. "Today, we say goodbye to the old, archaic way of ruling this paradise," he said. "Today, we say goodbye to the violence that has taken so many people who called this place home. Today we say goodbye to the brutal ways of the Cazador past, which saw people enslaved, murdered, and killed."

Hushed voices buzzed, and angry shouts called out as his words were translated.

Rolo raised his hand.

"I understand this might upset some of you, but if you look

around this arena, you will see something missing," he said. "From where I stand, I see children, I see elderly, and I see many women, but I do not see very many men. You see, you have lost almost an entire generation of warriors in the name of expansion and war."

Layla felt her heart sink at the truth, but not for the same reason. For her, there wasn't anyone left to challenge Charmer, except for Sergeant Jamal. But the Cazador and his Wave Runners seemed content with whatever Charmer had already paid them off with.

"War is the reason our Old World ended. To survive, we must burn this human habit out of us and focus on peace," Rolo said.

Charmer nodded and said, "Captain Rolo is a man of peace, a leader who will unite us all under a new banner. But that does not mean we won't have security. I am proud to announce that Sergeant Jamal will be promoted to general if Captain Rolo becomes king."

Jamal stepped up into the booth. Unlike Charmer, he wasn't smiling. He glowered over the crowd.

Layla understood now. So that was what they'd promised Jamal: promotion to general.

And everyone else? Charmer and Rolo had coaxed them with the promise of food. Those who didn't look convinced would soon be, through Jamal's intimidation.

"We gather here today to elect a new king," Charmer said. "I have already nominated Captain Rolo and now offer you the chance to do the same. Is there anyone else who knows someone deserving of such an honor? Someone who will feed us, keep us safe, and lead us into a brighter future?"

Layla looked around the arena. No one would challenge Charmer or Rolo at this point, especially with the malevolent Jamal looking on.

"Is there no one else?" Charmer asked.

Only the distant keening of a seagull came in answer.

Charmer smiled again, wider now. "Seeing no one else, I move to put this to a vote," he said. "All in favor of electing Rolo as king, raise your hand."

Layla looked around as hands shot up across the stadium. Within moments, virtually every hand was in the air.

"This is a proud day in our history," Charmer said. "All hail King Rolo!" He stepped to the side and went down on one knee.

All around Layla, the crowd bowed and took up the chant.

Layla refused to kneel. Bray babbled away, oblivious.

Rolo held up both hands. "Thank you," he said. "This is a great honor, and I'm proud to retire as captain from the airship *Vanguard*, to focus on restoring our home that we may live in peace. But before we can do that, we must first bring someone to justice for the crime of killing Oliver and his son, Nez."

Charmer looked over at Layla, his smile gone.

"Tomorrow, the trial of Chief Everhart will begin," Rolo said. "Then we can move on with the future of our home—a bright, peaceful future."

Humming sounded in the distance, and all looked skyward when a shadow passed over the arena. Once called the *Hive*, it was Layla's former home.

Long, narrow rods protruded from the ship's hull. As Layla squinted into the sun, she realized that these were machine-gun barrels. They had turned the airship into a weapon, along with the rooftop of the capitol tower. *Peace through superior firepower,* she thought. That was the future of the islands.

Bray looked up at the ship that his parents had dived from countless times to keep humanity alive. This was no longer that ship.

Layla turned her attention to Charmer. A woman stood next to him now, and she could see it was Jacquelyn. She kissed Charmer on the lips, then waved out to the crowd.

Layla's heart sank. How was she ever supposed to get to this woman?

Now more than ever, she knew that proving her husband was framed would be nearly impossible. The only way to save him was to break him out and flee this place.

Once again, they would have to find a new home.

* * * * *

"We're ready to launch," said Lucky.

Kade held up the radio. He had been waiting in the bunker's stairwell for several hours after receiving a message to stand by. Apparently, Bulldozer hadn't fixed the chopper after all.

Now it seemed the bird was ready to fly.

"Copy that," Kade said.

He climbed the stairs to the top blast door. Each step took him closer to death. He knew his odds of surviving this were worse than for any dive he had ever made into the wastes. But he had survived situations where most people would have died. In that way, he was like King Xavier. Tonight, he would stick to the plan he always used when he went into danger: stow his fear out of sight.

Fear was what got other men and women killed. Fear made you lock up and freeze when you could be fighting or running. Fear made you do irrational things to save your hide.

Fear had stopped ruling his life after he lost his family. Before then, he had feared death because he would miss out on the rest of their lives and be unable to protect them. With them gone, he was freed from all those cares.

Of course, he feared losing Tia and Alton, but he could do nothing for them right now.

Kade raised his rifle as he approached the top of the stairs.

The blast door was secure. He tapped in the code Lucky had given him, then stepped back, raising his rifle.

He had ninety hollow-point rounds. And he had his Monster Hunter revolver with three bullets. Each one must count if he was to have any hope of survival.

The thick door groaned open.

"Get ready," Kade said into the radio.

In the green hue of his night-vision goggles, Kade saw the airfield. A pack of Sirens patrolled about two hundred feet away, their eyeless faces flitting, sniffing, listening for prey. He had only seconds before they detected his energy signature, which would lure them like sharks to blood.

Kade walked out into the rain and lined up the iron sights on the beasts flying above the roof. Lightning flashed, backlighting their sinewy muscles and pale, cadaverous flesh.

A dozen of the creatures sailed under the clouds, their frayed wings beating hard to stay airborne in the storm. More sat perched like gargoyles on the hangar over the bunker.

An electronic wail came from the airfield.

Kade turned toward the pack of beasts on the asphalt. The leader was already clambering over the broken runway toward him. Three more creatures dashed out from the rubble, following the leader.

The beasts on the hangar took wing. Kade fired in their direction, hoping to keep them back. Then he turned toward the Sirens on the runway and sighted up their leader. He squeezed off a burst of hollow-point rounds, and the head flew apart.

The other three Sirens scattered, but not before Kade took out two more with calculated shots to center mass. With the fourth Siren on the run, he aimed his rifle back to the sky and was shocked to see all the monsters swooping down toward him at once.

"Go," he said into the radio. "NOW!"

Kade winged the leader of the formation, and it spun down into the asphalt. The next one took a head shot and dropped from the sky. By the time it smacked into the broken tarmac a few feet away, he had already maimed two more.

Screeching behind him prompted Kade to bring his rifle around to a gaunt-looking Siren coming at full speed. He closed his eye, aimed, and fired. The Siren leaped for him at that same moment, claws out. A burst ripped through its chest. He squeezed the trigger again, but the magazine was out.

The beast hit the ground, rolled, and skidded to a stop inches away. Backing up, Kade ejected the spent mag and punched in a fresh one.

Two more packs came sprinting across the runway to flank him. He searched for cover as the cries from the sky drew nearer.

When one was close enough to touch, he brought up his rifle and fired into its gaping mouth. Blood and gore flecked his entire front as he went down on one knee. He sighted up two more Sirens descending on his position. Two quick bursts put one on the ground and sent the other flapping away.

Lightning forked across the horizon. In its glow, he saw more of the monsters swarming toward the airfield. Their distant wails rose in an electronic chorus.

They were surrounding him from the sky and the ground. He sighted up the nearest beast on the asphalt and missed twice before finally bringing it down.

The *whop-whop* of rotors finally sounded as the chopper rose out of the underground hangar. He started toward it but stopped when he saw that the troop hold doors were shut.

Were they planning on leaving him here?

Of course. They figured you for a dead man!

"I'm on the runway!" he shouted into his radio.

The radio crackled but gave no response.

Sirens flew toward the Sea King, one hitting the disk of the tail rotor in a pink puff of gore.

Kade picked off two more of the monsters swooping down toward the chopper. Lowering his rifle, he raced after the bird as it began to wheel around.

"Down here!" he shouted. "I'm down—"

Something meaty hit him from behind.

He smacked the asphalt hard on his stomach, dropping his rifle in the process. A Siren's claws grabbed his helmet, scratching the visor as it tried to crush his head.

Kade reached down to his right thigh for his pistol as the beast squeezed his helmet. His fingers touched the grip, but the Siren brought its fists down on his visor, making him flinch. Finally, he got a purchase on the grip and brought the pistol barrel up under its chin. One of his last three bullets blew off the top of the eyeless skull. The body slumped off, but a live one was coming at him.

He raised the weapon, watching in what felt like slow motion as the jaws snapped and snarled. The creature slammed into him, knocking him onto his back again. Saliva and blood dripped onto his helmet as, in his peripheral vision, he saw more of the beasts surrounding him.

Trying to buck the beast off, he glimpsed something else that chilled him to the core. The chopper was lifting into the sky.

Kade should have known this was a suicide mission. Maybe deep down, he had wanted it to be. Maybe deep down, he had a death wish.

For a fleeting moment, he gave up, allowing the Siren to get a scaly hand around his neck. It squeezed, and his vision blurred.

Blood dripped onto his visor as he heard a loud crack. He reached up and wiped it clear as more cracks rang out. Gunshots.

He raised his pistol and fired at a Siren bounding for him, hitting it in the shoulder. It slid to the ground in front of him, and he bashed the skull in with the weapon's metal grip.

More shots cracked in the distance.

Kade looked to the sky, expecting to see the chopper, but it was nowhere in sight. He turned toward the destroyed hangars and saw a figure on the collapsed roof.

It was Lucky, firing a long-barreled sniper rifle that had to be Zen's weapon. He was damned good with that gun, picking off two beasts as they came at him.

Kade holstered the pistol and grabbed his rifle as a Siren ran out the doorway of the hangar Lucky was perched on.

"Watch out!" Kade called out.

Lucky turned and fired at the beast skittering up the mound of debris. A body shot knocked the creature off the slope. Then Lucky slip-slid down the rubble, pausing at the bottom to dispatch two Sirens chasing Kade.

They met in the middle of the tarmac, coming together back to back. Creatures surrounded them, some with wings, others without.

The beat of rotor blades buffeted Kade's ears as he palmed in his last magazine. He looked to the east, where the Sea King was lowering with a Siren attached to the cockpit.

Lucky aimed and fired. The beast fell off, and the chopper hovered overhead. The troop door opened, and a rope dropped down.

"Go!" Lucky shouted over the rotors.

Kade grabbed it and was pulled upward. In the opening, General Jack fired a mounted M60 at the fleeing monsters.

The second Kade was inside the bird, he collapsed on the deck, gasping. He watched as they pulled Lucky up. Nobu and Zen grabbed the knight by the back shoulder plates and hauled him in next to Kade.

General Jack shut the door, sealing out the wind and rain. He loomed over Lucky and Kade. "Risky move, Gaz," he said.

"Paying my debts, General," Lucky said. He got up as the chopper fought for altitude.

"Nice shooting," Zen said.

"Nice rifle," Lucky said, handing the rifle back to Zen. Nobu reached down and helped Lucky up. Kade remained sitting, still panting.

"Maybe we should be calling *you* 'Lucky,' instead of 'Hell Diver,'" said General Jack.

Still breathing hard, Kade dragged himself up into a seat. The chopper banked hard to the left, nearly knocking him back onto the deck.

Zen took his sniper rifle to the closed door to watch for hostiles. Nobu joined him, water dripping off his armor. It took Kade a few minutes to shake off the shock of the battle on the tarmac. He still couldn't quite believe he was alive.

But they weren't out of this mess yet.

Gail-force winds beat the hull, threatening to smack them back down onto the radioactive ground. Thunder boomed like gunfire in their ears.

The chopper jerked and shuddered violently, losing five hundred feet in an instant, then catching a lift back into the sky.

"I think we got a problem!" Bulldozer shouted.

"Yeah, I know! You can't fly for shit!" the general yelled back.

"It's not my flying!"

The general staggered up to the cockpit as Bulldozer tried to keep them steady. Kade made out two words over the engine and rotor noise: *losing* and *fuel.*

General Jack retreated back into the troop hold and grabbed a black shotgun with a painted image of a smiling blond woman in a flower dress on the barrel.

"Gonna need good ole Sally the Slugger for this run," he said. "We're fueling up at the Sunshine Castle."

FIFTEEN

"We're heading home," X said.

Magnolia tried to raise her head, and the sheet fell away from her neck. He pulled it back up to keep her warm.

A deep groan rumbled through the hull, sounding like a monster groaning. That wasn't impossible. During the attack back at the Sunshine Coast, a giant water bug had somehow gotten aboard, damaging the lowest deck of the ship the sailors referred to as the orlop deck. It remained there now, lurking in the shadows, no doubt feasting on the corpses of the two scouts they had sent to track the beast.

For now, they had the entire area sealed off, but they must deal with it at some point to address damage to that compartment. Until then, they had to travel at half speed.

So far, the *Frog* had already traveled two hundred nautical miles. Only another eight thousand or so to get to the Panama Canal, and then another seven hundred to get home.

We can make it, X tried to tell himself.

"X," Magnolia whispered, trying to reach out to him.

"Don't try to talk," he said. "You're okay. We're on our way to Panama."

Shivering, she turned from side to side, glancing around the dim room where ten other patients slept. X had looked at all their charts overnight. Most of these people had broken bones, but a couple had radiation poisoning like Magnolia's.

"Rodger..." Magnolia mumbled, no doubt still hallucinating from the fever.

"Go back to sleep, kid," X said. "I'll come check on you later."

He turned to look for General Forge, who had come for a final casualty count. Magnolia's eyes were closed. He stayed there watching for a bit longer, then went to Valeria's bedside. She was resting peacefully in the bed that Lieutenant Slayer had vacated. He and Sergeant Blackburn were back on duty somewhere on the ship.

Miles sniffed Valeria's bandaged hand as X checked her chart. She had a mild concussion, a sprained wrist, and three bruised ribs. After the beating she'd taken, she was lucky to be alive.

He put her chart back and was leaving when he heard his name.

"King Xavier." X turned to find Valeria awake.

He went to her bedside as she tried to sit up. "At ease, Corporal."

"Miles..." she whispered.

"He's fine," X said. "Right here, actually."

Valeria smiled as Miles licked her hand, his tail whipping back and forth.

"Thanks for what you did," X said. "You protected him."

"We amigos." She reached down to pat the dog.

X just watched them for a few moments. Never had the animal taken such a shine to anyone but X and Magnolia.

Miles even seemed to want to stay with Valeria when X stood up. That was okay with X.

He motioned for the dog to sit, then crossed the room to

check on the other injured. Most of the soldiers seemed to avoid his gaze, and one turned away.

Not the respect he was used to, but he understood. They blamed him for their current predicament.

X met with General Forge in the corridor. "What's the total count?" X asked.

Forge clenched his jaw. "Nine dead and twenty-one injured. Almost half our soldiers are out of commission, but we have another massive problem, sir."

X braced himself.

"Our food reserves are all but destroyed," he said. "A cyclops smashed through the food stash to get to the soldiers and contaminated everything. Some kind of fast-growing mold took hold, and now we have two days of rations left—and that's if we stretch it."

"You got any *good* news for me?" X ran his hand through his greasy hair.

"We're moving again. But we have to go faster if we want to get to Panama before we starve... or worse."

"Worse as in..." Despite his exhaustion, X understood. The general was worried some of the warriors might return to their old ways of cannibalism. And it wasn't just *human* flesh the soldiers would be tempted by. Miles would be looking quite tasty.

Heaving a breath, X did everything he could to keep it together.

"Let's go talk to Two Skulls and see what it'll take to get us moving faster," he said.

Sebastian and Nicolas accompanied him and Forge back to the CIC, avoiding the corridors that had been sealed off due to radiation and toxins. One lay just ahead, marked by plastic sheets and guarded by sentries with spears.

In the next intersection, crew members in hazard suits worked to seal off contaminated passages that were already cleared of carcasses. A sailor with a mop cleaned the blood trail, and another sprayed chemical mist to sanitize the passages.

"We have used up most of our chemical supply," Forge said. "The other contaminated areas must be kept sealed."

They were low on everything, it seemed. X was too exhausted to waste energy cursing.

When he entered the CIC, one look in the eyes of the officers around him said they were losing faith in him, like the injured soldiers in the sickbay.

Sergeant Blackburn and Lieutenant Slayer stood at the ready with three other soldiers, all armed and armored. But even the elite Barracudas had a certain aloofness about them. It seemed they, too, thought the Immortal had doomed them.

They could still make it back. He could still save his people.

X wasn't sure he believed it, but he had to try. He had to make sure the sacrifices that had gotten them this far would enable him to get home and bring Captain Rolo and his fellow miscreants to justice.

"Captain, sitrep," X said.

"Ship is crawling, sir, and until we can secure the orlop deck, I don't want to push her harder," Two Skulls replied. "We need to send a team down there to deal with the monster."

"Down there," X repeated.

"Yes, an experienced hunter-killer team," said the captain.

"We don't have any left," said General Forge in a heated voice.

"What about the Barracudas?" Two Skulls gestured to Slayer and Blackburn.

"They aren't in any shape to take on a beast that size right now." Forge strode forward, his posture tall, strong, and angry.

"We can fight," Slayer said.

The captain and Forge had a brief, heated exchange in Spanish.

X flashed back to finding the Barracuda soldiers in the submarine. He pictured them shrouded in webs and hanging from the bulkheads while the bristly limbs of a freak sea creature sucked their lifeblood.

"Stop," X said.

Two Skulls seemed to back down some, and Forge did as well. Both men, along with everyone else in the CIC, looked to the king.

Send a monster-hunter team down to die, X thought.

That was essentially what Two Skulls was asking. Anyone they sent to the orlop deck would be facing the beast in close quarters.

A voice boomed, "I go hunt bug."

It was the gruff, heavily accented voice of Gran Jefe. The Hell Diver and former Barracuda was standing in the CIC with a bandage over his face.

"King Xavier, I hunt bug," he repeated. The Cazador bowed slightly.

X weighed other options, but it seemed the best was standing right in front of him.

"Okay, go; I will meet you down there," X said. "General Forge, have a supply of the best close-combat weapons delivered—axes, cutlasses, blasters, stabbing spears—and see that the hatches are secure until Gran Jefe gets there."

Forge gave the order over the radio while X hurried out, not wanting to give the general a chance to protest his decision to head belowdecks. Sebastian and Nicolas followed X through the uncontaminated corridors, passing more sullen, gloomy soldiers.

"Sir?" Nicolas said.

X stopped.

"Is it true?"

"What?" X asked.

"Is our food supply really down to two days?"

X couldn't lie to these young men. The truth was out already anyway.

"Yes, it's true, but we'll make do," X said.

"If you say so, sir," replied Nicolas. His shifting eyes and the tone of his voice seemed at odds with his words.

Sebastian simply shook his head and followed X.

On the deck below them, three Cazador soldiers patrolled with Hell Divers Edgar, Tia, and Sofia, carrying crossbows.

X stopped to acknowledge them.

"King Xavier, how's Magnolia?" Edgar asked.

"She's hanging on," X said. "Don't worry, she's going to be okay, and we're going to make it home." He looked to Sofia. "You will see your son again."

"I better," Sofia replied.

The tone of her voice had X wondering if even some of his closest allies were rethinking his leadership.

"We're heading to secure the last deck," he said. "Once it's safe, you all get some rest."

The divers nodded, and X left with his guards.

They arrived at the orlop deck a few minutes later. A fire team of six soldiers was there with monster-hunting equipment. Short spears, stun grenades, a tranquilizer gun that could sedate an elephant, and electrical livestock prods like the ones the Cazadores had used on X years ago in Florida. Gran Jefe had arrived and was already equipped with his choice of weapons: two short spears, two cutlasses, and a sawed-off blaster.

At the heavy clomp of boots from X and his two guards, the soldiers looked up. Heads nodded, and a couple of them even bowed.

But those signs of respect weren't for X. They were directed at Gran Jefe as he opened the hatch leading to the orlop deck ladder.

Tales of the big man's valor at the Sunshine Coast had spread through the ranks. From taking on a pair of Tasmanian devils in the shipwreck on the beach, to battling the alpha cyclops on the *Frog*. X had seen that impressive fight with his own eyes.

He heard a hatch shut behind him.

"I'm sorry, King Xavier," said Nicolas. "But you have brought us to death."

The warm surge through his veins was one that X knew, from a betrayal many years ago. It was a mixture of fear and fury.

He turned to find the young guard gripping a cutlass up in his shaking hand.

Gran Jefe moved in front of X with his two spears.

"You a brave warrior, but some think you are..." Gran Jefe paused. "How do you say *maldito*...? *Cursed*, I think." The husky warrior shrugged his shoulder plates. "*No sé*. I no know if you are cursed or if you are *inmortal*."

"If you're going to kill me, you're going to have to work for it," X said, thumbing off the leather loop that secured his hatchet.

The six Cazador soldiers formed a wall behind X in the wide corridor, spears leveled at his back while Gran Jefe stood in front of him. A memory surfaced in his mind: when an ambush by Cazador soldiers loyal to el Pulpo had left Rhino dead.

He had given his life for X, just like so many others.

And now X was going to die like Rhino, struck down by the blades of betrayers.

Holding his hatchet, he mentally fell into battle mode.

From the other side of the hatch, deep within the lower deck, came a percussive clicking noise. The sound echoed over and over.

Gran Jefe walked around X, giving him a wide berth as he joined the other soldiers.

"Don't turn your back to me, you big ox!" X said. "Kill me yourself if you think you can."

"You failed us," Nicolas said. "We've lost so many of our brothers and sisters, and now we have no food."

"We will make do," X said. "We will survive."

He knew that his words meant nothing now. That these men had made their decision. In seconds, they would cut him down right here, leaving him to bleed out and fight for his last breaths.

"There is one way to prove that," Gran Jefe said. He turned with his spear, then tossed it in the air to X.

X dropped his cutlass and caught the spear.

"Prove you are the Immortal and not the Cursed One," Gran Jefe said. "You kill the bug, we follow you. You die, we follow me."

The other soldiers kept their spears up, blocking the only way out of the passage. Behind X, a loud, rhythmic clicking erupted from the depths of the orlop deck.

A message from Forge came over the comm, asking for an update.

X could have told the general the truth: that he was being forced to fight and could be going to his death. But that would only make things worse.

And anyway, X didn't plan on dying.

He rested the spear against the hull before picking up his cutlass and sheathing it. Then he unlocked the hatch. Turning on his helmet lights, X headed down the stairwell, spear in hand.

"Good luck, King Xavier," Gran Jefe said.

X closed the hatch, then jammed his tac knife into the locking mechanism to prevent any and all from coming to help him.

To regain the warriors' respect, he must do what he had done for a decade on the surface. He would go it alone.

* * * * *

Two guards came for Michael at dawn. Steve was already awake, sitting up in his bunk.

"Stay calm today, Chief," he said. "Don't let Charmer bait you."

But as the guards led Michael away, Steve seemed to have a hard time following his own advice. Grabbing the cell bars, he yelled, "You're making a mistake, dickheads!"

Michael followed the two guards to the airship's cargo hold, where again he was lowered to the same pot-fishing boat. An open purple tent had been erected on the afterdeck, hiding it from view.

When his boots touched down, Michael saw a dozen metal chairs set up in front of a large wooden armchair. This would be the courtroom.

His eyes went to the pots and then the rail where Eevi had been sunk in the ocean and drowned. It was hard to keep his composure when all he wanted to do was kill those responsible. Most of them were standing on this very deck.

Jamal walked over to Michael. Two more soldiers joined him, including the long-bearded man with the throwing knives.

They took him to the same storage area where they had held Eevi. Jamal lifted the grate and nodded toward a ladder.

"No," called a voice. "He waits up here."

Charmer stepped out of the two-story cabin and smiled down at Michael.

"We are civilized, after all. Right, Mr. Everhart?" Charmer asked.

Michael clenched his jaw.

"Have a seat. It's going to be a little while," Charmer said, pointing at two crates stacked on the deck.

Michael remained standing, facing the rail where they'd thrown Eevi overboard. His muscles tensed with rage.

Charmer wasn't keeping him up here out of any humane motive; he wanted Michael up here to look at the place Eevi had died, so that he might ponder his own fate.

Instead, Michael subtly scanned the boat for a way to escape. If this was where his trial was going to be held, then he needed to plan.

The lobster boat was a hundred feet long, and the aft weather deck was only a few feet above the water. Two Cazadores stood guard between him and the pots stacked in the stern.

The two-level enclosed cabin overlooked both stern and bow. Michael looked down at his bound hand and prosthetic arm. Even if he could break his bonds, what then? He would have to take out multiple guards and then swim to a rig without being caught. And there wasn't a rig in sight. He looked around the boat, searching the water.

"Nowhere to go," Charmer said. "Don't even think about trying."

Michael ignored him.

Engine noise drifted on the ocean breeze. Three boats approached off the starboard quarter. One had been the war boat of el Pulpo, then of King Xavier. Flanking it were two Jet Skis, each bearing two Cazadores. Behind these, a fishing boat carried those who would decide Michael's fate.

The war boat pumped dark smoke into the air, the engine growling and rumbling. Jamal opened a gate in the starboard side and extended a broad aluminum gangplank from the lobster boat to connect the two vessels. And out of the war boat's cockpit came someone Michael wasn't expecting to see.

Captain Rolo crossed the plank with two guards, a female servant, and a scribe in tow. Jamal, Charmer, and the other Cazadores bowed—something else Michael wasn't expecting to see.

"All hail King Rolo!" said Charmer.

Michael watched in shock as the newly coronated joke crossed the deck. Seeing Rolo wear the crown was a real gut punch.

This was meticulously planned, every tiniest move. They had plotted to remove the islands' rightful king, take out Michael, and help themselves.

Charmer stared at Michael as if to say, *Don't open your*

mouth. Only the threat he held over Layla and Bray kept Michael from springing forward and killing Rolo where he stood.

The coward king walked over. "A sad day, Michael," he said. "But justice will be served, one way or the other."

A hiss came from behind Michael—Jamal, telling him to kneel before the king. But Michael would never abase himself before this dung smear that called itself a man.

"It's okay, General," Rolo said.

Now Michael did look over at Jamal, curious to see what shiny new armor or fancy hat came with his promotion from sergeant all the way to general. Whatever he had been given, it was no doubt also part of Charmer's grand scheme.

"Considering you were instrumental in my still being alive, I suppose I shouldn't expect you to kneel," Rolo said. "This is also why, unlike Eevi, you are getting a trial."

He stepped around Michael and said to Charmer, "Is everything ready?"

"Yes, but . . ." Charmer looked out over the port rail, then leaned close to Rolo, though Michael could still hear most of it. "I'm not sure if having this out in the open is a good idea after what happened . . . Both men are still missing."

Michael also heard Rolo reply, "Keep searching, and keep all forces on high alert. The trial will be conducted here."

Jamal took away the gangplank, and the war boat motored away as the next boat approached. The first jury member walked across the platform.

It was Martino, a businessman Michael had met with not long ago. He had been grateful to Michael for granting his nephew mercy over a stolen battery.

The portly merchant dabbed his forehead with a silk handkerchief as he stepped onto the deck of the boat, which he probably owned.

He looked to Michael, sighed, and took a chair.

Next came the Cazador soldier called Salamander. He glared at Michael with undisguised hatred. The scribe, Ensio, seemed indifferent as he glanced at Michael.

Finally, the sky people came. First Donovan, from Kilimanjaro, and then Bailey, from the former *Hive*. Bailey seemed to look at Michael with pity, but Donovan seemed neutral for the moment. They all sat in front of Rolo.

"Thank you for coming today," Charmer said. "I am tasked with prosecuting the trial of Michael Everhart, former Hell Diver, councilman, and chief engineer of the Vanguard Islands."

"And father and husband," Michael said.

Charmer held up a hand. "You will have your time to speak."

Captain Rolo took a drink of wine and looked out over the water, like a man already bored.

"This trial will last two days and will start with the prosecution," Charmer said. "The second day will give Michael a chance to call witnesses and present his defense. Does everyone understand?"

Nods all around. "Then I will call our first witness."

Charmer motioned to Jamal, who walked across the platform connecting the two boats. A squirming boy was brought over in the grip of two Cazadores.

"Alton," Michael said.

"Chief!" the boy wailed. "Chief!"

Michael tried to move, but two hands on his shoulders yanked him back. The guards were even rougher with the boy. One of them grabbed the back of his neck, prompting a screech of pain.

"You pricks!" Michael yelled.

The outburst of anger drew the reproachful eyes of the very people who would decide his fate. This was exactly what Steve had warned him about.

Don't let Charmer bait you...

But Michael couldn't help it. He wanted to break out of his cuffs and go on a murdering spree, starting with the simpering one-eyed pretender in front of him. Charmer looked at Michael, his lips curled into his customary insolent grin. This was exactly what he wanted.

With a deep breath, Michael tried to calm his body and his mind.

The guards brought Alton in front of the jury and the king.

"Kneel before the king and state your name," Charmer said.

When Alton refused, one of the guards pushed him to the deck.

"*That's* not a king," Alton said.

Charmer scratched the back of his head, then leaned down to the boy. "King Rolo is your king, and soon you will come to understand that, but I wouldn't expect you to right now. Now, state your name."

Alton looked to Michael, who nodded.

"My name is Alton."

"And Alton, how do you know Michael Everhart?"

"He saved my life. He saved your life, too, and yours," Alton said, looking at Rolo, who took another sip of wine.

"Would you say you are friends with Michael Everhart?" Charmer asked.

Alton glanced over to Michael.

"Yes," Alton said. "He is a good person and my best friend."

"Answer the question and only that, got it?" Charmer said.

"Yes."

"Good. Tell the jury what you heard and saw the night Oliver and Nez were murdered."

Alton hesitated.

"Take your time," Charmer said.

"I heard a cracking noise, a cry of pain, and then when I looked out of my stall, I saw a man leaving."

"And what was this man wearing?"

"A militia suit."

"And was there anything specific that you noticed?"

"One of his arms was metal."

"As if it was *made* of metal?"

Again Alton hesitated, then nodded.

"Would you say it looked like the prosthetic arm that Michael Everhart has attached to his shoulder?" Charmer asked.

Alton checked Michael, lowered his gaze.

"Yes or no?" Charmer said.

"Yes," Alton replied. "But it wasn't him. It *couldn't* have been Michael; it was someone dressed up to look like him. It had to be!"

"That is all. Thank you, Alton."

"Wait. I don't get to question him?" Michael asked.

"You talk when—" Charmer spluttered.

"Go ahead," Rolo said.

Michael wasn't expecting that answer. "Alton, did you get a look at the killer's face?" he asked.

"No."

"Did you see what his hair looked like?"

"It was short, I think."

"He thinks," Charmer said. "But you're not sure?"

Alton looked up as if trying to remember but said nothing.

"Anything else from the defense?" Charmer asked.

"No," Michael said.

Charmer waved for Alton to step away. The guards grabbed him when he tried to run over to Michael.

"I'm sorry, Chief!" he yelled.

"It's okay," Michael said. "Everything's going to be okay."

The Cazador soldiers took Alton back to the other boat, then brought out their next witness. It was Lilyn, the woman who had lived in the stall opposite Alton's. She too confirmed she'd seen a man with a robotic arm leaving on the night of the murder. But when Michael asked her, she also admitted she had not seen the killer's face. She avoided Michael's gaze on her way back to the boat.

"Two witnesses place a man with a robotic arm at the scene of the crime," Charmer said. "But I'm sure you're asking yourself, what motive would Mr. Everhart have to kill Oliver and Nez?"

Charmer looked to Michael.

"Why would this man, a hero to us all, decide to do something so heinous? Something so horrible?" Charmer asked. "A husband and father himself..."

"I wouldn't, as you well know," said Michael. "I was framed."

"I won't ask you again to stay quiet until it's your turn."

Michael snorted.

"There is no denying that you and Oliver had a turbulent relationship and that you were even in an argument after his son and Alton got into a scrap," Charmer said. "Isn't that correct?"

"I intervened in that incident because Oliver became violent with Alton. But I had no reason to kill Oliver or his son. I've never hurt another human who didn't deserve it."

"Deserve it..." Charmer said. He walked back to face the jury. "As you now have seen, not only was Michael spotted the night of this evil crime, but he and Oliver had an altercation just days before."

Charmer wagged a finger and turned back to Michael.

"The altercation wasn't your only motive to kill Oliver," he said. "We learned about the hidden food supply long before General Jamal went to bring you to justice."

Michael narrowed his eyes. Everything thus far, he had been prepared for and anticipated, but not this.

"Oliver found out about your secret food cache, didn't he?" Charmer asked.

"No one knew about the food. I was instructed by King Xavier to make sure of that. For the safety of the islands."

"That may be, but you failed. Oliver told me he followed you to the prison rig and then to the silos on the island where you hid the food."

Charmer had to be lying, but there was no way to prove it. He continued to build a motive, and this was a solid one.

Dread gnawed at Michael as, for the next hour, Charmer laid out his case, explaining how Michael had lied countless times, about the food and other things, making him untrustworthy even to his own people.

"Soon, he will stand here and argue he is a hero who rescued us all from the machines," Charmer said. "He will say he was a Hell Diver long before he was the chief engineer and a council member, and that this should absolve him of his crimes."

Michael wanted to jump up and argue that he'd never committed a crime, but he kept seated and calm, patiently awaiting his turn.

"Today, I had the unfortunate job of proving that he isn't the hero we all thought," Charmer said. "Don't forget what he did to Oliver and especially to young Nez. This is the real man, sitting on the deck of this boat. A murderer and a liar."

Michael stared ahead as the jurors all looked in his direction.

A radio crackled. Jamal took it from his vest and stalked off, clearly agitated by the message.

"Tomorrow you will all hear Michael's defense," Charmer said. He looked to Michael. "You will be able to call one witness on your behalf. Do you have someone in mind?"

Michael thought on it. The only person who could testify he hadn't been at the rig when Oliver and Nez were killed was his wife. But they wouldn't possibly trust Layla. It might be a waste of his one witness, but it also might be the only way he would see her again.

Before he could respond to Charmer, Jamal came running over with two guards, prompting King Rolo to stand.

"What is it?" he asked.

Jamal and Charmer spoke quietly.

"What!" Rolo repeated. "Tell me now, Carl."

Charmer rubbed his forehead in distress. "There's been an unfortunate discovery just a few minutes ago," he said. "We believe the two missing Wave Runner troopers may have been killed. Flotsam from a shot-up Jet Ski was found, including a bloody seat cushion."

Hushed voices broke out among the jurors. Salamander said nothing, just glared at Michael.

"Because of this morbid find, I believe we should move the final day of the trial to a new location as soon as we can guarantee security," Charmer suggested.

"I agree," Rolo said.

Charmer nodded and looked back to Michael. "Have you made a decision on a witness to call?" he asked.

Michael took another moment to think. Then he stood and said, "I call my wife, Layla Everhart."

SIXTEEN

The old Sea King sat in the pounding rain on a rusted platform between two stone walls at the Sunshine Castle. Kade sat in the troop hold as Bulldozer worked outside, securing the fuel tank that had leaked most of their reserves during takeoff.

General Jack and Nobu guarded their mechanic and only pilot. Zen had climbed with his sniper rifle up into a turret overlooking the fortress—the same spot where X had stood a week ago. Or was it longer?

Kade had lost track of time. But he hadn't forgotten what had happened directly beneath them. The Barracudas had been attacked by the spiderlike humanoids that dwelled within those walls. Kade had already warned the knights, but they knew all about the monsters. These were the same creatures that had forced their troops to abandon the old base years ago. Fortunately, they still had fuel here—and it was treated with a hybrid stabilizer that Bulldozer claimed would work.

The cockpit radio crackled. Lucky grabbed it. "Copy that," he said.

Then he returned to the troop hold, where the other knights waited.

"They've finished sealing the tank and are adding petrol now," Lucky said. "We'll be out of here shortly."

Kade checked his HUD—his battery was at 30 percent. Plenty of time left to get back to the Coral Castle. That was a relief. In this storm, he'd be dead without his filtration system.

He watched out the starboard side as Bulldozer uncoiled a long black hose. Lucky watched the rest of the knights.

"So this was a bastion?" Kade asked.

At first, Lucky seemed reluctant to talk, but then he opened up.

"It was many years ago," he said, still looking outside. "My father was stationed here. He trained many warriors inside these walls. Held off the monsters for many battles. Long before the Forerunner sent him to Panama." He looked over to Kade briefly. "Where'd you learn to fight?"

"I was a teenager," Kade replied. "There were two types of fighters on an airship: militia, to keep the passengers in check, and Hell Divers. I started in the militia, but I didn't like beating starving people. So I decided to beat starving monsters instead."

Lucky chuckled.

"Hell Divers are trained on the ships but also on the surface," Kade explained. "It's the best training, because it's realistic. Problem is, most don't survive it. They threw me out of the airship at twenty thousand feet and gave me a beacon locator for a supply crate that landed in a crater with—"

A distant shriek made him pause.

Heart pounding, he moved closer to the window.

"Hear that?" Lucky asked.

"Yeah," Kade said. "One of those spider things."

Lucky unslung his rifle and went to the cargo door. Outside, Nobu and the general had their weapons trained on the eastern wall. Kade squinted but didn't see anything moving along the parapet.

Another shriek sounded over the howl of the storm. But this one came from a different direction. Kade went to the cockpit and scanned the walls. He squinted at movement on the exterior of a tower.

"Oh, son of a bloody..." he whispered.

Lucky saw it, too: a pair of hairy, human-size spiders scaled the exterior of the tower next to the one Zen was sniping from.

"Zen, watch out!" Lucky shouted.

A muzzle flashed from the lookout Zen perched inside. Once, then twice. Both monsters lost their grip and tumbled back to the ground.

Shrieking came from somewhere behind the chopper.

"Give me that rifle back," Kade said.

Lucky hesitated.

"Come on, you need my help," Kade argued.

"Fine. Grab one."

Kade pulled from the rack the same rifle he had used on the runway. By the time he grabbed two magazines, Lucky had the troop hold door open. Another spider was climbing the tower Zen remained inside.

Raising his rifle, Kade scoped the beast, which was bleeding from multiple bullet holes. This was one of the two they had already shot off the walls. It seemed determined to get Zen.

"Get out of there!" Kade yelled.

Nobu and Lucky took calculated shots. Bullets slammed into the scuttling arachnid limbs and the all-too-human head. Then, as it neared the top, Kade fired a bullet that hit it in the head, just behind two of its eight eyes. The beast reared and reached back with two of its limbs to paw at the wound.

As Kade was lining up another shot on the head, Zen hung

out the side and blasted the creature in the face. It plummeted to the bottom and smashed on the pavement.

"Get back here, Zen!" Lucky shouted.

"Bulldozer, how much longer!" the general yelled.

"Dunno!" yelled the mechanic, crouching with the hose nozzle by the fuel tank.

"We just need enough to get back to the Coral Castle! Lucky, Kade, stay here. Nobu, with me!"

They trotted off across the parapet as Zen climbed down from his turret.

Kade and Lucky retreated back to Bulldozer, who was still gassing up the bird.

"Get back to the cockpit, Dozer," Lucky said. "I'll finish."

The mechanic didn't need to be told twice. He went back to the cargo hold door and climbed in. Kade shouldered his rifle as Jack and Nobu reached Zen two hundred feet away. They started running back through the rain.

Kade heard a strange animal hissing. He checked the walls and parapets. Bending down, he looked through the platform grate, finally seeing motion in the courtyard right below.

"Guys!" Kade said. "You better take a look at this."

Lucky turned in time to see three of the spider-hybrid creatures darting through the weedy courtyard. The leader leaped onto the side of the wall. It clawed up the sides, preparing to cut off the general and his two knights running across the walkway above.

Kade fired a heads-up, drawing the general's attention a second too late. The first monster hopped down from the stone parapet behind Nobu, who held rear guard.

"Watch out!" Kade yelled.

"Enough fuel!" Bulldozer shouted over the comms. "Let's get out of here!"

Kade centered his sights where the eight bristly black legs joined at the strangely human torso, but knights were in the way. Two more of the nightmarish creatures jumped over the broken stone trim of the roof's barrier, flanking the men.

Nobu shot two legs off the first creature. It flopped on the stone pathway as the other two scampered around it.

General Jack leveled his shotgun and blasted off a face, pumped in another shell, and blew off a front leg. "Don't bloody mess with Sally!" he shouted. "She's beautiful, but she will blow off your knickers!"

The chopper lifted a few feet off the ground, and Kade heard Bulldozer screaming from inside. Nobu and Zen retreated while the general's shotgun blasted away at more of the hideous creatures coming over the wall.

Kade aimed at a beast perched on the wall that seemed to be scanning for new prey. He squeezed the trigger, erasing the bulging eyes. The creature flipped over the wall and landed in the courtyard.

Lucky waved Nobu and Zen into the troop hold, then joined Kade to cover the general.

"Let's go!" Lucky shouted.

Seeing no hostiles on the walls behind them, Kade swung up into the cargo hold. Then Lucky climbed up, and General Jack arrived a minute later. He went to grab a handhold, but just as he did, a longish white glob hit his extended arm. It pulled, yanking him backward and away from the chopper.

Bulldozer pulled up as more webs shot out from the walls, sticking to the hull along the left side. Four creatures stood on the wall to the east, their limbs extended with the thick, sticky string.

One of them had General Jack lassoed and was dragging him across the platform. Kade was already moving after him, grasping at the big man's kicking legs. The beast that had him was pulling him toward the edge of the metal landing pad. If the general went over the side, the fall might not kill him, but the monsters certainly would.

Gunshots cracked from the chopper, where Nobu and Zen fired from the open troop hold. Kade glimpsed the target on the wall. The beast that had the general darted across the stone, mostly avoiding the gunshots.

Kade finally caught up and grabbed the general by a boot. Lucky crouched down with a knife and sawed at the sticky, elastic rope that held the general. When the serrated knife got through the web, he yelled, "Get 'im up!"

Kade set his rifle down and hauled the general to his feet. He leaned on Kade on the short trek back under the chopper. Nobu swung his sword at more sticky rope that thwacked into the hull as Bulldozer lowered toward the three men.

Zen reached down and hauled the general up into the troop hold. Lucky went next, with Kade right behind him. Kade swung up just as a sticky white rope smacked him on the shoulder. A slash from Nobu's sword severed it before the monster could yank Kade back outside.

Lucky grabbed Kade and pulled him to the rain-slick deck. The door closed, sealing out the wind and rain but not the noise.

The storm battered the rusted helicopter as Bulldozer struggled to pull up. Another howl sounded, drawing Kade's attention to General Jack. The other knights crowded around him as he squirmed on the deck. Lucky was already removing a plate of armor from the general's arm while Zen fished through a medical pack.

The general howled in agony. "I'm cactus," he said. "I'm cactus!"

Kade had heard that word used before. It was another way of saying dead, or fucked. From what he could see, the general was in major pain but not mortally wounded. Maybe he had a broken arm or something unseen to Kade.

Nobu tried to hold him down, but Lucky had to pile on to keep the big man still. Smoke whisked away from the removed wrist gauntlet that clanked on the deck next to Kade. He moved for a better view, finally seeing the general's arm. The sticky webbing had melted not only through the armor but into a line deep across his flesh.

Kade looked down at his shoulder plate, where a web had hit him, but saw only slight charred remains. Not enough to burn through. Hopefully that was the case with the hull of the aircraft, which had taken multiple hits before they'd cut off the strands.

The chopper jolted hard, and General Jack gave a high-pitched yelp as his arm bone snapped along the line of weakness. It didn't take long for the webbing to burn through the rest of it.

Another roar filled the chopper as the general's arm split off above his wrist.

"Bloody shit!" Zen shouted.

The screaming distracted Bulldozer, who looked over his shoulder. "Someone do something!" he yelled. "You can't let him die!"

Kade hung back, watching as the knights worked to save their leader. They stuffed pads of gauze against the gushing stump. But it wasn't just the loss of blood killing the man. It was clear he had toxins in his system.

By the time Bulldozer called out the approach to the Coral Castle, the general was gasping for air.

"Take... take off my helmet," he mumbled.

Lucky eased the helmet away from the swollen face. Purple blood vessels bulged across his cheeks and forehead. He turned his bloodshot eyes to Kade.

The other knights looked over as the general grabbed his wrist.

"You … are a good man," he said. "I'm sorry … for—"

The Sea King set down with a hard jolt. Kade looked up to see they had landed on a large platform somewhere in the ocean. When he glanced back down, the general had stopped breathing.

Lucky checked his pulse, then shook his head.

"I'm sorry," Kade whispered.

Zen opened the troop hold door, letting in a wet blast. A fire team of six knights strode through the storm and led the survivors to an elevator that took them below the surface.

Kade was still reeling from the trauma of the attack and watching Jack die when the elevator came to a stop. Lucky grabbed him by the arm and helped him out. They were entering in a different location from when he'd first been brought to the Coral Castle. Still shaking, he was led through another area of the underground facility—a lab of some sort. The new soldiers took them into a large shower area, where they were hosed down.

After the chemical bath, Kade was taken into a smaller chamber that contained a single seven-foot-tall upright pod with a glass lid.

"Strip down and get in," said a guard.

The lid opened as Kade shucked off his armor and suit. He cautiously climbed inside, and straps automatically buckled over his wrists and ankles. Another stretched over his chest. The lid closed, and a cold, gelatinous fluid hissed out of jets in the tub, slowly filling the capsule and submerging his naked body.

Something curious was going on. Tiny black beads oozed through the thick fluid. Blinking, he tried to study them. A dozen of them found his flesh and clung on. He could feel their cool, metallic touch.

The black beads spread over his body, some migrating up to his head. He clamped his lips shut, but the beads just moved on until they found his nose.

The tiny legs tickled as they crawled up his nostrils. More went for his eyes, one even squeezing under the lid.

"No! Stop!" Kade whimpered. "What are you doing to me!"

His heart pounded with the memory of a similar event in his life. He was transported back to the machine camp, when he had found himself strapped down and moving toward a fiery oven.

But unlike then, Kade didn't want to die.

For the first time since his family had died, he wanted to live.

* * * * *

X had spent hours hunting the beast that lurked somewhere on the orlop deck. He had long since shut off his comms, ignoring the incessant requests from General Forge to report in. The creature had X's full attention.

He heard it skittering about on its hard insectile claws. Although he wasn't completely familiar with this deck, X vaguely remembered seeing a blueprint. Most of the six compartments were for storage.

He was in a long space filled with coiled electrical conduits that resembled metal snakes. Most of the lights down here didn't work, but there were enough that X didn't need his night-vision goggles. He moved quietly through the maze of flex tubing and skidded on something wet.

From experience, X knew better than to look down for more than a beat. But when he did, he found what he was looking for.

Just like the other two bodies he had found, this corpse lay flat on the deck, like a deflated balloon, draped over a coiled chain.

Spear in hand, X crept closer while listening to the not-so-distant skittering and rustling.

He approached the body—if it could be called that. It looked as if someone had made an inflatable life-size figure of a Cazador and then let all the air out. The helmet visor was cracked open, the shrunken face frozen in a mask of horror with an open mouth and wide eyes.

X kept going, still trying to process what he had seen.

A sharp, crackling sizzle came from behind him, the way he had come. *Son of a bitch,* he thought. Someone was trying to cut into the hatch and save him!

He kept moving, around more stacks of cables. With his prosthetic arm out in front and his spear in hand, he stalked between the piles of metal conduits until he heard a hiss.

Claws scrabbled somewhere in the dark space. X turned around, unable to tell which way it was coming from. He couldn't just stand out in the open and wait for the attack. He looked up at the closest stack of coils and started climbing.

At the top of the pile, he crouched and looked around the dimly lit room. And there it was.

The dome-shaped carapace came scuttling out of the shadows at the other end of the compartment on four jointed legs, brandishing a pair of foreclaws like hay hooks. The thing was three times his height, maybe even larger.

X raised his spear while studying the beast for a chink in its armor. The back had a black-and-yellow chevron pattern on the rigid shell. The triangular head was covered with the same chitinous shell.

He watched it move, exposing patches of orange flesh along the neck as the head rose and lowered. It scrambled toward his location, chittering and hissing.

"Come on, you ugly mother…" X whispered.

The bug scrambled down the rows of flex coil. The red compound eyes and the short antennae didn't seem to detect him perched above. For a moment, he watched it as those long antennae flicked back and forth. Perhaps it knew he was here, could sense him, but couldn't find him.

Finally, it turned and went back the way it had come, toward a hatch leading out of the compartment.

Surely, it couldn't get through, could it?

Armored wing covers suddenly lifted off the shell, revealing more bright-orange flesh below. It was trying to squeeze through, X realized.

The sizzling noise behind him grew louder.

After seeing the mammoth creature, part of him wanted to sit tight and wait for reinforcements. But he couldn't let it escape to another area of the ship. They had to kill the thing, secure the orlop deck, and get the engines running at full throttle.

X jumped off the cable and ran toward the hatch, spear in hand. This was his chance.

The monster began to squeeze through the opening.

"No, you don't!" X yelled.

The creature turned to have a look, exposing the soft flesh of the neck. X hurled the spear, and it hit with a satisfying thunk. Orange liquid bled out as the creature hissed and kicked with its jointed legs. Claws scrabbled against the metal deck.

X pulled his blaster, aimed at the neck wound, and fired, creating another explosion of juices. The beast squirmed, kicked, and tried to pull itself through with its front claws. X fired again, breaking the rib of a wing while most of the projectiles bounced off the hard carapace.

He flipped open the breech to reload. By the time he got the next two cartridges chambered, the creature had squirmed through the hatch into the next compartment.

X ran after it into a room stacked with interlocking crates too high to see over. The goliath bug moved fast for being injured. He pursued the orange blood trail to a dark part of the deck, where the lights were out.

He didn't need them to see the monster. It was in the corner, head down.

X approached cautiously, then flicked on his helmet lights. The spear he had thrown into its back was sheared off, its haft lying in the growing orange puddle.

Still aiming his blaster at the head, X stopped about ten feet away. With his chin he turned on his comms.

"General Forge, I've got one big dead *cucaracho* for you," he said. "We can secure the deck now. Send in your crew."

"King Xavier, where the hell are you?" Forge replied.

X looked around for a marking on the hull and caught motion in his periphery. He had just enough time to jump back to avoid a jointed hook that swiped out at him. Almost reflexively, he fired the blaster at the giant bug, right at a red compound eye the size of his fist. The monster chittered, rising up on four jointed legs and striding toward him, brandishing its scythe-like foreclaws. His back hit a stack of crates, blocking any further retreat.

An indistinct message from General Forge crackled in his ear.

As he ducked, the scythe-like pincers scissored right above his head. He fell on his butt and scrambled away with the blaster still in hand.

He got up and dashed for another stack of crates. They tumbled as the behemoth insect slammed into them. A crate hit him in the back, knocking him to the deck. He flopped from his back onto his stomach, then rolled away from a clawed foot that stomped the deck.

X brought up his blaster and fired the other shell, blowing out the other eye. The bug rose up, screeching in anger. Rolling up to his feet, X made a run for the open hatch. The deck trembled under the pursuing monster's footfalls.

He was almost to the hatch when he saw armored figures in the next compartment. A group of soldiers, led by General Forge and two Hell Divers, raced toward him.

X ran harder, but just as he was about to burst through, something hit him in the back of the helmet that knocked him off kilter. His visor smashed against the bulkhead with enough force he went down like a sack of potatoes. He lay on his side, too stunned to move. A warning flashed on his HUD, but he couldn't make it out.

After sucking in a breath, he managed to roll onto his back. The angle gave him a view of the monster bug waving its pincers together not six feet away. They scissored the air, antennae searching for him now that the thing was blind.

The creature chittered and reared back, slashing with its front legs. A spear shaft protruded from the neck, another now. Orange fluids gushed onto the deck, splashing all over X.

Suddenly, a heavily armored man moved in front of X with a spear in one hand and a cutlass in the other. The warrior parried the pincers with the sword and ducked a helmeted head crested with a red feather.

"Forge," X muttered.

The general held his ground in front of X, hunching under another swipe from a pincer. As the creature recoiled the limb, Forge thrust his spear into the soft area below the bug's tubular mouth. Orange fluid squirted out.

Chittering echoed through the entire space, followed by a low hissing as the creature collapsed with a tremor that shook the deck. X curled on his side to watch the beast draw its last breath.

Then strong hands heaved him up and carried him to the corridor. There, he was placed on a stretcher. He tried to pay attention to the soothing voices, but his pounding head made that impossible.

The last thing he saw was a group of men standing against a hull. He couldn't see their faces, but the hulking figure bringing up the rear was Gran Jefe.

"*Muy bien, King Javier,*" he said. "*Usted es inmortal.*"

SEVENTEEN

Loud barking pulled Magnolia from fevered dreams.

She batted her eyelids at the bright lights inside a cold gray room. Chemical smells hit her nose—the first clue to her location.

Sickbay...

Her blurred vision filled with people at the end of the room. Heavy footsteps as they came inside.

The barking continued as Miles darted away from her bedside to two soldiers carrying a stretcher.

She gasped when she saw a prosthetic arm hanging over the side. Another pair of soldiers rushed inside. The knot of armored bodies obstructed her view as they rolled King Xavier in.

"Someone get that dog back!" yelled Dr. Keller.

Miles barked louder as a soldier tried to hold him back.

Lifting the blanket off her chest, Magnolia tossed it aside. The rank smell of urine overpowered even the chemicals.

Another day, she might have been horrified that she'd pissed herself, but not today. Today she was horrified that the king had been wounded.

She glimpsed him through a gap in the cluster of armored bodies lifting him onto an operating table.

Summoning what little strength she could, Magnolia swung her feet over the side of the bed and scooted off. As soon as her feet hit the cold deck, her knees gave way and she collapsed.

Red encroached on her vision. The last thing she saw before her world went dark was the surgical bay door closing.

She didn't know when she woke up again, but she was back in her bed. Her eyes shot to the door where she had last seen them taking X. It was open now. She blinked to see inside.

Her pounding heart settled when she saw Miles curled up at the king's feet, watching the open hatch. Edgar and Sofia were also there, sitting in chairs just outside the private room.

Mags licked her dry lips and scratched her head. A strand of blue hair came away. The radiation poisoning had wreaked havoc on her entire body, but as soon as she sat up, she felt stronger.

She stood and took a step.

"Commander Katib," Dr. Keller called out.

"I'm okay," Magnolia said. She took another step and wobbled but didn't fall.

"Not really. You're weak and need to stay in bed. The meds I gave you will wear off soon."

"The king," she said. "What happened to X?"

"Mags," said a soft female voice.

Sofia came over and helped Magnolia walk.

"King Xavier," she said again. "What happened?"

Keller looked to Sofia.

"He went belowdecks to kill a beast," Sofia explained. "When he was found, he was unconscious from a nasty head wound."

Before Magnolia could ask for more details, Keller said, "He's a fighter, that's for sure, but he has some brain swelling, and we have to get that under control."

Even from here Magnolia could see the bandage around X's head. An oxygen mask covered his nose and mouth. She started in that direction, leaning on Sofia for support. Halfway across the space, she felt stronger and walked on her own.

Edgar stood in front of the king's room with Sergeant Blackburn and Lieutenant Slayer. "Commander, how are you feeling?" he asked. "You look better."

"Don't lie to me, Cervantes," Magnolia said.

He snorted. "Okay, you look like Siren shit on a hot day."

"I've been through worse," Magnolia said.

"Yes, and you will get through this," Sofia said.

"Does she know what happened?" Edgar asked.

Sofia shook her head.

Magnolia looked up at her best friend. "I thought you told me…"

Edgar motioned for her to join him in X's room. Miles was now standing on the bed at the king's feet. But he didn't greet Magnolia with the usual eager wag of his tail. The animal seemed to understand what bad shape his best friend was in.

As Magnolia looked down at the unconscious king, Edgar told her what had really happened to X.

"Gran Jefe and a group of Cazadores forced the king belowdecks to kill that giant bug," Edgar said. "On his own."

"Wait, what…" Magnolia said. She looked back to Slayer and Blackburn.

"They weren't there, and Forge has posted them here to guard X," Sofia said.

"Guard him from what?" Magnolia asked.

The radiation poisoning had clouded her mind, but she began to understand. There had been a coup—happily, an unsuccessful one so far.

"We saw him going down there with his guards, Nicolas and

Sebastian," Sofia explained. "But we had no idea they were planning anything until it was too late."

"Those fucking bastards," Magnolia whispered.

"Seems the Cazadores believe the king is cursed, and said they'd only follow him if he killed the monster on the orlop deck," Edgar said.

"There is more," Sofia said. "Food supplies are almost exhausted. We lost most of them during the attack."

Magnolia scratched her itchy head again. Everything had fallen apart. She staggered over to the king's bedside and put her hand on his arm. A bloodstained bandage was wrapped around his skull.

"What did the doc say?" Edgar asked.

"He said there's some swelling of his brain," Magnolia muttered, hardly able to say the words.

Sofia helped her sit on a chair. "Let's leave them alone," she said to Edgar.

They left Magnolia alone with Miles and X. The dog rested his head on his paws, watching Magnolia as she held X's hand in her frail fingers.

"You can't die," she whispered.

Miles let out a low whine.

"X, there's something I want to tell you," Magnolia said. "Something I wish I'd said a long time ago."

She looked at his scarred features, each mark with its own story to tell. Anger raged through her like wildfire. This man had given so much for his people. Always putting others first, going through hell to keep humanity afloat.

And people continued to betray him. Captain Rolo, the Cazador soldiers, even Gran Jefe...

She sniffled. "You've been like a father to me," Magnolia said. "When I was younger, you filled a role that I never knew about—looking after me, teaching me, training me, protecting me." A tear fell from her eye. "Now it's my time to protect you."

Which meant she couldn't just sit here.

Magnolia got up and went to Edgar and Sofia. "Don't leave until I get back."

"Where you going?" Sofia asked.

"To see if we still have friends."

Magnolia got her Hell Diver suit from the chest under her bed and took her time getting into it. She also got out her curved blades, which she had insisted on having here after the last attack. Feeling weak and loopy, she staggered out of the sickbay.

With various sections of the ship closed off, it took her a while to reach the CIC. Plastic sheets with radiation warning signs blocked entire corridors. Her headache pounded with each step on the slog up through the decks.

When she reached the CIC, she was on the verge of passing out. Two guards posted in front of the hatch looked in her direction, but neither offered to help.

They crossed their spears when she tried to pass.

"How's that?" she said.

"No enter."

"I'm here to talk to Captain Two Skulls and General Forge."

"No enter," the same man repeated.

She looked at the Cazador who had spoken. He was almost a foot taller than she. He stared at the hull as if she did not exist.

"Get out of my way, or you'll be explaining to your friends how you got your sorry ass kicked by a *girl*," Magnolia said.

The guards kept their spears crossed. She took a deep breath, reached over her shoulder, and drew one of her curved blades. That got their attention.

Magnolia felt her knees wobble. Sweat dripped down her brow, stinging her eyes.

"Stand down!" boomed a voice.

A wiry soldier came around the corner, repeating himself in Spanish.

Both guards lowered their spears, but not soon enough for Lieutenant Slayer. He grabbed them both by the chest armor and yanked them away from the hatch, tossing them to the deck.

The two guards, chastened, pushed back up to their knees and bowed their heads.

"*Lo siento, teniente,*" said the one who had denied her access.

"This is Commander Magnolia Katib," said Lieutenant Slayer. "You disrespect her at your peril. She is a warrior who has killed more monsters and men than either of you ever will."

The soldiers nodded ruefully.

"Sorry," one said.

"*Lo siento,*" said the other.

Slayer looked to Magnolia. "Glad Edgar told me to come check on you," he said.

The hatch to the CIC opened, and General Forge strode out into the corridor, taking in the scene.

"What's going on here?" he asked. "*¿Qué pasó?*"

Neither guard answered, and Forge looked to Magnolia.

"I came to see you, but . . ." She blinked from a fresh wave of dizziness.

Forge looked at the guards, then nodded at Slayer. "Go back to the king, and don't leave."

"Yes, sir," Slayer said.

Forge motioned for Magnolia. "Follow me, Commander," he said.

The general took her into a private conference room

they had been using as a war room. As soon as he shut the door, she went to her knees and emptied her stomach in the wastebasket.

After wiping her mouth, she got up and looked to the general. "You've lost control of your soldiers," she said.

Forge blinked his eye. "They know the truth now."

"And what truth is that?"

"We have fuel to get to Panama, but not the food." Forge gestured to a chair.

She sat and pulled her thinning hair back. "The human body can survive weeks without food, as long as it has water," she said. "We have that, right?"

"Yes, but if we don't find food in Panama, we'll be weak by the time we get back to the Vanguard Islands."

"How long to Panama?"

"Another week, six days if we're lucky," Forge said. "I have injured men who will likely not make it that long, I have men who have lost their will, and I have men who question not only the king but my own leadership."

"This isn't the first time someone questioned the king, and it's sure not the first time someone's tried to kill him." Magnolia took a deep breath. "But every single time, he has survived, and every single time, he has led us home."

"For now, the men who betrayed him are in the brig. I have taken their rations, but that presents another problem."

"We'll need them to fight if we make it to the Vanguard Islands," Magnolia said. She got out of her chair, fighting another wave of nausea. "I want to see Gran Jefe."

"Commander, I respect your strength, but you should be resting," Forge said. "Let me take care of things."

"And all due respect, General, but if you had been with King Xavier, this might not have happened."

He raised a brow, and for a fleeting moment, Magnolia feared she had overstepped.

"You're right. This should never have happened, but the king is stubborn," Forge said.

She chuckled. "Ya think?"

"Slayer and Blackburn will protect him."

"They're still recovering from their own injuries."

"Yes, but no one will harm them," Forge said. "I'm sure of that."

"Why?"

"Because they are respected, and because even the traitors know we need them." Forge gestured toward the door. "After you, Commander Katib."

They left the war room and headed down to the brig. Magnolia had to rest three times on the way. A guard stood outside the hatch to the brig when she arrived. He came to attention with a sluggish salute.

"Take us to Jorge Mata," Forge said.

The guard led them through the dark compartment, past several hatches, to the one at the very end of the space. Light from the dim corridor spilled into the small space, where Gran Jefe sat on a bunk.

He stood while the guard unlocked the gate.

"Please leave us," she said.

Forge hesitated, then moved away with the guard as she stepped into the small cell.

"I trusted you," she said.

Gran Jefe scratched at his chin.

"You think I wouldn't find out? You thought you'd get away with what you did?"

The Cazador man walked up to her, inches from her face. She could smell the tuna jerky he'd eaten last.

"Your king bring us to *un mundo de la muerte*," he growled. "A world of death. He have to prove himself."

Magnolia swallowed. "He's fighting for his life," she said. "He might not make it."

Gran Jefe shrugged his shoulder. "He immortal, be okay."

"He'd better be."

She took a step back, and Gran Jefe heaved a whistling sigh through his pierced nostrils. "You let me out of here now?"

"Ha!"

"General no keep us here *siempre*."

"Oh yeah? Why is that?"

"You need us to win war."

"We don't need shit from you," Magnolia said. "As far as I'm concerned, you can rot in here. No, wait—I got a better idea."

Gran Jefe lifted a brow in anticipation.

"Your men can eat your fat ass!" Magnolia said. "There. Problem solved—now we have enough food to get home!"

She backed out of the room as he chuckled in the shadows.

"You sick. Many sick. You come back on your knees for my help when the time is here," he said. "Army need me. Without me, you don't win war."

Magnolia scoffed. "I never get on my knees."

"*Puede sí, puede no, Comandante.* We shall see…"

* * * * *

Layla sat on her bed with Bray and opened his favorite book, based on the nursery rhyme "Twinkle, Twinkle, Little Star."

Her son touched the faded cover featuring a green field under a dark sky with a glowing yellow star. A man stood with a boy in the field, holding his hand, both of them looking up at the star, their scratched and worn images barely visible. Bray touched them with his fingers, just as so many children, including Layla, had done before him.

When she was a child, her mother would read this book to her before bed every night. She had lost track of it during her youth, then found it again one day in the library on the *Hive*. Now the tradition continued.

Bray reached for the page featuring a dark sky and a bright-yellow star. "Star," he said.

He patted the page, giggling. Layla usually laughed also when he played like this, but she found herself staring at the drawing of the night sky. She imagined herself and Michael diving into the black void.

"Then the traveler in the dark," she sang, "thanks you for your tiny spark. He could not see which way to go if you did not twinkle so."

She turned to a page featuring a scene with a beach and palm trees under the dark sky.

"Ocean," Layla said. "Ocean."

She always tried to teach him words, and now, going on a year and a half of age, he knew quite a few. But recently, he seemed to have a favorite.

"Da-da," he said.

"We're going to see Da-da soon," Layla said. "He's on a mission."

Bray cocked his head to one side, put his pinkie in his mouth, and chewed on it thoughtfully.

"That's right, a mission," Layla said. "He's part of the reason we no longer live in the darkness—why we live here now, in the sun."

"Sun," Bray said.

"Yes."

She turned to the last page, with a bright-orange glow

crossing the dark horizon. The sunrise spread its soft glow over a forest of evergreen trees at the base of jagged mountain peaks.

"Until tomorrow," she said. "Time for night night."

She put the book down and picked Bray up, holding him against her chest. She rocked him until he settled, limp in her arms.

Gently she laid him in his crib and closed the door.

When Layla turned from the door, she found Victor standing in the small living room. She brought a hand up to her chest.

"Sorry," Victor said quietly. He waved her into the kitchen. "Message from Pedro, here."

It took her a second to spot the pigeon sitting on the open windowsill. The people from Rio had once used birds to carry messages back in their massive bunker, and also to warn them of danger.

Victor went over and unwrapped the wisp of paper from around its leg. He handed it to Layla.

"What does it say?" Victor asked when she paused.

She read it out loud. "No sign of Raptor. One transmission about moving the bird again."

"'Raptor' is Michael?" Victor asked, bringing the bird inside.

"Yes."

The news wasn't good. They still didn't know where her husband was being held, and the soldiers holding him were moving him from location to location.

"What are we going to do?" she said to Victor. "If we can't find him, we can't…"

"We will find him," Victor said.

She sank down on the couch and buried her face in her hands, trying to keep it together. Not only did she not know where Michael was, but she still had no idea where Charmer and his people had taken Rhino Jr.

"You need sleep," Victor said.

Layla lifted her head up and nodded. He was right: the best thing right now was to get some rest.

"I'll keep watch," Victor said.

"Thank you, Victor, for everything."

He held her gaze a second—long enough for her to see the pain in his eyes.

She knew he was hurting. He had lost his best friend, Ton, and the king. Everyone he loved was dead, except for Michael.

"You are a loyal friend," Layla told him. "I'm lucky to have you with me."

"I'm the lucky one," he replied. "What I do, your people have done for mine a hundred times over."

"Try and get some rest too, okay?"

"Okay."

Layla went to her bedroom and took off her boots. She took out the sheath knife she had used to kill the Cazador, and put it under her pillow.

Banging brought her back. She shot up in bed, groggy, scanning the darkness of her room. In the doorway stood the lean, muscular frame of Victor.

"Soldiers," he said. "Three, in hall."

Layla had hoped this was a bad dream, but the banging was real. She fingered the knife under her pillow, wondering if somehow the Cazadores had found out that she'd used it to kill one of their own. Or maybe someone had seen the pigeon fly up here.

Squalling came from Bray's crib. She rushed into his room and picked him up, trying to soothe him.

"Open!" shouted the same soldier who had taken her to the Sky Arena.

She looked back to Victor.

There was no time to escape, and even if they could somehow slip out the window, where would they go?

She backed away from the door, and Victor opened it.

The three men barged inside. The man who had taken her to the Sky Arena wasn't grinning this time.

"You come," he growled.

"What's this about? Where are you taking me now?" Layla asked.

The man handed her what looked like a black hood and gestured to put it on.

Victor stepped beside Layla.

"Back, *cabrón*," said the soldier. He held the hood out to Layla.

Bray reached out for the hood and giggled. But Layla knew this was no game.

The last time they took her, she had agreed to save Victor, and also because they let her take Bray with her. This time, it was clear he wasn't coming. It was also clear they didn't want her to see where she was being taken.

A cold lump formed in her gut, telling her if she left her child, she would never see him again. She eyed the other two soldiers, both holding the hilts of their cutlasses.

If she told Victor to fight, he would do it. He was ready to lay down his life for them.

It was possible, if she and Victor struck first, they could kill these three Cazadores. But not without injury to themselves, and not without putting Bray at risk.

A year and a half ago, she would have given Victor the nod, but everything had changed when she became a mother. Now Bray was her main priority.

Layla handed the child to Victor. Bray reached back to her with his tiny fingers.

"It will be okay," she said. "Victor will look out for you. I won't be gone long, right?"

She looked to the soldier, who didn't reply to her question.

"He should be good until morning for food," Layla said. "If I'm not back by then, give him some bananas and orange slices."

Layla kissed Bray on the face, then whispered to Victor, "If something happens to me, you have to take care of Bray."

Victor nodded as she took the hood from the soldier and slipped it over her head. The other two soldiers grabbed her by the arms and guided her out the door to the sound of Bray's wailing. This time, he wasn't crying out for his father; he was screaming, "Ma-ma!"

EIGHTEEN

"King Xavier, can you hear me?"

X opened one eye to a bright glow and slammed it shut.

"King Xavier," repeated the same voice.

Groggy, X slowly opened his eye again and was dazzled once more by an intense light.

"King—"

"Get that damned thing out of my eye," X grumbled.

He heard laughter, then a familiar female voice that said, "No brain damage after all. That's definitely the king."

Brain damage... X tried to look toward the voices but saw only blurred shapes. The other eye wouldn't open at all. He reached up with his hand to his swollen-shut eyelid, wincing at the touch. Then something warm and wet hit his other arm that had to be the tongue of Miles. The dog jumped up on the bed, landing a paw in X's gut.

"Oof," X cried.

The dog licked his face while X took in several ragged breaths.

"How do you feel?" came a faint voice to his other side.

X turned to Magnolia.

In a moment of clarity, he managed to focus on her face. Dark skin sagged under red eyes. Even her swatch of blue hair seemed washed out and thin.

And for some reason, as sick as she looked, she was wearing a black Hell Diver suit, a duty belt, and her twin curved blades over her back.

"Mags, you—"

"I'm fine," she said. "And you're going to be fine too."

"Yeah, but I need to do some tests to make sure the swelling is gone, and you all need to give us some space," said Dr. Keller. He leaned over to X. "King Xavier, you've been heavily sedated for the past two days. Do you remember what happened?"

X shook his head. "Where are we?" he asked.

"On the *Frog*," Magnolia said.

"I know, but how far from Panama?"

"At least another five days."

Keller glared at her.

X cleared his throat. "Doc, I understand you need to do tests, but I need an update on what's going on. Last thing I remember, we were leaving the Sunshine Coast and . . ." A memory of the attack emerged. The cyclops monsters boarding the ship, the radiation contamination, the trip belowdecks to fight the bizarre giant water bug.

In his mind, faded images of somber-looking Cazadores surrounded him.

"Where is Gran Jefe?" X asked.

"Hopefully in a dark room, but I'm not sure of all the details yet," Magnolia said.

"I need to see General Forge. Where is he?"

"You need to rest, King Xavier," said Dr. Keller. "You almost died."

"He's right. I'll go find General Forge," Magnolia said.

She paused on her way out to whisper something to Edgar, Sofia, and Tia while Miles nudged up to X to be petted.

"King Xavier, I'm going to check your head, okay?" Dr. Keller asked.

X leaned forward, and the doc peeled back the bandage around his head.

"Can you see out of your right eye at all?" Keller asked.

"Just stars floating in the darkness."

"Do you feel any pressure in your head right here?" The doctor gently touched the right side of X's skull, prompting a yelp of pain.

"That stings, and I got a splitting headache," X said.

Keller shined a light on the injury. More memories entered X's mind. He was on a lower deck of the *Frog*, searching for the monster bug. He recalled finding the bodies of the Cazadores who had gone before him, looking like some sort of deflated rubber dolls.

An image of the monster came to his mind. The red eyes and the wicked front hooks, and that chittering...

The door to his room opened, and General Forge stepped in.

"King Xavier." He took off his helmet, exposing his scarred face. "I'm glad to see you awake."

"Leave us," X ordered.

He waited for the room to clear.

"Did I prove myself, or do the soldiers still want my head on a pike?" he asked.

"It doesn't matter. Those responsible will pay for their treason."

"What?"

"Nicolas and the others, including Gran Jefe, are locked in the brig," Forge said. "Their rations have been distributed to the rest of the crew, but I'm afraid we're almost out."

X cursed, not just because they were low on food but because punishing Gran Jefe and the other Cazadores would accomplish nothing good.

"Shall we execute them?" Forge said.

"No," X said.

"¿Qué? What if they try again?"

X sat up and slowly dragged his legs over the side of the bed. He was weak, but he had been in worse shape before.

"King Xavier, those men could have killed you. I can't have traitors in my ranks," Forge said. "We can't let the rot fester."

"You're loyal, and I'm grateful for that, General, but if I were a Cazador, I would have lost faith in my leadership, too."

"What happened is not your fault."

"Bring the prisoners to the mess hall, and gather everyone else. I have something to say."

Forge put his helmet back on and left, replaced by Magnolia.

"What's going on?" she asked.

"Tell Keller I need to see him again."

She returned with the doctor a few minutes later.

"Doc, I need you to give me something to help me function for an hour," X said. "Preferably, something that will allow me to walk."

"Just a new body, then?" asked Keller.

X chuckled. "That would be nice, but some sort of stim should suffice."

"Why? What do you have planned?" Magnolia asked.

The PA system crackled with a message in Spanish, then English: "All hands to the mess hall in one hour."

"This isn't a good idea," Magnolia said. "People are hungry, tired, and sick."

"Which is exactly why I need to speak to them," X said.

Magnolia took a seat at his side. "X, when I saw you lying here the other day, I told you something I've never said. Do you remember?"

He shook his head.

"I said you're like the father I never had."

Unsure how to respond, X reached out and patted her on the shoulder.

"I'm telling you this because I don't want to lose you," she said. "I know you'll never do it, but I think it's time for you to sit back and let General Forge run military operations."

"Soon, but I got unfinished business first."

A little while later, Dr. Keller returned with a cup of water and a pill. "You're going to feel like a new man after taking this, but after it wears off, you'll crash hard."

"Got it, Doc. I promise to be back in bed by then."

X took the pill and washed it down. Miles snuggled up next to him as Keller left again.

"Don't get too comfy, pal," X said.

He got up. But even with the stim, he was weak and unbalanced, nearly falling as he picked up his suit. Magnolia went to help, but he waved her off.

She turned around as he took off his pants. He struggled a little but eventually managed to slip his legs into the suit. When he was finished, he bent to get his armor from the case.

"Let me," Magnolia said.

Picking up his chest rig, she staggered too.

"Look at us—the picture of physical vigor," X said, lifting his arms.

Magnolia chuckled. She put the chest rig over his head and fastened the pieces together.

X stood as straight as he could, but his aching back made that difficult.

Magnolia handed him his helmet, then reached up and brushed a hair from his brow. Then she stepped back and nodded.

"How do I look?" he asked.

"Like you're ready to persuade us to jump into hell again," she said.

He grunted. "I wish I didn't have to…"

Miles jumped down to the deck and followed them out of the room.

Edgar, Sofia, and Tia all came to attention, shocked to see X in his armor. Slayer and Blackburn both bowed. X nodded back, then followed everyone out of sickbay.

The mess hall was packed with crew and soldiers.

Gran Jefe, Nicolas, Sebastian, and the other Cazadores who had forced X onto the lower deck to fight the goliath bug were standing together with their wrists cuffed. Stripped of their armor and weapons, they looked frail and somehow smaller. Even Gran Jefe seemed less menacing—almost pathetic, really, with his gut hanging over his belt.

None of them saluted X as he crossed the room, but the rest of the soldiers and crew gave a sharp salute. Nonetheless, he could smell the distrust.

Miles walked up with him, also on guard. General Forge, Lieutenant Slayer, Sergeant Blackburn, and the Hell Divers stood with them. The gaze of a hundred people hit X.

There were sharks all around him, and he was bleeding in the water. He looked like a walking ghost. But he had the stim and would utilize it while he could.

"I asked you all here to tell you the truth," X boomed in his loudest voice. "I've made many mistakes during my life—as a husband, friend, soldier, and especially as a king. While diving and searching for supplies and food, I have seen countless people die, both on the airships and on the ground. I don't know why I'm still here when better men and women are not, but I can tell you right now, I'm as mortal as anyone here."

He looked down at Miles. The dog looked up with eyes

clouded by cataracts, as if to remind X that his best friend was not eternal either.

"I will die someday, maybe someday soon," X said, lifting his gaze back to the soldiers and crew. "But before I die, I will take the islands back from Captain Rolo, Charmer, and the miscreants who aided them. I swear this to you."

This brought several grunts and nods.

"Then my time as king will end," X said. "I will pass the torch to someone more capable, whom you all support. You have my word."

General Forge turned to look at X.

"Gran Jefe, step forward," X said.

The big man took one step.

"You asked me to prove to you that I am not cursed," X said. "Now I ask you to prove yourself."

X looked to the other prisoners. "I ask you all to prove yourselves by preparing for Panama and for what awaits us back at the Vanguard Islands. To follow me one last time into battle."

The men all stared at X. He looked at them in turn again, then motioned for General Forge.

"Free them," X ordered.

Forge seemed to hesitate, then followed the order.

"We have one last chance to save our home," X said. "I won't screw up again. This time, I will lead us to victory, or I will die trying."

All across the room, heads nodded.

X felt the stim pill wearing off. His head pounded, and his legs felt weak. "Get some sleep," he said. "When we get to Panama, we'll deploy teams to search for survivors and supplies."

The room began to clear, and X called Gran Jefe.

The Cazador lumbered over, rubbing his wrists.

"Don't speak," X said.

Gran Jefe shrugged a shoulder.

"I don't blame you for what you did to me," X said. "You have every right to challenge me. But I need your support when we get home. Not because I am afraid of dying by your sword or of death at all. I'm ready to die, but if you turn on me again, I will send you straight to hell."

The big Cazador snorted. "You think I want *la corona?*" He wagged his finger. "I no want crown."

"Then what do you want?"

"*Justicia.*"

* * * * *

Two days after entering the capsule with the little black beads, Kade was starting to go stir crazy. He remained suspended in the slimy material, watching as the tiny bots skittered over his skin.

It had taken him a few hours to understand what they were doing, but now he was convinced they were cleaning him of toxins and perhaps even removing radioactive material his body had absorbed.

He had read about this technology many years ago but had never seen it in action. His nose tickled from the bots still in his nostrils. More were inside his ears, mouth, and other places he didn't care to think about.

Besides the itching, it wasn't all that bad. His captors had opened the lid once to give him something to eat and added what he heard was an anesthesia to help reduce his discomfort. He felt no pain at all and was glad to know he was being cleansed, even if it was taking forever.

As he lay bound by the straps inside the capsule, his mind drifted from past to present. Thoughts about his family and his time in the machines' camp.

Kade snapped out of it when he felt new currents and eddies in the soup around him. Something had changed…

The gel level in the pod began to drop, the tiny bots vanishing right along with the gel. Minutes later, his naked flesh glistened.

Finally, days after he'd been sealed inside the capsule, the lid opened. He blinked, his eyes adjusting in the bright glow of an overhead light.

Standing in front of him was a bald man in a black lab coat with a trident symbol on the collar. He held a tablet. Next to him was Lucky, whom Kade almost didn't recognize without armor. The knight wore a blue uniform over his muscular body. He had shaved all but his mustache, exposing a square jaw and the half-moon scar on his right cheek. On his duty belt was a holstered pistol with two extra magazines, and the hilt of his long sword rose over his right shoulder.

"How do you feel?" asked the man in the lab coat.

"Good as new," Kade said. "Mind taking these straps off so I can get some clothes on?"

The scientist looked up from his tablet to scrutinize Kade. Then he checked a monitor built onto the capsule.

"He's clean," remarked the man.

Lucky nodded back. "Let him out."

The straps retracted, freeing Kade. He stepped out, nearly falling. After getting his balance, he slowly walked over and leaned on a table for support.

"Take a few minutes, then put this on and follow me," Lucky said. He handed Kade a suit.

The tingling sensation in his limbs burned for the first few minutes, bad enough he clenched his jaw. When they finally passed, he took the suit and began to dress.

Lucky led him out of the room into a long corridor wide enough for vehicles. More scientists in black lab coats walked past, some of them eyeing Kade skeptically.

"Where are we going?" Kade asked.

Lucky didn't respond. That was unusual since their bonding journey, but perhaps something had changed since they got back.

Of course it has, Kade thought.

These people had lost a knight, a pilot, and General Jack. It was no surprise Lucky had closed off.

They walked into another corridor with glass walls. As they drew closer, Kade saw movement on the other side.

Fish swam by, some of them darting away from the viewports when Kade stepped up to look. He watched the fish retreat to the colonies of corals. Orange, red, and pink polyps grew in shelf upon shelf inside the tank.

"We call it the Fish Bowl," Lucky said. "It's where we get most of our protein, including new seaweed harvests."

Kade recalled the tanks of seaweed he had seen when he first arrived here.

"It's an important part of our ecosystem," Lucky said.

They walked past several scientists who were working at monitors built into the walls. A woman with a tablet seemed to be monitoring some of the sea creatures outside the viewport on the left.

It was fascinating to Kade, but they didn't stick around.

Lucky didn't stop until they got to a section of labs with more glass windows. Soldiers with automatic rifles stood outside the double doors. A sign read *Advanced Research and Testing*. On the other side, two scientists worked at lab stations. Both wore bulky hazard suits. Those suits told Kade that whatever they were working on was far more dangerous than some radioactive material.

He followed Lucky down a connecting passage that ended at a steel hatch with a keypad.

Lucky stepped up to it but hesitated.

"I'm taking you to the Forerunner," he said. "Answer what you are asked, and don't speak out of turn."

The knight paused to look Kade in the eye. "Do you understand?"

"Yes," Kade said.

"Good, because your fate is no longer in my hands. If the Forerunner decides to kill you, there's nothing I can do."

Kade swallowed hard as Lucky tapped in the key code. The hatch buzzed and swung open to a concrete stairwell with dim lighting. The cavernous passage felt as if it dropped ten degrees in temperature while they descended four flights of stairs.

At the bottom landing, Kade caught a whiff of what smelled like burning hair.

Lucky went to the next keypad and typed in another code. He opened the thick hatch, and they entered the recessed chamber with the circular platform over the top that Kade remembered from his first visit to meet the Forerunner. Nobu and Zen were there, dressed in the same uniforms as Lucky. They stood at trident-shaped podiums overlooking the chamber. The other four were empty—no doubt previously assigned to Mal and the other knights killed recently.

Lucky stepped up to his podium and drew his sword. "I am here to serve the Trident," he boomed.

"To serve the Trident," repeated Nobu and Zen.

A half-synthesized voice answered them. "Have you brought the Hell Diver?"

"Yes," Lucky replied. He motioned for Kade to step up to the extended platform.

Kade moved out and looked down at the weathered face of the cyborg searching the darkness for him.

But it wasn't just the Forerunner down there.

A body lay on a gurney, with tubes hooked up to multiple

ports in the pale flesh. Kade almost didn't recognize the man until he saw the severed arm.

Stepping up closer to the edge, he saw that it was indeed General Jack Campbell.

The tubes snaking away from his chest were connected to a machine with a monitor. A heartbeat showed in a zigzagging green line on the screen.

"I saw him die," Kade whispered.

"He did, and the Forerunner brought him back."

"How?" Kade looked on in awe. "How is that possible?"

"Because we are creators, not deestroooyers!" yelled the Forerunner in a voice that seemed more synthesized than human.

Risers lifted the elderly leader and his wheelchair, along with the medical equipment supporting his frail body.

The liver-spotted bald head and wrinkled brow came into focus under the bright glow of dangling lights. The platform rose directly in front of Kade. He went down on one knee in a show of respect.

"I am told you're not an enemy," said the old man, this time sounding more human. "I am told you performed many heroic actions to save some of our knights, even risking your own life on more than one occasion."

Kade kept his head down, avoiding eye contact.

"I wonder how many of my warriors would have died out there if it weren't for you," said the Forerunner. "However, a better question is whether your heroism makes up for the horror your people brought to our lands."

"I'm truly sorry for what's happened," Kade said.

"Look at me."

Kade raised his face to meet the gaze of this mysterious, ancient being. The Forerunner pushed a control on his chair, rotating it toward the mounted monitors. Most of them flickered to life. On the screens, views of the Sunshine Coast lit up the room.

Kade looked at the different monitors, seeing some that appeared to be underwater. There were also screens with live views of the labs he had passed earlier.

"The damage from the radioactive fallout is worse than I feared," said the Forerunner. "It has poisoned our water and is already showing up in the tanks of seaweed and coral that sustain our food sources. We are using all our technology to prevent lasting damage, but it might be too late."

The Forerunner came closer to Kade, his wrinkled face just inches away. Kade braced for punishment from this man of unknown powers.

"Your king escaped the fallout and the monsters, which is impressive," the Forerunner said.

A flood of relief washed through Kade. He tried to keep his emotions from showing.

"Where will your king go now?"

Kade was afraid to tell him what he believed, in case of retaliation. But from what he had seen, these people had no way of mounting an offensive. Chances were good they didn't even have the means to hunt down the *Frog* with more than a dozen knights. Still, he couldn't risk telling them where the Vanguard Islands were located. It was simply too dangerous.

After a brief pause, Kade decided to give a half truth. "Panama, to our outpost, a place called Gateway," he said. "He will probably try to refuel and stock up there before hunting down Captain Rolo, the man responsible for what has happened to your lands and resources."

"He won't return to your home? These Metal Islands?"

Kade was surprised to hear the Forerunner invoke the former name of the Vanguard Islands.

"Speak quickly, Hell Diver," Lucky said.

"I do not know," Kade said.

"I suppose you don't know the location of the Metal Islands, either, do you?" the Forerunner asked. The cyborg came closer, his rancid breath hitting Kade.

"I do not know the location. It has been guarded closely, like the location of your home here," Kade said.

The Forerunner seemed to study Kade for a long moment. Normally, Kade didn't fear men, but the creature in front of him wasn't entirely human. He was part machine—something that Kade did fear.

Kade saw the Forerunner shift his eyes—one cybernetic and the other human—away and over to Lucky.

"Do you believe these words are true, Lieutenant Gaz?" the Forerunner asked.

Kade couldn't help but look over. Had Lucky been promoted?

"Yes, I believe the Hell Diver speaks the truth," Lucky replied.

"Then you have new orders," said the Forerunner. "Prepare a Sea King chopper for a long journey to this Outpost Gateway. Find this king's forces, and activate the Trident."

In his peripheral vision, Kade saw Lucky stiffen.

"Do you understand?" the Forerunner asked.

"Yes," Lucky replied. "Find the king and activate the Trident."

NINETEEN

A week had passed since the *Frog* escaped the Sunshine Coast. The ship was now mere miles from the Panama Canal and Outpost Gateway.

Magnolia stood in the crow's nest with X. They were both on the mend, but the radiation poisoning still lingered for Magnolia. She was hungry, exhausted, and sick with worry about what they would find here.

X had suffered a concussion from his fight with the water bug, and like everyone else on the ship, he was frail from lack of food.

General Forge climbed up with them. "We have not picked up any radio transmissions from the outpost," he reported.

"Understood," said X. "Keep radio silence."

"Are you sure?" Magnolia asked. "What if the crew had to abandon the outpost?"

"Yes, I'm sure." X cleared his throat. "We don't know if Captain Rolo sent forces here, and we can't risk alerting him to our presence if he or some of his people are here."

"I agree," said General Forge.

X looked at the sky. "We still don't know what we picked up on radar."

"Whatever it was, it's been gone for days," Forge said.

"I know, but I don't want any surprises. My gut says Rolo returned to the islands, but we can't let our guard down."

Magnolia held up her binos, searching the horizon for the shore.

Her heart pounded at the first sight of land, which came with a lightning strike. She had waited over a week to get back here and learn the fate of Rodger and the outpost.

Please be there, Rodge. Please...

She held on to a sliver of hope that he was still out here, but hope had betrayed her before.

"We're here," she said.

King Xavier took the binoculars and held them for a long scan.

"Okay, anchor us out here and prepare the assault teams for recon," he said.

"Aye, aye, sir," replied General Forge. He took the ladder down, leaving X alone with Magnolia.

She took the binos back.

"Mags, no matter what we find here today, don't forget, the fate of our people rests in our hands," X said.

"I know that."

She turned away, but he grabbed her by the shoulder. "Hold up," he said. "You said some stuff when I got hurt a few days ago. Now I'm going to say a few things to you, and you're going to listen."

She sighed. "Okay."

"We've known each other a very long time, and we've been through a lot of shit together on this crazy journey. Lost a lot of people. Before this is over, we're sure to lose more."

He pulled his hand away.

"I don't want to lose you," he said. "I'm not sure I can handle that. You understand what I'm saying?"

She nodded. "I'll be careful when we get to the outpost."

"Okay, then. Let's go see if we can find Rodger."

They went back down into the CIC, where Miles waited. From there, they trekked to the aft cargo hold, where they had fought the cyclops just days earlier. Corporal Valeria was there, holding Jo-Jo on a chain. The animal, unlike everyone else, was well fed, having eaten much of the spoiled food that would make the sailors sick.

That was good. The last thing they needed was a starving, angry monkey.

Miles trotted over to say hello to his friend as X and Magnolia went to the soldiers waiting in the cargo hold. The fire team of six trusted Cazadores was ready to go. Each man, including Sergeant Blackburn and Lieutenant Slayer, was handpicked by General Forge.

Edgar, Sofia, and Tia were also here, ready to deploy with the team.

Not one of these people had eaten in three days. Magnolia had felt hunger in her life, but now, combined with the lingering effects of radiation, she felt like a walking zombie.

"Get ready," X announced. "We're heading to shore for a recon of Outpost Gateway. I'm bringing the animals for extra protection and to see if they can sniff out what happened."

The vines, Magnolia thought. She recalled the SOS for the thousandth time, trying to imagine what could possibly have happened to Rodger and the rest of the outpost.

"Everything is set," Forge said.

"Good. Don't take your eyes off Gran Jefe and the others while I'm away," X said. "I also want a rescue team on standby to deploy."

"Good luck, sir."

X went to Valeria, who insisted on coming despite her injuries. "I help," she said. "Please, King Xavier."

After a brief hesitation, he allowed her aboard the assault craft with a nod.

Magnolia followed them to the elevator deck, where Jo-Jo knuckle-walked over to Miles. The dog was coming along, which surprised Magnolia some, but apparently X felt better bringing him along than leaving him behind with a crew of hungry Cazadores. Perhaps that was why Jo-Jo was coming, too, especially with Gran Jefe staying behind.

The monkey really seemed to dislike the Cazador. X had told Magnolia about Jo-Jo's second attack against Gran Jefe, this time during the fight with the cyclopes, and Magnolia was starting to think maybe the first attack wasn't a fluke. That maybe the animal sensed something off about Gran Jefe.

Magnolia didn't understand *how*, but if that wasn't the case, she was bewildered at what would cause the monkey to behave that way. There had to be something, and it wasn't just because the Cazador smelled bad.

The elevator in the stern cranked and began to lower. Magnolia took a breath of filtered air and boarded the assault craft bobbing in the choppy water. Heavily armored Cazadores piled onto the afterdeck they had used to transport APCs back in Brisbane. With all aboard, the engine roared to life, and the craft motored away from the *Frog*.

Miles sat on his haunches next to Magnolia, wagging his tail under his hazard suit. She found herself patting him on the head while the boat started toward the outpost. It helped calm her mind and soothe her heart during the ride.

"There it is," someone called out.

Magnolia stood up for a better view but saw only the faint outline of land in her night-vision optics.

"I'm coming, Rodge," she whispered.

She reached into her vest and pulled out a stim pill she had stolen from sickbay. It would make her crash hard, but she needed to be sharp until then.

As the shore came into focus, she lifted her visor and popped the pill. A sip of water washed it down.

When she clicked her visor back into place, she had a canal view of Panama City. Piles of debris that were once high-rises and resorts lined the shore. The view from the port side was much the same. The Cazador pilot steered toward the sand where they planned to beach the assault craft.

By the time the bow hit the surf, the stim pill had taken effect. Magnolia felt a flood of warmth in her system, along with a massive boost of energy.

"We move slow and careful," X said loud enough for everyone to hear.

The assault craft plowed through the waves and slid up onto the beach. Magnolia hopped over the side—first one off.

"Mags, remember what I said," X called out. "Jo-Jo will take point."

Valeria took the chain off the beast and let her roam. Jo-Jo loped up to the top of an embankment to scan the area while the remaining Cazadores got off the craft. The pilot pulled the assault craft away, motoring back into the darkness for cover.

Edgar and Sofia ran up with Magnolia while the soldiers fanned out. X stayed in the middle of the pack with Miles as they worked their way up from the beach and into the former resort area. Slayer and Blackburn stuck close to X, rifles up.

The group moved into the concrete jungle of ruined hotels. Magnolia looked west, still unable to see the outpost.

On the trek through the streets, Jo-Jo moved along on her knuckles, her spiky back hair lying flat. She stopped to sniff a hole in the ground, then continued toward the shells of decomposing vehicles filling the road—a perfect place for the spawn creatures to hide in ambush.

Magnolia brought up her infrared scope to search for the crablike monsters, but no heat signatures flickered. She clicked on her wrist computer to check the Geiger counter. The radiation was no different from what she remembered from her last time here.

They made it through the ruined resort zone without contacts. Not a single creature prowled in their sights. They were getting close to the canal. She checked on X, Miles, and the Hell Divers. X was telling Sofia to come up with Magnolia, probably in the hope this would keep her from straying ahead.

But Magnolia just couldn't hold back. When she started to feel the stim wearing off, she picked up her pace.

"Mags," Sofia said.

She heard X curse.

She didn't slow and instead ran past Jo-Jo to the top of a hill—where she froze. An open field was all that stood between them and the canal's banks—widened and deepened two centuries ago. The first thing she noticed in the water was the *Osprey*, sitting right where she had seen it last.

Throwing up her rifle, she did a quick scan with the infrared scope again but saw no heat signatures. She moved her sights back to the rusty ship for a closer inspection. Unlike the *Frog*, the *Osprey* showed no sign of damage or a fight.

X trekked up the embankment and stood beside Magnolia. She half expected an ass chewing, but he just scoped the area.

Valeria returned with Jo-Jo. Then came the rest of the soldiers, moving into combat intervals across the field, toward the bridge that still crossed the canal.

At the bridge, X went ahead with Miles while Sofia again joined

Magnolia. Finally, the group trekked across the bridge and reached the other side of the canal. The stacked containers remained in a wall around Outpost Gateway, but not a single soldier guarded them.

Magnolia studied the terrain, not seeing any bodies of spawn or the gargantuan breeders. There were no twisting vines or fiery radioactive beasts. Jo-Jo's hair remained flat, still indicating no perceived threats. There was nothing out here, it seemed.

The Cazador fire team and the Hell Divers advanced around the containers to the front gates, which stood wide open. Tents, some of them unzipped, flapped in the breeze.

Slayer flashed hand signals, and the Cazadores moved out. Magnolia staggered inside the outpost, her heart pounding.

Please, she thought. *Please somehow be okay, Rodge.*

The fire team scoured the inside of the fort, checking every building and tent. Magnolia resisted the urge to scream for Rodger.

Stay calm, Mags. Stay calm…

"Maybe they evacuated," X said.

"And went where?" Slayer asked. "The *Osprey*'s still here."

"Let's head to the bunker."

Magnolia started in that direction, following the Barracudas down a ramp and underground. These doors were open too, just slightly.

Slayer led them down a passageway, playing his flashlight beam over an empty hall. Severed vines lay curled up like dead snakes. Magnolia hurried after them, and Slayer held up a hand.

"We got a body," he said. "Or what's left of it."

She squeezed ahead, moving up to a small pile of armor and bones. There was no way to tell who it was, but the armor said *Cazador.*

"Something got inside and picked it clean," Slayer said.

X went up for a look, then told the group to split up. "Valeria, Blackburn, you take Jo-Jo that way," he said. "Slayer, Mags, with me."

They parted, and Miles trotted along with Magnolia, X, and Slayer. In the next corridor, they located three more sets of remains, each a Cazador soldier.

Slayer reached the command room to find the door locked.

"Stand back," X said, drawing his blaster. He shot the lock, destroying it, and Slayer kicked the door open to a room in disarray.

The wall had caved in on the right side, spilling half a dump-truck load of dirt across the floor. Monitors and computers lay strewn about, chairs and decks upended. Two sets of remains lay scattered throughout the space.

"Something got in," X said. "Something big."

"Spawn?" Slayer asked.

X bent down and picked up a femur. Part of it broke into lumps of grit. He scooped it up, letting it sift through his fingers. Miles bent down to sniff it through his suit and gave a whine.

"I was right," X whispered.

"About what?" Magnolia asked.

X glanced up. "There was a dive, a very long time ago. I was with Aaron Everhart. We encountered carnivorous vines."

"We've all seen those."

"Yeah, but these were different." He stood up, brushed his hand on his leg. "I don't think it was spawn that picked these bodies clean…"

A grunt drew all eyes to the open doorway. Jo-Jo knuckle-walked inside with Valeria and Blackburn.

"Find anything?" X asked.

"*Nada*," Valeria said.

"Maybe the outpost was abandoned after the vine attack," Edgar said. "Maybe they all went back to the islands."

Magnolia wanted to believe that.

"Something broke into the bunker," Sofia said, looking at the caved-in wall. "The doors were open, so maybe he's right—maybe people did flee and the soldiers stayed behind to cover their retreat."

Tia went over to check the wall, next to another pile of clothing, armor, hair, and bones.

"Careful," Edgar said. "Watch for a spawn hole."

He joined Tia with his rifle and tactical light trained on the darkness. Sofia went with them while Magnolia searched the room with Slayer, X, and Miles.

"I think spawn have used this tunnel," Edgar announced. "There's more bodies in here—looks like they were dragged out."

"So maybe the vines broke in, and the spawn came after to feed?" Slayer asked.

Magnolia was growing impatient. "We need to keep searching," she said. "There could be survivors."

"Okay," X said. "Let's head topside."

"Wait," Edgar said.

Magnolia was already heading out of the room when she heard her best friend cry out.

"Oh no," Sofia murmured.

She was standing next to Edgar at the mouth of the tunnel. He seemed to be holding something.

Sofia blocked Magnolia as she rushed over.

"What?" she asked. "What did you find?"

Edgar kept his back turned.

"What is it?" Magnolia asked. She forced her way past Sofia, nearly pushing her out of the way to find Edgar holding a twisted pair of eyeglasses.

Magnolia stared at them a moment, realization setting in as she finally reached out and took them gingerly from him.

"Where did you find these?" she asked.

Edgar pointed his chin at the bones in the cavernous hole. Most had been smashed to little hills of ash.

Magnolia looked again at the glasses, confirming they had belonged to Rodger. A tear rolled down her cheek as she slipped them gently into a vest pocket. Then she went down on her knees in front of the tunnel opening. She reached inside with both hands, scooping up the ash in her palms—all that remained of her lover and best friend.

"No," she mumbled. "Oh God, oh, please no."

X walked over. "Mags, I'm…"

She brushed his hand off with a shake of her shoulder before collapsing in tears.

"Rodger, I'm so sorry," Magnolia said. "Rodge…"

A shriek interrupted her sobbing.

At first, she thought it was her own voice.

"What is that?" someone asked.

"It's coming from…" Slayer said.

Magnolia noticed a glowing orange light under her visor. She slowly glanced up as the tunnel brightened.

Slayer and Blackburn ran over to her with rifles up, aiming down the corridor. She went back to scooping the ashes into a pile as carefully as she could.

"Mags," X said. "Mags, we have to go."

Magnolia remained on her knees in front of the tunnel, collecting the ash into a waterproof bag she often used for electronics.

The shrieking grew louder, the orange glow more intense.

"King Xavier, we need to get out of here!" Slayer said. "Something's coming… fast."

Hands reached down and picked Magnolia up. Ash sifted down from her hands.

"No!" she wailed.

Edgar and Sofia dragged her out of the room, moving into the passage just as a glowing humanoid figure with bark-like skin emerged in the tunnel entrance where Rodger had perished. The alarm from the Geiger counter chirped at a major spike in radiation.

X raised his rifle.

The incandescent creature pulled itself out of the tunnel and dropped to all fours. It got up, staggered forward, moaning and reaching out with burned limbs. Tattered, blackened clothes hung off the hardened muscles and flesh, which seemed to glow and pulsate between the grooves. The once-human creature moved toward them on legs that were nothing but bones.

Not bones, Magnolia realized. They were prosthetics.

"It's … Bromista," Slayer said in disbelief.

He lowered his rifle as the much-altered lieutenant stumbled through the command room groaning, his eyes burning like candle wicks.

"Bromista, stop!" Slayer shouted. "Stop. We're going to help you."

X kept his rifle up but didn't fire at the glowing monster that was once the funniest Cazador. This was no longer the jocular though supremely competent warrior they had left in charge of the outpost.

"There's no helping him," X said. "The only thing you can do now is show mercy."

Slayer held his weapon in shaky hands, aiming it at his best friend. "*Lo siento, hermano.*"

Magnolia closed her eyes, gripping the bag of ashes to her chest as machine-gun fire and another cry of death rang out.

TWENTY

Thunder rattled the barred windows of the circular room. Outside, sporadic lightning captured the beetle shape of the airship, hovering in the darkness over the prison rig once known as the Shark's Cage.

Soon, the second and final day of the trial would kick off. In just a few hours, Michael would be reunited with his wife, perhaps for the last time.

He watched the airship from the viewports in the top of the tower, where he stood with his hands bound. A chain ran from the cuffs to ankle bracelets.

The irony wasn't lost on him. This was the exact room where X had stored hundreds of barrels of food from the supercarrier *Immortal*. Ton and Victor had slept here for days, protecting the location, before they decided to move it.

Now it would be the venue for the second and final day of the trial that would determine Michael's life or death.

This place, a former prison, had held some true human monsters guilty of murder and rape. Some of those prisoners had spent hours and months in this very room, making ammunition and explosives.

The metal chairs where those prisoners once sat now supported the five jurors of the trial: Martino, Salamander, Ensio, Donovan, and Bailey.

Two Cazador soldiers stood guard at the single door to the room. It opened a few minutes later, and Charmer walked inside with a new scribe.

"Imulah," Michael whispered.

The bearded scribe hardly even glanced at Michael.

"My apologies for all the delays," Charmer said. "Between the weather and security challenges, it's been difficult, and for that reason the king will not be joining us."

Another heavy thunderclap shook the floor.

"That's a cue to get started, I'd say," Charmer said. "Proceed whenever you're ready, Mr. Everhart."

Michael shuffled to the front of the jury with all eyes on him. It was obvious Bailey felt pity for him. In his preparation, Michael had decided to focus on convincing the former *Hive* citizen, along with the businessman Martino, of his innocence.

They were his best shot.

He wouldn't waste energy on getting Salamander's vote, probably not Donovan's either. The sky person from Kilimanjaro had known Oliver. There was nothing but anger in their gazes. Michael wasn't sure about Ensio, but the Cazador scribe would be the tiebreaker, if Martino and Bailey found him not guilty.

For days, Michael had had the time to go over what he would say, but now that it was time, the gravity of his situation gave him pause. On a dive, his body and instincts kept him alive. Today, he needed words.

"I stand here in front of you as a guilty man," Michael said.

Brows rose among the jurors.

"I'm guilty of failing to see the bad in people," he continued. "For my entire life, I have put others first, risking my life to keep the *Hive* in the sky, then in a war against el Pulpo to liberate the Metal Islands and turn them into what you know today as the Vanguard Islands. After that, I spent years traveling the world to rescue survivors, but you already know all that."

Michael looked at each juror in turn.

"I stand before you, framed for a crime that I would never commit," Michael said. "The evidence against me is circumstantial at best. Did I have an altercation with Oliver? Yes. Did multiple people see someone with something that looked like this?" He raised his prosthetic arm. "Also true."

Michael lowered his arm again. "But Alton and Lilyn never saw this killer's face," he said. "Anyone could have put on armor to make it look like me."

"Is that so?" Charmer asked.

"Yes, absolutely."

"I see."

The trial slogged on for the next hour, with Michael explaining where he had been the night of the crime. Soon, his wife would confirm that he had been at home with her. He remembered the night well because he'd had a nightmare about armored soldiers coming to their apartment.

"My wife will confirm all this," Michael said.

"Very well," Charmer said. "Let's take a short break, then reconvene with the defendant's witness."

The jurors left the room with Charmer and one of the guards, but Imulah stayed. He walked over to the viewports to look out the windows.

Both men knew how dangerous it would be to talk. For all Michael knew, Charmer had hidden cameras or mics in here, but there was one question he didn't fear.

"Imulah, if I am found guilty, what options do I have?" Michael asked. "Can I request judgment by combat?"

"I'm afraid not. The Cazador ways are over. Violence is prohibited in a new law signed by King Rolo. He has declared an end to the old ways."

"So my options…"

"I'm sorry, Chief—er, Michael. I'm also sorry about King Xavier. He was a brave leader," said the scribe. "But he knew the risks when he decided to go to Panama and beyond."

Michael wondered if Imulah had any idea about the truth. "There was a woman, Janga, on the *Hive* when I was growing up. She believed it would take a prophet of great strength and resolve to find a safe place for us to live." Michael shifted in his chains. "The challenges X survived to get us here and to ensure our survival will echo in eternity."

"That's true," said a voice from behind them.

Charmer had returned.

"The former king's contribution to the islands will assure his place in history with his predecessors," he said. "El Pulpo and those who came before were warlords, and fortunately for us all, humanity's time for war has finally passed." That famously insolent grin spread across Charmer's face. "We are building a new, peaceful home here, led by a man of peace, King Rolo."

Michael stared at Charmer, astounded at the man's endless fount of lies. Rolo was worse than all his predecessors for his actions in Brisbane. Not even el Pulpo would have detonated a nuclear bomb to further his aims.

Footsteps approached, and Jamal and two other soldiers entered the room with a shorter person wearing a hood.

Michael froze as Jamal lifted the hood.

"Layla," he cried.

She blinked, looking for him, then bolted away from Jamal and another guard.

Michael started toward her, shuffling in his chains and nearly tripping. Layla got to him before the guards could catch up. She wrapped her arms around his neck.

"It's okay," he whispered. "Everything's going to be okay."

"Back!" Jamal shouted. He reached out to grab Layla, but Michael turned her away.

"Touch her again, and it'll be the last thing you ever do."

Charmer held out a hand in front of his chest. "Give them a minute," he said before lowering his voice. "It could be their last."

Michael nearly broke at Layla's touch.

"Bray misses you so much," she said.

"Okay, enough," Charmer said. "Please stand over here."

Layla took in the room and the jurors. Imulah opened his book and prepared to take notes.

"State your name," Charmer said.

"Layla Everhart," she replied.

"Do you promise to tell the truth?"

"Of course."

Charmer nodded to Michael.

"Layla, can you tell us where you were the night Oliver and his son, Nez, were murdered?" Michael asked.

"I was at home sleeping, with you," Layla said.

"And do you remember anything specific about that night?"

"I recall you waking up from a nightmare, the same one you had many nights."

"And what else do you remember?"

"I remember you getting up at dawn and kissing me goodbye, and Bray. Then you went to work, like you always do, day in and day out, protecting the islands. And before that, you protected our airship."

"Please stick to the questions," Charmer said. "Do you under-stand?"

"Yes."

Michael switched to the next part of his defense. He had established an alibi, but that wasn't going to be enough. After his lie about the food reserves, his character was in question.

"Layla, you have known me since we were kids," he said. "Did you ever know me to hurt another human who wasn't directly threatening my life or the life of someone else?"

"No, never. The only times you have ever been forced to violence were in war. Against the skinwalkers, Horn, and el Pulpo, who captured our people and tortured them."

Michael looked to Salamander. The guy had fought for el Pulpo and had no doubt eaten human flesh over his lifetime. Nothing they said would convince the guy of Michael's innocence.

But Martino was a cultured, sophisticated Cazador, and so was Ensio. Maybe hearing about who Michael was as a man would help them realize that he simply could not do what he was accused of.

Bailey already knew most of this, but it was useful history for Donovan, the sky person from the machine camp, to know.

Layla looked in his eyes. "My husband went to Mount Kili-manjaro and risked his life to save your people. He went to Rio de Janeiro and multiple other locations to do the same thing."

Charmer scratched his jaw but, to Michael's surprise, didn't intervene.

"My husband has spent his life protecting others, rescuing others, and diving so that humanity survives," Layla said. "To murder Oliver or his son would go against everything he stands for."

Her wild eyes flitted around the room as she grew more exasperated. Michael needed to rein her in before she looked too panicked.

"Layla," Michael said.

She seemed to relax at his calm voice.

"Is there anything else?" Charmer asked.

"My husband is a good man, and you all know that," Layla said. "He would never kill a child."

Finally, after another hour, Michael finished his defense.

"Is there anything else?" Charmer asked.

Michael thought for a moment, then shook his head.

"Okay, thank you for your time, Layla," Charmer said. "You are free to sit over there."

She was led to a chair.

"In a slight change of plans, I'd like to call a witness before you make your final remarks," Charmer said. "As long as that's okay with you…"

"Who is it?" Michael asked.

"Steve Schwarzer. Do you agree to have him here?"

Michael couldn't think of a reason not to bring Steve before the jury, but Charmer must have a reason. Still, it could be to Michael's benefit to interview one of his closest allies—a man who could vouch for his character.

"Okay."

Steve entered the room, looking as surprised as everyone else that he should be here.

"Steve," Charmer said, "Michael has accepted our offer to interview you and will be able to ask you questions now. Then I will follow them up."

"Okay," Steve said.

"All yours," Charmer said.

"Steve, do you remember where we were on the night before the murder?" Michael asked.

"Yes, we were working on several projects, including one at the rooftop school."

Michael went on to ask several questions that added to his character defense. It helped that Steve was a Cazador. It couldn't hurt his chances with Ensio and Martino.

When Michael finished, Charmer said, "You are a master bladesmith, correct?"

"Yes, for the past thirty years," Steve replied.

"What does this job entail?"

"A bit of everything. I've forged weapons, armor, and—"

"How about *this*?"

Charmer walked over to Michael and pointed to the prosthetic arm.

"Have you ever constructed something like this?" Charmer asked.

"I've built prosthetics before," Steve said. "I built one for King Xavier."

"I understand, but have you ever built one like this?"

"No, that prosthetic is beyond my abilities."

"And why is that?"

"Because it is bionic, and connected to Michael's nerves."

"I see. So no one else has one just like this, that you're aware of?"

The question sent a chill up Michael's spine. Now he understood why Charmer had called Steve: to refute the defense that his arm looked like normal body armor.

"No," Steve admitted.

"Thank you," Charmer said. "No further questions from my end."

He turned to the jury. For the first time today, they were fidgeting in their seats and raising brows.

Michael looked to Layla, his heart pounding.

His fate had just been sealed. They had two people who had seen his arm at the crime scene, they had two motives, and they had no other suspects. The jury would find him guilty. The only way to save him would be for Layla and a few of his friends to risk everything.

Michael couldn't let that happen. He had to accept his fate without fear. It was the only way to save his family.

* * * * *

Miles followed X to the edge of the canal. A pair of Cazador soldiers stood with Sergeant Blackburn at a construction site, where an earthmoving machine sat idle.

Clumps of dirt surrounded holes where the vines had burst through the canal's sloping walls.

X studied the scene, tracing the humps in the ground back to the outpost walls. Magnolia was with Sofia somewhere, grieving over Rodger. But right now X had no time to grieve. He had to keep it together, for Magnolia's sake and for the survivors with him. Their number two priority right now was to find food.

Half the fire team was spread out searching for provisions while the rest kept on the first priority, which was always security. X was trying to get a clear picture of what had happened. It was the only way to make sure it didn't happen again.

After a few hours, he believed he had pieced together the puzzle. The evidence led him back inside the outpost, to a collapsed metal building over the water-desalination plant.

In his mind's eye, he imagined the scene. Rodger and his people had turned on this machine, triggering the vines to burst out of the canal. The glowing red tendrils had squirmed over the surface, snagging anyone in sight.

Lieutenant Bromista must have told everyone to retreat to the bunker, where he thought they would be safe. But the vines had burrowed, breaking through the interior walls and engulfing the people who sheltered there.

Somehow, Bromista had turned into one of the radioactive beasts. How, X wasn't sure, but the soldiers with him now were prepared to put down any more of their former friends who had made the unnatural transformation.

There was a reason the Cazadores had vanished when they came this way decades ago. X had known the risks, and still he had come here. He had thought that once they cleared the monsters from the canal, they could support an outpost here. His mistake had cost them too many lives.

"Sir?"

X turned to Slayer.

"We've scoured the outpost, and so far we've found very little food," he reported. "I don't think it was the vines that destroyed it, either."

"What, then?"

"I mean, someone was here before us," Slayer said.

X looked at the sky. "That chickenshit son of a bitch…"

Again he pictured what had happened, imagining the airship on its way back to the islands. They had stopped here on a raid, taking everything.

"FUCK YOU, ROLO!" X shouted. "I will obliterate you!"

He kicked the metal side of the building, scaring Miles. The dog jumped back, then looked up at him.

"Damned son-of-a-Siren's-bastard, scum-sucking Rolo," X said. Closing his eyes, he drew in a breath and held it as he counted to ten. Just as he used to when he was a kid.

"Sorry," he said, exhaling.

Slayer simply nodded. "We have yet to check the *Osprey*," he said. "Maybe there is something useful on board."

"I'm surprised Rolo didn't have someone sail it back."

"He may come for it yet."

X bent to scratch behind Miles's ears. He looked up at the

old ship that Yejun's family had sailed here years ago. "I'm sorry, boy," he said.

"The good news is, the outpost is secure," Slayer said. "The vines seem dormant."

"Okay, bring up the *Frog*," X said.

Slayer jogged away to give the order while X went with Miles to find Magnolia. It didn't take long. She was inside the outpost with Sofia, Tia, and Edgar.

Miles ran ahead to Magnolia. She was on her knees, head bowed, clutching something tightly in her hands. The dog nudged up against her, tail wagging inside his suit.

Edgar joined X beside a sagging tent.

"How's she doing?" X asked.

"Not so good," Edgar said.

"We need to get some food in her, but…" X resisted the urge to curse again. "So far, we haven't found any."

"He came here because of me," Magnolia said. She turned and looked at X. "He died because of me."

"That's not true," X said. "You know it isn't."

She got up, and X could see the mangled spectacles in her hand. "It's the truth, and I have to live with it."

"Time will heal this," Sofia said. She put her hand on Magnolia's shoulder, but Magnolia shrugged it away.

"Time doesn't fix the fact this is my fault," Magnolia said. "He should have been with us."

"He could still be dead if he'd been with us," X said. "Look at what happened to Arlo."

"No. Things would have been different."

X sighed. He didn't know what to say, not that anything he said would make a difference at this point. Sofia was right: only time would help.

"We're bringing up the *Frog*, and we're going to check out

the *Osprey* for supplies," X said. "It's our only hope at this point. Rolo got here before us, took every bloody thing."

"You got to be joking," Edgar said.

X shook his head. "I'm going with the Barracudas to check out the *Osprey*."

"We're coming," Magnolia said.

"No, you—" X started to say.

"I know the ship. So does Edgar."

"Yeah, but—"

Again she cut him off. "I want to see where Rodger lived when he was here. Give that to me, X, okay?"

Even with the threat seemingly gone, she was a liability out here in her present state of mind. But he wasn't going to say no. She deserved to take anything of Rodger's back to the islands with them.

"Okay," X said. "Let's make this fast, though."

He kept close to Magnolia on the walk out of the outpost, back to the canal. The rest of the Cazadores had gathered there with Jo-Jo. Slayer was pointing out to sea, where the *Frog* was now within view.

The assault craft they had used to beach in the resort zone was speeding back toward the shoreline. It arrived a few seconds later, pushing up a wave in front of it, ready to extract the group.

The group started down the bank, with Jo-Jo again on point. The animal sniffed across the construction site, where Rodger and his team had run pipes from the canal to the desalination plant. The *Osprey* was just a short hike beyond the disturbed soil.

When they got to the ship, Jo-Jo loped up the ramp to the weather deck.

The rest of the team followed.

"Okay, we split up," X said. "Slayer, you take the lower decks with Jo-Jo, I'll head up to the top levels with the divers."

"Got it."

They parted, and X opened a hatch to an internal ladder.

"The mess is on this level," Magnolia said. "Go there. I'm going to Rodger's room."

X turned to Sofia. "Go with her."

Sofia nodded.

The group split up further, X heading for the mess hall.

Please, please have food, he thought.

When he rounded the corridor and saw the debris in the next passage, the anger rose up again, threatening to take over. Someone had already been here.

Pans, plates, and trash littered the passageway.

X went inside the mess hall with Miles and found the space a complete disaster.

Not a can was left on the shelves. They had even taken the utensils.

X felt his stomach growling. The hunger pains were getting worse. They might still make it back to the Vanguard Islands, but they would be exhausted and weak.

He looked down at Miles. The dog had to be starving, too, but that didn't seem to affect his attitude much.

"There's nothing here," X said.

"Maybe Slayer found something belowdecks," Edgar said.

They went back down the corridor toward the cabins, where Rodger had apparently lived while running the outpost.

X heard sobbing down the hall.

He stopped just shy of the open doorway. Magnolia sat at a desk covered in carvings and wood shavings.

Sofia looked back at them as X started toward the hatch. He hesitated there, not sure what to say or do. He hated seeing Magnolia like this.

A scream came from somewhere aboard the ship. Then came a crack.

"That's gunfire," Edgar said.

Magnolia shot up from the desk and looked out the port window. X rushed into the room and squeezed between her and Sofia. It didn't take long to see a Cazador opening fire across the weather deck below. What his target was, however, X couldn't say.

"What the hell's he shooting at?" he asked.

The Cazador was firing at stacked shipping containers on the port side. Whatever was out there seemed to be using them for cover.

X saw a flash of motion—red feathers, then maybe a pincer. But this was no giant bird, spawn, or vine. This was a person.

As X watched, a figure in a ghillie suit and a beaked helmet slammed into the Cazador, knocking him to the deck.

Two more soldiers came running across the deck, rifles blazing.

"Hold your fire!" X shouted. "That's Yejun!"

TWENTY-ONE

A week had passed since Kade returned to the Coral Castle after the mission in the wastes. He had spent most of that time back in the original jail cell like a caged animal.

Lucky had come to visit him a few times, bringing him food and a new blanket. On those visits, Lucky explained that they couldn't leave until the Sea King helicopter was completely repaired and updated with a hybrid fuel-and-battery system to power the flight. After all, it was a very long way to Outpost Gateway.

Kade spent most of the downtime resting and working out to regain his strength. Push-ups, sit-ups, squats, and lunges were about all he could do in the small cell.

Each passing day, he grew more and more anxious about the impending trip. He couldn't help but wonder if he was betraying King Xavier by going with the knights to find the *Frog* and "activate the Trident," whatever that meant. But they were hunting X with or without Kade, and it was his only chance to get back to his people—maybe even help them.

He thought of Tia, Alton, Magnolia, and everyone else he

cared about. Kade was desperate to be reunited with them and to take his revenge on Rolo.

Finally, on the seventh day after returning to the Coral Castle, Lucky showed up in his armor. In one hand he held his helmet, in the other a duffel bag and a gray uniform. The guard opened the cell door, and Lucky set the bag and uniform down.

"How do you feel?" Lucky asked.

"Bored stupid and ready to get out of here," Kade replied.

"Good. Put this on. We're leaving in a few hours, and I have a stop to make."

Kade threw on the uniform, unsure why he was tagging along with Lucky but happy just to be out of the cell. It didn't take long to get his answer.

They left the brig and headed up into the communal area, which Kade had passed through when he was first brought here. Above him, the multilevel decks were lit up and buzzing.

Kade heard what sounded like music—drums and a guitar. Then came the scent of barbecue. Fish and some sort of meat. The aromas were mouthwatering.

He was hungry after being fed only some sort of fish cakes over the past few days. The clumpy yellow patties were better than what the machines had fed him, but not by much.

To Kade's surprise, instead of leading him through the blast door, Lucky went to a closed gate before a ladder. "Stay close to me," Lucky said. "People haven't seen a foreigner for many years, and I'd prefer not to get any attention, but we have to go this way."

He unlocked the gate by punching a code into a keypad. Then he started up the rungs, boots clomping on metal.

For the first time since he'd arrived, Kade saw firsthand where these people lived. The first floor was an open market a warren of small stalls and people bartering eggs, fish, soap, and clothing.

Most everyone he saw spoke English, with similar accents to what Kade had grown up hearing on his airship.

Curious eyes found him right away. People backed away as he walked with Lucky down an aisle of small shops. On the right were chests of ice, with fish neatly arranged on top. On the left was a butcher's block, with a man holding a cleaver. He swung it once, hacking off the head of a red fish with big eyes. The head slid off, and a young boy plopped it into a bucket. The kid reminded Kade of Alton.

"Come right back," said the butcher. And the kid hurried off to a woman stirring a huge metal pot. Lucky and Kade moved on as the man wiped the blood off his cleaver with a rag.

Raised voices came from the end of the aisle, where a large woman stood behind a table of stacked wooden crates. Her great jiggling arms were folded in defiance across a sweatshirt that read *Crab Cakes* in faded red letters.

"Moira, just open the buckets," said the man with her. He wore gray pants with a matching shirt that bore a trident logo on the collar and cuffs.

"Open them," said another man, also in a gray uniform and armed with a sword. The woman finally lowered her arms and twisted a lid off a bucket packed full of frozen crabs.

The official waved a wand with a glass tip over the orange-and-white pincers.

Kade guessed he was some sort of scribe, like those at the Vanguard Islands, responsible for keeping track of food and other essentials.

The tip of the wand blinked red, and the man frowned. "I'm sorry," he said, "but you can't sell this. It's been contaminated. Let's see the others."

"Shit," Lucky said. He and Kade walked past just as the official moved to the next bucket.

"Lieutenant Gaz," he said with a slight bow.

"Hey, Hugh," Lucky replied. "You think the entire batch is bad?"

Hugh waved the wand over the next bucket and sighed. "Afraid so."

"How can that be?" Moira asked. "I've never had a contaminated catch before!"

"Irradiated," Hugh explained. "Radiation has ruined those crabs."

Moira looked down, perplexed. It struck Kade that most of these people had no idea about the radiation yet.

"What am I supposed to do?" she asked. "I need to sell those, and people need to eat."

Hugh didn't answer, instead motioning for the soldier to confiscate the buckets as Lucky and Kade walked on.

A small crowd had gathered around them, and not because of the irradiated crabs. They were all looking at Kade.

"Come on," Lucky said, and Kade followed him out of the market. They went up a flight of stairs to a corridor with apartment doors on both sides. Halfway down, Lucky stopped and knocked.

It cracked open, and a woman looked through the gap. "Gaz!" she said in surprise.

She opened the door to a small living space where a mattress lay with its covers in disarray. Against the wall was a table with two chairs. A candle burned in a glass jar, dimly lighting the room.

"Come in," the woman said.

Kade followed Lucky inside, holding his duffel bag.

"Came to check on you. I also wanted to introduce you to my friend Kade Long."

She turned on an electric lamp that highlighted her features. Kade guessed she was in her forties, though she looked younger. Her dark-brown hair was pulled back into a ponytail, a few strands falling over her blue eyes.

"Kade, this is Sabrina, my sister," Lucky said.

She grinned and stuck out her hand.

Kade shook it. "Pleasure to meet you."

"Gaz has told me a lot about you."

"Yeah?"

"He says you're from the sky and that your people call you a Hell Diver."

"Among other names," Kade said.

"Here, take a load off your feet," Sabrina said. She pulled out the chairs from the table.

"We can't stay, but I'm also here to tell you something," Lucky said.

"Then have a seat."

Lucky frowned. "Sis, I really don't have the time."

"You never do. Come on, stay just a bit," she wheedled. "Care for some tea?"

"That would be lovely, ma'am," Kade said. "If that's okay with you, Lieutenant."

Lucky looked at his watch and gave a half shrug.

Kade set his bag down and took a seat with Lucky at the table.

"How about you, Gaz?" Sabrina asked from the small kitchen.

"Save your rations," Lucky said.

She returned a moment later with two glasses and set them on the table, then sat at the edge of the mattress.

"I'm doing fine on rations," Sabrina said, passing a glass to Lucky. "Don't worry about me."

He passed it right back to her. "That's another reason I'm here," he said. "Things are going to get ugly here for a while— maybe for a long while."

"What?" Confusion darkened Sabrina's pleasant features. "I don't understand."

"You will soon, but I'm not authorized to say anything else," Lucky said.

"I'm your sister. You can't tell me the truth?"

"The truth is not for me to say, to anyone."

Sabrina huffed with frustration.

"I'm leaving tomorrow morning on a long trip, and I'm not sure when I'll be back," Lucky said.

"Long trip where?" she asked. Then she looked at Kade. "To the place he's from?"

"I'm sorry. I wish I could tell you more, but things have gotten bad. We've lost people, and..." Lucky shook his head. "I'll be back as soon as I can."

He stood up, and Kade followed suit.

"Give us a minute," Lucky said.

Kade nodded.

"Nice to've met you, ma'am," Kade said. He bowed his head politely before stepping out into the corridor.

Two boys, of perhaps eight and six years, came running down the hall, skidding to a stop when they saw him.

"Who the heck are you, mister?" said the younger one.

"Yeah, I've never seen you before," added the older kid.

Both shaggy-haired kids stared at Kade.

"Well? You a mute or something?" asked the older boy.

The door opened and Lucky stepped out.

The kids backed away when they saw the knight.

"Keep moving, guys," Lucky said.

They took off, getting a last look over their shoulders as they walked.

"Okay, let's go," Lucky said.

He guided Kade down ladders and hallways, past two soldiers in fatigues. Both saluted Lucky.

Dozens of people in gray jumpsuits worked on the helicopter. Bulldozer was in the cockpit, barking orders.

"We're leaving soon," Lucky told Kade. "Go wait over there."

"I'll help."

"Fine."

Kade went over to the stacks of supplies and decided to help load up. The other people inside seemed to be technicians and engineers. None of them seemed to pay much attention to him as he picked up a plastic crate of fish protein wafers and dried bananas. The other boxes of supplies were variously labeled *Electronics, Tools,* and *Ammo.*

He had loaded ten crates when a regular beeping made him pause. Everyone stopped what they were doing and turned to a monitor that bore the weathered, ancient face of the Forerunner.

"Sons and daughters of the Trident," said the sampled robotic voice, "as your steward, I am tasked with sharing some news that pains me. The rumors you may have heard are true. Our food source has been threatened by the actions of a hostile enemy."

Kade felt the burn of eyes on his back. When he glanced around, he saw almost everyone staring at him as he held the crate in his hands. He slowly lowered it to the floor.

"We have planned for a situation like this," the Forerunner continued, his voice taking on a more purely electronic tone. "We have *preeeeepared* for this."

The workers went back to watching the screen.

Kade could see the concern on every face. Most of these people probably had families. Wives. Husbands. Children.

They wanted a simple thing for their loved ones: to survive.

Something that was not in the cards for Kade's family.

"For the first time in over a decade, I am deploying a knight and crew into the wastes beyond our known territory," said the Forerunner. "Their mission is to find the hostiles responsible for our current plight."

* * * * *

Magnolia stood outside the open gates of Outpost Gateway. In her hands, she gently held Rodger's twisted eyeglasses as she stared, entranced, at the storm over the Panama Canal. She recalled landing here months ago, clearing the zone of the monstrous radioactive breeders and their ravening spawn in a pitched battle. It had cost the Vanguard army many Cazador and sky fighters, but they had ultimately secured this area, preparing it for the outpost and opening a way to the Pacific Ocean.

Or so they all had thought.

She remembered the firewalker beasts on the *Osprey*. They would have killed her and the other divers if not for Yejun.

He was the only person who had understood there was a deadlier threat than the breeders and their spawn. Yejun had watched the vines consume many of the people he'd come here with, leaving nothing but bones or ash. He had also seen his family and others transformed by the radiation into firewalkers like Lieutenant Bromista.

Magnolia blinked at the industrial zone across the canal. Yejun was still out there somewhere. Maybe there were others…

She tucked Rodger's glasses back in her vest, holding on to the slender thread of hope that he had simply lost them when fleeing the bunker. That somehow, against all reasoning, he had escaped. That the ashes she had picked up in her hands were not his but the remains of some less lucky soul.

But deep down, Magnolia knew hope was a heartbreaker. The chances of Rodger being alive were slim to nil. If anyone would know the truth, it was Yejun. Magnolia had to find him.

Crunching footsteps ended her reverie. The last soldiers had finished their search of the *Osprey*. They carried a few boxes but nothing substantial. Nothing to feed the survivors on the *Frog* or prepare them for war at the Vanguard Islands.

Magnolia was beyond hunger, with stomach cramps and a truly seismic headache.

Sofia, Tia, and Edgar looked on, clearly under orders from X to keep an eye on her. But Mags wasn't the only one near a breaking point.

X swore another long tirade when Slayer and Blackburn gave him the news.

"We searched the entire vessel," Slayer said.

Magnolia slogged over to join them. The assault boat waited in the unlit waters of the canal.

"Okay, listen up," X said, tilting his head up at the *Osprey*. "It didn't have supplies, but it's full of fuel. General Forge is sending a crew from the *Frog* to board the vessel, and then we're out of here."

"What about Yejun?" Magnolia asked.

"Yejun is welcome to come with us, but I'm not sending anyone out looking for him," X said. "Too bloody dangerous."

"He's never going to come after we just shot at him," Edgar said.

X grunted. "The kid never wanted to leave in the first place."

Magnolia looked across the canal again. "We can't leave him here," she said.

"I can. And I will."

"And take his ship? X, that was his *home*."

"Mags, we don't have time to argue. Yejun's the least of my worries right now."

"You're right, and I'm not arguing. I'm going to look for him." She started away.

"Magnolia, stop!"

She stopped walking but kept her gaze across the canal.

"Is this really about Yejun?" X asked. He walked around until they were face to face. "Rodger's gone, Mags. I'm sorry, but that's the truth."

"Maybe he's with Yejun," Magnolia said. "Maybe Yejun saved him…"

"You know that isn't true."

"We don't know for sure. I only found his glasses."

"The ash—I'm sorry, but that was Rodger."

She walked away as X cursed another blue streak.

"We don't have time for this, and you promised me," he said. "Slayer, Blackburn, go with her. Edgar, Sofia, you too. If you see vines, you fucking run right back here."

"You got it," Slayer said.

"What about me?" Tia asked.

"Come with me," X said.

Boots crunched after Magnolia. Edgar and Sofia came up on her flanks while Slayer and Blackburn went ahead.

"Mags, can I talk to you real quick?" Sofia asked.

There was a caution in her tone. Magnolia didn't want that. "Go for it," she said.

"I came on this mission to find a new food source for the islands," Sofia said cautiously. "That is why I left my son with Layla."

"I know."

"I was judged by many for this, but to me, helping meant saving him."

"I never judged you."

"Not what I'm saying. I'm saying I want to see my son again. He needs his mother. I'm so sorry what happened to Rodger, but you are still alive. Your life is valuable, and so is mine."

"You don't have to come with me if you don't want to."

"Another thing I'm not saying, Mags."

The group was already approaching the bridge across the canal. Slayer bent down to look at tracks on the ground.

Edgar said, "I think Sofia's simply saying you need to be extra careful soon as we cross the canal."

"No worries there," Magnolia said.

"Come on," Slayer said, waving them over the bridge.

The crew moved across, over the dark water. On the other side, Slayer followed tracks into the salvage yard. Their flashlight beams raked over rows of rusted shipping containers, then over stacks of salvaged iron.

Magnolia recalled the last time she had tracked Yejun down. And the time before that, when he tracked her down, freeing both her and Edgar.

"Tracks end here," Slayer said.

"He must have climbed onto one of the containers," Edgar said.

Magnolia noticed a warning on her HUD. "Sudden spike in radiation," she said.

"How bad?" Slayer asked.

"Just a small one."

"Not exactly small," Edgar said. "These readings are on the line between yellow and red zones."

Magnolia looked out over the mounds of scrap. She had no idea if Yejun was hiding in here or how he would act if they found him. He might try to kill them in self-defense. And with the radiation, vines, and ravenous beasts, she realized how dangerous it was out here.

"Sofia," Magnolia said.

Sofia stopped. "Yeah?"

"Go back across the bridge. Edgar and I'll go with the Barracudas."

"No, it's okay; I'm with you. Just saying be careful."

"I know, but we can handle it."

"Mags, really, it's okay."

"Blackburn, escort her back, please," Magnolia said. "Edgar, Slayer, let's keep going."

"Copy that," Slayer said. As Blackburn took Sofia back toward the bridge, Magnolia looked over her shoulder and nodded. Sofia nodded back.

Slayer took point into the salvage yard. Their lights raked over the rusted containers as they advanced.

After a few minutes, Magnolia whistled to Slayer. He stopped and looked back.

"If he's out here, he knows we're coming," she said. "I say we just call out."

Edgar nodded, as did Slayer after a short pause.

"Yejun!" she shouted. "Yejun, we aren't going to hurt you!"

The distant oscillating sound of a Siren call answered.

Both men turned their rifles to the sky. Lightning speared through the clouds but didn't reveal the monster to Magnolia.

Another ethereal wail sounded, this one from the ground. Magnolia resisted the urge to call Yejun again.

Slayer and Edgar started through the maze of containers, with Magnolia right behind them. She looked for prints on the ground where Yejun hopped down.

For the next thirty minutes, they ghosted through the area, searching every container. Magnolia pulled open a heavy, creaking steel door. A nearby thunderclap made her flinch. It faded to the sound of a transmission over the comms.

"Mags, give me a sitrep," said King Xavier.

"No sign of Yejun yet," she replied.

"The *Frog* is in the canal. We're almost ready to go."

"Copy that. We'll come back soon."

"Thirty minutes, Mags. Max. Got it?"

"Got it."

Magnolia joined Edgar and Slayer at the bottom of a hill on the eastern border of the salvage yard. They trekked up the slope for a better view.

"We've searched this entire area," Edgar said. "He must have kept going into the industrial zone, maybe even into the city."

Magnolia looked out in that direction. Rusted shipyard equipment littered the area for a mile eastward. It would take hours to search the area safely.

"I'll call out for him one more time," she said.

"Yejun!" she shouted into the wind. "Yejun, it's me, Magnolia!"

She scanned the skyline with her rifle scope but saw nothing. Edgar hissed and pointed, directing her to the winged body of a male Siren, flapping in their direction.

Two more, sitting perched like cathedral gargoyles, took wing over the ruined city.

"We should go before they see us," Edgar said.

Slayer didn't argue.

Magnolia swept the infrared scope across the terrain one last time for the teenager. A wave of dizziness came and went. *Yejun, where are you?*

"Come on, Commander, we gave it our best shot," Edgar said. "The kid doesn't want to be found."

"Gotta go," Slayer said.

Magnolia lowered her rifle as the men retreated down the hill. She stared into the darkness, fighting the dizziness. Yejun was out there somewhere, but in her heart, she knew that Rodger was gone. She finally turned away with Edgar and Slayer.

They crossed back through the salvage yard as a light rain began to fall.

The electronic discord of a Siren rose into a wail, and she turned to see three of the beasts circling nearby. That made her pause.

"Magnolia…" Edgar said.

She turned around for a better view as the dizziness grew worse.

"Commander," Edgar said.

One of the Sirens dropped into a dive. It struck her then: the creatures had done what she'd failed to do.

"Shit! They found Yejun," she said.

The realization gave her a sudden jolt of energy. Ignoring shouts to stop, Magnolia lit out running back through the salvage yard and up a low hill.

All three Sirens had dived out of sight. She finally saw one perched on a crane, its wings folded around its spiked back.

"Magnolia," panted Edgar behind her, trudging up the hill with Slayer.

"They found Yejun," she said, pointing to the crane. "He must be there somewhere. Maybe there are other survivors too."

"Magnolia, you have to let g—"

Gunfire cut Edgar off. Slayer shouldered his rifle as the Siren slumped off the crane and fell to the yard below.

"It's Yejun. We have to help him. Those things found him because of my yelling," Magnolia said. She did a standing glissade down the scree slope.

Rifle up, she ran as more gunshots cracked in the distance.

A Siren gave an agonized howl and flapped back into the sky. Magnolia high-stepped over a fallen beam and ducked under the jib of a toppled crane.

She slipped and went down. Looking up, she saw one of the eyeless creatures about two hundred feet ahead. It was trying to pry the door off a truck that lay on its side, its bed half-buried under loose earth.

Yejun...

Eyes alert, ducking under warped beams and squirming between concrete slabs, she got closer to the truck.

The lights of Slayer and Edgar moved just behind her over the muddy terrain. She sighted up the muscular beast at the back of the truck door that it had pried open. A yell came from inside, then another gunshot.

The Siren pushed inside.

Magnolia held up her hand to hold fire.

Reaching over her shoulder, she pulled one of her curved blades.

"Cover me," she said.

Edgar and Slayer searched the sky and ground while Magnolia stalked toward the beast at the truck. She was ten feet away when the eyeless face whipped around.

Magnolia walked toward it with her blades gripped tightly. The creature leaped down off the back of the truck, claws swiping at her helmet.

The sickle blade flicked out, severing a taloned hand.

Then she silenced its screams with a swift decapitating blow. She had a clear view into the back of the truck.

Yejun crouched inside, holding a rifle.

Walking over to him, Magnolia heard Slayer and Edgar approaching, but there was another sound: the whoosh of wind.

She looked up as a Siren streaked down from the sky. Another came skittering down the crane's mast.

Laser bolts appeared—narrow, bright planks of sizzling blue light, flashing through the leathery wings and into the night for miles beyond. Magnolia had barely enough time to bring up her blade. Then there was darkness and a squeezing embrace. It took her a moment to realize that the beast was wrapped around her.

"Hold your fire!" Edgar shouted.

Magnolia blinked at the eyeless face of the creature hugging her inside its laser-tattered wings. She slammed her helmet against the jagged teeth snapping in her face. Then she sliced and sawed with the curved blade. The creature's electronic wails hurt her ears. Finally, sensing the battle was lost, the beast released her and limped away with ragged, useless wings.

Magnolia collapsed onto her back as Edgar and Slayer bent down. It wasn't just them.

Yejun came out of the truck and put down his rifle. He crouched in front of her while Slayer suddenly went to the back of the truck.

"Holy shit!" said the Cazador. "Take a look at that!"

Magnolia reached up to Yejun.

"Yejun," she said. "You have to come back with us. You can't stay."

Edgar helped Magnolia up before she could finish the words. Pain riddled her muscles. Everything seemed to hurt.

She tried to fight her blurry vision as she stood on wobbly legs. Yejun walked over to her side, and Magnolia saw what had Slayer so excited. The truck was packed with crates of food and jugs of water.

It wasn't Captain Rolo who'd raided the *Osprey*. Yejun had. Bringing the items from his old home all the way out here.

The comm channel crackled.

"King Xavier," Slayer said. "We found Yejun. He's not alone."

"You found more survivors?" X answered.

"No. We found the food stash from the *Osprey*." Slayer backed away from the opening. "This is the sound of me chewing. Tell everyone to get ready for a feast."

TWENTY-TWO

Layla waited in a cell on the prison rig, sick with worry. She sat on the concrete slab that served as a bed, waiting to learn the fate of her husband.

The Cazador guards had brought her here hours ago. She wasn't sure what time it was, but it had to be morning soon. There would be no indication of that here. This rig was outside the light, cloaked in storms and perpetual darkness.

As time crawled by, she tried not to worry about Bray, trusting that Victor would take care of the child.

Footsteps approached. She went to the bars. But the man approaching wasn't a guard.

It was Charmer.

"It's time," he said. "The jurors have been deliberating for the past few hours and have now made their individual decisions."

Layla felt her heart skip. "What... what did they decide?"

"I don't know, but I am allowing you to be there when they announce it—as long as you promise to behave yourself."

Layla glared at Charmer, who was talking to her as if to a toddler.

"Can you do that?" he asked.

She managed a nod.

"Excellent."

He motioned, and a guard came and unlocked the gate. She followed them up a stairwell to the top of the rig.

The makeshift courtroom was dark when they arrived. The lights were turned back on, and the only person inside was her husband. He sat in a chair, looking more exhausted than she had seen him in a long time. Seeing her, he perked up and stood as best he could in his shackles.

Layla felt the guard's hands on her shoulders.

"Stay put, Michael," Charmer said. "The jury has reached a verdict. Before we hear it, I wanted to bring your wife to you. No matter what the decision, it would benefit you both to remember that justice will be served."

"If he is set free," Layla said.

"Perhaps, or if he is found guilty." Charmer raised a brow. "You promised to behave, but I see I need to be clearer. If the latter happens, you and any allies will refrain from violence and accept this outcome, or you put yourselves at risk."

"If you kill my husband—"

"Then you will accept it, Layla, as hard as it may be, for the sake of our son and our friends," Michael said.

Layla gaped at her husband.

"You must accept whatever happens," he repeated. "For Bray."

"Shall we bring in the jurors?" Charmer asked.

Layla felt her stomach churning as if she was going to be sick. This was it. After over a week of waiting, they were about to announce his fate.

Martino waddled into the room. Next came Salamander and the scribe Ensio. Finally, Donovan and Bailey entered.

Bailey's averted eyes told her everything she needed to know. The former resident of the *Hive* was going to vote guilty. She had no reason to suppose the others would vote differently.

"Thank you again for your time," Charmer said. "In a moment, you will each announce your decision of guilt or innocence. It will take a majority to convict or free Michael."

Layla looked to her husband. He nodded slightly, as if to say it would be okay.

"We will start with Martino," Charmer said. "Please stand."

With an effort, the well-fed Cazador businessman rose up, using a cane to steady himself.

"How do you find the defendant?" Charmer asked.

"I find Michael not guilty," Martino said.

Layla let out a breath of relief.

"Salamander," Charmer said next.

"Guilty, guilty," said the retired soldier before he even got to his feet.

"Okay," Charmer said. "Ensio, what's your decision?"

The scribe stood, looked at Michael, and even looked at Layla before announcing his decision. "Not guilty," he said.

Salamander threw up a hand and cursed.

"*Silencio, por favor*," Charmer said. He nodded to Bailey next.

When the man avoided her gaze, Layla knew better than to hope.

"Guilty," Bailey said after a short pause.

Tied, two against two. Michael's fate was down to Donovan, a man he personally had rescued from the machines at Mount Kilimanjaro.

Please, please… please, Layla thought.

"Donovan, your decision?" Charmer said.

The sky person looked at Charmer, then at Michael.

"You saved me, and my family," Donovan said.

"The decision only," Charmer said. "Guilty, or not guilty?"

"I'm sorry, Michael, Layla," Donovan said.

Layla clutched her chest.

"Guilty," Donovan said.

Charmer nodded and faced Michael. "You have been found guilty of murdering Oliver and Nez. Thus, King Rolo sentences you to death. You will be executed at a time and place of his choosing."

The announcement sent a hot flash through Layla. She felt a quivering in her knees and an urge to scream out.

Michael looked over at her, eyes wide with concern.

Charmer gestured for the guards. "Take him away," he said.

Layla started over to Michael, but a soldier grabbed her.

"Tell Bray I love him!" Michael shouted.

Everything happened so fast, she lost complete control. Layla spun out of the guard's grip. He flailed for her as two others grabbed Michael to escort him out.

Layla smacked the man's arm away and rushed toward her husband. The room seemed to slow around her. She could see Charmer saying something, but it came out in a low, slow, robotic tone.

Another guard rushed into the room as Michael bucked the first two off, knocking them into the chairs.

Someone grabbed Layla and pulled her to the floor.

She watched Michael's fist slam into a guard's jaw. Teeth flew in a spray of spit and blood.

"I will kill you all!" he screamed.

She heard a loud metallic snap, and the cuff around his robotic arm snapped off. He swung his freed prosthetic arm, clotheslining a guard who had just gotten up. The guard bounced off the wall and didn't get up.

Two more guards burst through the open door.

"Michael!" Layla shouted.

He turned just as one of the men swiped at him with a knife. Robotic fingers caught the guy by the throat and flung him away like a rag doll.

The fourth soldier thrust a cutlass at Michael, who deflected the blow with his bionic arm. He then threw an uppercut under the soldier's chin, lifting him off the floor and sending him to slumberland.

Layla felt the cold steel of a gun against her temple.

"Stop, or your wife dies!" Charmer yelled.

Michael whirled toward them.

"Do you want your boy to be an orphan?" Charmer called out.

"Let her go!" Michael shouted.

"Then stop resisting!"

Layla scanned the room, searching for a way out of this. She could maybe duck under the gun and surprise Charmer. She had mere seconds to make a decision.

Shouts and the pounding of boots outside echoed into the room. One of the guards Michael had injured was starting to get up, knife in hand.

"Michael," she mouthed.

He stood there, fists clenched. Courageous and strong—the man she had known since he was just a boy in a tinfoil hat.

"I'm sorry, Layla," he said.

She watched as all the fight left him. His hands fell to his sides. The circling soldiers waited as Jamal motioned them back. He strode up behind Michael with a hatchet in his hand.

"No!" Layla shouted.

Jamal raised the weapon and slammed the flat of the blade against Michael's head. He fell unconscious to the floor.

Charmer grabbed Layla, keeping the gun to her head.

"Relax," he said. "It will all be over soon."

And then Michael was gone, dragged out of the room by his ankle shackles. The hatch shut with a loud clank.

Layla sank to her knees in front of Charmer. He put the Uzi back in his tunic and let out a long sigh.

"He made the right decision," he said. "You will be spared, and so will your son. I'm a man of my word."

She glanced up at the jury, crowded behind the chairs at the other end of the room. They all looked shocked except for the grinning Salamander.

"Take her home," Charmer said.

Moments after Michael was taken away, a guard who had stayed behind hauled Layla up to her feet.

She walked down the stairs to the docks. With each step, her breaking heart thumped harder. And with each step, she felt the dread leaking out of her. Replacing it and filling the void was anger.

This wasn't over. Now was the time to plan—and, soon, to fight. When she got home, she would find a way to get a message to Pedro. Then they would come here and break Michael out, and they would leave the islands with their son. There were plenty of places they could go to survive. Places like the bunker in Rio de Janeiro, where Pedro and his people once survived for over two centuries.

Living in darkness was better than death, as long as they were a family.

The guard loaded Layla back onto the runabout that had brought her. She slumped against the stern while the guard fired up the engine.

As the boat pulled away into the rain, she looked at the tower where Michael was being held. Lightning split the sky, illuminating the top of the rig.

Layla peered at the beetle shape above the tower. The airship *Vanguard* hovered below the clouds. Michael wasn't being held in the tower after all—he was being held on the airship. Good to know.

Layla felt the hint of a smile forming on her face. They assumed no one could get to him there. Bad assumption.

It was Charmer's first mistake, and he would never recover from it.

* * * * *

The *Frog* pushed through the canal, heading north. X stood in the CIC, marveling at the feat of engineering it had taken to carve out and widen this artery connecting the two oceans. Humans had once been great creators. But damned if they weren't even better destroyers!

Maybe X had that in his DNA, because he had inflicted more than his fair share of destruction during wars to save his people. And he would do it again if it meant keeping his loved ones alive. He would hunt men like Rolo to the farthest corners of the wastes until his last breath.

He looked out over the rubble lining the waterway and the distant ruined city. Miles sat by his side, chewing on a stick of jerky they had recovered, oblivious to anything else.

The dog was happy, and X was too. Finally, they had a win, thanks to Yejun.

X planned to talk to him soon—not just about what had happened but also to thank him. If not for the lad, the crew would be in dire shape.

The teenager was waiting inside the war room, but X was waiting for Magnolia before going to visit him. She was one of the very few people Yejun seemed to trust.

She arrived a few minutes later. Her thinning hair with its cobalt-blue forelock was still wet from the decon shower, a bright strand hanging across one cheek. With bloodshot eyes, she searched the room.

She had always had pale skin, but at first glance, X felt as if he were looking at a ghost. That was what losing someone so close to you could do. He had stood in her shoes many times.

X went over and enveloped her in a hug. "There will be a time to mourn," he said. "Right now, though, we have to save our home. Let's go talk to Yejun."

They walked to the door, where Miles sat down on his haunches to finish off his treat. X opened it to find Yejun sitting at the table and Lieutenant Slayer standing guard.

Yejun shot up from the chair.

"Relax—we just want to talk to you," X said into his wrist computer. The device translated, but that didn't seem to calm the youngster.

Magnolia tried. "I'm sorry to hold you here, but we couldn't leave you behind."

Yejun shook his head, talking fast. The device translated his angry words.

"I wanted to stay there, on my ship, my home."

"Your ship is coming with us, and you are, too," X said.

Yejun's distrustful eyes narrowed at X, then went back to Magnolia.

"We need you to tell us what happened after the vines, and if anyone survived," X said. "That's all. Then you can go home."

Slayer shifted, drawing Yejun's gaze. The boy was clearly nervous, blinking rapidly and shaking.

"Lieutenant, please leave us," X said.

"I'll be right outside," Slayer said.

After the door shut, X said to Yejun, "Were there any other survivors before you fled?"

Yejun ran a hand through his long, greasy hair.

"Please," X said.

"A group of soldiers," he said. "They ran when the vines came."

"Where did they go?"

"The other people killed them."

"The firewalkers?" Magnolia asked.

Yejun shook his head and pointed to the sky.

"Rolo," X said. "Slimy bastard."

The anger in his voice seemed to bother Yejun, who backed away slightly from the table.

"I'm sorry," X said. "You're safe with us."

He went through more questions, asking Yejun what had happened that day and growing angrier with each answer. Rolo had indeed landed and taken supplies from the outpost before returning to the islands.

After thirty minutes of asking Yejun everything he could think of, X pulled Magnolia aside. "Do you mind spending some time with him?" he asked. "See if you can get anything else out of him."

"Where are you going?" Magnolia asked.

"I have something I've gotta do."

X thanked Yejun and left.

Breathing in deeply, he tried to let his anger subside. Miles looked up at X, tail whipping.

X pulled a piece of jerky from his vest, bit off half, and tossed half to Miles. The dog caught it in midair.

"Yeah, good stuff, isn't it," X said, slowly feeling his energy return. His perpetual headache was still there, but the swelling had gone down. By the time he got back to the islands, his swollen eye would be open. That was good. He wanted to have binocular vision when he watched Rolo die for his crimes.

Soon.

But they weren't back to the islands yet, and when they got

there, they would face another massive fight. X had to plan their next moves carefully to have any shot at winning.

That meant avoiding another mutiny, preparing his troops, and coming up with a strategy to defeat the enemy.

Having the *Osprey* would certainly help. X was already coming up with a plan on how to use the ship when they got back to the Vanguard Islands. Whom to trust with this information, however, was another question. It was imperative he figure out if he could trust certain soldiers.

X went over to Two Skulls. "How's it looking, Captain?"

"We'll be in the Caribbean in three hours," he said.

"Keep me updated," X said.

He went to General Forge next. The man was looking over maps of the Vanguard Islands. X filled him in on what Yejun had said.

The unscarred side of the general's face turned red.

"He will pay, General, don't worry," X said. "Come, I'm going to eat with the troops. I've always believed breaking bread with another man—or woman, for that matter—is the second-best way to relate to them. The best being to fight beside them in battle."

"I agree, sir."

"Let's go see who I can still trust."

Miles trotted with them out of the CIC.

They went belowdecks to the mess hall, where the cook was preparing the crew's first real meal in a week.

So far, everyone had eaten just jerky and other snacks to get some calories and kick-start their digestive systems. Dr. Keller explained that easing back into it would keep them from getting sick. Soon, the cook would serve a stew that the doc said would be easy to digest.

Walking down the corridor to the mess hall, X heard laughter.

Morale was way up since they'd discovered Yejun and his cache of supplies.

Forge and X entered the mess hall side by side. Maybe fifty people were sitting at tables across the space, talking, laughing, and drinking. The scent of a salted potato stew wafted from the kitchen.

All over the room, conversations died. Everyone rose from their seat and saluted.

X stopped in front of everyone, flanked by Miles and Forge. For a moment, he debated sharing news of what Rolo had done to the Cazadores at the outpost, but he decided not to ruin this moment. Now was a time to celebrate.

"Who's ready to eat?" X boomed.

Shouts rang out all around, with glasses hoisted in the air. X realized that the soldiers and crew weren't drinking water. They were drinking ale and shine from Yejun's supplies.

X led Miles over to Gran Jefe. The big Cazador was sitting at the head of a table filled with six male Cazador soldiers. They had just sat back down, but hopped right up again as X approached.

"As you were," he said.

"As *qué*?" Gran Jefe asked.

X gestured for them to sit. They didn't.

"*You* sit," Gran Jefe said.

X moved to the other end of the table to take the chair opposite Gran Jefe. The burly Cazador still looked bad, with yellow bruises and cuts across his forehead and chin.

"You look like shit," X said. "But hey, so do I."

The men around the table looked at Gran Jefe, waiting for him to react. The Cazador warrior cracked a smile, then laughed.

Everyone at the table chuckled nervously.

Gran Jefe took a slug of his drink, then wiped his mouth.

"Big bug try to bash your brains in," he said. "Big monkey try to bash *my* brains in."

A bell rang, drawing all eyes to the kitchen. The three crew members commandeered by the cook put the first bowls of soup up in the window.

"Come and get it!" one of them yelled. "Line up, though—no stampeding, ya damned animals!"

X remained sitting while the rest of the table emptied, all but Gran Jefe. This was a perfect opportunity to get a read on him.

"We're lucky to be going home," X said.

"*Sí,* lucky for *la comida.*"

"Indeed, we need our strength." X scratched his beard and said, "When we get back, we're going to have the upper hand against our enemy, but we will be vastly outnumbered. We have to be united to defeat Rolo and the others."

Gran Jefe took another drink. "I said I fight," he said.

X looked into his eyes, trying to read him. Gran Jefe seemed to have been hiding something for a while. But exactly what, X did not know.

A soldier brought a bowl to Gran Jefe and one to X. Another brought mugs of ale.

X stared longingly at the foamy liquid. He could almost taste it. But the moment he did, he would lose control. And considering what awaited them, he couldn't afford to do that.

He lifted a spoonful of the steaming potato soup to his mouth, savoring that first bite.

All around him, men were shoving food into their mouths. The talking had quieted, replaced by slurping and contented sighs as the starving warriors scarfed down the first substantial food in a week.

X watched them, imagining how bad it might have been if they hadn't discovered Yejun's stash. There were few things in this world more dangerous than a starving man with a weapon.

As bellies filled and mugs emptied, the soldiers around the

table began to loosen up. Some of them looked at X with respect in their gaze. Others, like Nicolas and Sebastian, no doubt felt guilt for what they had done. But others still didn't seem to trust him.

X didn't blame them for that. After failing to find the Coral Castle and failing to see Captain Rolo's betrayal coming, he didn't quite trust himself. Maybe it was all the talk of X being an immortal. Maybe he had begun to believe it.

"*¡Un brindis!*" Gran Jefe exclaimed. The Cazador lifted his mug into the air, ale sloshing over the side. "*¡Viva el Rey Javier!* All hail King Xavier!" Gran Jefe shouted. "The Immortal!"

X picked up his mug, not wishing to show disrespect. Across the room, the ship's crew and warriors stood toasting a man whom many had wanted to see dead.

Perhaps some still did.

X couldn't help wondering if this was just Gran Jefe trying to regain his trust. But it also didn't matter. Gran Jefe knew the truth that there was no point in denying. X needed him.

He raised his mug up and nodded at the Cazador fighter.

"Fill your bellies; then rest," X said. "In a few days, we will once again draw our swords—one last time."

Shouts rang out, voices hungry for revenge.

Gran Jefe tipped back his mug and sucked down the contents, then dragged his wrist across his mouth. He stared at X, who had yet to take a drink.

X tilted his back and took a gulp. The ale went down smoother than he remembered. Laughing and shouts echoed across the room.

X felt revived, but he also felt a lingering dread. This moment was as fragile as life in the wastes. It could lead them to victory or end in death.

That wasn't the only threat. X could also slip back into the darkness of the bottle. He couldn't let that happen.

Sitting down, he pushed the mug away and pulled his bowl of soup back under his chin. But before he could begin, General Forge walked over.

"Sir," he said. "We need to go to the CIC."

X looked up, knowing it had to be an emergency. He excused himself with a nod and then tapped his thigh for Miles to follow him out of the mess hall.

"What's this about?" X asked when they were in the corridor.

"We've picked up a broadcast, but it doesn't make much sense."

X double-timed it back to the CIC with Miles and Forge.

A group had gathered around the comm station, where Tiger was leaning over a screen.

"What do you got?" X asked.

"A broadcast, sir," replied the corporal. "I'm working on it. Please stand by."

"Who from?"

"Vanguard Islands, we think…" After a few agonizing minutes, Tiger straightened in his chair. "Okay, let's try this."

He tapped a button and turned up the volume. A voice crackled from the speakers.

"To the subjects of the Sun Empire, this is King Rolo with the daily address. This morning, the jury reached a verdict in the murder trial of Michael Everhart."

X stepped closer to the comms station. The huddle broke to let him in.

"The former chief engineer, council member, and Hell Diver has been found guilty of murdering Oliver and his son, Nez," Rolo continued. "I have sentenced Michael to be executed in three days for this atrocious crime as my first act toward achieving a peaceful future. There is no room for violence in the Sun Empire. We are all children of the same home."

X stared at the radio, not wanting to believe his ears.

"How far from the islands are we?" X asked.

"Sir, several days, at best," said Tiger.

X had already known the answer. The realization filled him with a rush of something he didn't recognize. This wasn't anger or dread. This was fear. His worst fear.

There was nothing X could do to save Michael from the evil that had taken root back home.

TWENTY-THREE

Coughing from the back of the troop hold woke Kade from a deep sleep. His eyes adjusted to the sporadic flashes of lightning outside the cockpit. The Sea King rattled violently under storm clouds, passing over the ocean.

Kade had dozed off despite the turbulence, the noisy aircraft, and the fact that they were searching for the king. The Forerunner wanted to find the hostiles responsible for their current plight. Which meant he wanted the people responsible for the radiation now poisoning their home. Sitting in the chopper seemed like a betrayal because Kade was, in a way, helping the knights hunt the *Frog*. But this was a potential opportunity to help X and his people. This was his ticket back to them.

Whether it was a betrayal or not depended on what the Forerunner planned to do. Kade had spent the past day pondering the mysterious cyborg's intentions. Were they to engage in a conflict for food? Or to negotiate some sort of trading pact?

Only one person would tell Kade the truth...

He looked across the hold to Lucky. The knight was bent

over, vomiting into a bucket. For most of the flight, he had been clutching it in his lap.

Lucky glanced up with swollen red eyes, snot dripping into his mustache. He wiped it away, dragging a strand across his half-moon scar.

There was still a lot Kade didn't know about this man—how he'd gotten that scar, for instance. Maybe he could gain Lucky's trust enough to ask what *activating the Trident* meant. His gut told him it was a beacon that would notify the Forerunner when they found the king so that the knights would know his location. But maybe it was something more than that. Maybe it was a call to arms. And if so, was that a fight the knights and the Forerunner could win?

Back at the Coral Castle, Kade had seen ten more of the elite knights, and a handful of guards who seemed to be less for fighting and more for security. All in all, the forces were not nearly enough to mount an assault against the forces King X controlled on the *Frog* alone.

Moreover, this chopper wasn't exactly a war machine. It had a machine gun and some ammo, but not nearly enough to put up a fight against the *Frog*. The fuselage sounded as if it were coming apart at the seams, and he didn't exactly trust the ancient-looking batteries in the back either.

Still, if somehow Lucky and Bulldozer did have intentions beyond finding the king—perhaps even trying to reach the Vanguard Islands—then Kade would stop them. Even if that meant using violence.

He hated thinking about that, but damned if he would lead them to his home.

Lucky said something, but Kade couldn't make it out over the racket. "Can't hear you!" he yelled.

"How the hell did your people live up here for so long?" Lucky shouted back.

"It wasn't this bad. And you get used to it, mate."

"Like I could get used to being kicked in the yarbles!" Bulldozer yelled from the cockpit. "It's like being cramped inside a Tasmanian devil's pouch, but with lightning trying to fry us."

Kade unlatched his harness and started toward the cockpit.

"How much farther?" he asked Bulldozer.

"Not long. Maybe an hour to the southern entrance of the canal."

"Mind if I sit?"

Bulldozer shook his head. "Knock yourself out, Hell Diver."

Kade took the copilot's seat and fastened in. He searched the ocean on the horizon, using the flash of lightning to scan for land. So far, there was no sign of it.

King Xavier and the *Frog* were out there somewhere. Kade hoped they would find the ship before they made it home.

Home... That was what the Vanguard Islands were to him now.

Memories of the past billowed up in his mind like passing storm clouds. He knew how lucky he was to survive all that he had. But surviving without those you loved was a curse too.

A hand gripped the back of his shoulder and snapped him out of his daydream. Lucky looked as pale as a ghost.

"Something wrong?" Kade asked.

Lucky shook his head. "I don't think I got anything left in my guts."

"You should try and eat something," Bulldozer said.

He tilted the nose down into another patch of turbulence. Lucky held on to his seat as the pocket rattled the chopper. He heaved again into the bucket wedged between his feet.

"Don't chunder to death, mate," Bulldozer called back.

Lucky groaned.

They flew another thirty minutes before the knight staggered up into the cockpit.

"Better?" Kade asked.

"Yeah, I think I got it all out."

"Good. We're five minutes out from the remains of Fort Kobbe," Bulldozer said. "That's where this outpost is, right?"

Kade nodded.

"Anything else we should know before we get there?" Lucky asked.

"There are—or were—fifty Cazador soldiers stationed there, plus the same number of civilians."

"Do they have any antiaircraft weapons?" Lucky asked. "Anything that could take us out?"

"With a lucky shot, a rifle could take us out," Bulldozer said.

"Then you best keep clear of any sharpshooters."

"Aye, aye, sir." Bulldozer threw up a half-assed salute and muttered something about having carnal knowledge of a kangaroo.

Kade couldn't help but chuckle. The pilot was a weirdo for sure.

"Hold on," Bulldozer said.

The chopper picked up speed as they flew over the last stretch of ocean to Panama. Kade watched the horizon like a hawk until he finally saw the dark outline of land.

"There," he said.

Bulldozer curved west and began to pull up toward the clouds. Lightning sizzled across their flight path.

Kade searched the shoreline and quickly identified the broad maritime highway that ships had once used to transport goods around the world.

Lucky held up a pair of binoculars, bracing himself against the dashboard. "I don't see any vessels in the canal," he reported.

"Where's the outpost?" Bulldozer asked.

"There," Kade said. He pointed to what looked like bricks: the containers surrounding the base.

Lucky's binos went there. "Nothing moving that I can see," he said. "Circle a few times, but keep this altitude."

The pilot began to cut around the base for a second pass, then a third. Nothing moved except a few mutant palms in the breeze.

"Take us down a little lower," Lucky said.

Bulldozer descended toward the canal. The waterway was clear, and the outpost seemed unmanned. The gate was even open.

"They must have abandoned it," Kade said. "The king must have continued north…" He let his words trail off.

"To your home?" Lucky asked.

Kade hesitated.

"We know it's somewhere in the Caribbean; trust me on that," Lucky said.

The chopper hovered over the outpost, rotor wash whipping tents and equipment.

"Want me to put down?" Bulldozer asked.

"I'll go have a look," Kade offered.

"Negative, we keep going," Lucky said. "Our mission is to find the king, and Kade already told us that he continued up the canal."

Lucky leaned over Bulldozer. "We good on fuel?"

"For now. About a quarter tank left; then it's all the batteries."

"No, that's too risky," Lucky said.

"What do you mean?" Kade asked.

For a beat, it seemed Lucky didn't want to say. Then he went ahead. "This bird runs on mostly batteries but requires some petrol as well. We used up the tank that supplemented the batteries on the ride here. Now we gotta refuel."

Kade nodded as if he understood, but he wasn't sure how the setup worked. All he knew was they had switched it to hybrid power right before taking off.

"We'll put down in Colón to refuel the tank," Lucky said. "Then we keep looking for the king."

Over the next hour, the chopper flew just under the clouds.

It crossed over Gatún Lake, closing in on the northern stretch of the canal, and the Caribbean coast.

"Where we puttin' down?" Bulldozer asked.

"Let's find a place in Colón," Lucky said. Hunkered over the display panels, he brought up the digital map, pointing to a city. "How about here, on the piers?"

"Copy that," Bulldozer said after taking a glance.

He mumbled under his breath and flew the chopper over the ancient Gatún locks, made obsolete over two and a half centuries ago when the canal had been bored out to eight times its former volume. From this altitude, Kade could make out two canals running parallel. They connected with Limón Bay. Lightning illuminated the ragged skyline that had once been Colón.

"Croc shit on a stick!" Bulldozer shouted.

"What?" Lucky asked.

Kade peered out the cockpit windows at the ruined cityscape.

Bulldozer pointed downward. "Check that out!" he yelled.

A glowing sea creature the size of a warship swam beneath the surface, illuminating the dark bay waters.

"A leviathan," Kade said. "A pod of them attacked us on our journey to the Coral Castle."

"What is it?" Lucky asked.

"Cross between a giant squid and a whale, or something. I'm not sure."

"Keep way clear of it."

Bulldozer nodded. "Don't have to tell me, LT."

"Put us down over there," Lucky said, pointing toward a peninsula along the coast of the city. "Kade, get ready. I want to make this fast."

"Okay." Kade went to the back of the troop hold and put on his helmet. Lucky met him there, also donning his helmet and grabbing a rifle.

"I'll secure the area; you fill up the tank," he said.

"Got it, mate," Kade said.

He went to the secured tanks of gasoline. He loosened the harness around one of the canisters as the chopper lowered.

"Prepare for landing!" Bulldozer yelled.

The chopper set down with a jolt. Lucky opened the sliding troop hold door and hopped out. Kade hurried right behind him with the fuel and a funnel. They had put down on a pier that had once berthed large ships. Some of those ships were still moored here.

Kade looked out over the harbor, where shipwrecks protruded from the water like the bones of ancient beasts. Then he followed Lucky around to the gas tank.

Lucky stood guard while Kade unscrewed the cap, put the funnel inside, and started to pour. He watched Kade for a few moments, then stepped away to look out over the lighthouse.

"You know, this is where it happened, not far from here," Lucky said.

"Where what happened?"

Kade kept his eye on the funnel, making sure no fuel sloshed out as he tipped the canister down.

"The lighthouse over there is where the Cazadores from the Metal Islands lured my father," Lucky said.

Kade was so taken off guard, he wasn't sure what to say. Instead of replying, he searched the shoreline as he carefully filled the tank. It only took a few moments to identify the rusted tower that once guided ships in and out of the bay.

"I always wanted to see this place," Lucky said. "And I have always wanted to meet the barbarians who killed my father. They might be—"

Kade interrupted. "Those men are all gone, Lieutenant. The barbarians died with el Pulpo, the last king of the Metal Islands."

Lucky scoffed. "So what do you call your people, then?"

When Kade didn't respond, he laughed. "That's what I thought, Hell Diver." Lucky shook his head. "Your people dropped a goddamned nuke on the new king and his army of Cazadores. It's hard to bloody believe we could trust any of you."

It was no wonder Lucky felt the way he did. The sky people had poisoned his home, and the Cazadores had killed his father. If Kade were in his boots, he wouldn't like any of them either. But with all that said, Kade felt it was good to remind him of something.

"You trust me now, right?"

Lucky waited a beat before shrugging. "I trust you aren't going to slit my throat when I'm sleeping."

"Look," Kade said, "I know I'm at your mercy, but hopefully I have gained enough respect to ask you something."

"Ask away, but keep fueling."

Kade tipped the tank in the rest of the way to drain the rest of it.

"This Trident—it's a beacon, right?" Kade asked. "When you activate it, it'll send out a signal to the Coral Castle about the location of the king and the *Frog*?"

Apparently, Lucky didn't trust Kade enough to give an answer. He looked at the lighthouse, then walked away.

"If you came for a fight, I don't think you can win it," Kade called after him.

The knight kept walking, toward the lighthouse.

Kade sighed and set the empty canister on the ground. He hurried back into the troop hold to retrieve another canister. When he got back to the tank, he heard an alien cry over the wind.

Bulldozer hopped out of the chopper. "Crap," he said. "They got those things here too?"

"Sirens," Kade said.

"You think they saw us?"

Lucky ran back over.

"Did they see us?" Bulldozer asked again.

"Not sure, but we're not sticking around to find out," Lucky said. "Hurry it up, Hell Diver. And Bulldozer, get ready to fly."

The pilot got back into the chopper and shut the cockpit door.

Lucky aimed his rifle toward the noise coming from the heart of Colón. Ruined high-rises lined the skyline like the jagged teeth of the Cazadores who had eaten the knight's father.

Kade watched the sky as he poured in the fuel, some of it sloshing out of the funnel despite his best efforts. That was hard to do when he spotted a formation of the monsters. He counted twelve circling on the horizon.

Kade finished off the canister and went for another. By the time he got to the fifth one, the Sirens were starting to flap away from the city.

"Those bloody beasts are coming this way," Lucky said. "Bull-dozer, how we lookin' on fuel?"

"Got a half tank now if the gauge is right," he called back over the channel.

"That good?"

"Maybe. I don't know."

Lucky turned to Kade. "Do one more; then we're outa here."

Kade dropped the canister on the ground and ran back into the troop hold. He rushed back to the tank and started pouring. The Sirens were closing in, electronic voices screeching.

Lucky aimed at the leader. "Hurry," he hissed.

"I'm hurrying!" Kade replied.

The V formation of blind, screaming beasts dived toward the piers.

"Almost there," Kade said. "Almost—"

"Let's go. We got to get the hell out of here!" Bulldozer said over the channel.

The rotors swung overhead, the blades passing once, then twice. Kade finished off the last of the fuel canister. Then he followed Lucky back into the troop hold.

They went to close the door, but both fell back to the deck as Bulldozer lifted off. Kade fought his way up to a seat, grabbing on.

"Hold on to your biscuits!" Bulldozer yelled.

He banked hard to the left, pulling over a rusted ship's hull, then over the harbor. Lucky managed to get up and over to the door. He began to close it as one of the Sirens flapped right for the opening.

"Bulldozer!" Lucky shouted.

"I see it!"

The chopper pulled to the right, dipping almost on its side. They heard a thump, and fluid peppered the windshield.

Kade held on to the seat and watched the Siren gore drizzle down the windshield after its losing encounter with the blades.

Bulldozer let out a laugh.

"Got it!" he said. "Roadkill, or *rotor*kill!"

Kade went over to help Lucky shut the door. They were flying low over the water, with the other Sirens still pursuing them but falling behind.

"Look, it's one of those beasts," Bulldozer said calmly.

Kade and Lucky held on to grab handles and watched in awe as they passed over a single leviathan in Limón Bay. The glowing abomination burst through the surface as they passed overhead. Squid-like arms suddenly fired up at the chopper.

"Oh, bag o' dingo shit!" Bulldozer yelled.

The bird jerked hard again as Bulldozer got them higher. Lucky lost his grip and flailed toward the open door. In a swift move, Kade grabbed him and hauled him back into the chopper.

Lucky landed on the deck and heaved the door shut with a thud. He stayed there, looking out the porthole at the bay below. The limbs curled back into the water as Lucky pushed himself up and grabbed a handle for support. The glow of the monster vanished under the surface like a dying light bulb.

"That was too bloody close," Bulldozer said.

"Yeah," Lucky said, still panting. "I guess Kade here is seriously my guardian angel."

"Just returning a favor," Kade said.

"Storms, winged beasts, sea monsters the size of a ship—what's next?" Bulldozer said. "Oh, I know, we got to worry about getting blasted out of the sky by this crazy king, or getting blown up when we hit the Metal Islands."

He twisted in his seat. "I didn't sign up for this bullshit!"

"When we hit the Metal Islands?" Kade asked. "The hell does that mean?"

Bulldozer looked back to the cockpit, and Lucky said nothing.

"What's that mean?" Kade asked.

Realization came over him when he still didn't get a reply. How had he not seen this?

They weren't just searching for the king; they were searching for his home, which they already knew about because the Cazadores had killed Lucky's father.

If they found the king, the *Frog* might lead the knights right back to the Vanguard Islands. Kade slumped in his seat as they flew toward the Caribbean. He couldn't let that happen.

I won't let that happen.

He would have to make a decision sometime, perhaps very soon, on what to do if they did find the king and tried to follow him.

TWENTY-FOUR

Michael stood on the top of the prison rig, letting the rain wash off the blood caked to the back of his head. The cool water felt good on the aching wound.

He wasn't sure how much time had passed since a Cazador soldier knocked him unconscious. He wasn't even sure what had hit him, but it had enabled them to take his only weapon.

He looked down at his shoulder. Blood seeped from where his prosthetic arm had been removed when he was out.

His eyes shot back to the two Cazadores guarding him on the rooftop. Dressed in full armor and holding their cutlasses aggressively, they clearly would love to slash him down.

He would have taken them all on earlier—probably killed Charmer, too—but it would have been at the price of Layla's life. He couldn't let her die. He couldn't leave his son an orphan.

Overhead, he heard the turbofans slow, lowering the airship to take him into the sky one last time to await his execution.

He felt like screaming, but he would be just a voice in the void, with no one to hear him.

The verdict should never have been a shock. The trial had

been rigged against him all along. But part of him had clung to that thin wisp of hope that he might be spared.

That would have been the peaceful way back to his family. He had also tried violence, but it was too late for that. Now he had lost his last advantage: his arm.

He was nothing but a broken man on this rooftop, waiting to die.

Maybe he should just get it over with, go down right this moment. He could whirl around and take on both these soldiers. Rain sluiced off their black helmets and down their visors. Behind those glass plates, their eyes were no doubt watching Michael, hoping he would make a move.

The turbofans hummed louder as the airship descended. A rope with a harness dangled down, and one of the guards strapped Michael in and raised his hand.

The pulley system jerked Michael off the rig and into the storm. He looked down at the rig and the water surrounding it. The boats at the docks were long gone now. Layla would be back at their home, holding Bray. The sun would be up over the islands, spreading its bountiful golden glow over the last bastion of humanity.

The thought filled Michael with sorrow. He would probably never see that sun again, or his family. He hung there in the dark sky, his tears lost in the rain.

Two militia soldiers waited for him in the airship's cargo hold. They pulled him up and unbuckled his harness. From there, they led him down a passageway to the brig.

When they got there, Steve hopped up and grabbed the cell bars. "Chief," he said.

The master bladesmith didn't need to ask what the verdict was. The look on Michael's face and the missing arm left little doubt.

"Sons of bitches," Steve growled.

Michael kept his mouth shut. The guards locked the cell gate and left him alone with Steve.

"You okay?" he asked, looking at Michael's shoulder. "Your head…"

"It's nothing."

Steve gestured for Michael to lean down. "Nothing, my ass. You need stitches." He looked out the bars, left and right. "It ain't over, Chief," he said. "I got a plan."

"Not if it involves you dying for me," Michael said.

"I'm old. I've lived a long life. Dying to set you free and kill Charmer would be a nice touch."

Michael smiled at his old friend. They didn't come more loyal than this.

"So you want to hear my idea, or what?" Steve asked.

"It's over," Michael said. "Without my arm, I can't fight."

"You don't need your arm for my idea, so you want to hear it or not?"

"Indeed, I do," came a familiar silky voice.

Steve groaned as Charmer appeared in the passageway.

"Am I interrupting?" Charmer asked.

Neither prisoner responded.

"You're not going to tell me your idea?" Charmer asked.

"I am, actually, because it's for you," Steve said.

"Interesting." Charmer stopped in front of the gate. "Enlighten me, then."

Michael looked over at Steve, wondering what he had up his sleeve.

"The seeds Rolo brought back from the Hell Diver mission," Steve said. "They're a good start to keeping the population fed here."

"A solution to our problems."

"And you see, that's where you got it all wrong."

Charmer's grin hardened. "Speak, then," he said.

"The solution isn't food, because the storms will continue to ravage these rigs," Steve said. "I've seen it over all my years here. El Pulpo knew it. That's why he tried to find alternative sources and expand like King Xavier. While X never resorted to cannibalism, King Rolo might have to."

"That will never happen."

"No? What happens when the next crop is wiped out?"

"It won't be."

"Bullshit. You know it will happen again and again."

"What, pray tell, is your solution? To fix the skies?"

"Well, since we seem to be going all Shakespearean now, why, *yes, sirrah, verily.*"

Charmer chuckled. "You're old and crazy, but smart. Now, Michael, I'm here—"

"Old, not crazy," Steve said. "I'm talking about the weather modification units. If you're going to kill Michael, why not send him to turn them on? I'll go with him. We might die, but it'll give us a shot at restoring the weather across the globe."

Charmer eyed Steve, then Michael. "Tempting offer, but we can't let you have the airship," he said. "And letting Michael go free would set what kind of example for other murderers?"

"How can you use that word on me?" Michael asked. "We know you killed your friend and his son to frame me, and we know what Rolo did to King Xavier and the Vanguard army."

Charmer smirked. "You can't prove a thing."

"It doesn't matter what I can prove. You know what I say is true." Michael shook his head.

"If you knew the struggles my people went through, what I went through, you wouldn't judge me," Charmer snarled as he leaned in closer to the bars. "You saved us from hell, but we were already dead."

"Listen, no one will give a shit what Michael allegedly did if the storms go away," Steve said. "We don't need the airship either—just a boat with supplies."

Charmer seemed to consider the offer. "It's not a bad idea. If it were up to me, I'd let you take a crack at it. But it isn't up to me, and Michael must pay for his crimes."

"Let me save the islands like I saved your people," Michael said. "Please, give me a chance."

He didn't care that he was practically begging. If he was going to die, he wanted it to mean something, to help his family survive in an uncertain future.

"No one has to know. They can all think I died," Michael said. "I will never return. Layla doesn't even need to know."

Charmer studied Michael, and for a moment Michael saw what might be considered empathy. He had seen a flash of it right before the Cazadores threw Eevi into the water.

"I'm sorry, kid," Charmer said. "Everything that has happened to you and to your people is because of your king. Don't blame me. This is just business. And unfortunately, it means you have to die."

* * * * *

It had taken Magnolia two days at sea to muster the courage to go through the belongings she had recovered from Rodger's room. She sat cross-legged on her bunk on the *Frog*, staring at the wooden box and feeling the hum of the ship as it sailed closer toward home.

She held her breath and opened the lid.

Inside was a collection of hand-carved animals. She held the box up to the light to see the newest addition: a deer with antlers. There were also a barracuda, a rhino, and a giraffe.

She set the box down and took out the elephant that Rodger

had carved for her back at the Vanguard Islands. Closing her eyes, she thought back on good times she'd had with Rodger. She had never met anyone like him. He could make anyone laugh—sometimes inappropriately, like when they were in the wastes with danger besetting them on all sides.

But the more she thought about it, the more she saw how he had slipped away from her over the past year. Ever since he got injured by the skinwalkers in a blast that had ended his career as a Hell Diver.

The past few months especially, Rodger had joked less, laughed less, and slipped into darkness. Magnolia could now see with excruciating clarity all that she had ignored then. She had been occupied with the mission to expand to Panama and then beyond. She had become obsessed with finding the Coral Castle, in the process abandoning Rodger when he needed her most.

She tried to hold on to the good memories, but the guilt was too much. She had to find a way to live with it before she could look back upon their relationship with a happy heart. That wasn't going to happen anytime soon.

She reached for the tactical vest under her bunk. After dragging it out, she pulled out the sealed bag of Rodger's ashes. She set the bag inside the box, next to his bent glasses.

"Mags?"

Sofia walked down the aisle of bunk beds.

"You okay?" she asked.

Magnolia nodded.

"Good. Just remember…" Sofia pursed her lips, then changed the subject. "I heard there was a broadcast picked up from the Vanguard Islands. You know anything about that?"

"No, nothing, but I've been down here … Haven't talked to X for a while."

Magnolia bent down and tucked the box under her bunk.

Doing it made her light headed. The effects of the radiation poisoning lingered, but she had gained some of her strength back with the food from Yejun's trove.

"Let's go see if it's true," she said.

They didn't talk much as they walked down the dim passageways of the ship, some of which were still sealed off due to radiation. When they closed in on the CIC, Magnolia stopped.

"What?" Sofia asked.

"You hear something?" Magnolia asked.

It was faint, but they could hear shouting.

"Is that X?" Sofia asked.

This time, the two guards gave Magnolia no trouble and opened the hatch at once. Inside, officers stood at their stations, looking in the direction of the war room.

"That son of a bitch!" X shouted.

Pounding followed—sounds of fists hammering the hull.

Magnolia opened the hatch of the war room to find General Forge, Slayer, and Captain Two Skulls standing at a table. On the table were maps of the Vanguard Islands, a bottle of shine, and three glasses.

X had finally removed the bandage around his head. Sutures protruded from the shaved strip on his skull. The bruised flesh was purple fading to yellow and brown.

Miles nudged up against his leg, but not even he could calm X down.

The king turned his red face to Magnolia. Maybe he had been drinking. Maybe he was just really mad.

"It's all my fault," he spluttered. "My fault..."

"What?" she asked. "What's going on?"

X looked to Forge and nodded. The general leaned down to the tablet on the table and tapped the screen.

"Per decree of King Rolo, Michael Everhart will be hanged

from the capitol tower tomorrow morning for all to see," said the announcer. *"The future of the Sun Empire is a future of peace. This will end a violent history."*

"What! No... that can't be real," Magnolia said.

"It's all my fault," X repeated. A tear outlined the scar on his cheek. "They framed Michael for the death of Oliver and his boy," he said. "It's their way of removing the last opposition to King Rolo and his handler, Charmer."

"We will stop them," Magnolia said. She went over to him, but he pulled back.

"You don't get it, Mags. We can't."

She looked at the map and saw a red line that was their route. They weren't even halfway back from Panama to the Vanguard Islands. They wouldn't be there in time to save Michael.

Not only that, but the *Osprey* was far slower than the *Frog*. The carrier ship would take an extra day, if not longer, to reach the barrier of light and darkness.

"There has to be a way to save him," Magnolia said.

She had never seen the king in such distress. She felt it, too—a horrible, painful dread that seemed to be eating her from inside. She had lost the most important person in her world. And soon, X would lose Michael, the son he'd never had.

"Rolo, Charmer, and their allies have tried to destroy everything we've built," X said. "They will stop at nothing to take the islands for themselves, even if it meant killing two of their own—one just a child—and framing Michael for it."

X's voice shook.

"There's no way we will make it in time to help him, unless..." X said. His voice cracked and he cleared his throat. "I will send a radio transmission to Rolo and tell him if he spares Michael, I will never return to the islands. I will take Miles into the wastes, and no one will ever see us again."

"What?" Magnolia blurted. "X, you do that and they still might kill Michael, and we lose the element of surprise."

"It's a risk I'm willing to take."

Magnolia tried to pick her words carefully, then realized at this point it didn't matter. He needed truth right now, just as she had needed it back at Outpost Gateway.

"You can't save Michael this way," she said. "Just like I couldn't save Rodger. But we can save others. We can save our home. We have to make sure their deaths aren't in vain."

X glared at her. "I can save Michael."

"Not doing what you just proposed."

"She's right, King Xavier," Forge said. "You send that transmission, and they will be waiting for us with the airship when we arrive."

X leaned over the maps, scrutinizing them for an answer to their problems.

"We have food, we have soldiers, and you have regained the trust of our warriors," Forge said. "We must take this momentum and strike at Rolo and his people before they can prepare."

"I love Michael like a brother, and I know his heart," Magnolia said. "He would want us to take care of his family and not risk their lives to save him."

"His family and my son," Sofia said. "Rhino Jr. has been with Layla, and I fear what they will do."

X looked up from the maps to Sofia. He seemed to be attending to a distant memory, perhaps of General Rhino, the great warrior who had given his life for X.

He took in a deep breath, then shook his head wearily. "How did it come to this?" he whispered. "The greed of our species is a fucking cancer that just won't die."

"It might not die, but we can remove it," Magnolia said. "We owe that to children like Rhino Jr. and Bray, and all the people who died getting us this far."

"The element of surprise will allow us to crush our enemies without hurting innocents," Forge said. "We go in silently, and we can save families like Michael's and Sofia's."

X looked from face to face, stopping last on Magnolia.

"If I know Layla, she won't let them kill Michael," she said. "She'll try on her own, and maybe she'll find a way. There's hope."

"Or she too will die," X said. "I should have been there to protect them."

"And I should never have left Rodger." Magnolia swallowed hard.

She put a hand on his shoulder and thought of something that they both needed to hear right now.

"Accept your past without regret. Handle your present with confidence. Face your future without fear," she said. "Remember that motto from the fortune cookie that Michael got at the trading post in the *Hive* many years ago?"

X quickly nodded. "He gave it to me before a dive."

"Yes, and we all have used those words for strength when things got dark. Now is that time again. We must fight through the darkness."

For a fleeting moment, despair seemed to grip X. Then his features turned to steel and his eyes took fire. "Gather around, and let's talk about this final fight for our home."

Everyone crowded around the map.

"Go ahead, General," X said.

"The capitol tower is where they will have concentrated their forces," Forge said. "We arrive at night, sending assault rafts to the tower to off-load four fire teams. Meanwhile, the *Frog* will take out the airship with its front cannons."

"We're going to destroy the *Vanguard*?" Magnolia asked.

"If we have to," Forge said.

She shuddered at the thought of shooting down their former home. But if it had to be done, so be it.

"The *Osprey* will arrive here," Forge continued. He pointed to rig 15. "The ship will be used as a blockade to prevent any smaller boats from heading to the capitol tower in aid of Rolo. Everyone will be given a chance to surrender. If they choose to fight, we show zero mercy."

All nodded.

"Questions?" Forge asked.

Hearing none, he looked to King Xavier, who was scowling and scratching his beard.

"General Forge and Lieutenant Slayer will put together the fire teams," X said. "We have two more days to get battle ready. I want everyone fed, rested, and ready to fight."

"What about Gran Jefe?" Magnolia asked.

"What about him?" X asked.

"Do you trust him?"

"Does a turd trust an asshole?"

Magnolia snorted. "No."

"Does a turd *need* an asshole?" X asked.

"At times, I guess."

"There's your answer."

Magnolia was glad to hear X having a little fun.

"I will watch Jorge," Slayer said. "If he tries anything, I'll put an arrow through his heart."

X looked over the maps one more time, then nodded.

Everyone started out of the room, but X called out for Magnolia to stay.

X came around the table with Miles. Magnolia scratched the dog's head.

"If Michael dies…" X seemed unable to finish the thought.

"There's still hope," Magnolia said. But she knew that wasn't true. Michael had about as much hope of surviving as Rodger once had.

X glanced at the bottle of shine on the table. He wasn't the only one giving it longing looks. Magnolia had considered drowning her sorrows, but the hangover would be gruesome.

"Don't," Magnolia said. "We need the best of you in this fight." She grabbed X and embraced him. "We'll get through this," she whispered.

"They're really going to kill him?" X asked.

Magnolia pulled him tighter.

"If they do, we'll make them pay," she said.

"Oh, they're going to pay regardless," X said. He wiped a tear from his eye and transformed from a defeated man back into the warrior Magnolia had known all her life.

King Xavier stood taller, chest out, eyes filled with strength.

"We face our future without fear, together," Magnolia said. "I'm with you to the end, X, whatever it may be."

TWENTY-FIVE

At three in the morning, Layla made final preparations to save Michael. She'd had little time to plan, but she had managed to get a pigeon out to Pedro with a message.

They had planned to pack a boat full of supplies and sail away from the islands after rescuing Michael. But when she learned Michael was on the *Vanguard*, she thought, *Why sail away in a boat when you can steal an airship?*

It had everything they needed to survive. The old lifeboat had been their home, and it seemed fitting to take it from the ungrateful people they had brought here on it. The brazen plan to steal it back included bringing Bray—a massive risk, but she had no other option.

Her heart pounded at the thought of leaving without Rhino Jr. But Charmer and the Cazadores were holding the child somewhere in the capitol tower. She had considered trying to rescue the baby, but it was too risky.

All she could do was hope they would love him as much as she did.

With a sigh, she zipped up her padded black Hell Diver suit

and bent down to check her gear. On the floor of her apartment were the booster and parachute that would get her to the airship. Next to these, a tactical vest was stuffed full of flares, rope, carabiners, and the knife she had used on the Wave Runner soldier.

She moved to a backpack that contained everything she needed for the rest of her life. It had been odd filling the small pack, but items like clothing, jewelry, and valuables from the Old World had never been important to her. Now they meant nothing at all.

All that mattered were the few sentimental items: the pictures of her family; the *Twinkle, Twinkle Little Star* book; a fortune cookie saying, which Michael had given her long ago; and a few other small trinkets. These were the things they needed if they were going to survive in the darkness again.

But all she really needed was to be with Michael and Bray. She didn't care if she had to live in a cave for the rest of her life if it meant being together.

Victor came in from the kitchen.

"Layla," he whispered. She got up and went to the kitchen window, half expecting to see Pedro and Cecilia climbing through. When Victor got there, he pointed to the sky.

Layla looked up at the airship. It was moving into position for the execution. An image of Michael hanging from the rooftop flashed into her mind. She used that horrifying image to energize her in what she was about to do.

"Let's run through it again before Pedro arrives," Layla said. "I'll go up first using my booster. Once the altimeter shows I'm seven or eight hundred feet above the airship, I'll cut away the booster, deploy my chute, and pull one toggle to spiral gently down onto the airship and land. If I make it up, you follow with Bray and do the same thing."

Victor nodded sternly, but she could tell he was nervous,

having trained only a few hours with the greenhorns months ago. Layla was trying her best to keep it together. She desperately wanted to be the one to take Bray, but it was far too dangerous to take him up with her. She had to go first, make sure the way was safe.

"You sure I can do this?" Victor asked. "I only landed three times before I hurt my ankle and washed out of Hell Diver class."

"I'm sure." Layla smiled and held both his arms. "We only need to get this right once. You got it right three times."

Victor nodded, resigned. He stepped back from the window while Layla left to see Bray. He was sleeping peacefully when she poked her head into his room. She didn't want to disturb him, but she couldn't leave without saying goodbye.

This could be the last time she ever held her child.

She reached over the side of the crib and scooped him out.

"I'm sorry, my love," she said. "Soon, you have to be very brave and very quiet, okay?"

He rubbed at his eyes and let out a babble, something about apples and Da-da.

"I'm going to save Da-da," she said.

"Da-da," Bray mumbled.

Layla turned as the door opened.

"Pedro is here," Victor said.

Layla hugged Bray, kissed him on the forehead, and put him back in his bed. She gently shut the door and went to the kitchen. Inside, Pedro stood there dressed in all black, with booster packs and parachutes slung over both shoulders. He hauled more gear up on a rope and pulled it through the window.

"You weren't spotted?" Layla whispered. It was hard to imagine he could get all this gear up here without being noticed, but he shook his head.

If he had been seen, the guards would already have burst

inside. Two were out in the hallway, both sleeping the last time Layla checked.

Pedro began unloading his gear. "I got three parachutes and three boosters, just like you asked," he said.

"Three?" Layla asked him.

"I'm coming with you," he replied. "Michael saved me and my people; now my turn to save him."

Layla smiled again. "Thank you."

"Thank me when we free him."

Pedro pulled out a holstered pistol with a silencer attached. Then he took a second pistol from his bag. There were two magazines for each. Layla took the suppressed weapon, and Victor took the other.

"Let's hope we don't have to use these," she said.

Layla put on her tactical vest and then secured the booster over her back. Finally, she put on her backpack. She looked out the window. Luck was on their side tonight. Clouds blocked off the moon and stars.

"Remember, steer clear of the turbofans, and come up the hull on the opposite side of the ship. Those turbofans will..." She couldn't finish her sentence. The mere thought of what those whirring blades would do to them made her wince.

"I should climb up to the rooftop first," Pedro said. "I'll take over one of the searchlights so you aren't, how do you say . . . a sitting duck."

His idea wasn't bad, but it did put him at risk.

"Be very careful, and good luck," she said.

"You too."

Pedro uncoiled his rope.

Victor clasped his arm in a sign of respect. Slinging his crossbow across his chest, Pedro grabbed the windowsill and climbed back out. He looked down at the water, then up at the rooftop.

"I'll signal when I'm ready," he said. "Look for a quick up-and-down movement of the light. Same goes for you, Victor. Once Layla is up and ready, I will signal for you to launch with Bray."

Then Pedro was gone, scaling the building as Layla had done. She climbed out after him and looked down. There was no sign of patrol boats, but the searchlights overhead would be a problem. One lanced downward, then back up into the sky.

Scarcely daring to breathe, Layla watched Pedro climb. All the planning and preparation had kept her occupied up to this point. Now that the moment of action was on her, she felt her heart kick into a faster gear.

Pedro made good time up the side of the building. But all it would take was one casual glance, one person to see him and sound an alarm.

Layla took a quick inventory of her gear, as she always did before a diving mission. Her pistol was holstered on her duty belt, along with a KA-BAR knife in a sheath. All her pockets were zipped, and the booster and parachute were secure over her back. She checked Victor's rigging.

"You're all set," she said. "You got this, Victor; I know you do."

She pulled the black mask down over her face and checked on Pedro by looking up and out of the window. He was approaching the top of the roof. When he reached it, he coiled his rope around one leg, then clambered up over the side.

Layla pictured him belly-crawling through the crops up top. He would likely stash some of his gear there, then sneak over to the guard tower that had the searchlight.

The wait wasn't long, and she would have missed the light if she had blinked for more than a second.

The spear of light flickered up and down, just as Pedro had said.

"He made it," Layla said to Victor. "I'll see you and Bray soon."

Reaching over her back, she hit the booster. The canister fired and the balloon filled with helium, lifting her off the window and into the sky. She kicked away from the window to get some distance, seeing the beetle shape of the airship directly above.

"Hold on, Michael," she whispered. "I'm coming."

The balloon pulled her higher. In a minute, she would be at the top of the tower and in view of the guards. But at least she didn't have to worry about the searchlight hitting her. If one of the others somehow did, she hoped her black outfit would keep her from being spotted. She hated leaving so much to chance.

She searched the balconies along the tower as she rose. It sure beat climbing them one by one. Almost all the rooms were dark, but a candle burned in a gap between the curtains in Imulah's apartment.

The balloon pulled her higher, giving her a view of the old scribe, on his knees, his head bowed in what appeared to be prayer.

"Goodbye, Imulah," she whispered.

As if in answer, he looked up, stood, and went to the window. If he saw her, he made no indication.

Layla looked up at the rooftop as it approached. Cannons protruded off a platform almost directly above. Not far to the east was a .50-caliber machine-gun turret.

She trembled at the sight. Not because she had to get past the barrel unseen but because Victor had to with Bray. She suppressed any images of what would happen if one of those half-inch-thick bullets hit them. This wasn't dangerous; it was bloody insane.

And that's why it's going to work. No one would expect them to try something so batshit crazy.

The searchlight Pedro had commandeered raked across the sky to the west. Everything was going to plan.

She was fifty feet off the eastern edge, directly under the stern of the airship.

The machine-gun emplacement was farther away, just near enough that she could see the soldier looking over the sandbags to the water below.

She felt a stab of fear. What if this was a trap? What if they were waiting for her?

Stop being so paranoid. They had Michael in the airship for a reason. Charmer didn't think anyone could get to him there. Soon, he would understand his mistake.

Layla floated higher, holding her breath as she passed over the rooftop. She pulled out her suppressed pistol and pointed it at the soldier, who was still looking down over the sandbags. It would be a tough shot to make with a pistol while moving.

The soldier turned from the view and grabbed the machine gun.

No, no, no…

The shot would be easy for a machine gun with a full belt of ammo. It would turn her to pulp.

Layla moved her finger from the guard to the trigger.

She was about to squeeze when she heard a distant voice. It wasn't coming from the man with the machine gun. The balloon pulled her higher, above the orange grove that grew just beyond the machine-gun nest.

"*¡Hola, Yuca!*" shouted a voice.

Layla followed the voice to a silhouette of a person emerging from the orchard with a spear in one hand. He tossed an orange to the machine gunner.

"*Gracias,*" he called back.

Layla let out a sigh. Neither of these guys had seen her. The guard in the grove went back inside to watch for fruit thieves, and the machine gunner sat down to eat his orange.

She rose higher into the sky. One hundred feet above the

roof. Three hundred. At five hundred, she was comfortably out of sight. She holstered her pistol as she came up on the airship's port side.

Almost there…

The balloon pulled her above the hull, just feet away from the windows that were installed during the airship's restoration after the war with the Cazadores. Next, she passed the reinforced panels that protected against the storms.

Finally, she rose above the curved back, higher and higher, until she was about seven hundred feet above the airship *Vanguard*. She cut away the balloon, kicked her left heel against her right shin, and threw out her pilot chute. The low-porosity canopy shot out and pulled her up short. Pulling one toggle, she spiraled down and stepped onto the domed roof without making so much as a thump.

She went down on all fours and clambered over to a hatch. She decided to try it before pulling out her KA-BAR. To her surprise, it was unlocked. More good luck. *Take it when you can get it.*

Layla stood and waved down to Pedro, hoping he could see her. She could make out the twenty-foot watchtower he was on and the searchlight beaming away from it.

That light suddenly flitted. The signal.

Victor and Bray would be heading up now.

She waited a minute, then two.

In the darkness, it was almost impossible to see anything on the capitol rig below its rooftop. She pulled out her binoculars and focused on something she could see: the machine-gun nest sitting dark and motionless midway along the roof's edge.

Her heart jumped when she saw movement. Multiple guards were fanning out from the gardens to the three machine-gun nests and the two low searchlight towers.

"No, no! Shit!" Layla gasped.

She zoomed in on the soldiers, who seemed to be moving casually. No one was even running.

It was the shift change, she realized.

Jumping to her feet, she waved to Pedro, hoping he would see her and get out of there before the replacement soldier found the other gunner missing.

Shouting rose over the whir of the turbofans. Distant and faint, but several voices.

Torches suddenly lit up every hundred feet along the rooftop. In the glow, she saw frantic movement. One of the torches began to move toward the watchtower where Pedro was now manning the searchlight.

As she watched through the binos, Pedro climbed up onto the flat roof of the watchtower. He crouched there as a guard climbed up and looked inside the unmanned cabin.

More shouting followed.

The soldier left in a hurry.

Layla pointed the binos down to where Victor and Bray would be rising with the balloon. Along that eastern edge of the rooftop, the searchlight caught something in the air.

"No, oh God, no," Layla said.

Through the binos, she could see Bray secured against Victor's chest. The machine-gun nest was just above them. The soldier was gripping the weapon, ready to light them up.

Her mind raced to find a way to help. A distraction wouldn't work; it would just draw more eyes up here. Firing her pistol from this distance would be a waste of bullets, maybe... But it was all she could do.

She pulled out the pistol, aimed, and fired at the nest. She fired again, shot after shot, emptying the magazine. Victor's booster was almost up to the machine gun's field of fire. As the big fifty's barrel swung toward him, she lined up her final shot. She felt the trigger against her finger pad, but as she started to squeeze, the gunner slumped face first over the sandbags.

Layla dialed the binos in to find an arrow sticking out of the gunner's back—no doubt from Pedro's crossbow. When she searched the middle distance for Victor and Bray, they had risen halfway up to the airship.

She put the binos back on Pedro. Sure enough, he was still crouched atop the searchlight tower, loading another bolt into his crossbow.

Layla watched him a moment before again turning the binos back to her son and Victor. They were nearing the bottom of the airship now.

"Come on, please, please," she whispered.

All hell seemed to be unleashed on the rooftop below. Gunfire rang out, with shouting in the pauses.

She dialed in on the roof again and saw pinprick muzzle flashes in the darkness. Pedro had fired off another bolt and was hunched down again, reloading.

"Get out of there," she said. "Come on, Pedro, move!"

He put another bolt into the bow as the soldiers searched for his location.

Layla moved the binos back to Victor. He would soon pop up over the top of the airship with Bray.

Seeing them, she let out a cry of relief. The uneasiness returned as the booster took them higher, hundreds of feet above the airship. Then, abruptly, the booster lifted off them and they fell a hundred feet. And then, as if by some miracle, a parachute popped out above them, and they were gliding her way. Victor pulled his left toggle and corkscrewed down to the airship's dome roof. Six feet up, he flared as Layla had, and landed on his feet, though not as gracefully.

To Layla's surprise, Bray smiled. "Ma-ma," he said.

She kissed him on the head.

"Pedro's in trouble," Victor said.

"I know." Layla aimed her binos at the watchtower where she had last seen Pedro.

He was in the air now, the balloon pulling him up.

"He's on his way," she said.

Layla held the binos on Pedro. In a blink, the balloon vanished. Muzzle flashes from the forest told her what had happened to it.

Flailing, Pedro fell fifteen feet back to the rooftop. Flames from torches surrounded him as soldiers closed in.

"Pedro…" she whispered.

She zoomed in. He was still alive and trying to get up. A half-dozen soldiers moved in, beating him with fists and rifle butts. She flinched, feeling each blow.

"We have to keep moving before they figure out what he was doing," Victor said.

Layla forced her gaze away and led them back to the hatch she had opened earlier. Victor followed her down the ladder, Bray babbling on his chest.

The hatch closed overhead, sealing them inside the dark shaft of her old home. Soon, if she was lucky, this would be their sanctuary once more.

But first they had to take out the soldiers on the ship, and they had to do it without Pedro. He had given his life to get them this far.

Layla would make damned sure it was worth his sacrifice.

TWENTY-SIX

It was hard to believe that the lighthouse had ever been white. Kade had climbed to the blackened top of the California Lighthouse on the northwest tip of Aruba, looking for hostiles. He had a sprawling view of the Arashi Beach and Sasariwichi Dunes. The Sea King sat on the road below. Bulldozer was asleep inside, and Lucky was watching the chopper. They had landed here three hours ago after spending another twelve hours in the air doing a grid search for the *Frog*.

Each time they put down, danger lurked. It wasn't ideal, but they couldn't stay in the sky forever. The chopper needed maintenance, and Bulldozer needed sleep.

Kade, however, had rested plenty on the journey so far. He was wide awake and searching the dunes for any sign of hostiles. For now, he didn't see any, but there were monsters out there. There were always monsters.

That wasn't the only thing on his mind, of course. What Bulldozer had let slip back in Panama haunted Kade. They saw King Xavier as the enemy, and they would follow him back to the Vanguard Islands. The knights had a larger plan that they were hiding from him.

What if activating the Trident meant actually launching a weapon at the *Frog*? Or at the Vanguard Islands?

What if the chopper had a nuke that they planned to drop on his home?

Kade swallowed hard at that possibility.

No way, not possible. If this bird had a nuke, you'd know.

It was just another reason Kade had to stay vigilant and ready for anything.

He was more useful here, trying to stop a war, than sitting in a cell back at the Coral Castle. He would do whatever it took to keep his people safe.

Wind gusted against the lighthouse. He opened the door to the gallery that encircled the faded blue cupola, checking with a boot to see if it would hold his weight. The metal creaked, and a screw popped off and fell to the ground below.

Kade swore, tested his footing again, then cautiously started out on the wraparound platform, the wind whipping against his armor. He walked around the gallery, scanning the beaches, dunes, and ruins of resorts in the distance with his night-vision optics. Unlike in Panama, he didn't see any Sirens flapping across the sky.

It was oddly peaceful up here, but judging by the corroded batteries and stripped and blasted wires back inside the lighthouse, this hadn't always been the case. This lighthouse had been part of the Cazador empire under el Pulpo. It was one of many places the old cannibal's raiders had used to lure survivors and monsters alike.

People like Lucky's father.

Kade looked down at the chopper and noticed that Lucky was no longer in view. He walked all the way around the platform but didn't see the knight anywhere below.

As Kade went back inside the lighthouse, he heard the clomp of boots. Lucky emerged at the top of the stairs with a small wooden crate in his hand.

"You see anything up here?" he asked.

"Negative."

Lucky set the crate down, then bent down to the batteries and wires.

"Cazadores?" he asked.

"A long time ago," Kade said. "How much longer are we staying here?"

"Not long—just need to let Bulldozer catch a few more z's. Hunting for this ship of your king's is turning into a bloody nightmare."

"You mean hunting for my home?" Kade said.

"We're looking for your king," Lucky snapped back. "That's our mission—you heard the Forerunner. Bulldozer has got a few kangaroos loose in the top paddock—you've obviously seen that."

Kade wished he could see the knight's eyes through his helmet visor and gauge whether he was telling the truth. But his gut told him Bulldozer wasn't lying and that it was Lucky holding back the truth.

Lucky set the crate down with a thud. "I'm gonna try to get the radio signal booster up before we leave, to see if I can pick up anything from your king's ship." He turned away without another word.

Kade had even started to hope they could be allies, maybe even friends someday. But even after so many close scrapes together, Lucky still saw him as a prisoner and not much more.

The knight opened a portable satellite dish and unfolded the legs. Then he took out a control panel with a screen and knobs.

"Keep your eyes peeled while I try this out," Lucky said.

"A'ight," Kade replied.

He went outside with Lucky, who held the dish. He secured it to the railing around the cupola, then positioned the booster dish to the northeast. Next, he put on a headset that connected by wire to the control panel. Once everything was set up, he turned on the screen and started twisting knobs.

Walking around the platform, Kade scanned for threats. That was the most important thing right now: to stay alive so he could deal with whatever was going to happen later.

He checked the Sea King and spotted Bulldozer through a window, snoring away. Waves slapped against the shoreline in the distance. Kade couldn't help imagining what sorts of creatures were out there. He thought of the spawn back at the canal, and the cyclops monsters of the Sunshine Coast. Everywhere he traveled, different life-forms had adapted to their deadly environments.

The food chain out here was stacked high, and humans were nowhere near the top.

Kade went back inside the lighthouse after finishing his scans. "Got anything?" he asked.

Lucky shook his head. "Go down and wake Bulldozer up," he said. "We're leaving in thirty minutes."

Kade descended the stairs spiraling inside the ancient lighthouse. Red moss grew in some of the damp areas where water seeped in from cracks or broken windows.

At the bottom of the tower, vines wrapped around the exterior, snaking upward around the grimy gray concrete.

He trekked across the rocky terrain to the road, where the Sea King sat parked. With his hand on his holstered pistol, he searched the dunes on the other side. He was down to his last bullet, but it was better than nothing.

The waves slapped the beach, rising up over the sand and then receding. Seeing nothing, he walked around the chopper to the cockpit. He grabbed the lever and opened the door, but that didn't wake the pilot.

"Dozer," Kade said.

That didn't wake him either.

Kade rapped with his gloved knuckles on the window three times before Bulldozer jerked awake and reached for his pistol.

"Whoa, relax," Kade said. "It's just me."

"What's wrong? Are those winged freaks back?"

"No. Lucky told me to come wake you up."

"I just fell asleep, though." Bulldozer lifted his wrist and stared at the watch. He shot up. "Shit, I've been out three and a half hours? Where's Lucky?"

"Up there, using the dish."

Bulldozer glanced up at the tower. "Oh. Probably trying to contact the Fore…" Bulldozer didn't finish his sentence. He leaned forward and started to flip buttons.

Kade backed away and looked up at the circular deck atop the lighthouse, where Lucky was still fiddling with the dish. But now he had it pointed in the opposite direction, back the way they had come.

Of course. He's trying to contact the Forerunner. But why had Lucky lied to him about that?

"How much fuel we got left in the canisters?" Bulldozer asked.

Kade walked around the chopper to the left side, facing the beach dunes. He searched them again for trouble before opening the sliding hatch and climbing inside.

The inventory took him a few minutes. They still had nearly a quarter of their reserves.

Kade made his way up to the cockpit to report the number as Lucky came running around the chopper with the crate.

"I picked something up with the dish," he said.

"From who?" Kade asked, expecting it to be the Forerunner.

"Something about King Rolo and an order for the Sun Empire militia to be on high alert," Lucky said. "That mean anything to you?"

"*King* Rolo?" Kade asked.

"Who's that?" Bulldozer asked. "What's the Sun Empire?" They both looked to Kade.

"Rolo was the captain of my airship. He's the one who nuked the ship back at Brisbane, trying to kill King Xavier. But the Sun Empire? I've never heard of…"

"What?" Lucky said.

A memory surfaced of being on the bridge of the airship *Victory* with Captain Rolo before Kade dived to Mount Kilimanjaro all those years ago.

"Soon we will start a new life under the sun," Rolo had said. *"A new empire for humanity."*

"Empire of the Sun," Kade muttered. "Rolo must have got himself crowned king and has renamed the Vanguard Islands."

"So this Rolo is in charge now?" Bulldozer asked.

"I guess so."

"The guy that nuked your army? That's great, really bloody great," Lucky said. "Come on, let's get back in the air."

Kade knew this shouldn't have come as a huge shock to him. It was hard to stomach that he had once trusted his old captain. But those days were a lifetime ago, before the machines had robbed them of their humanity. Some of his friends had never gotten theirs back.

Kade strapped back into his seat. The chopper lifted off, leaving Aruba behind and flying over the dark Caribbean Sea as Kade pondered what to do when they found the *Frog*. Several hours passed, and at some point he must have dozed off, because a loud pop over his headset snapped him awake.

"I got something on radar," Bulldozer said. "Not one but *two* ships."

Kade looked down at the blips on the screen.

"See if you can get us a view, but stay in the cloud cover," Lucky said.

"You got it," Bulldozer said.

He lowered the helicopter through the clouds, and the ocean exploded into view, dark waves and whitecaps stretching to the horizon.

"There," Lucky said.

He pointed east at a long wake from a ship with containers stacked on the deck.

"That's a carrier ship," Bulldozer said.

"Yeah, but that isn't..." Lucky said. "Is that the—"

"The *Frog*," Kade said.

He smiled at the sight of the ship. X was still alive, and they had obviously found supplies, as well as the cargo ship in Panama.

"Get us back into clouds before they see us," Lucky said.

"Let me hail King Xavier," Kade said. "I can broker a conversation between him and your Forerunner."

"You will do no such thing," Lucky said.

Kade squirmed as the knight began to wrap a rope around him from behind.

"No! Stop!" he shouted.

"Hold still," Lucky said with a grunt. "Don't make this any harder on yourself."

"What are you doing!" Kade said, although it was clear he was being restrained. It was also clear that all hope of being allies with the knights was dwindling fast.

"I had to lie to you," Lucky said. "I don't like it, but orders are orders." He cinched the rope around Kade's waist and the chair, then bound his ankles to the front legs. "I'm sorry. I know you're a good man, not like the rest of your people."

Kade cursed himself for not trying to do something earlier. He had wasted one opportunity after another, hoping that Lucky would see reason, especially after Kade had saved his life so many times. But that didn't seem to matter to the knight.

Lucky went to a crate and popped the lid.

"What are you going to do?" Kade asked.

"I'm sending an encrypted transmission back to the Forerunner," he said. "We've finally found your king. Now we're going to follow him back to your home."

* * * * *

X knew he was dreaming. This was a memory from almost fifteen years ago. Or maybe not—he couldn't quite remember.

What he did remember were the steaming orange noodles he always bought from the noodle bar at the trading post on the *Hive*—Tin's favorite meal.

After a long day of training the newbie Hell Divers, X was glad to be heading back to his apartment with the food. Some of the trainees were already driving him nuts. Especially this Magnolia, or Mags, the conscript with an attitude, a wave of blue hair, and way too much eye shadow. He had no idea how he was going to keep her or any of the other greenhorns alive when the time came to dive again.

And it would come again. They always needed divers.

The curious eyes of passengers followed X as he walked the painted corridors of the *Hive* with his plate of food.

He slowed as he came up on the Wingman bar. Marv was wiping down the surface with a filthy rag. The lights flickered.

He sure needed a stiff drink right now, but that would have to wait. He had other responsibilities after the loss of his best friend, Aaron Everhart. The thought of how Aaron had died made X want to down a few mugs of shine. He wanted to block it out. He *needed* to block it out.

As X walked the empty corridor, recurring images of the ill-starred dive played through his mind like a familiar motion picture. It started in the launch tube, at the last second, when X had realized this was no green-zone dive.

Team Raptor had launched right into an electrical storm that the *Hive*'s ancient sensors had failed to detect. Maybe human error was in there too; X still wasn't certain. But one by one, the beacons of his team members went offline. Victims of the storm.

X made it through the strikes, exploding out of the storm above the skyline of a ruined metropolis. Aaron broke out of the clouds not long after.

For a moment, X had thought they both might make it to the surface.

"I can't see!" Aaron had screamed.

X had tried to guide his friend safely to the surface. Past the jagged tips of scrapers. But one of those sharp girders snagged his chute. The sound of Aaron's body hitting the concrete would stick in X's memory banks forever.

In a matter of minutes, Team Raptor had been eliminated. But X was still alive, and he had a job to finish. His mission would determine whether the *Hive* could stay in the sky.

The images continued to play through his mind. He pictured the first Siren nest, then the electronic wail of the beasts that haunted his dreams.

But it was what had happened at the very end of the dive that had seared itself into his memories. The ravenous creatures with the rubbery flesh and ropy, muscular bodies had chased him to the corpse of his friend.

X had been forced to launch into the clouds while the beasts disassembled Aaron's body in short order, dragging his limbs and trunk away to feed their young.

He lingered outside his apartment door, torn between going inside and marching right back to the Wingman. That dive had broken X. He was in no shape to raise a boy.

He opened the hatch to find Michael sitting on the torn carpet, wearing his tinfoil hat. He glanced up from a robotic vacuum cleaner in pieces.

"Don't worry, I'm fixing it for you," Michael said.

X held up the bag of food. "Hungry?"

The dream faded from his mind, replaced by a flood of other memories. The *Hive* flying away on the horizon while X hung from his helium balloon. Then finding Miles in a cryo-tube and being so lonely that he had broken his own rule of never opening a capsule. The dog had saved his life, helping him survive on the surface for a decade.

Those ten years were mostly just fragmented memories. Hiding from and fighting the abominations of the wastes: rock monsters, water snakes, giant bugs, Sirens. And then humans...

He remembered the bulky armored suits of the Cazadores who had taken him captive. And he could almost feel the pain of the cancer and radiation poisoning that had followed in the years after his escape.

Somehow, despite all odds, X and Miles had survived. Even more miraculously, they had managed to find Michael in Florida. Half-crazy, malnourished, and on the edge of giving up, X had been a broken man back then. Just as he had been a broken man after losing all of Team Raptor a decade before. And once again Michael had brought him back from the darkness. Taught him to live again. To love again.

X awoke from the dreams to find himself in a dark space. Miles slept beside him, deeply enough that X didn't even wake the old dog when he sat up.

Cold despair filled X as the confusion wore off and he remembered he was in his private cabin on the *Frog*. That despair metastasized through him when he also remembered what was about to happen. He snatched his wrist computer off the table. In a few hours, Michael would be dead, executed by the very people who were alive only because Michael had saved them.

X put the wrist computer down and tried the hatch. It was locked from the outside, on his orders.

"Don't let me out," he had said to Magnolia and General Forge. "I will be my own worst enemy and yours too. Don't let me close to the radio or a bottle of shine."

They both had agreed, and Magnolia said she wouldn't be far when the time came.

X paced in front of the hatch, drawing Miles's attention. The dog let out a whine.

No matter how hard he tried, X couldn't help but picture Michael being murdered. Morbid images clung like cobwebs in his mind.

Soon, Michael would join the ghosts of the countless people X had failed over the years. Divers like Michael's father and X's best friend, Aaron. People like Katrina, whom X had loved more than any other woman.

Rhino. Les. Arlo. Ada. Rodger... The list seemed to have no end.

Many had believed the prophecy that X was an immortal. Maybe he was, but whatever the case, his survival had become a curse. He continued to live while the people he loved were killed.

X closed his eyes and counted to ten, but it was no use. The anger erupted like an exploding can of gasoline. He rushed to the hatch, pounded on it.

"Let me out!" he shouted. He pounded the metal again with the bottom of his fist. "Mags!" he yelled. "Mags, let me out!"

His voice echoed over his pounding fist. He slammed his forearm against the hatch. Each blow sent a jolt of pain through his beaten and sore body.

"Shine! I need shine!" he shouted.

Oblivious to Miles's sad whining, he pictured Michael on his knees, a sword above his head in the grip of a Cazador executioner.

"Let me out!" he screamed.

X grabbed the handle and strained against it. When that didn't work, he slammed his head against the hull. Blood trickled down his forehead. He didn't care. He hit his head again.

Miles barked at him to stop, then howled as if to say, *I'm still alive—don't leave me!*

X fell to his knees in front of the hatch, sobbing. He wished for something to numb the pain. Something to take away the guilt and clear the horrific images of Michael's impending death.

It's your fault. You couldn't save him.

Again X slammed his head against the hatch, leaving a smear of blood. Miles latched onto his arm, pulling him back. The dog pulled harder, until X fell away from the door.

He went up on his knees, face to face with the wet muzzle of his best friend. Miles licked his face and whined.

And it all came crashing down on X. He put his arms around the animal and hugged him, listening to his pounding heart through his furry coat.

"I'm sorry," X groaned. "I'm so sorry, boy."

A knock came on the hatch, followed by a voice. "X, are you okay?"

It was Mags.

"Yeah," he grunted.

"I can't let you out," she said. "You know why. You told me to—"

"I know."

X let go of Miles and crawled over to the bed. The dog followed him and hopped up onto the mattress.

"I won't be far," Magnolia said. "We'll get through this. Remember what you said. We have to focus on those we can save."

X let out a sigh and fell back on the bed. His head pounded, and blood dripped down the side of his head onto the pillow. He was a wreck.

Miles lay against his side.

"We sure have been through a lot together, haven't we, boy?" X asked.

But none of those times compared to how helpless X felt now. Another morbid image of Michael made him wince.

"Fucking hell," X mumbled. He sat up and forced his eyes open. Closing them was worse.

Over the next hour, he was tortured with the images. He went from the bed, to pacing, to resisting the urge to smash his skull into the hatch.

As he stared at the drying spot of blood on the hatch, he heard footsteps outside. Several pairs, moving fast.

They stopped right outside the hatch.

"He said to keep it locked," Magnolia said.

"I know, but this is urgent," said General Forge.

The locking mechanism clicked, and the hatch creaked open. X stood looking at Magnolia, Slayer, and General Forge.

"Sir," Forge said. "I'm sorry to disturb you, but—"

"What is it?" X asked.

"We're picking up radio chatter at the Vanguard Islands— something about an attack on the rooftop of the capitol tower."

X narrowed his eyes and looked to Magnolia. His mind was muddled, but the report could mean one of only a few things.

"You thinkin' what I'm thinkin'?" X asked.

"Someone's trying to save Michael," Magnolia said.

"There's something else, King Xavier," said General Forge. "Captain Two Skulls has reported something on radar again."

"The airship *Vanguard*?"

"He doesn't think so, but one thing is certain: we're being followed."

TWENTY-SEVEN

Michael lay in his bunk, awaiting his fate. In a few hours, the new day would dawn at the Vanguard Islands. It would be his last sunrise.

Unable to sleep, he had stared at the bulkhead most of the night, remembering better days with Layla and Bray. He had given up the thought of breaking free or being saved. No one was coming to help him, and without his bionic arm, he wouldn't be much in a fight.

He wasn't the only one who couldn't sleep. Steve was sitting up at the end of his bed, looking out through the bars.

"You awake?" Steve asked.

"Yeah."

"I think something's going on."

"What do you mean?"

"I don't know, but the guards left."

Swiping the hair from his eyes, Michael walked over to the cell door. Steve was right; no one was posted in the corridor.

"Shift change?" Michael asked.

"No, that would have happened a while ago." Steve stroked his beard. "I think I heard yelling earlier. That's when I woke up."

"Yelling?"

"Shouts. I don't know. You didn't hear anything?"

"No."

Michael listened but heard only the usual ship sounds. When he was a kid, the soft noises at night had made him imagine a sleeping giant that lived beneath the decks.

He sat back down on his bunk, recalling those days.

Steve's head dropped in despair. Maybe he had thought someone was trying to save Michael.

"Promise me something," Michael said.

Steve looked up.

"When you get out of here, don't try and avenge me," Michael said. "Look after my family, and tell them I wasn't scared to die. Tell them we'll see each other again someday."

"Chief…"

"Promise me."

"Promise."

Michael lay back down on his bed, one hand under the back of his head. He recalled good times with Layla and Bray. Bray's first smile. His first laugh. First word, first hand wave, then clapping.

He would give anything for more time with his wife and child, and he counted himself lucky to have even had this much time with them. Far more time than most people had. His parents and so many other families from the *Hive* had lived their entire lives never once seeing sunshine.

He sat up at the sound of panicked voices. Steve got up to stand in front of the bars; Michael too.

Distant voices called out in both English and Spanish.

"Where?" one of them said.

"*¡Ataque!*" yelled another. "*¡Hay un ataque!*"

The voices drew closer, and metal clattered somewhere in the brig. Two masked men rushed over, holding swords. These weren't the militia soldiers who had brought Michael here. These were the Cazadores who had helped Charmer and Jamal murder Eevi.

One of them held two throwing knives in his hands.

He spoke in rapid, angry Spanish to his comrade and pointed a knife at Michael.

"What's he saying?" Michael asked.

Steve hesitated. "He says there is fighting on the rooftop and he should kill you right now."

The two guards continued their conversation outside the cell. The one with the knives seemed hell bent on executing Michael here and now, but the other guy didn't seem to agree.

"He says Charmer will gut them if they kill you now," Steve said. "And King Rolo will hang them both."

The man with the knives pushed the other Cazador away from the cell door. He tripped and fell on his back. The knife wielder waved a blade in his face.

Steve yelled something in Spanish, and the guy turned and shook the knife at Steve, screaming back.

Michael understood bits and pieces—something about killing them both.

The guard who had fallen on the deck got back up, still yelling, while his comrade took out a key to unlock the gate.

"Stay back," Steve said to Michael.

"This could be our chance," Michael whispered back.

The Cazador unlocked the gate and kicked it open. "¡Fuera!" he yelled. "Out!"

Steve moved in front of Michael, shouting back.

Michael came around Steve to fight them, but the other guard had turned toward the entrance to the brig. Reinforcements arrived—two people in black rushing through the dimly lit passage.

The soldier with the knives slashed at Steve, who jumped

back. But this warrior was fast. He thrust at Steve with his other knife, then elbowed him in the face, smashing his nose.

The older man went down hard on the deck.

Michael watched the soldier's rage-filled eyes as the two blades sliced the air. With little room to maneuver and only one arm to parry the knife thrusts, Michael backed away as the blades carved ever-closer arcs.

He felt the cell bars against his back. The Cazador had him now and knew it. Laughing, he cocked a tattooed arm for the fatal thrust.

This was it, then—the last moment of Michael's life. But it sure as hell beat hanging in front of everyone.

As the Cazador chuckled, toying with him, Michael did what the soldier probably least expected. He threw a forward elbow, unhinging his attacker's jaw and knocking the man backward.

He heard a thunk, and warm blood flecked his cheek. The big soldier fell onto Michael, knocking him to the deck, on his back. He tried to heave the dead weight off and noticed a rod sticking out the side of the knife wielder's head. Not a rod—an arrow.

Voices called out from the corridor. Indistinct shapes moving in the darkness. A tall, lean man in black holding a crossbow. And a shorter figure, also dressed in black.

Steve leaned down, holding his gushing nose, blocking Michael's view. He hauled the dead Cazador off Michael and helped him up. By the time they were both standing, the two people in black were standing over the other guard.

"No, no!" begged the soldier. He had his hands up, and the smaller masked figure held a pistol to his head. The mask came up.

And there, in the brig with him, was the smile he had fallen in love with years ago.

"Layla," he said.

"Not much time!" she said.

He stumbled out of the cell and around the living guard. That was when he heard a voice he had given up all hope of ever hearing again.

"Da-da."

Michael leaned over and kissed the small boy cradled against Victor's chest. "Bray," he repeated. "Oh my God, I can't believe it's you."

"We have to move!" Layla insisted.

She already had the surviving guard hog-tied and gagged. Steve dragged him to the cell and locked him in with the dead Cazador.

Layla handed Michael a suppressed pistol. She pulled another pistol out of Victor's vest. A crackling radio echoed from the cell.

"Grab that walkie-talkie," Layla said.

Steve reopened the gate and fished inside the pockets of the dead guard until he pulled out a bloodstained radio.

"See if you can pick up any enemy chatter on that," Layla said. "I'll be right back."

She went to the exit with her pistol as Victor bent down to reload his crossbow. Bray reached from the carrier, and Michael held one of the tiny hands, still not quite believing this was real.

A furious voice surged from the radio. Michael didn't recognize it at first, because he had never heard Charmer lose his cool composure.

Layla came back during the transmission.

"...One hostile in custody," Charmer said. "We believe he was going for the airship to rescue Michael. Guards have searched Layla's apartment, which is empty. All teams, be on the lookout for Layla, her son, and Victor."

"Who's the hostile?" Michael asked.

"It's Pedro," Layla said. "He was captured trying to get to the airship."

Michael swallowed hard at the thought of his friend dying for him.

"He wanted to free you," Victor said. "For what you did for his people."

Layla sighed, then motioned for them to follow. "The corridors are clear for now, but we have to hurry."

"What's the plan?" Michael asked.

"Head to the bridge," Layla said.

"Wait—what? We're not..."

"We're leaving," Layla said.

"Leaving... the islands?"

"I'll explain on the way. Come on."

"Wait," Steve said. He bent down and put his hand on the deck. "Do you feel that?"

"Feel what?" Michael asked.

"The airship... Shit, it's moving. They must be trying to land."

"Let's go," Layla said. She led the way out of the brig, clearing the corridor first. Victor went behind her with Bray on his back, still reaching out to Michael.

Michael couldn't hold back a smile, but he kept the pistol aimed down the hallway as they advanced.

"We can't let the ship put down on the rooftop," she said. "Pedro was our only defense down there."

"It's just you three?" Michael asked.

"Bold move," Steve said.

"We've been lucky," Layla said. "Most of us."

Michael thought again of Pedro, who had likely given his life for Layla, Bray, and Victor to get here. They couldn't let his sacrifice mean nothing.

"Hurry," Michael said.

He went ahead of Layla and the others. No one else was dying for him today.

He ran down the empty corridor. They were almost to the bridge, but they had only minutes before the ship put down.

Approaching the next intersection, he slowed to listen for footsteps. Layla was right behind him. They stopped and went to hand signals, just like old times during dives. Then they moved around the corner, clearing both sides.

Michael turned back to Victor and Steve. "Stay there," he said. "Layla, with me."

She followed him to the closed hatches and tried the keypad. The doors to the bridge hissed open, unlocked.

Michael aimed his pistol and went inside the white space. At the bottom of the two-level bridge, he saw Ensign Dmitri Vasilev and Lieutenant Olga Novak at the main controls.

"Down!" Layla shouted.

Michael dropped as an arrow whistled past his head. He lined up the sights on a militia soldier who had been waiting for them behind a desk. A bullet to the helmet ended the threat.

Layla fired two shots, taking out the other militia soldier who had been waiting to ambush them. They were the same two guards who had escorted Michael to the brig—both sky people.

"Raise the ship right now!" Layla shouted.

Pistol up, she made her way down the stairs dividing the bridge. Michael followed her while Victor entered the room with Bray, Steve right behind them.

He shut the door and locked it from the inside.

As Michael made his way down to the lower level, he saw the mirrored feeds from cameras on the monitors. The airship was hovering right above the rooftop, and the gate was lowering toward a dozen armed soldiers.

"Get this ship into the sky NOW!" Michael shouted.

Layla put her gun muzzle against Olga's head. "Do it."

When Olga didn't move, Layla murmured, "Nothing would

delight me more than to blow your feeble brain all over that monitor. So please, try me."

"Okay, okay! Relax!" Olga slowly reached down.

The airship jolted.

Michael looked at the monitor relaying the view from the bottom troop hold. It was maybe ten feet above the soldiers, who were armed to the teeth with spears, swords, and rifles.

"Pull up!" Michael shouted.

"Last chance to keep your brains inside your skull," Layla said through clenched teeth.

Olga throttled up on the turbofans, blasting the soldiers as the ship finally began to rise.

Michael was watching on the monitors with the live camera feed when a loud grunt came from behind him.

He whirled about to find Victor hunched over with an arrow sticking out of his belly. To his left stood the militia soldier Michael had shot in the head. Bizarrely, the bullet had penetrated the top of the guard's helmet, missed his skull, and exited through the back.

The man was on his feet and trying to load another bolt into his crossbow—so engrossed in the task that he didn't notice Steve until it was too late. He came up behind the man with a knife and traced it across his throat.

The guard slumped to the deck, holding the spurting wound. Victor was down on one knee, grimacing in pain. Bray reached out from the carrier, bawling.

"Layla, go!" Michael cried.

She bolted up the stairs while Michael moved the gun from Dmitri's face to Olga's.

"How many more people on this ship?" he asked.

"Only a few engineers and maintenance people," Olga said.

"How many?"

"I don't know, five, six…"

"And guards?"

Olga hesitated.

"Answer me!" Michael shouted.

"Four total."

"They left only four? I don't believe that." He turned to Steve. "Make sure that door is secure!"

"It is, Chief."

Layla got to Victor and unstrapped Bray from the carrier.

"Is he okay? Is he okay?" Victor kept asking.

She held Bray up, looking him over, then clutched him to her chest.

"Victor turned to take the arrow and protect your child," Steve said.

"Don't try to pull it out," Layla told Victor. "Just breathe. You're going to be okay."

Michael said, "Olga, open a comms channel to everyone on this ship."

She activated the PA system with a tap to a monitor. "Okay, go ahead," she said.

"To the guards and anyone else still on this ship, this is your one opportunity," Michael said. "Lay down your weapons and head to the cargo hold. We will let you off so you can return to the islands, but only if you go there now."

Michael backed slowly up the stairs, his nerves on fire. At the top, he took his eyes, but not his gun, off the officers to check on the others. Victor was gasping in pain and Layla was still comforting the child, who seemed unharmed.

"Hold the wound," Layla said to Victor. "We have to stop the bleeding."

"I got you, brother," Steve said, easing him into a more comfortable position.

The comms suddenly crackled with Charmer's enraged voice.

"Dmitri! Olga! What the hell are you doing? You were ordered to put the ship down on the rooftop!"

"Don't answer that!" Layla yelled to the officers.

The speakers in the room blared again. "Olga, Dmitri, do you copy?" Charmer said.

"The ship is no longer under their control," Michael said into the radio. "I will release the officers in exchange for Pedro."

There was a slight pause. Then a response crackled from the handheld.

"Michael—that's you, isn't it?" Charmer asked.

Michael had much that he wanted to say, but there was no time. "You have five minutes to get Pedro to the rooftop," he said. "We will lower a rope; you will secure him and send him up."

"Pedro isn't going anywhere, and if you try to escape, we will shoot you down."

Holding Bray, Layla went back down the stairs to Olga and Dmitri. "Keep pulling up," she said.

Michael could see the rooftop on the monitors. The soldiers there had their weapons aimed at the ship but held their fire.

"I will shoot you the fuck down! Don't test me!" Charmer screamed over the comms.

"And I will turn you into shark chum, and the capitol tower into an artificial reef," Layla said into a different radio. "Try me, you one-eyed fucking shit-weasel. I don't need an excuse to cleanse the earth of your sorry carcass."

There was no response.

Victor groaned as Steve put a cup of water to his lips.

"Is there someone in the med bay?" Michael asked the officers below.

Olga shook her head.

"Hang in there, Victor," Michael said. "Soon as we get out of here, we'll get you into the medical bay."

"What do we do about Pedro?" Layla asked Michael.

He took a moment to consider their options while she rocked their skittish child. On the monitors below, he saw an army waiting to kill them. But how could he just leave Pedro?

"Michael," Layla entreated.

An idea came to him. "Olga," Michael said. "Bring Timothy back online."

"I can't do that," she said.

"Try," Michael said.

"I don't know how."

"Okay, maybe Dmitri can and you are just worthless to us," Layla said. She aimed the gun at Olga's head.

"Okay, okay." The officer sat at a terminal and tapped the screen. After a few moments, she pressed a key and glanced up.

A familiar, polite voice surged from unseen speakers.

"Hello, my name is Timothy Pepper. How may I assist you?"

"Timothy, I need you to arm the missiles," Michael said.

"Ah, Chief Michael Everhart—"

"Pepper, do it fast, and target the capitol tower."

"Sir, may I ask why you are targeting—"

"Do it, now, Timothy!"

"Stand by, sir."

"Tell Charmer what you're doing," Michael said. "Tell him if he doesn't send Pedro up, we'll take out the tower."

Layla held the radio up, but before she could get off the transmission, the airship jolted hard, shaking the entire room.

Michael stared down at the monitors, which showed flashes of light sparking across the rooftop. The room jolted violently, nearly knocking Layla to the deck with Bray in her arms.

"Missiles are armed and pointed at the rooftop," Timothy announced.

The radio sparked to life with another message from Charmer.

"Lower the airship, or we will blow you out of the sky," he said. "Those first shots were a warning. There won't be another."

Layla looked back up to Michael for permission, it seemed, to turn the capitol tower into an artificial reef as she had threatened. But Michael couldn't give that order to kill the innocents there—people like Imulah, Pedro, and innumerable other friends.

Charmer had called their bluff.

A strong tremor rocked the ship from another impact. The lights flickered. They continued to rise away from the tower, but they wouldn't make it if Charmer made good on his threat. Even with the reinforced armor plates on the hull after the last retrofit, the airship could take only so many hits from the cannons.

Warning sensors flicked on across the bridge. Alarms blared, one announcing a water leak. He had to get the ship out of here before Charmer blew them out of the sky. He had seconds to make a decision. Looking at Layla and his son was all he needed.

Michael talked into the nearest radio. "Charmer, we have every piece of weaponry on this ship aimed at the capitol tower. If we go down, you go down. I've already given the order to Timothy to fire if you shoot so much as another arrow at us."

"You won't get away with this," Charmer seethed. "I will hunt you, and I will find you."

"Oh, you won't have to hunt me, because one day you will wake up, and there I'll be. I want to look in your eyes when I kill you, but if you'd prefer to die now, it'll be a lot quicker and won't hurt as much. Your choice, Polyphemus."

Michael switched off the radio. "Timothy, get us out of here," he said.

Timothy's hologram emerged. "Where to, sir?" he asked.

"Into the storms."

TWENTY-EIGHT

At midnight, the *Frog* pushed through the darkness, closing in on the Vanguard Islands. After three days of travel, the troop hold was full of eager warriors ready to fight for their home.

Magnolia sat on a plastic gear crate, sharpening one of her curved swords with a block.

Sofia was sitting beside her, head bowed. Tia and Edgar were standing and talking.

"You don't have to come with us," Edgar said.

"I want to. These are my people, and they tried to kill me," she said. "I want to be there when Charmer goes down."

Magnolia switched to a fine-grit hone. She didn't plan on using her blades on Charmer even if she got to him first. Everyone knew to leave that to X. Charmer's and Rolo's fates would be up to the true king.

Precombat sounds filled the long room.

Each soldier dealt with the final minutes of waiting in their own way. Some thought of a loved one, as Sofia was probably doing. Some prayed. Others joked nervously.

Slayer walked around to check on the troops, giving some

words of encouragement here, cinching down a strap there, checking suit integrity.

When he got over to the Hell Divers, he abruptly stiffened and saluted.

Everyone stopped whatever they were doing when General Forge walked into the room.

"All hail King Xavier!" he shouted.

"Just 'Xavier,' my friends, or better yet, just 'X.'" He entered the troop hold with Miles, but the dog wasn't wearing a combat suit, which told Magnolia he wasn't coming today.

She got up and studied the king.

For the first time this week, she saw the true X in front of her. His hair and beard, though unruly, were not too wild. The color had returned to his face, and he looked as though he had actually slept.

He strode forward in shiny armor and polished boots.

"The moment is upon us," X said. "We don't know what awaits us, but we do know there was an attack at the capitol tower several days ago. Since then, there has been complete radio silence. And whatever aircraft we detected on radar has long since vanished."

Magnolia was still curious about that, but maybe it was some sort of glitch with their equipment. Whatever the case, they were almost to the islands.

X walked in front of the troops and pulled out the hatchet that Steve had made for him before they headed to Panama.

"If we're lucky, that attack will have cut the cancer of Rolo and his minions out of the Vanguard Islands," X said. "But if it failed, then I will hack it out myself."

He paused to look at the faces around the cargo hold.

"This will be the last time I go to war," X said. "The last time

I lead men and women into battle and experience the horrors that we humans are capable of…"

He turned the blade over.

"But I promise you one thing. If today we have to fight, I will lead you to victory." He held the hatchet up higher. "Who is with me!"

Angry and excited voices rose throughout the troop hold. Magnolia didn't even recognize her own voice among them.

"Grab your weapons, and prepare to take back the Vanguard Islands!" Forge shouted.

Most of the soldiers moved over to the racks of rifles and spears, but Slayer gestured to Gran Jefe.

"Jorge," Slayer said.

Gran Jefe stepped away from the line. The hulking warrior had swapped out his Hell Diver gear for traditional Cazador armor. An axe with a curved blade hung over his back. On his duty belt, he wore a saw-toothed cutlass. But those were the only two weapons he was going to get. Slayer explained this to him in Spanish, and to Magnolia's surprise, Gran Jefe didn't curse or argue.

"I no need gun," he said with a laugh. "*They* need gun."

The giant walked away just as General Forge gave the order for the fire teams to move to the weather deck. He put on his red-feathered helmet and walked with King Xavier through the doors—repaired since the cyclopes had broken them open. Thirty-two warriors followed them outside into a light rain.

Lightning forked across the dark sky. If Magnolia didn't know better, this could be anywhere in the world. But the Vanguard Islands were mere miles away.

Not far behind, Magnolia could see the *Osprey* trailing off the *Frog*'s starboard quarter. She couldn't make out the twenty soldiers on the deck, all headed to oil rig 15 to take it from the other sky people.

Yejun had been moved back to the ship, where he would spend the attack locked away in his cabin for his own protection.

Shouting in Spanish rang out across the weather deck of the *Frog*. Forge barked orders to the soldiers, who marched in lines to the aft elevator. On it, four black assault rafts waited to ferry them to the capitol tower. The former Zodiacs had been found in storage on the *Immortal* supercarrier and transferred to the *Frog*.

Magnolia followed Edgar, Sofia, and Tia onto the elevator with the Cazadores and X. They would be in the first wave, tasked with taking out Charmer and any guards unwise enough to fight back.

Of course, they had the Wave Runners to deal with, but Gran Jefe had already assured King Xavier and General Forge that he would handle his cousin Jamal, their leader.

Magnolia wanted to believe him. She had fought with Gran Jefe long enough to know that he wasn't evil. He had saved her life on several occasions, and he had felt the loss of Arlo. She had to trust that he wouldn't betray them when the time came.

The real wild card was the airship *Vanguard*. It was the only real threat to the *Frog*, and Captain Two Skulls had been ordered to deal with it by any means necessary, even if that meant shooting down the airship.

"One mile out!" Forge shouted. "All teams move into position!"

The teams boarded their motorized inflatable assault rafts as the elevator clanked down toward the ocean. Miles stayed on the deck above, barking.

"It'll all be over soon, boy!" X called out. "See you in a few hours!"

He got into a raft with the Barracudas, which included Slayer, Blackburn, Gran Jefe, and four more soldiers. General Forge got into another boat with a fire team of six Cazadores, and Magnolia and her Hell Divers joined six Cazadores in yet another raft. A fourth raft was being boarded adjacent to them.

Memories of fighting el Pulpo and his cannibalistic warriors surfaced in her mind as she took a seat next to Sofia. But so much had changed since then. They each had lost their best friend and lover.

And yet, there was still life to be lived.

"We will find Rhino Jr., don't worry," Magnolia said. "He's going to be fine."

"I can't lose him. I should never have left him in the first place."

It was the first time Magnolia had heard Sofia show any regret. She had been firm in her belief that heading to Panama and Australia was the best thing for her son.

"Accept your past without regret," Magnolia said. "You'll be with him again soon. I promise you that."

"I'll be with you," Edgar said.

"Me too," Tia said.

Magnolia bowed her helmet with the other three divers, clacking them together in solidarity. She still didn't know Tia that well, but she had shown a lot of bravery since Brisbane and losing Kade.

The elevator lowered the rafts to the choppy water, and as soon as the deck submerged, all four craft headed out.

The boats fanned away from the stern of the *Frog* and spread out over the waves, leaving the warship behind for now. Only a handful of soldiers remained on the ship with the crew, with cannons and machine guns ready to fire. Soon it would begin its search for the airship *Vanguard*.

Magnolia feared what would happen to her former home.

The thought of it being blasted from the sky again was hard to stomach. But this was a fight for their home. They had to do whatever they could to save it.

The boat's twin engines roared, skipping it over the waves in the darkness. All four inflatables sped toward the invisible wall that separated the wastes from paradise. Behind them, the *Osprey* chugged along.

It was just after one in the morning when they caught the first lights from the distant rigs. Magnolia prepped her laser rifle and looked quickly back to see the *Frog* as it continued its hunt for the airship.

She watched X, standing casually in the bow. The next instant, he was gone. The boat had passed through the barrier of darkness into light. Magnolia's raft did the same a few moments later. She cursed when she saw an almost full moon glowing above them.

"There's a rig," Tia said. She pointed west, to a tower with three wind turbines churning lazily in the mild breeze.

Magnolia thought of Michael, who had overseen their construction to generate more energy for the islands.

The thought of losing Michael, on top of losing Rodger, made her broken heart ache. Yes, there was that ghost of a chance that Tin was still alive, but she had learned better than to hope.

She patted the pocket where she had placed Rodger's mangled glasses. *I'm sorry, Rodge. God, I'm so sorry...*

Seeing Sofia beside her reminded Magnolia that she had to keep strong for her friend. For the people who were still alive: Rhino Jr., Layla, Bray, X, Edgar...

The raft motored around another rig. Pinpricks of light outlined each level. This was a civilian tower that a thousand Cazadores called home.

Magnolia brought her rifle scope up and zoomed in. She raked the sights over the decks—only a few people were still awake on the various levels.

Lowering the weapon, she focused on the open water and the sky. They had yet to see the airship *Vanguard*, but if Magnolia had to guess, it would be hovering over the capitol tower.

She checked over her shoulder, searching for the *Frog*. That she couldn't see it in the moonlight was a good thing. She hoped that meant no one else could either.

Until it's too late for them…

Magnolia stared up at the rig. This was the largest of them all. Bridges connected the two towers of concrete and rusted steel. It was not so long ago that she had passed under the bridges on a small boat after she was captured by the Cazadores. She remembered those hostile, barbaric-looking people clacking their sharpened teeth and looking down at her as if she were an alien.

In the glow of torchlight, she saw guards with spears patrolling the bridges and the various decks. No one seemed to notice the boats, though. They gave the rig a wide berth as they passed.

"Almost there," Edgar said.

Magnolia studied the horizon until she saw the dome of the capitol tower. To her surprise, the airship wasn't hovering overhead. It wasn't mounted there either.

"What's that?" Tia asked.

"The capitol tower," Magnolia said.

"No, over there." Tia pointed to the left.

Magnolia followed her finger to a tiny dot moving across the water. It wasn't one of the other rafts.

She raised her rifle and zoomed in on a Jet Ski zipping toward them at full speed.

"Shit, we got company!" Magnolia shouted.

The other boats didn't seem to notice.

"X!" she yelled.

Slayer turned toward them from the king's boat. Magnolia pointed in the direction of the Jet Ski. The rider had eased off and was standing with a pair of night-vision goggles.

"Oh, no, you don't," Magnolia said.

The Cazador soldier lowered the glasses and began to turn his Jet Ski.

"Don't let him get away!" Edgar shouted.

"He's a Wave Runner," Gran Jefe yelled.

"Shoot that fucking Jet Ski!" Slayer ordered.

Gunfire immediately cracked from two different rafts. The hostile rider slumped off the idling Jet Ski.

Gran Jefe went to the edge of his boat, looking out as if he were in shock.

It struck Magnolia then: the Cazadores with X were going to have to kill other Cazadores—and they already had.

"Let's hope he didn't get a radio transmission off," Sofia said.

The boats kept motoring over the water, leaving the unmanned Jet Ski still idling in the water. Magnolia searched in all directions for other Wave Runners. Seeing none, she looked ahead, to the capitol tower. All the floors were lit up except for the rooftop.

She zoomed her night-vision goggles in on what looked like new construction. It was hard to see, but she could make out platforms protruding off the deck with sandbags and...

"Holy Siren shit," Magnolia whispered.

She located two cannon emplacements and two machine-gun nests. The scope wouldn't allow her to zoom in any farther, but there were surely more.

A geyser of water rose up twenty feet from the boat, showering them all. Again fire flashed from the rooftop, and she understood what was happening.

"Incoming!" Edgar shouted.

More cannons across the roof blazed, one by one. Shells burst under the water around the rafts, sending up more geysers into the sky.

"Faster! Faster!" Magnolia shouted. "Get under their artillery!"

The Cazador pilot needed no coaxing to open up and go at full throttle over the waves.

Magnolia aimed her rifle at the rooftop, but it was still too far away to bother wasting any shots. She slung the weapon and grabbed a handhold instead as the boat bounced along. More shells exploded as they closed in on the tower.

Bright-green tracer rounds arced away from machine-gun nests.

The boat carrying X curved away, right into a huge, foaming explosion in the water. Magnolia held her breath as the newly formed crater in the ocean slammed shut, sending up a pillar of water.

In the green view of her HUD, she made out the boat, and its occupants still miraculously on board. One Cazador hung over the side but was hauled back in.

Machine-gun fire forced her down, bullets whizzing right over their boat. She glanced up over the edge as screams rang out behind them. The other boat went up in the air, bodies cartwheeling in all directions. Magnolia stared for a horrified second.

Now that their stealth approach had been blown, the comms fired with a message from X. "Frog One, we're under heavy fire," X said. "Do you have eyes on the airship?"

"Negative."

"Fuck. Then head to the capitol tower. We need covering fire now!"

Magnolia kept low as the boat sped toward the objective. She pulled Tia down to the bottom of the raft.

"Stay down!" she shouted.

The Cazador pilot was doing a crackerjack job keeping them away from the machine-gun spray, but it was guesswork where the artillery would land.

Another shell burst somewhere in front of them, showering the craft with water. Magnolia looked up. The rooftop was within accurate firing range now. But her muzzle flash would give away their position again. The only thing to do was stay down and hope they could get to the marina without being blown up.

"*¡Miren!* Look!" shouted the Cazador on the motor.

He was pointing at more Jet Skis ahead. A dozen of the little speedsters were spreading out from the marina of the capitol tower.

Gran Jefe's voice came over the open channel. Magnolia listened, trying to pick up something useful but not getting much.

"What's he saying?" she asked Sofia.

"He's telling Jamal to stand down, to join us," she said.

Magnolia watched the riders approaching, hoping they would listen to Gran Jefe.

The response came in the form of bullets as every rider opened fire with small arms.

"Down!" Edgar yelled.

Magnolia ducked down with everyone else on the boat.

A gruff voice came over the channel in reply. It was Jamal, according to Sofia, who translated.

"He says he is general and for us to stand down," she said.

A scream came from behind Magnolia. She turned to find one of the Cazadores shot in the gut.

The other soldiers needed no further motivation to fire back. Magnolia sure as hell didn't. She aimed her rifle at a Jet Ski, then pulled the trigger. The laser bolt flashed a three-inch-wide tunnel through the rider, who splashed into the water as the Jet Ski skidded to a stop.

Magnolia searched for her next target, waiting for the boat to even out. When it steadied, she pulled the trigger. She only got off a few shots before she was suddenly rising up in the air with the boat somehow still under her.

She didn't know what had happened until she hit the water.

Another shell burst fifty yards away, sending another massive column of water into the sky. She flailed in the waves, her armor weighing her down. Machine-gun fire striped the ocean around them.

Magnolia kicked and struggled to stay above the waves. She slipped under, bullets whizzing around her. Reaching down, she shucked off her left boot, then the right.

It didn't help much, but at least she could kick now.

Breathing the oxygen supply from her helmet, she took another terrifying moment to pull off her chest armor. It was the second-heaviest thing. Losing it was tough, but it was no decision, really—either this or death.

Probably death, no matter what.

She broke through the surface, treading water and searching for the others from her boat. Two Cazadores had resurfaced, and Sofia was also treading water.

A round of bright explosions lit the rooftop. Debris rained down, along with a burning soldier, kicking as he fell.

Magnolia looked for Edgar and saw that he had surfaced with Tia. Behind them, a ship was moving across the water.

Fiery bursts from cannons and muzzle flashes from machines guns lit up the deck of a warship. Magnolia braced herself to be obliterated. But the shells and bullets screamed and zipped high overhead.

The weapons weren't aimed at the Hell Divers or Cazadores

fighting to stay above the water. They were aimed at the capitol tower.

"It's the *Frog*!" someone shouted.

She kicked around and watched explosions across the rooftop.

Still, they weren't safe yet.

They still had to swim to the marina, break inside the capitol tower, and take it back from forces that knew they were coming.

TWENTY-NINE

"We're almost there," Bulldozer said over the short-range comm channel.

"Be ready for anything," Lucky said.

With every mile that brought them closer to the Vanguard Islands, Kade's fury grew.

"You're an asshole, Gaz," he said. "You lied to me all this time."

Ignoring him, Lucky stared out the helicopter windshield.

They had spent the past day following the *Frog* and the container ship through the Caribbean. Bulldozer had kept the bird at a distance, keeping to the turbulent storm clouds to avoid being spotted. That made the last stretch of the journey rough, to a nauseating degree.

"I could help bring peace between our people," Kade said.

"Your people started a war," Lucky replied. "The only way there will be peace is if those responsible are dead. I swore an oath to the Trident, to protect the Coral Castle and all the souls living there, and that is exactly what I'm going to do."

Kade fell silent. There was nothing else he could do now. His actions that had saved Lucky multiple times were meaningless.

The knight was putting his people first, and for that, Kade couldn't blame him. He wanted to do the same thing.

Unfortunately, his actions were doing the exact opposite. He had put his people at risk by helping the Forerunner track down King Xavier. Soon, the Knights of the Coral Castle would know the location of the Vanguard Islands.

The chopper rattled and banged through a pocket of turbulence. Lightning flickered in the distance, the low roll of thunder lagging far behind.

Kade focused on his breathing, trying to keep calm. His mind went to Alton, Tia, the Hell Divers, and King Xavier. He had failed them all.

"Hold on, I'm taking us lower!" Bulldozer said over the comm channel.

The Sea King speared down through the shelf of clouds. Rain beat against the windshield while gusting wind buffeted the chopper this way and that. Kade willed his food to stay down. He would rather not taste that seaweed again.

Lightning broke into a thousand kinks of white light across their flight path. Lucky peeled back his helmet and reached for the bucket. He hurled into it as Bulldozer fought to keep them steady.

"Just don't miss!" the pilot shouted.

The wall of darkness seemed to lighten ahead of them.

Or maybe it was just Kade's eyes playing tricks on him?

He squinted at what appeared to be streaks of light dancing on the horizon.

The chopper cut through the final wall of black and flew under a brilliant moon. They glided through the last of the rain until there was none at all.

The last drops sluiced down the windshield.

Distant thunder faded away, leaving only the steady thump of the main rotor. Moonlight captured the dark bulk of oil rigs in the distance. But it wasn't just the bright light of the moon out there.

A mile to the east, orange explosions bloomed at the top of a rig. By its height, it had to be the capitol tower.

"There," Bulldozer said.

"Bloody hell," Lucky said, the bucket sloshing between his feet. "Get us higher on approach."

Bulldozer pulled up as they flew toward the battle.

Tracer rounds arced from the tower rooftop, and cannons blazed from multiple locations at targets on the water. One of those targets fired back.

Kade didn't need his night vision to see the *Frog*'s dark bulk silhouetted in the moonlight. The guns on the decks blasted the tower of concrete and steel.

"Bloody oath!" said Bulldozer. "This isn't a battle; it's all-out war!"

Hours earlier, when they'd found the *Frog* and the cargo ship again, Kade had seen soldiers gearing up on the weather decks. He had hoped they were about to ambush King Rolo.

But it seemed their surprise attack had gone horribly wrong.

The rooftop turrets continued to fire down on the water. Kade tried to see whatever they were shooting at, catching glimpses during the rocky ride. He made out Jet Skis dead in the water and two capsized rafts.

The chopper dipped lower, providing a clear view of the marina at the capitol tower. A third raft had made it to the dock, and Cazador soldiers from it were running up the piers with rifles blazing. People were flailing in the water. He could tell by the helmets, these weren't all Cazadores. One looked a lot like a Hell Diver.

The thought of Tia being down there made Kade fight against his restraints.

"Let me out!" he yelled. "I have to help!"

"Keep us clear of those cannons and machine guns," Lucky said.

Bulldozer pulled up, carving back into the sky.

"No, let me out!" Kade said. "My friends are being slaughtered down there!"

"What do you plan on doing?" Lucky said. "If they spot us, they could blow us out of the sky. Both sides will think we're the enemy."

"Then get me low enough to the ocean, and I'll jump, then swim—"

"Stop talking," Lucky said forcefully. "I won't let you throw away your life—ours either."

Kade worked his hands against the rope. He couldn't just sit here and do nothing.

"Incoming!" Bulldozer shouted.

The chopper banked hard to the left, pressing Kade against the window.

An arcing line of small round holes appeared in the side of the Sea King.

"Fuck me dead!" Bulldozer shouted. "We're hit! Shit, we're hit!"

"Get us out of here!" Lucky yelled back. "Go low if you have to!"

Out the port window, Kade saw tracer rounds streaking down at them from a machine-gun turret. The arcing line of projectiles ceased when a fireball on the tower rooftop swallowed up the machine-gun nest. Several smaller explosions puffed across the edge of the roof.

Lucky fell as he tried to move back into the troop hold. He got up and scrambled over to the same wooden crate he had lugged up the lighthouse back in Aruba. He opened it, pulled out a dish, and unfolded the legs.

The knight was going to activate the Trident.

To Kade's astonishment, he got his thumb knuckle out from

under the rope he'd been working at. A minute later, he had freed his left hand. For a fleeting moment, he was too surprised to do anything. Then he made short work of the rope binding on his right hand and went quietly to work on the ankles as Bulldozer flew them low over the water.

Now with his feet free, Kade sprang up and lunged straight for the cargo hold door as Lucky pulled something from his duty belt.

"Don't do it!" Lucky shouted.

Kade turned to find a pistol aimed at his head. The chopper roared upward.

"Hold on!" Bulldozer shouted. "I'm making a run for the clouds."

"We're getting out of here and activating the Trident," said Lucky, still crouched on the deck. "I'm sorry, Kade, but your people are savages. That is fucking clear!"

"Not all of them!"

"Really? 'Cause from where I sit, they look like a bunch of cavemen!" Bulldozer yelled.

In the cockpit, an alarm blared.

Lucky looked past Kade. "What is it?"

"We got a problem," Bulldozer replied. "I'm losing hydraulic fluid!"

The chopper whined and shook as the pilot fought to keep it on an even keel.

"I can't control..." Bulldozer grunted over the comm.

Lucky fought his way up to the seats and buckled in not a moment too soon before the chopper began to rotate clockwise. Kade tried to suppress the nausea as he hung on, muscles quivering from the effort.

Bulldozer was doing his level best to control the bird, but they were going down. "I'm gonna try to land on the tower!" he shouted.

Lucky looked back at Kade, who said nothing.

Moonlight streamed through the cockpit, illuminating their two very differently designed armored suits. In a flurry of muddled thoughts, Kade marveled at how they had come from different civilizations and were both just trying to survive in a world gone mad.

A view of the rooftop came into focus through the cockpit. Kade could make out trees and a field of crops below.

Bulldozer managed to slow the rotation just as the rooftop came leering up at them.

"Brace yourselves!" he shouted.

The trees reached up at struts that somehow just cleared them.

The Sea King burst over the edge of the orchard and smacked into the dirt with enough force that Kade lost his grip and slammed against the hull across from him. His helmet absorbed some of the impact, but it still hurt like hell.

Plants rose up and slapped against the cracked windshield. And on they slid, across the rooftop for several agonizing seconds.

Finally, the machine came to a stop.

More alarms blared, and something sparked under the dashboard. Tangled wires hung from the open overhead. Moonlight shone through the gaping holes from high-caliber rounds in the fuselage.

Kade flopped onto his stomach. He pushed himself up to his knees to find that Lucky was no longer in his seat.

Kade soon found him in the hold, where he had been tossed and now lay pinned beneath two heavy cargo crates. A touch to his neck confirmed he had a pulse.

"Kade," Lucky whispered.

"I'll be right back," Kade said. He went up on both knees and turned to the cockpit.

Bulldozer was slumped over the controls, not moving.

His helmet had smashed into the windshield. Blood spatter surrounded the cracked glass, which had pushed inward. Kade stumbled over to check the pilot.

He checked for a pulse. Nothing.

"Shit," he mumbled.

"Kade..." Lucky called out from the back of the wreckage.

Kade made his way through scattered supplies across the hold. There were muffled voices in the distance, and gunfire he could hear over the ringing in his ears.

He pulled out his revolver and pulled back the hammer. Then he staggered to the door and looked out at the rooftop.

"You have to help me," Lucky said. He reached out to Kade, then pulled his hand back with a whimper of pain.

Kade went aft. "How bad are you hurt?"

"I can't feel my legs," Lucky said. "I..."

Kade looked for blood but saw nothing. It sounded like a spinal injury. That meant moving him now, alone, was too dangerous.

"I'll come back for you," Kade said.

"No," Lucky groaned. He grabbed Kade's arm.

"I have to... have to activate the Trident," he said.

Kade looked at the crates, then back to the knight. He felt a trace of empathy for Lucky, but he wasn't going to help him activate the Trident; that was for damned sure.

"Please help me, mate. Please..."

Kade got up and banged open the side door.

"I've been risking my biscuit to help you," he said. "And you still treat me like a criminal. Well, from here on in, you dag-snapping mongrels are on your own. It's time for me to help my people and our king."

* * * * *

Two days after leaving home, the airship *Vanguard* cruised through storm clouds just above twenty thousand feet. Lightning flashed beyond the viewport, illuminating mounds of clouds that looked like dark ocean waves.

Layla had never thought she would be looking at this view again. It was a far cry from the sunshine and clear water of the Vanguard Islands.

She had traded the view to be with her family and didn't regret it one damned bit. Being with them was a gift.

"A gift, right, Bray?" she asked.

The child hung in the harness on her chest. He reached up and patted her chin.

Michael was belowdecks with Steve, fixing panels damaged during the escape from the capitol tower. They would soon know just how bad that damage was.

"Timothy, you there?" Layla asked.

Bray waved at the hologram of Timothy that emerged in front of them.

"Well, hello there, Bray," Timothy said. "And Layla Everhart, how are you?"

"That depends on the condition of the ship. How about a sitrep?"

Timothy blinked while digesting information for the report. She already knew most of what he explained. The ship had taken severe damage to sections 14 and 15, directly under the water-treatment plant, rupturing a pipe and causing it to leak over 20 percent of their water supply. The water had also caused a power outage. Steve and Michael were checking it out now.

Layla let out a sigh, which Bray mimicked.

"What else?" she asked.

"The damage to panels thirteen through eighteen and

eighty-five through ninety-one is severe," Timothy said. "I'm not sure they will protect us from a direct lightning strike."

He walked closer, waving to Bray.

The child laughed and raised a finger to point at the AI's hologram.

"The good news is, the damaged panels can be replaced, and with the proper wiring, Chief Everhart and Deputy Schwarzer should be able to get the plant back online. But of course, that means…"

"Diving," Layla said.

"I'm afraid so."

"Understood." She heaved a breath. "How about transmissions? Have you picked anything up from the islands?"

"Still nothing. My guess is, King Rolo has gone radio silent out of self-preservation," Timothy explained. "They are likely preventing any long-range transmissions, too."

"Which means we can never explain what really happened to King Xavier and the *Immortal* in Brisbane."

"Correct."

Layla still had trouble understanding how Rolo could have betrayed everyone the way he had. Launching a nuke on their own people and killing not only King Xavier but all of their friends and hundreds of Cazadores just didn't seem possible. Then again, she had seen what Charmer had done to her husband. It seemed Rolo was just as bad.

Timothy had confirmed it was all true, and Layla had even seen the footage of the missile launch that destroyed the super-carrier *Immortal* back at Brisbane. Her heart broke for Eevi, who had tried to stop it all, only to be murdered by the Wave Runners once the ship returned to the islands. Tears welled in her eyes as she thought of her friend, but Layla fought them back. Now wasn't the time to cry.

"Is there anything else I can assist with at this time?" Timothy asked.

"No, you have the bridge. I'll be back later," Layla replied.

She left the room with Bray and headed through the ship. The colorful passages evoked memories—some good, some bad.

"Elephant," Layla said to Bray. "Magnolia loved those. Rodger carved her one out of wood once."

More memories flashed in her mind as she stood holding her child. Soon, she would paint new images on these walls. Bray would paint with her, so they would never forget the Vanguard Islands despite all that they had suffered there.

Maybe someday, they would return home. But for now there was no turning back.

Layla walked the dimly lit corridor to the sickbay. The doors whisked open, and she entered pure darkness.

"Timothy, lights," she said.

The overhead turned on. At the end of the open room, she could see Victor sleeping peacefully.

"Dim lights," Layla said.

She moved as quietly as possible down the aisle of empty beds to Victor's side. He was alive thanks to Timothy and one of the crew members, who had agreed to help in exchange for being let go.

Ten people had been on the airship when the escapees took it. After the crew's surrender, they were lowered to the ocean in a raft and allowed to return to the islands with a written message to Charmer from Michael and Layla.

Your time is coming. Someday—maybe not today, maybe not tomorrow, maybe not even a month from now, but someday—you will wake in the middle of the night to a knife at your throat. Or perhaps you will stroll through the gardens in the moonlight when a figure steps out from behind a tree . . . Someday, when you least expect it, we will return, and we will make you pay. Depend on it.

Layla checked Victor's vitals. His heart rate was faint, and his oxygen level was down. He wasn't out of the woods yet.

"Hi," Bray mumbled. He reached out and waved.

Victor cracked open an eyelid. He managed a smile when he saw the child.

"Sorry, we didn't mean to wake you," Layla said.

Victor tried to sit up but grimaced and reached down to the bandage around his waist.

"Take it easy," she said with a warm smile.

"Hi," Bray said again.

Victor reached up to meet Bray's tiny fingers.

"How are you feeling?" Layla asked.

"I'm okay," Victor said. "How... how is the ship?"

"We're still figuring that out, but it seems we're going to have to put down for parts sooner rather than later."

"I feared this."

"I know, but don't worry. Do you need anything?"

Victor shook his head.

"Okay, get some sleep," she said. "I'll be back later."

Victor rested his head back on the pillow and waved at Bray.

She left the sickbay with her son and turned off the lights before heading to her next stop: the farm. The hatch creaked open to the long space. The grow lights blasted the room with a brilliant glow.

"Nana," Bray said, pointing over her shoulder at the crops growing across the space.

"No banana, but plenty of other fruit. Like a strawberry?"

Bray chirped—a sound that always made her smile. He was like a little monkey, the way he clung to her and loved fruit.

She walked out for a better view of the crops. It was plenty of food for the small crew, but it wouldn't survive without water. Neither would they.

Layla went down several levels until she got to an open hatch. Clanking and voices sounded inside. She stepped into the entrance, feeling a draft of heat that made her back up.

"Michael?" she called.

"Yeah, in here," he replied.

She stayed outside the hatch, looking at the machinery that Michael knew better than anyone. He emerged, covered in grease, from behind a boiler unit. Steve walked out after him, carrying a toolbox.

They followed Layla into the corridor, where both men took off their breathing masks.

"Damn, it's a furnace in there!" Michael said.

"Sorry to disturb you at work, but Timothy has an update," she said.

The AI flickered to life in front of them.

"We have to get the water-treatment plant on," Michael said. "It's the only way we and our food supply survive."

"So where do we get the supplies we need?" Steve asked.

"We could go to Rio, but that's too predictable," Michael said. "If Pedro is alive and they force him to talk, he'll likely tell Charmer that's where we might go."

"Yeah, but will Charmer send people to find us there? I highly doubt that."

"We can't take that risk," Layla said.

"I quite agree," Michael said.

"Okay, then, where should we go?" Steve asked.

"If I may, I think the question is, where *can* we go?" Timothy said. "The current status of our ship makes journeying to most places a difficult and perilous undertaking."

"Do you have any suggestions?" Michael asked.

Timothy's hologram paced a few steps in front of them, blinking as he searched some archive or database. Layla could tell, when he stopped and massaged his beard, that even the AI was nervous about their options.

"Outpost Gateway should have everything we need," Timothy said. "However, the last message received spoke of an attack. I fear that something terrible has happened there."

THIRTY

King Xavier pulled himself up onto the dock, feeling as if he might cough up a lung. Gunfire ripped over the piers and sparked off decks and rig pillars. He took a moment to catch his breath. He had nearly drowned after their assault raft capsized. Fortunately, most of his team had made it to the docks after the initial attack from the Wave Runners.

He searched for Magnolia and the Hell Divers but didn't see them anywhere on the piers. A bullet whizzed past his head as he searched the moonlit ocean surface. Idle Jet Skis bobbed in the water, their riders draped over the handlebars or missing altogether.

About fifty feet out, he spotted swimmers. Edgar, Magnolia, Tia, Sofia, and three of the six Cazadores from their raft were floundering to stay afloat. From what he could tell, they had shucked off at least some of their armor—enough for them to thrash their way to the dock.

"We have to get off these piers!" Slayer yelled.

He and Blackburn crouched down with shields to protect X as bullets slammed into the dock.

X turned toward the hostile gunfire. The rest of his teams had taken cover behind boat hulls and stacks of supplies. General Forge and his men were farther up the docks, closer to the entrance to the capitol tower. Some were even inside boats, firing from concealment at the tower's defenders.

It was clear now that Gran Jefe had failed to get his cousin to stand down. There was a civil war going on between the two different Cazador factions: the insurgents, led by Jamal, and the loyalists, under General Forge.

So far, things weren't going to plan, but in war things rarely did. For the first time, X feared that they might somehow lose this battle, especially now, having lost the element of surprise. He also feared that if the enemy had Michael captive, they would try to use him as a bartering tool. If Tin was still alive, X had to find him.

First, though, they had to get into the tower. At the other end of the docks, five hundred feet away, he saw the main double doors leading into the rig. Two defenders lay beside the doors, both riddled with arrows from Forge's soldiers.

Another hundred feet off to the right was a smaller door that led into the enclosed marina, where he had once stored his boat and the *Sea Wolf*. That door was sealed off now.

X looked up for the elevator cage. It was halfway up the tower and carrying the last of the dock's defenders, who had abandoned the area. The rest lay bleeding on the dock or had already sunk beneath the waves.

The biggest rooftop defenses seemed to be idle now, thanks to the *Frog*'s naval artillery. But X had already told Captain Two Skulls to forbid them from shooting into windows or balconies. They could take out snipers there, but only if they could keep their projectiles outside the dwellings. It was too dangerous with civilians inside.

Due to their low numbers, X and his forces had to move

across the piers and inside without much covering fire. The Hell Divers and surviving Cazadores from their raft joined him on the dock.

"Lay down covering fire from this position," X said. "Barracudas, on me!"

Slayer and Blackburn ran with X, holding their shields out front. Gran Jefe moved up with them, jerking slightly when an arrow hit his shoulder plate. He used his axe to break the shaft off. He laughed but did drop down into a crouch-run as he advanced, still the biggest target in this battle.

Muzzle flashes came from multiple windows and balconies on the rig above them—shadowy figures taking potshots. One took return fire and fell over the rail, plummeting twenty floors before splattering into nothing more than viscera and gore on a dock piling.

As X advanced, more of his forces moved out from cover to join him, forming an armored phalanx moving up the center pier.

An arrow struck the deck in front of X; then a second streaked between his legs.

"Sir, get to cover!" Forge shouted from behind a stack of crates up ahead, waving.

X glared up at the cascading balconies on the rig.

"Can you hear me, Rolo?" X shouted. "I'm coming for your scalp, you conniving old fuck!"

X kept moving, searching for a way into the tower. The soldier to his right fell with a sniper bullet through his head.

"Take that shooter out!" X yelled.

Several Cazadores stopped and fired as X pushed ahead with the Barracudas and General Forge. Bullets pounded the side of the building, the balcony, and, finally, the sniper, whose lifeless body slumped down against the metal railing.

Gunfire exploded from several windows about ten floors up.

More allied warriors fell around X as they bolted for cover. He slid down behind the crates with Forge about two hundred feet from the main doors.

Glancing over his shoulder, X saw Magnolia and the other divers behind him, working their way up the dock. None of them had a chest rig on.

"Stay back!" X yelled.

Forge pulled on him to get down. "Sir, we have to take out those other snipers," he said.

X sneaked a glance at the tenth floor. A shot immediately forced him back down. They were pinned here.

"Two Skulls," he said into his comm. "Lob one to the tenth floor—we got snipers. But make sure that shell is accurate, got it? We can't afford a short round."

"Copy," came the reply.

X kept down, breathing heavily, hoping this wasn't a mistake. He had little time to question his decision.

The gun muzzle on the Frog's foredeck flashed, a shell screamed overhead, and the tenth and eleventh floors of the tower vanished in a massive explosion. Fire belched out the side of the impact area.

X stood up and watched the billowing smoke. No enemy fired at him. His ears were still ringing when an idea seeded in his mind.

"Two Skulls," X said over the command channel, "I need you to blow the doors at the bottom of the tower. Use the same gunner. He's good."

"Stand by."

"Everyone, down!" X shouted. The soldiers and Hell Divers took cover wherever they could find it on the open terrain of the dock.

While waiting, he bumped on a different channel to the

Osprey. He reached Ensign Tiger, handpicked by Captain Two Skulls to command the vessel.

"What's your status?" X asked.

"Light resistance," Tiger replied. "Our soldiers have boarded the rig and are securing the decks. We captured a militia soldier who says Rolo and Charmer are at the capitol tower, over."

A flash came from one of the cannons on the deck of the *Frog.*

"Incoming!" Forge yelled.

The projectile screamed over the docks. The blast came behind X before he could turn.

When he did, both doors were gone, blasted inward, the two defenders outside blown to nothing.

"On me!" X shouted. He wasn't sure how loud he was due to the worsening ringing in his ears, but apparently, he was loud enough. Forge, Slayer, Blackburn, Gran Jefe, and a squad of Cazador soldiers ran up with him toward the cloud of smoke.

X walked right in. If anyone had been behind the doors, they were no longer a threat. The door to the interior stairwell was open, and X cleared the first flight and landing. It had been abandoned, but they would meet defenders as they advanced.

Alarmed shouts came from the dock below.

X moved back down through the still-dissipating smoke and looked out the blasted doors. Half his forces were running back down the dock and firing at incoming targets.

"Son of a bitch," X whispered when he heard the whine of the approaching Jet Skis. Either Jamal was still alive, or he still had more troops.

Three war boats raced toward the *Frog,* firing mounted machine guns at the small warship. A shoulder-fired rocket streaked away from one of the war boats and slammed into the hull of the ship in a brilliant blast. The armor could withstand plenty of machine-gun fire, but those rockets could do real damage to the superstructure.

Gran Jefe emerged from the smoky stairwell, sword and axe in hand. It seemed that since he couldn't recruit his cousin, he would deal with him in a different way.

Magnolia and the Hell Divers piled into the stairwell.

Someone pulled X back into the fire-gutted interior. He looked around him at the chaos of confused soldiers. General Forge was directing some of them down a corridor. Tia and Sofia joined Magnolia and Edgar at an open door on the next landing up.

"We have to split up," X said to the remaining Barracudas huddled around him. "Forge, take four men up the stairwell at the other end of this passage. Hell Divers and the rest of the Barracudas, with me."

Forge nodded, but as he moved away, X said, "Rolo and Charmer are mine. You find them, I want them alive."

"Understood, sir."

"And look for Michael and his family. No indiscriminate firing."

"Yes, sir."

Slayer raised his shield and started up the stairs, toward sounds of distant shouting and panicked voices.

"Expect an ambush," X said.

He remained right behind Slayer, with Magnolia trying to push up between them, but the narrow stairway really allowed only one fighter up at a time.

"Mags, keep back," X said.

She flattened herself against the wall to let Blackburn up with his shield.

They reached the next landing to find the door locked. Slayer kept going, up the next flight, while a team moved in to clear the floor below.

He checked his HUD—only fifteen minutes had passed since the battle started. Still, it was time enough for Rolo to escape.

But there was nowhere the bastard could run that X wouldn't find him.

At the third landing, Slayer raised his shield to deflect a hurled spear.

"Kill 'em all!" someone shouted.

Gunfire rose over the voice.

Slayer fell back, knocking X into the person behind him. He tried to get free, but his rifle was pinned between his chest and Slayer.

Letting go of the stock, X pulled his blaster from its thigh holster. He raised it up over Slayer at a militia guard who was leveling a machine gun at them. There was no time to hesitate. X didn't.

A dozen buckshot pellets slammed into the man's chest, and he slumped over on the stairs. Another militia soldier jumped down onto the landing, firing as Slayer raised his shield into the blast.

X fired the second buckshot round into the soldier's knee. He screamed in agony, reaching up as Slayer thrust his spear. The blade pinned the outstretched hand to the soldier's chest as it impaled him. Bracing a boot against the dead man's ribs, Slayer jerked the shaft free, then continued up the stairs holding the bullet-riddled shield.

As he pushed up the stairs, X looked down at the two dead men. He hadn't asked for this and didn't want it, but these people had made their decision.

X strained to hear past the ringing in his ears. The gunfire faded away, and Slayer called "Clear!" around the next corner.

They kept going, tracking bloody prints and drips up to the fourth floor, then the fifth. The door to a corridor was open. Frightened civilians looked out their doors, some ducking away when Slayer shouted, "Where is Rolo?"

"Gone!" someone yelled back.

"Keep climbing," X said.

The team advanced up the stairs to the sixth floor, to the sound of more voices, all in English.

X moved around the corner with Slayer and Blackburn, both with shields up. No arrows, spears, or bullets came at them. Through a gap in the shields, X saw more civilians: women, a few children, and two unarmed male sky people of advanced years.

"Where is Rolo?" X shouted.

A familiar voice came from the landing above. X whirled to find Imulah standing on the stairs, gripping his stomach.

"King Xavier..." he rasped.

X caught the old scribe as he fell. "Get me a medic!" he yelled over his shoulder.

He gently put the man down on the deck while soldiers rushed up to establish security. He examined Imulah to find blood welling out from between his fingers.

"Who did this?" X asked.

"Charm... Charmer did."

"Where's Michael?"

"He..."

Magnolia squatted down beside them and put a hand on Imulah's shoulder. His eyes flitted up toward her.

"Stay with me," X said. "Where is Michael?"

"Gone."

X felt his heart shatter in his chest.

"What... what happened?" he stammered.

"He escaped with his family in the airship," Imulah rasped.

X's broken heart skipped a beat. For a moment, he couldn't believe what he had heard. Time seemed to stand still around him.

He opened his mouth like a fish out of water, trying to get air. Then he looked at Magnolia. She nodded at him, as if to confirm what they had heard was real.

"Michael and his family are alive?" X asked just to be sure.

"Yes. But how are you ... alive?" Imulah whispered.

"Call it shithouse luck," X said. "Where's Rolo?"

"Rooftop ... with guards."

"You're going to be okay," Magnolia said. "Just keep pressure on your wound."

"Imulah," Sofia said. She pushed closer as the knot of warriors moved up the stairs. "Where is my son?"

"Jamal took him, but he is here," Imulah said. "In the tower."

"Where?"

"I don't ... I don't know."

"We'll find him," X said.

He tried to rise, but Imulah grabbed his wrist. "You are the Immortal," said the scribe. "Kill Rolo. Save the islands."

"I have to find my son," Sofia said.

Magnolia said, "I'll go with you."

"Edgar, Tia, go with them," X said. "And take two of Forge's men."

Then he was moving with Slayer and Blackburn up the stairs. On the way, he bumped on the command channel to the *Frog*.

"Two Skulls, give me a sitrep," X said over the radio.

No response.

He tried again, then again.

Either they had lost comms with the ship, or the ship was in major trouble.

"Someone get eyes on the *Frog*," he called out. "I want to know what the hell is going on out there!"

"Aye, aye, sir," came a reply.

X pressed on, his mind racing. Michael was alive, and they were winning the fight for the tower. But the Wave

Runners seemed to have damaged the *Frog* at the very least, and they had the means to ravage it beyond all hope of repair.

No, the Frog *is still in this fight. And Miles is fine!*

Still, X feared the worst, especially with the *Osprey* so far away and unable to help. He bumped on the channel to the ensign in charge.

"Tiger, what's your status?"

"Rig fifteen is secure, sir."

"Good work. Proceed to capitol tower to provide backup."

Filled with new confidence, X moved up the rest of the stairs like a teenage boy who thought he was invincible.

Each landing was clear. It seemed Rolo and everyone else had fled.

By the time they reached the last few flights, X was feeling it. He slowed to catch his breath, wanting to be fresh for what could be an ambush. The door at the top was open and bathed in soft moonlight.

A blast sounded in the distance. A truly massive explosion, and it wasn't coming from the rooftop.

X signaled to advance.

Slayer and Blackburn started up the stairs and vanished through the door. X was right behind them with more Cazador soldiers, and General Forge following. They filed out into the night at the edge of a scene of devastation.

Smoke plumed away from craters in the rooftop where shells had burst. Trees burned along the eastern edge of the roof. In the center, at the end of a long gouge carved in the dirt, lay the wreckage of what appeared to be a helicopter.

"Where in hell did that come from?" X said. Something clicked in his mind. Was this the craft that had been following them, showing up on the radar?

He moved out with the soldiers, searching for Rolo and his guards.

"The *Frog*!" someone shouted.

X ran to the eastern edge of the roof. The sight took his breath away. The ship was venting smoke and surrounded by small watercraft. X counted eight Jet Skis and two war boats. Soldiers on boats loosed shoulder-fired missiles at the *Frog* while their mounted Miniguns dumped a hundred rounds per second onto its weather deck and superstructure. Sparks danced across the hull and the command tower. At the top, smoke plumed into the sky.

X had his answer why Two Skulls wasn't answering on the comms.

A single cannon was trying to engage the two war boats while Cazador soldiers on the bow and stern fired small arms and two mounted .50-caliber machine guns. One of those gunners went down, his legs blown off by an enemy rocket-propelled grenade.

They wouldn't be able to hold out much longer.

X said to Forge, "General, take half the soldiers and head back to the docks. Get up there and take command. I want those Wave Runners dead on the water."

"Understood."

Forge took off with three men, leaving X with ten, led by Slayer and Blackburn. They advanced across the roof, through the smoky darkness, and into a forest, their weapons sweeping the shadows.

Slayer came out of the forest and stood in a field of peas. "Over there!" he shouted.

The soldiers cleared the area, moving past the wreckage of the helicopter. X saw the pilot still inside, blood smeared against the cracked windshield.

He moved around it and saw five or six people just past the Sky Arena. They seemed to be trying to find a way off the rooftop.

Slayer led the Cazador soldiers toward them, with X running to keep up. On approach, he saw the white hair of the man he had been hunting since Brisbane.

Rolo stood with his hands up, a pistol muzzle at his head. Five of his guards were pointing their rifles at the man holding that pistol. That man was a Hell Diver.

"Drop your weapons!" Slayer shouted.

The guards with Rolo turned their barrels on the approaching Cazadores. They needed only a moment to see they were outnumbered.

They lowered their weapons as Slayer and Blackburn moved in with shields and spears. X switched to his axe as he stared at the Hell Diver, who kept his pistol to Rolo's face.

"Why?" asked the diver. "Why did you do it?"

That voice. That accent.

Could it really be...

"Kade," X whispered.

He looked back to the helicopter. Kade had somehow taken the bird and returned from the dead.

"You!" Rolo shrieked, spittle forming at the corners of his lips. He raised a shaking finger at X. "You, you are a demon!"

"You're the demon!" Kade said. He pushed the rusted barrel of the revolver between Rolo's wild eyes.

"Look what he's done to your home!" Rolo roared. "It burns because of him, and it has burned before because of him. I am the only one who can save you all! You must slay this evil beast of a man!"

Rolo pointed at X, ranting to the men surrounding him.

"If it weren't for me, he would have destroyed this place, destroyed everyone! Destroyed humanity!"

"You dropped an atom bomb on the Vanguard army, you crazy old bat," Kade said. "You killed hundreds of innocent people and poisoned the land—"

"That land was already poisoned, and those *innocent people* would have killed us all if they had the chance," Rolo snapped back. "You must kill him! You must kill X before he dooms us all! Charmer was right. He has to be removed to save us all!"

Charmer, of course. So the cunning bastard was behind this all along. Rolo was just a puppet, and Charmer was the one pulling his strings.

Now that puppet ranted on, trying to justify his actions. His panicked eyes flitted about. He was like a trapped beast with nowhere to flee.

"Kade, you know me. You know that everything I've done is for our people," he stammered.

"Maybe that was true once," Kade said. "But after we got rescued and brought here, everything you've done has been for you and that simpering turd you listen to. You lost your way, Captain. You lost sight of your humanity."

Rolo turned to his guards, but they all backed away. They knew that it was over. That their "king" had never been anything but a hollow imitation of a man.

"I gave everything for you; I dived into hell," Kade said. "These people saved us, pulled us from that hell, and *this* is what you do to repay them? By murdering them, jailing them, and taking their home? You have no honor and don't deserve to draw breath."

"You're blind, Kade," Rolo said. "X has corrupted your mind."

Kade slapped the insolent face with a resounding smack, turning the pudgy man ninety degrees. When Rolo looked at him again, he seemed to be in shock, reaching up to hold his cheek with one hand. Kade pulled the hammer back on the pistol.

"My mind's pretty clear," Kade said. "I see you for who you are with my own eyes."

"Put the gun down, Kade," X said. "This walking shit heap is mine."

Kade looked over his shoulder at X. In that instant, a snarling Rolo lunged and grabbed Kade by the wrist in an attempt to snatch the gun.

A shot cracked. Rolo staggered back, his crazed eyes locked on Kade. He stumbled away as a cherry-size hole blossomed in the center of his chest.

The former airship captain took another step back, then another, right into the railing, where his momentum carried him over the side.

X ran over with everyone else as Rolo hit the water twenty stories below.

It was the most anticlimactic way X could have envisioned to kill the bastard, though he did get the desired outcome. And X was still standing.

"The reign of Rolo is over," someone said. "All hail King Kade Long."

X turned toward Kade, who held the pistol in his shaking hand. Of course! A memory flashed from the day he'd killed el Pulpo, inheriting the crown. It was Cazador custom. But there hadn't been two kings back then.

A few of the soldiers looked confused.

Gunfire cracked in the distance, and not just sporadic shots. The battle wasn't over yet. Any questions of royal succession would have to be dealt with later.

"Come on," X said. "It's time to find Charmer."

THIRTY-ONE

"Where's my son?" Sofia yelled in English and then Spanish as she rushed down the hallway, frantically banging on doors. Magnolia was just behind her with Edgar, Tia, and the two Cazador allies assigned to help them.

They had searched an entire floor already, but the only information they had was from Imulah, and no one else was talking.

Magnolia passed a door that was slightly open. A young woman looked out through the gap.

"Hey," Magnolia said.

She went over to the door, but the woman closed it right into Magnolia's boot. With a kick, she launched it back open. The young woman staggered back, wearing an expensive low-cut dress and turquoise jewelry.

To Magnolia's surprise, it was Charmer's lover, Jacquelyn. She had seen them together a few times before leaving for Panama months ago.

"Hands up," Magnolia said. She had her laser rifle up, just in case Charmer was around.

But if she had to guess, the sneaky shit was long gone.

After a quick search, Magnolia lowered the barrel.

"I'm not going to hurt you," she said. "We're looking for a baby named Rhino Jr."

Jacquelyn turned slightly to the window. "Why?" she said. "Why are you killing us?"

Magnolia thought about the quickest way to explain what was happening. "Ask your boyfriend," she said. "He started this war together with Rolo. It is a war that my people will win. You should consider which side you're on, and tell me where the baby is."

Jacquelyn hesitated again.

"Charmer left you," Magnolia said. "Why would he? Because he knows it's over. Now, tell me where the baby is."

Heaving a sigh, Jacquelyn looked down. "I saw him with the Cazador soldiers a floor below us. I heard he was being kept there."

"Which room?"

"I don't know."

An explosion outside drew Magnolia to the window. It wasn't the best angle, but she could see the naval battle between the Wave Runners and the *Frog*.

The ship continued to put up a fight despite two fires burning on its weather deck. Muzzle flashes came from the last defenders in both the stern and the bow.

The Wave Runner soldiers circled the beleaguered vessel, firing small arms from Jet Skis to keep the gunners on the *Frog* busy. A well-aimed rocket streaked away from one of the war boats and slammed into the command tower, which was already spewing flames.

The last cannon on the deck swung around toward the two war boats. The barrel blazed, firing a shell that burst in front of the boat. Water geysered up.

Footsteps approached.

"Mags, come on," Edgar said.

She left with him and joined the others in the hallway. Sofia searched for her child while Tia held security with two Cazador soldiers.

"I think I know where he is," Magnolia called out to her friend.

Sofia whirled about. "Where?"

"Maybe one floor below us."

"Let's go!" Edgar said.

Magnolia rushed back to the stairwell and loped down the stairs with the other Hell Divers and Cazadores right behind. She yanked the door open to a dark corridor that seemed abandoned.

Sofia moved out in front of her, and Magnolia yelled, "Be careful!"

Just as Magnolia had ignored her friends' cautionary words in Panama, Sofia ignored hers now. "Where's my son!" she shouted.

Magnolia and Edgar ran to keep up with her while Tia hung back with the two guards to hold rear security.

Sofia pounded on doors. None opened.

"Open up!" she shouted. "Open or I'll blast my way in!"

Magnolia ran to catch up, then skidded to a halt at the sound of gunfire ahead. Bullets ripped through the door across the hall from where Sofia was busy knocking. She cried out and fell on her back.

"Sofia!" Magnolia shouted.

She raised her laser rifle and flashed a bolt through the door to the room where the shots had originated. The gunfire stopped.

"Cover me!" she shouted to Edgar.

He moved over with her as Magnolia went to Sofia. She was on her side, reaching down to her legs. Blood ran from bullet wounds to both calves.

Magnolia immediately put pressure on the wounds. She could

tell by the steady blood flow that no artery had been nicked, but that didn't guarantee survival.

Edgar kicked the door off its hinges and went inside to the sound of a baby crying. Sofia tried to sit up.

"No, don't move," Magnolia said.

"I have to get to my son. I have to..."

Magnolia looked over her shoulder to a body sprawled behind the broken-down door. Edgar moved inside, sweeping with his rifle for contacts.

"Clear!" he shouted.

The crying grew louder and closer.

Edgar emerged with Rhino Jr. in his arms. He cradled the child and bent down to Sofia, who reached out as Magnolia kept pressure on the wounds.

"Tia! Med kit!" she said.

Tia got down on one knee and started pulling out supplies.

"My baby, my baby," Sofia kept saying. She hugged her crying child as Magnolia and Tia applied tourniquets.

"You're going to be okay," Magnolia said. "This is gonna hurt, though..."

Sofia cried out as Magnolia tightened the tourniquet just below the left kneecap.

"I'm sorry," Magnolia said. "One more, okay?"

Sofia managed a nod while squeezing her wailing baby even tighter to her chest.

Magnolia tightened the second tourniquet to another grunt of pain. Then she pulled back to check her work. Her friend had lost blood, but she would survive.

Bumping on the comms, Magnolia called for a medic. A response fired back.

"We need all teams to the marina," Forge said. *"Taking heavy casualties!"*

"We're pinned down on floor eighteen," X replied. *"Civilians are blocking our way, and several of them have weapons. Magnolia, report position, over."*

"On floor three," she replied. "Sofia's been wounded, but we found her baby and he seems fine."

"Copy that. Stay put," X replied. "General, I'll be there as soon as I can!"

Things weren't sounding good, and with so much going on, Magnolia could hardly concentrate.

"Mags," Sofia whispered.

"I'm right here. Everything's going to be okay."

"Go help the others. We have to win this fight. We can't—"

"We aren't going to lose." Magnolia stood up, bloody to her elbows. "Tia, you stay here with her and the guards. Edgar, with me."

They raced back down to the marina two floors below. At the blown-out doors to the dock, smoke was still thick.

More gunfire and explosions rang out across the piers. In the respite, she could hear the clang of weapons and armor.

Wounded soldiers called out for help; others moaned their last.

Magnolia shouldered her laser rifle and stared out in the darkness, using the moonlight and flickering fires to guide her aim. Along the dock to her right, an entire row of small fishing boats burned. One was in the process of sinking.

A midsize trawler blazed at the end of the dock, its glow backlighting the figures of soldiers fighting. These men were down to swords and spears, fighting hand to hand.

"Stay close," Magnolia said to Edgar.

They started the trek back the way they had come, moving in a crouch with rifles up. Cazador soldiers with the Vanguard logo on their armor lay sprawled along the dock. Most were dead from gunshots, but a few had arrows sticking out of their armor. One man had a broken spear in his back.

As they got closer to the remaining fighters, Magnolia made out the red-plumed helmet of General Forge at the end of the dock on her left. He fought with two swords against a pair of Wave Runner soldiers. Another Vanguard soldier fought an enemy spearman. Several other pairs were dueling on other piers, but in the glow of the fires, it was hard to make out who was who.

Out on the water, the enemy continued to pound the *Frog* with gunfire and rockets. They seemed close to taking the ship.

Magnolia couldn't let that happen.

She ran the rest of the way to the skirmish at the end of her dock, where she recognized another soldier by his hulking form. It was Gran Jefe, fighting the Wave Runners.

A message came over the comms from X. They were still pinned down by civilians who had taken up arms. It would be a few more minutes before he could get to the marina.

Forge and Gran Jefe didn't have another minute.

Magnolia aimed her rifle to help General Forge as he ran an enemy warrior through with his spear. But the other soldier smashed a hatchet against his back, knocking him to the deck with the skewered Wave Runner.

The man with the hatchet strode over to finish off the general.

"Over here, dickhead!" Magnolia shouted. She sighted him up and squeezed the trigger, firing a bolt that cleanly took off the top of his head.

Gunfire forced her and Edgar behind a stack of scavenged wood planks.

She looked through a gap between the stacked boards to see the last of the soldiers allied with Forge go down. The general was wounded and trying to crawl away. Only Gran Jefe remained on his feet and fighting.

"Fuck, we're …" Magnolia started to say before she heard footfalls behind her.

By the time she turned, it was too late. Wind ruffled the charred jacket of an injured Wave Runner. Not just any. This was their leader.

Jamal, the short, muscular Cazador general, approached with a submachine gun. Blistered arms raised the weapon, aiming at her, then swung it over to Edgar.

"NO!" she shouted.

Jamal fired a burst through Edgar's head. Some of it spattered on Magnolia.

She turned to look in horror upon the man she had spent years diving and fighting with. He was gone in the blink of an eye.

The Cazador turned the weapon to her but held his fire for some reason.

"Jorge!" he shouted.

There was a pause; then Jamal yelled in Spanish—something about a *puta*.

Magnolia stared at Edgar's ruined helmet. The visor had shattered, and smoke curled out of three holes.

"No. Edgar …" she mumbled. "Oh God …"

In a fit of rage, she jumped up and reached over her shoulder for a blade, only to find a Cazador cutlass at her throat. Jamal whirled her around, keeping the blade against her neck. She could smell his burned flesh.

"Jorge!" he shouted again.

Through the smoke, a huge figure emerged, holding an axe in one hand, a spear in the other.

An arrow stuck out of his shoulder plate, and blood dripped down his arm. He favored his right leg.

Magnolia looked over to Forge, still crawling away on the dock. The other Vanguard soldiers nearby were all injured or dead.

With X pinned down, no one was coming to save her.

Shouting rose over the crackling of flames. Magnolia followed it out over the water to the *Frog*, where the Wave Runners were trying to board by firing grappling hooks up to the deck rail. From her vantage, she could see they were climbing up in unguarded sections of the ship. There simply weren't enough sailors under Captain Two Skulls' command to hold back the Wave Runners.

If the enemy took the ship, the battle for the islands would be lost.

Magnolia thought of all the people they had already lost, from Rodger to Edgar. Her heart thumped with despair and, beneath that, rage.

She couldn't give up. She had to keep fighting.

She squirmed, and the blade cut into her neck, drawing blood.

"*No te muevas, puta*," Jamal said. "No move."

She pressed her chin down, trying to make it more difficult to cut her. This angle allowed her to see something she hadn't noticed before.

Jamal seemed to be wearing metal armor over his right arm. The armor looked a lot like Michael's prosthetic arm.

It all came clear to her in an instant. This was who had killed Oliver and Nez. Charmer had hired this scum to frame Michael.

Magnolia squirmed again, only to feel the blade bite into the skin of her neck.

Gran Jefe kept coming toward them. When he was ten feet away, he stopped and spoke in Spanish—something about letting her go and how this was between them.

She picked up more pieces of the conversation. Gran Jefe saying how Rolo had nuked the supercarrier and killed countless of their friends.

"No," Jamal said. "*¡Mentira!*"

It seemed he didn't believe Gran Jefe. Magnolia could

understand his skepticism, since the true king was back from the wastes.

Gran Jefe dropped the spear to the ground, then pointed his hatchet at Jamal.

"Let her go, and fight me!" he said in English.

Jamal responded with a name Magnolia wasn't expecting. "Ada." Something about how Gran Jefe had…

Magnolia narrowed her eyes with realization. Both these men had the blood of innocent people on their hands.

"You killed Ada?" she sputtered.

Gran Jefe took a step forward.

"Did you do it?" Magnolia asked.

"*Sí*," Gran Jefe replied.

"How could you?"

"For what she did to container with my cousin. I'm sorry. I… *lo siento*."

Jamal laughed. "Now you die, bitch."

"Stop!" Gran Jefe howled. He cocked the hatchet back and threw it.

Magnolia had barely half a second to move slightly. She felt the cutlass edge sting the side of her neck as the hatchet hit Jamal with a thud.

Magnolia sank to the deck and looked up. The axe's handle was cocked up in front of Jamal's face, its blade buried deep in his chest. Dropping to his knees, he reached up and grasped the handle.

Gran Jefe grabbed it, too, then pressed a boot against his cousin's chest and wrested the blade free.

Jamal fell back to the dock, hissing like a leaky air bladder as he tried to speak.

"*Vete a la mierda*," he wheezed.

Gran Jefe hawked and spat in the dying man's face. "*No eres mi primo*… No my cousin."

Magnolia kept her hand on her neck, which felt greasy with blood. Too much blood.

Her vision began to blur. She could see just enough to make out Gran Jefe finishing off Jamal by bringing the hatchet down on the top of his helmet, splitting it with another sickening crunch.

Then Gran Jefe bent down to her and put a hand on her neck.

"*Tranquila*," he said. "You don't die today."

* * * * *

When Kade got to the marina, X raised his damaged prosthetic arm, signaling a halt. The squad of six soldiers joined him. Slayer and Blackburn moved out in front with their shot-up shields.

Kade raised the assault rifle he had liberated from a dead enemy soldier. He trained the iron sights on the burning docks. Bodies were sprawled everywhere, even in boats. Vanguard soldiers. Charmer's militia. Wave Runners. The death and destruction were almost too much to comprehend. What the hell were they doing? With humans all but extinct, why were they fighting each other?

Maybe they were barbarians and savages as the Forerunner and Lucky had said.

Kade drew in a breath and let it out.

One of the two main instigators was dead, and Kade had been the one to kill him. He wasn't even sure that was what he had planned, but Rolo had forced his hand by lunging at him. Now it seemed that people thought Kade was king of the Vanguard Islands. That couldn't be the case, though—the true king was right in front of him.

X waved for the fighters to push down the docks. Kade followed him into the smoke, through the death. But there was also life to celebrate. He felt relief knowing Tia was still alive. Last he'd heard, she was on the third floor of the tower with Sofia, who had been shot in the legs. They were safer inside than out here.

Lucky was also safer where he was right now.

Kade had left the knight inside the helicopter, pinned under the crates, for his own good. If the Vanguard military won this battle, Kade would see that Lucky was taken care of. First, though, they had to pull off a victory—an outcome that was far from certain.

Smoke drifted across the path ahead. When he pushed through it, he saw the ongoing battle for the *Frog*. Kade couldn't see much, but someone else could.

"They're being boarded," Slayer said.

X brought up his scope to his visor. "Shit. Get going and spread out."

The fighters surged ahead, running across the adjacent docks. Kade was almost to the end of the dock when he heard a soldier calling out.

"Help!"

He recognized that gravelly voice.

"*¡Auxilio!* Someone, help!"

Kade followed the noise through another curtain of smoke. On the other side, he saw Gran Jefe on his knees beside a fallen Hell Diver.

"General!" Slayer shouted from the dock parallel to theirs, advancing toward the still form of Forge. The lieutenant bent down to check him, then yelled, "He's alive! We need a medic!"

X ran up with Kade all the way to Magnolia and Gran Jefe, who had a hand on her neck.

"Mags!" X cried.

Even from ten feet away, Kade could see the blood. It was everywhere: her hands, arms, legs. Less clear was whether all the blood was hers. If it was, then she would soon be dead.

Gran Jefe spoke to X in fast broken English mixed with Spanish. Something about how she'd had her neck cut.

As Kade arrived, he saw it wasn't just her. A Cazador with a hatchet in his head lay dead by her side. Behind them, Edgar lay slumped against crates, with half his head gone.

Two more Vanguard soldiers arrived. One had a medical pack.

"Help her!" X shouted.

Kade saw Magnolia's hand move. She was alive still, but it didn't look good for her.

"We have to get to the *Frog*!" someone yelled. "Charmer is out there!"

X looked out over the water, growling under his breath like a wild animal. He turned away and crouched to the medic.

"Don't let her die," X grumbled.

Then he got up and stumbled over to Kade and said, "I don't know how the fuck you're standing next to me, but I need you now, Cowboy."

"I'm with you, King Xavier," Kade replied.

"Let's get our raggedy asses to the *Frog*!"

The remaining soldiers boarded one of the surviving assault rafts that had brought them here. As the boat thumped away from the burning docks, Kade pulled out the magazine—ten rounds left. And his pistol was empty, its last round now inside Rolo's body, drifting toward the ocean floor.

Kade looked back at the rooftop of the tower he had crashed onto not an hour ago. Smoke tendriled into the air, and flames licked out from many windows.

The assault boat thumped over the waves. Kade checked his rifle and studied the ship in the green hue of his night-vision goggles.

Shots were coming from the *Frog*, but Kade didn't see any of the fighting.

The raft closed in on the stern of the ship.

"This is it," X said. "We secure the ship, and we will have our home back. Fail, and we lose everything!"

"So we don't fail," Slayer said.

The engines burbled as the boat slowed on approach. It bumped against a hull pockmarked with bullet scars. Slayer grabbed a dangling rope and started shinnying up the side.

The second the Cazador was up, he wiggled the rope, signaling X, who went next, followed by Kade.

By the time Kade was up, most of the gunshots had ceased. Shouting, most of it in Spanish, replaced the noise. That didn't tell him much.

He followed X over the rail and onto the deck, to a scene of carnage. Vanguard soldiers lay scattered everywhere he looked. He saw a few Wave Runners among the corpses, but not many.

Slayer flashed hand signals to the team. Fanning out into combat intervals, they began the search for Charmer.

It didn't take long.

His smooth voice called out from a platform two levels above them, where he stood illuminated in soft moonlight.

"Don't shoot!" X shouted.

A moment later, Kade saw why. Charmer stood with his boot on Miles's back, and he held a chain that was wrapped so tightly around the dog's neck, it could hardly snarl.

In his other hand, Charmer held an Uzi, which he pointed down at X.

Three sky people and two Wave Runners moved out from the two hatches at the bottom of the tower, their rifles pointed at Kade and the others.

"It's over—put your weapons down!" Charmer called down. "Do it, or I'll kill your dog."

"Carl," Kade said.

Charmer looked down to him.

"Rolo is dead," Kade said. "You've lost. It's time to end this bloody madness!"

"You can end it by putting down your weapons!"

"Let go of my DOG!" X snarled.

"I don't know how you did it, X. Maybe you are immortal."

Miles bared his teeth as Charmer pulled tighter up on the chain.

"All I know is, you aren't some guardian angel," he said. "Death follows you wherever you go."

"They saved you, Carl," Kade said. "Brought us out of hell and gave us life and hope."

"Which is all the more reason I had to do what I did. How do you not see that, Kade? They were trying to keep food from us, and they would have conscripted us all into a war that would take us back to the wastes!"

"I did what I did to keep our people alive!" X thundered. "We can't stay here forever, you simpering fool. Storms, famines, violence!"

"Rolo," Charmer started to say, but Kade interrupted him.

"Rolo nuked the supercarrier! He murdered hundreds, then tried to kill me and the Hell Divers he left behind," Kade said. "We all know the truth of what happened. I'm the truth. King X is the truth."

"He isn't king anymore," Charmer said. "And he never will be again."

"I don't need to be king to finish you," X said. "Fight me like a man. Hand to hand. No weapons."

Charmer turned his monocular gaze from Kade to X. "Me fight the great Immortal? Why, when I have your beloved pet? You have one choice: surrender, or your dog becomes fish food."

"You got four seconds to let go of him, shithead. Then the pain begins," X snapped back.

Somewhere above Charmer, Kade heard a faint, almost subliminal chittering sound. Above Charmer, a shadow seemed to float down the exterior of the superstructure.

"Three…" X said.

The shadow separated from the superstructure and dropped onto Charmer, knocking him over the rail. He fell the twenty feet to the weather deck, landing with his arm under him. X was on him before his first howl of pain.

"Fire!" Slayer shouted.

Gunshots rang out all around Kade. He blasted a Wave Runner with two to the head, then moved to the next target.

It was over in a few seconds. Somehow, Kade was still standing and unscathed. In front of him, the enemy troops were all down, two still whimpering in pain, the others dead.

Kade looked behind him. Slayer was also still on his feet. Blackburn and another loyalist soldier were on the deck, moaning in pain.

As Slayer went to finish off the wounded rebel fighters, Kade ran over to X, who slapped Charmer hard on the ear.

"Where did Michael go!" X shouted. He punched Charmer in the nose, breaking it, then slapped the other ear.

"Where did he take the airship!" X yelled.

"He…" Charmer tried to say. Then he grinned—a mistake.

A gloved hand slapped the grin away, along with a couple of teeth. X hit him again, then grabbed him by the throat and squeezed.

"Wait!" Kade yelled. "We need him alive to explain what happened. To admit to the truth. Not just about Oliver and Nez but also what really happened to the supercarrier."

X wasn't letting up, and Charmer's face turned a deep red.

"King Xavier, stop!" Kade shouted. "Slayer, help me!"

They grabbed X, but he had an iron grip. Charmer's eye bulged.

The two men finally yanked X away from his gasping, coughing victim.

"No!" X shouted.

He fought free and scrambled back to finish the job. Luckily for Charmer, Kade and Slayer managed to once again stop the enraged king from killing him.

Loud barking erupted from Miles, then excited utterances from Jo-Jo. The two animals made their way over to X as several figures emerged around the bottom of the command tower. Kade picked up his rifle and aimed at them.

"Hold your fire," Slayer said.

Kade lowered the weapon when he saw it was Valeria and a few sailors, including Tiger.

"Where's Captain Two Skulls?" Slayer called out.

"He didn't make it. Rocket hit the CIC, killed most everyone inside, and took out the comms," Tiger said.

"Damn," X said and heaved a great sigh. "He was one of the best of us."

A team of four Cazadores moved out to secure the ship. It took a few minutes before someone yelled, "All decks clear!"

Tiger walked over to X. "The *Osprey* is on the way here with reinforcements," he said.

"You did it, sir," Slayer said. "The islands are back under our control."

There was scattered applause across the deck. X didn't chime in, and neither did Kade, for different reasons. The king was likely considering the losses they had taken in the short battle. Kade was worried about a possible war on the horizon with the Knights of the Coral Castle. He had yet to explain everything he had learned while in their captivity, but he would soon. Now was the time to celebrate the victory and minister to the wounded.

Blackburn groaned as Valeria tended to his injuries.

"We have to put out those fires, or we're going to lose the ship," Tiger said.

"Same for the capitol tower," Slayer said.

"Over there!" someone shouted.

Kade looked to the horizon, where he saw the container ship *Osprey* sailing toward them. But the shouting Cazador was pointing at the top of the capitol tower.

Black smoke billowed up from the rooftop, snaking around a beam of blue light that shot straight up into the sky.

"What is that?" X asked.

Perplexed sailors and soldiers crowded around for a better view.

Kade stared with realization.

"The Trident," he whispered.

"The *what*?" X turned toward Kade.

Everyone did. All staring at him. It was time to start talking. To tell what he knew about the Coral Castle.

"We must prepare," Kade said. He studied the beam of light.

"For what, exactly?" X asked.

Kade swallowed hard. "For a new enemy."

EPILOGUE

The Vanguard flag, frayed at the ends, flapped in the breeze atop the capitol tower. A full day had passed since the battle for the Vanguard Islands, and X was preparing to speak to his remaining confidants about the future—not just theirs but his own as well.

He strolled through the gardens with Miles. The bodies of the dead had been removed, but much of the damage remained. Charred trees and scorched crops were all that remained of the lush, verdant landscape of the tower roof.

Already, they were replanting, using seeds from the vault in Brisbane.

Militia soldiers and Cazador warriors carried new sandbags to rebuild the machine-gun nests. Lieutenant Wynn, who had been imprisoned under Charmer and Rolo, was supervising their work. He walked over to the techs welding a machine-gun turret, repairing the weapons of war for whatever came next.

X looked out westward over the teal-green waves. Australia seemed a world away. Based on Kade's description of the Coral Castle and its denizens, if the knights came, the Vanguard army, even in its weakened state, would crush them.

Miles trotted over with an apple in his mouth. He raised it up, offering it to X.

"I'm good. Thanks, though, boy," X said.

He and the dog crossed the ravaged forest and the field where the helicopter had crash-landed, killing the pilot and breaking the back of the knight they now had in custody a few floors beneath his feet.

X walked up to the rail, to the spot where Kade had shot Captain Rolo.

X spat over the edge to commemorate the old bastard's ungraceful last and only dive.

"Sir," said a gravelly voice.

A half-dozen men approached with the late-afternoon sun behind them. He raised his hand to shield his eyes and saw General Forge, walking with a cane. He was lucky to be alive after a concussion and several stab wounds. The old warrior wouldn't be fighting again anytime soon.

Imulah, still recovering from Charmer's craven attack, was here, carried in a chair by three stout Cazador warriors. Also present were Kade, Slayer, Pedro, and Gran Jefe. They all looked the worse for wear, especially Pedro, who was as bruised and battered as any gladiator who'd ever fought in the Sky Arena. As X checked them in turn, he realized that they all looked like an old, worn-out Hell Diver he knew. *Like me.*

The men stopped in front of X. Lieutenant Wynn ran around the remaining trees to join them, but one person was still missing.

"Where's Commander Katib?" he asked.

"I don't know, sir," Imulah said.

"I guess we'll proceed without her, then," X said. "I'll make this short, since we all have work to do and places to be."

He looked back over the rooftop at the craters from the recent battle, some of the dirt dark with blood. So much death.

He sighed and looked to Kade. "You've told me everything about the Coral Castle you can think of?"

"Yes," Kade replied.

X hesitated. Maybe he was underestimating this Forerunner. "Do you think it's possible there are more knights you didn't see?" he asked.

"Maybe. There were probably other guards, but the knights seemed to be their own discrete fighting force. I counted another half dozen before I left. I didn't see any other aircraft, or navy. Just small boats."

"And this knight Gaz, or Lucky?"

"He's still not talking," said General Forge. "He won't say what the Trident is, but we think it's a beacon."

"So they know where we are?" X asked.

"Possibly," Kade said. "I'm sorry, I—"

"Not your fault. They would have found me and followed me regardless, and besides, that's what *those* are for." X pointed to the cannons that were positioned along the edge of the rooftop. "If the Forerunner's knights come looking for a fight in another chopper, they'll get shot down like the first one, and it won't be pretty on their end."

"I would be honored to lead a mission to the Coral Castle if we can beat the location out of this knight," Forge said. "Perhaps going on the offensive is better than waiting for them to plan an attack."

X rubbed his forehead. "Try and learn the location, but do not send out troops. The journey is too long and dangerous," he said. "Besides, we've been on the offensive too much. It's time to play defense. You're needed here, General. To protect the islands."

"Aye, aye, sir."

"Lieutenants Slayer and Wynn, I'm counting on you to beef up our forces and train new ones to help General Forge keep our home secure."

"We've already had new volunteers," Wynn said. "Sky people from Tanzania who said Charmer wouldn't let them help us when they arrived. Now they're eager to help."

"How many?" X asked.

"Thirty men and ten women."

"That many?"

"Yes, Charmer and Rolo instructed them not to work with us before. They didn't want *their* people dying on your missions, according to a few people I interviewed."

"It's a strong stock of able-bodied people," Slayer said. "Makes for easy training."

"How many of Charmer's forces are still missing?" X asked.

"A total of seven that are unaccounted for," Wynn said. "We're searching the rigs and every boat bigger than a canoe for them. We'll get 'em, though. I mean, where they gonna run to?"

X thought on it. These missing fighters could already be octopus food, or they might be hiding out there and still loyal to Charmer. "Best keep an eye out and watch your six," he said.

"Yes, sir," Wynn and Slayer said in unison.

X felt that the sky people's rebellion under Rolo and Charmer had been crushed, but he couldn't take any chances. Soon, Charmer would be forced to share the truth about every evil thing he had done, including hiring Jamal to kill Oliver and Nez. That would surely bring around the last supporters of the defeated would-be strongman.

After that, any remaining diehards could join him in hell. But X had other problems that had to be addressed so that a new peace could move forward among all survivors. He turned to look at the giant Cazador standing before him.

Gran Jefe shifted where he stood, looking anxious.

"You killed Ada," X said. "I know this to be truth."

The big man nodded like a scolded child. "*Sí*, King Xavier."

"Because Ada killed your cousin?"

"*Sí.*"

X shook his head wearily. He understood revenge better than anyone. Ada had done a terrible thing. She had repented and gone into exile, then agreed to serve as a Hell Diver, and he had spared her life. It was only right to give Gran Jefe the same opportunity.

"Do you swear to the Octopus Lords to protect these islands?" X asked.

Gran Jefe squinted as if trying to understand.

"Will you continue to fight for the Vanguard flag?" X asked.

"Sir?"

General Forge translated, and Gran Jefe snorted.

"*Comprendo, pero no comprendo.* I understand, but no understand. I killed Ada."

"Yes, and she killed your cousin, and instead of killing her, I sent her on a journey to hell," X explained. "When she returned, she served to pay for her sins. You've been to hell, you have served, and you have the option to keep serving."

Gran Jefe bowed, then went down on one knee.

"I serve King Xavier," he said.

"Not anymore, you don't," X said.

He walked over to the railing where Rolo had toppled over, ending his weeklong reign as king of the Sun Empire. And now the man who'd killed him would take over.

"Imulah," X said.

"Yes…" The scribe lifted his head.

"According to Cazador law, if a king is killed in battle, the person who killed him becomes king, correct?" X asked.

"Yes," Imulah said. "That is how you became king."

X looked out over the distant oil rigs. It was time to crown a new king of the Vanguard Islands—a man whom X trusted to lead this place better than he himself could. It was time to pass the torch, just as he'd promised back on the *Frog*.

The islands needed a fresh start.

"Kade 'Cowboy' Long, by killing King Rolo, you inherit the crown," X said.

Every eye turned to Kade, who took a step back.

"Bloody hell, I don't want to be king," Kade said.

"I don't blame you," said X. "But when you pulled the trigger and killed Rolo, you took that on. And to be honest, I'm glad you did."

"You are the true king of the islands, Xavier," Forge said. "Rolo was never a real king."

"That isn't precisely accurate," Imulah said. "He was voted in as king after X was declared dead in the wastes."

"I understand," Forge said.

"General," X said, "I've made too many mistakes to continue to lead the islands. I failed my people, I failed your people, and I failed Michael. Kade, on the other hand, survived hell in Australia, survived capture by these knights, and made it back here to avenge us."

X put his hand on the Hell Diver's shoulder.

"Kade, you are a hero," X said. "People trust you, and we need a new leader that can bring us together."

Kade tried to shrug it off. "I did what any Hell Diver would have done, but that doesn't qualify me to lead the islands," he said.

X rubbed the back of his sore neck. "I'm an old man," he said. "My days of leading are over. We need fresh blood. Yours, mate."

"But... you are the Immortal," Forge said.

"A curse, like Gran Jefe said."

"No," Gran Jefe said. "Jorge *incorrecto*."

Forge glanced down, then looked back up. There was disappointment in his eye. "We need you, sir," he said.

"Look, I understand," X replied. "It may seem like I'm running away, but Michael thinks Rolo's still king, and he also thinks I'm dead. This isn't the first time he thought I was dead, and I won't wait another decade to see him again." He heaved a sigh. "Once I find him and his family, I'll return. You have my word. Until then, you give the islands a fresh start."

X stuck out his hand to Kade.

"Good luck," he said.

Kade hesitated, then shook.

"I will arrange a ceremony to make this official," Imulah said.

X threw up a salute to Forge. Instead of returning it, Forge limped forward and embraced him.

"Take care of this place," X said. "Protect it."

"I will, sir."

Slayer, Wynn, Gran Jefe, and Imulah all nodded.

"Safe travels on your journey," said the scribe. "I hope you find Michael."

"Good luck," Slayer said.

"I see you again. We fight together someday," Gran Jefe said.

"I hope not, but better than fighting *against* you, ya big asshole." X chuckled.

He shook arms with Gran Jefe, who snorted like a bull.

When X turned to Pedro, the lean, rangy warrior stiffened. He had nearly died on the rooftop helping Layla and Victor escape with Bray.

"Sir, requesting to come with you," Pedro said. "If Michael did go to my home, I can show you where it is."

X thought on it and said, "Your people need you too, Pedro. You already gave a lot to help Michael and his family."

"I owe him."

"The debt is paid." X smiled and reached out to the warrior. "I will find him; trust me on that."

"I have no doubt, sir."

X looked at the rooftop one more time, taking in the beautiful view of the gardens and forest. Part of him expected to see Magnolia rushing over, but she was probably sleeping off her sorrow. Before leaving, he would see her and say goodbye.

"Come on, boy," X said.

He patted his thigh, and Miles accompanied him to the elevator. He pushed the lever, and the crate jolted and started down toward the marina.

The battle's aftermath was staggering: burned and shell-splintered docks, swamped boats, and grisly flotsam in the water. And the man responsible wasn't far.

X turned to the east, where a cage hung from a steel pole over the water. Inside was a half-naked prisoner, bright red from sunburn.

"How's the little parasite?" X chirped. "What, no smile today?"

Charmer popped up from lying in a fetal position to look at the lowering elevator. Both arms were in casts, but that didn't stop him from gripping the bars and glaring at X with one bloodshot, swollen eye.

"You want a parasol?" X asked. He patted his vest, then shrugged. "Oh, silly me, I'm all out."

"You're a demon," Charmer hissed through his broken teeth.

X wasn't sure that keeping the man alive was the right call, and he had really hated that they wasted medical supplies on him. But when they were back on the *Frog*, Kade had persuaded X to spare Charmer for now. They still needed him to admit publicly to all his wicked doings. And soon, Charmer would do that very thing at the Sky Arena, in front of everyone.

Then they would crown Kade as the new king.

X wished he could be here to see both things, but he and Miles would be long gone by then. Glancing down, he saw their old ride, the *Sea Wolf*, moored at one of the piers. The railings were wrapped with new razor wire, and stacks of crates waited on the deck, full of fruit both fresh and dried, root vegetables, and jerky. The robotic arm Charmer had stripped off Michael was also there, along with Cricket 3.0, which had been stolen when Jamal's Wave Runners took Michael captive. X looked forward to returning both to Michael soon.

The elevator clanked to the bottom, and he opened the gate for Miles to hop out. The dog trotted straight to the boat.

X spent the next hour inventorying everything he had and the things he still needed. Just as he was about to go belowdecks, he heard a croaky female voice.

"I'm ready to go when you are!"

X squinted into the sunlight. Someone was pushing a wheelchair.

Magnolia walked like Frankenstein's monster. Her hair was thin and wispy from radiation poisoning, and her neck was bandaged where Jamal had cut her.

In the wheelchair was Sofia, with bandages on bullet wounds to both legs. In her arms, she held Rhino Jr. Tia was also with them, carrying two bags.

At the dock, Magnolia took the bags from Tia. Then she walked across the platform to the *Sea Wolf* and dropped them on the deck.

"What in the wastes might you be doing?" X asked.

"I'm coming with you," she said.

X snorted. "Like hell you are..."

She put her fists on her hips. "I just heard the news you aren't king anymore, and last I checked, you aren't my Hell Diver commander, so you can save your breath telling me what to do."

He flashed back thirteen years, to Magnolia standing in the

launch bay of the *Hive*—insolent, insubordinate, and a general pain in his ass.

"Some things never change," X said.

"Michael and Layla need help, and so do you, old man," Magnolia said. "And there's nothing much left for me here anyway."

She turned to Sofia and her son. "Besides you two, that is. But hey, this isn't *goodbye*—it's just *see you soon*."

X scratched his beard as he took a moment to think. Although it didn't really matter. Magnolia was coming with him, and he had to accept it.

"Say goodbye, then," X said. "We sail soon."

Magnolia flashed what might have been a grin—it was hard to tell with all the bruising. She bent down to hug Sofia. Then she held up Rhino Jr., who cooed and giggled.

"I'll watch over them," Tia said. "Don't worry, King—"

"Just X," he said.

She nodded.

"Watch out for Kade, too," X said. "He will need you."

X kissed Rhino Jr. on the forehead. "Your father is proud of you," he said as he handed the child back to Sofia.

He had just boarded the *Sea Wolf* when a voice called out.

"Wait!"

X turned to find a kid running across the dock, holding a red baseball cap over his head. It was Alton, moving as fast as his small legs would take him.

"Wait!" he called out again.

When he arrived, Alton panted and took off his hat. "Are . . . are you going to find . . . Michael?"

"Yeah, kid, I am," X said.

Katherine Mitchells and Phyl ran across the piers, making their way past two guards, who lowered their spears when X shouted, "Let them through."

"I told you to stay with Katherine," Tia said to Alton.

"I'm sorry, but I wanted to give this to X to give back to Michael," Alton handed the red Marine Corps baseball cap to X.

"Full circle," X replied with a grunt. "Thanks, pal, but I'm pretty sure Michael would want you to keep it."

"Tell Michael it brought me luck and I want him to have it back for now."

X took the hat gingerly. "Okay."

"Please find him, sir."

Alton bowed slightly, then returned to Katherine and Phyl, who X was told had been instructed to look after Alton in a note from Layla. He waved goodbye one last time, then joined Magnolia in the cockpit of the boat.

Minutes later, the *Sea Wolf*'s sails caught the wind, propelling them over the teal-green waters. As the boat neared the invisible wall on the horizon, Miles was in the bow, wagging his tail and barking at a pod of dolphins that jumped and gamboled in the waves. X gazed into the swirling darkness beyond. He didn't turn for a fond last look at what he was leaving behind.

"Face your future without fear," he said.

"Accept your past without regret," Magnolia said.

She joined X behind the wheel. The sky seemed to darken in the distance, and the first lightning bolt snaked out.

"Another adventure into the wastes," X said.

"Just like old times," Mags replied. "We're going to find them, X, don't worry."

* * * * *

The airship *Vanguard* hovered before a towering dark fortress of clouds. Lightning flashed across the massive storm front, making the horizon seem eerily alive. Four days after leaving the islands, they were hovering over Timothy's first suggested stop: Outpost Gateway at the Panama Canal.

Michael tried to put Rolo and Charmer out of his mind. He had escaped them, and that would have to be good enough for now. Perhaps someday he would return for his revenge, but all that mattered right now was getting his family far away from those sick bastards. To do that, they needed parts for the airship. That meant someone would have to go down to the outpost.

On the bridge, Michael watched the dashboard of instruments with Steve while Layla sat at an idle station with Bray sleeping on her lap. They had shut down all noncritical systems to conserve power, and the ship had limped here for the parts to keep it in the sky. Michael knew that the outpost had the necessary items to repair the water-treatment plant, but it meant putting the airship down. And if that proved unfeasible, they must become Hell Divers once more. First, he needed to scope the scene out from above.

"Take us down, Timothy," Michael said quietly. "I want an aerial view."

"Copy that, sir. Please stand by."

The airship lowered through the gray swirl. Twenty thousand feet . . . fifteen thousand . . . At five thousand feet, the Panama Canal exploded into view. At a thousand feet, it was obvious the outpost had been abandoned.

Scanning the fortified camp, Michael didn't see anyone moving around the idle construction equipment or on the guard walls.

"What's that?" Steve asked, pointing.

Timothy dialed in long mounds of disturbed earth, like mole tunnels. They seemed to originate at the canal and ended at the outpost. Dozens of holes had burst through on the other side of the outpost walls.

"The spawn, you think?" Layla whispered.

Michael shook his head, unsure. Whatever had happened was a mystery they could never unravel from up here. He watched the screens closely for a few minutes but saw no sign of the beasts that had come out of those holes.

Perhaps it was safe now.

"What ya think, Chief?" Steve asked.

Michael looked up from the monitors. "I think we put down and scavenge for parts. Starting with that desalination equipment. It should have everything we need to get our water treatment back online."

"I'll get suited up," Layla said.

"No," Michael and Steve said at the same moment.

"I'll go," Michael said.

"Respectfully, I'd prefer that you both stay," Steve said. "You two have been through enough. Let me go. I know what I'm looking for."

"You shouldn't go alone."

Steve smiled. "Let me do this. I can handle myself. Just get me on the ground."

Michael didn't like it, but with just one arm and a banged-up head, he was in no shape to go. And he certainly didn't want Layla going.

"Okay," he finally said. "I'll be in the launch bay with a gun, watching your back. Timothy, take us down right above the outpost and do a life scan."

By the time Steve and Michael were suited up in the launch bay, the ship was a hundred feet above the ground.

"All life scans completed," Timothy said. "Nothing identified."

"I'm not taking any chances," Steve said.

He grabbed a shotgun from the weapons locker and slung it over his hazard suit. "Don't worry. I'm old, but I'm able."

Michael chuckled. "More than able, I'd say." He grabbed a pistol with an extended magazine—easy to fire with one hand.

In the launch bay, Steve got into a harness. Michael rigged a rope.

"Ready to go," Michael called over the command channel.

"Copy. Opening launch bay doors," Timothy replied.

The dual doors whisked open, letting in a gust of warm, humid wind. Steve went to the edge, turned, and rappelled down. When his boots hit the dirt, he unclipped and gave a thumbs-up, then set off into the compound.

Michael stood in the open launch bay, watching his friend jog away in the green glow of his NVGs. Nothing else moved among the mounds of dirt. He could only imagine what horrors had emerged from those tunnels.

Several minutes later, he was still peering into the darkness when he caught movement. It was Steve, running and waving. He stood right under the airship.

"I found more than we need!" he said.

"Bodies?" Michael called down.

"No, nothing."

Michael bumped on the command channel. "Timothy, prepare the cable winches to bring up supplies. I'm going down to help Steve load up. Don't worry, Layla, we'll be fast."

"Just be careful," she said. "Something could still be out there."

Rappelling down to the surface, Michael couldn't stop thinking about Rodger and his crew. Something had happened to them, and without the bodies, their fates would remain unknown.

On the ground, Michael unclipped from the rope and drew his pistol. Scanning the area, he followed Steve to the desalination plant. The facility had the most mound and tunnel activity of the entire site. This had to be the work of spawn. But where were all the bodies?

"This must have been during the night, when most everyone was sleeping," Michael said.

"Horrifying to think about," Steve said. "They didn't stand a chance."

Michael shined his light into a tunnel and saw nothing but some old, withered vines. He listened for activity and, hearing none, began to help Steve disassemble pipes and electrical relays. For the next few hours, they carried the salvage up and stacked it beneath the airship. After rigging a cable harness to their final load, Michael looked out over the outpost.

Wind swept the dry terrain, ruffling the tattered tents and scattering debris. It had been a dream of King Xavier's to bring this place online. But like the king, Outpost Gateway was dead. With it, Rodger was gone forever—another victim of the wastes.

"Okay, Chief," Steve said. "We've got the loads rigged so the winch can hook them without a ground crew. Let's get out of here."

They returned to the launch bay and went through the decon process before finally returning to the bridge, exhausted but happy.

"Mission complete," Michael said. "Timothy, lower us just above the ground and start winching up cargo."

"On it, sir," replied the AI.

"Did you find any sign of anyone?" Layla asked.

Michael shook his head. "Once we get the parts aboard, I'll start fixing up the ship with Steve. In the meantime, we need to figure out where we're headed next. Timothy, any ideas?"

"I have an idea." The voice came from behind them, and Michael turned to see Victor standing in the open hatch above the bridge. Still creaky from the arrow wound, he limped down the stairs to the lower level.

"My home," Victor said. "We go to my home."

Michael felt guilty not knowing where that was. "Where is it?"

"Canary Islands," Victor said.

Timothy pulled up a map of the area.

"This archipelago is located in the Atlantic Ocean, in Macaronesia," said the AI.

"Just off the coast of northwest Africa," Michael said.

"We live not on land," Victor said. "My family live... lived on boats."

"Boats?" Layla asked.

"Yes. A city of boats in a bay."

"Excuse me," Timothy said.

Michael ignored the AI. "How come you never told us about your home?" he asked Victor.

"Because my home was broken in a war with... ¿Cómo se dice 'piratas'?... Pirates."

"Like Cazadores?"

"No, these no Cazadores."

"But you were captured by Cazadores..."

"Yes, but first, Ton and me run away from that war on a boat. We came to America shore in search of new life. That is where we get captured."

"I'm sorry, I don't understand something else," Layla said. "If your home was destroyed—"

"Not destroyed," Victor said. "There was a resort on the on island once. Built by rich man that owned diamond mines. Underground in volcanic tunnels we find rooms of dried food that could last forever. Ton and I take what we need and go with some of our friends because we afraid the pirates find us. Some friends stay behind. They might still be there."

"Excuse me," Timothy repeated.

Michael finally looked over to the AI. "What is it?"

"I am picking up movement on the surface," Timothy said. "I'm retrieving the last batch of supplies, but we seem to have attracted some attention."

"People?" Michael rushed over for a look.

Not people. Glowing vegetation snaked out of the holes he and Steve had walked past just an hour ago. Stranger still, it was crawling like serpents, toward the airship and the bundle of pipe now dangling in the air.

"What in the wastes…" Layla began to say.

"I'm also detecting a huge spike in radiation," Timothy said.

"Get us out of here as soon as those supplies are up," Michael said.

"Finishing in ten… nine…"

Michael watched as the winch cable pulled the last load—a crate of insulators, electrical relays, and spools of wire and cable.

The turbofans clicked on, and the ship jolted away from Outpost Gateway. Michael stood riveted, watching the strange glowing flora still snaking out across the surface.

"Now we know what happened," Layla said. "Poor Rodger."

Michael pushed aside his sorrow for his friend. He had an airship to fix, and they couldn't do it here. They also had to figure out where they were going after they fixed the ship.

As they rose into the clouds, he felt the weight of that decision. "Let's put it to a vote," he said. "All in favor of Canary Islands, raise your hand."

Victor and Michael both raised their hands.

"If not for Victor, we wouldn't be here right now," Layla said, raising a hand. "If you want to try going home, I support you."

"Thank you," Victor said.

Steve seemed uncertain. "The Canary Islands is a heck of a long ways. I'll feel a lot better when we've got the ship up and running properly," he said. "After that happens, you got my vote."

"Timothy, how about you?" Michael asked.

"I am impartial by design," said the AI.

"Perhaps Bray would like to weigh in," Steve said with a chuckle.

But even if the boy could vote, he was sound asleep.

"Okay," Michael said. "We make the ship airworthy, then head to the Canary Islands. Timothy, find us a place to do the repairs."

"First we need to get through the storm front," Timothy said. "We're completely surrounded."

Michael went to the front viewports to watch the flashing boil of clouds, an idea already seeding in his mind. "Timothy, try to find a weak pocket that will let us go up and over the storm, like Captain Ash once did."

Layla looked at Michael. So did Steve, though they both trusted him enough not to question the suggestion.

The AI was less confident. "Chief, from what I understand, Captain Ash performed that risky maneuver when the ship was in much better condition than it is now."

"I understand that, Pepper, so you'd better find us a nice weak spot to fly through."

"I'll do my best, Chief. You'd better strap in."

Michael helped Layla and Bray into a chair, hoping not to wake the child. Bray babbled and batted his eyes, groggy. He reached out to Michael, then saw the dashboard.

Fascinated by the lights, Bray pointed his tiny fingers at the bright screen. He giggled and waved at Timothy.

Timothy waved back. "Hello, little guy," he said.

Michael helped secure a harness over his wife and their son. Victor winced as he buckled in. Steve took a seat in front of the weather station.

"Okay, Timothy," Michael said. "Take us up."

The viewport began to close, and the front cameras turned on to reveal the brooding storm clouds.

Bray tensed as the entire ship quivered.

"It's okay," Layla said. "Just a storm. Rain and thunder."

"We're going to be okay, buddy," Michael said.

The boy looked over to Michael, then back to Victor, and finally to Timothy, who smiled.

Bray smiled back and waved again.

"Keep doing that, Pepper. It's working," Layla said.

Bray, thinking it all a game, clapped excitedly.

The airship rumbled and shook, and again Michael questioned his decision. He had to trust in the ship. She had gotten them through many storms before, even when damaged.

He remembered crawling through a tunnel to fix a gas bladder. He could almost feel the heat and the fear. That fear had almost won back then, and it threatened to once again.

"We're going to make it," he said. "Pepper, keep us steady."

The airship rose toward the looming clouds shot through with threads of blue fire.

"Preparing to enter storm," Timothy said.

The bow pierced the scalloped gray mass, and every joint and rivet of the ship seemed to groan at once.

The monitors flickered. The main lights went off, diverted to emergency red, then flicked back on.

Bray reached out to Michael, his six-tooth smile gone.

"It's almost over," Michael said.

Warning sensors chirped as the storm lashed the hull. Thunder boomed, rattling the ancient ship's bones. Sparks rained down from a loose panel behind them. A fire sensor went off at a station on the second level.

"Got it!" Steve shouted over the alarms. He unbuckled and ran to get a fire extinguisher.

"Timothy, how much longer?" Layla asked, clearly trying to stay calm.

"We're at thirty thousand feet," replied the AI. "Only five thousand to go."

A massive tremor ran through the ship, and Michael knew at once that they had been hit by lightning. Two more alarms popped off.

"Fire in zone three," Timothy said. "Permission to use the water lines?"

Michael paused. Water spent quenching flames was water unavailable for drinking. They had already lost a fifth of their reserves during the escape from Charmer. But it was either use the precious water now or lose the entire ship to fire.

"Do it," he ordered.

Bray had finally gotten enough drama and began wailing with gusto. Layla tried to soothe him. Michael answered her worried glance with a reassuring nod, though he wasn't sure how many more jolts the old warhorse could take.

Steve's fire extinguisher hissed. The airship lurched, and he staggered but somehow kept his feet till he had stifled the flames.

"Buckle back in," Michael said.

The lights flickered off completely, and red emergency lights warmed to life, illuminating Bray's frightened face.

Michael put a hand on his son and prayed, if there was a God and if that God was listening, that they all be spared.

The alarms blared like a Siren streaking in for the kill. Had Michael's rash decision doomed his family? His heart thudded.

"Thirty-five thousand feet," Timothy announced.

The monitors flickered. Michael watched them, hoping the ship was through the worst of it. Another violent wind shear slammed the airship *Vanguard*.

And it was over.

The main lights came back online, then the monitors. Michael unbuckled his harness and stood. Layla spoke softly to Bray, who was pointing at the bright screens, his tears forgotten.

"Pepper, open shutters," Michael ordered.

"Aye, aye, Chief."

The metal shutters protecting the glass viewports slid down.

"Stah," Bray said.

"Yes," Layla said. "Star." She motioned for Michael to follow her to the viewports.

Victor walked over with Steve. Both men smiled.

"We're above the storm," Timothy confirmed. "Fire in zone three is out."

"Good work, Pepper," Layla said.

They all stood at the viewports with the AI, looking out at a dazzling sky ornamented with a brilliant silvery half moon. Michael put a hand on Bray while Layla sang:

> *"As your bright and tiny spark*
> *Lights the traveler in the dark,*
> *Though I know not what you are…"*

Bray pointed at the stars and turned to grin at Michael. The boy was too young to understand where they were going or why.

And to Michael, it didn't really matter. They were together, and that was enough.

HELL DIVERS XI

Don't miss the next installment of the Hell Divers series with *Hell Divers XI* coming soon!

ABOUT THE AUTHOR

Nicholas Sansbury Smith is the *New York Times* and *USA Today* bestselling author of the Hell Divers series, the Orbs series, the Trackers series, the Extinction Cycle series, the Sons of War series, and the new E-Day series. He worked for Iowa Homeland Security and Emergency Management in disaster mitigation before switching careers to focus on storytelling. When he isn't writing or daydreaming about the apocalypse, he enjoys running, biking, spending time with his family, and traveling the world. He is an Ironman triathlete and lives in Iowa with his wife, daughter, and their dogs.

Join Nicholas on social media:
Facebook: Nicholas Sansbury Smith
Twitter: @GreatWaveInk
Website: www.NicholasSansburySmith.com